PRAISE FOR THE
WORK OF JEFF MANN

"Mann conveys the experience that most rural gays go through as they attempt to negotiate their homosexuality in a place that often discriminates against them...."

TRAVIS A. ROUNTREE FOR *APPALACHIAN JOURNAL*

"The sounds of rock 'n' roll music wafting from the radio, or played on guitar, the feel and scent of leather, the smell and taste of good home cooking, the look, smell, and feel of a hairy man...Mann's vivid prose describes all these and more."

Keith Glaeske for CHELSEA STATION MAGAZINE

"Libraries that collect gay historical fiction, Civil War novels, and LGBT fiction will want these books as well as Mann's other works."

James Doig Anderson for the GLBT ROUND TABLE
OF THE AMERICAN LIBRARY ASSOCIATION

"As a gay Appalachian himself—or, as he might put it himself, a mountain man—the poet and scholar has used his own life experiences and inner journey as source material in examining what it means to be a man from the rural South who loves other men, and loves them with a certain (even specialized) vigor."

Kilian Melloy for EDGE MEDIA

COUNTRY

JEFF MANN

LETHE PRESS

Published by Lethe Press
118 Heritage Ave, Maple Shade, NJ 08052
lethepressbooks.com

ISBN 9781590212400

Cover Art: Alice Rutherford
Cover and Interior Design: Inkspiral Design
Author Photo: L.s. King

Library of Congress Cataloging-in-Publication Data

Names: Mann, Jeff, author.
Title: Country / Jeff Mann.
Description: Maple Shade, NJ : Lethe Press, [2016]
Identifiers: LCCN 2016025654 | ISBN 9781590212400 (paperback : alk. paper)
Subjects: LCSH: Gay men--Fiction. | Country musicians--Fiction. | GSAFD: Love stories
Classification: LCC PS3563.A53614 C68 2016 | DDC 813/.54--dc23
LC record available at https://lccn.loc.gov/2016025654

For STEVE BERMAN, *who gave me the gift of this plot.*

For the many country singers and country boys who've stirred my heart and my libido.

For country music stars TY HERNDON, CHELY WRIGHT, *and* BILLY GILMAN, *who had the courage to come out.*

For JONI MITCHELL, *whose example helped me become a musician and a poet.*

For my husband, JOHN ROSS, *who's made a home for this ornery country boy for nearly twenty years.*

*

Thanks to Cynthia Burack for decades of friendship as well as information about reparative therapy.

Thanks to Philip Rogerson for his kindness and his priceless wit.

Thanks to Jason Burns, John P. Mullins, Kevin Oderman, Jesse Kalvitis, Fran Whiteman, and Katie Fallon for the Morgantown visit.

Thanks to John P. Mullins for the snake-handling story, which I have repeated almost verbatim.

Thanks to Matt Bright for the fine book design.

PART
ONE

STIFF-BACKED AND HUNGOVER, BRICE BROWN, rubbing sleep from his eyes, trudged the sands on Thanksgiving Day of 1997. Near sunset, this stretch of beach was almost empty, save for a few wizened, brown Daytona natives taking brisk holiday walks and the occasional manic sandpiper picking through the wave-wash of low tide for dinner. Behind barefoot Brice loomed nineteen pink and yellow floors of condominium tower. Before him spread the Atlantic, rough and booming after recent storms. On the horizon, a white shrimp boat trawled for crustaceans. Above, a white-bellied osprey rode air currents, scanning the water for prey.

Brice, a burly man of six feet and forty years, had a broad, handsome face, blue eyes, and a close-cropped brown beard. He wore his favorite warm-weather clothes: a black baseball cap, camo shorts, and a baggy black nylon muscle-shirt chosen to show off his big chest and thick arms while concealing the booze-belly he habitually sported. Brice looked out at the ocean, tried to rub the blur out of his left eye, and failed. Shrugging, he massaged the throb in his temples, checked for new messages on his cell phone, found none, muttered beneath his breath, and looked out to sea again. When he stepped on a sharp fragment of shell, he stumbled. Sharp pains shot through his lower back, and he sank to his knees, cursing.

"Goddamn sacroiliac," Brice hissed. "This aging shit's for the fucking birds." Brow crimped up, he stretched his back out using a couple of yoga positions that Buddy, his bass player, had taught him, then rolled onto his side, wincing. His gaze roved along the beach, where breaking waves rolled up the sand, leaving at their farthest reach lacy clumps of sea foam that the brisk breeze blew sideways like tiny ships. Teeth gritted, doing his best to ignore the pain in his lumbar, Brice followed the progress of one such little galleon till it scattered and dissolved. Head pounding, he closed his eyes, listening to the surf and the rhythmic sounds of a jogger's shoes somewhere nearby.

After last night's concert and the partying afterwards, he was exhausted, despite having slept all day long. He was close to drifting off when a voice startled him.

"Hey, sir. Are you all right?"

Brice opened his eyes. Hunkered down beside him was a man in his twenties sporting a trim golden goatee and wearing nothing but gym shorts and running shoes. His muscular chest, heaving with exertion, was slick with sweat. Tattoos raced up and down his sinewy arms.

Holy fuck, you're hot, Brice thought. *Big yummy nipples. And going commando too. How about you come back to the condo with me?*

Brice sat up with a grimace. "Hey, I'm fine. Bad back, that's all." He pulled his glance from the boy's long furry legs and packed shorts. "Actually, I had a late night, and a date with a whiskey bottle."

Smiling, the boy stepped back. "You look familiar. You been on TV?"

Brice grinned. While he had grown used to fame, it still thrilled him when anyone handsome recognized him, as if Fate wanted him to get laid despite a life trapped in the closet. "A few times. I'm Brice Brown."

The boy didn't respond as Brice had hoped, with wide-eyed recognition and garrulous adulation. Brice mumbled something about the Country Music Awards, that duet he did with Pam Tillis that brought the house down, best ratings yet....

"Country? That's cool. I'm more of a hip-hop guy myself."

Brice scowled. "Hip-hop? I hate that shit."

The boy laughed. "That's what everyone over forty says. You want me to help you up?"

"Thanks," Brice said, offering his hand. Despite Brice's heft, the boy heaved him to his feet with little effort. Brice swayed a bit and kneaded his spine.

"My father has back problems too. Take care. Happy Thanksgiving." With a grin and a wave, the boy bounded off.

Brice groaned, watching the tanned broad back and athletically rounded buttocks recede down the beach. "His father. That ain't the kind of Daddy/boy scene I had in mind." He was stepping cautiously up the beach when his phone buzzed. He flipped it open, glad to see it was his manager.

"Hey, Steve," Brice said. "How's my favorite Yankee?"

"I am the bearer of good news, Brice. Not only is Molasses Mount eager to release your next CD but they're going to book you on a tour in the spring."

"Big venues, I hope? Not like that piss-ant pit I played last night."

"Big, big, big! You're on the verge of a comeback, I promise. Have you been dieting? I've found a fashion consultant perfect to help with the album cover and we both think you should wax your chest—"

"Hell, no. My fans want a real man, not a slick city boy. Let me look country."

"What sells in WalMart may be country but it isn't trucker—"

"Steve, leave me a few rough edges. Play up my outlaw status, or whatever you want to call it."

"All right, all right. Could you be more stubborn?"

"Ornery's the word we use down here."

"Ornery outlaw.... Maybe that should be a song title. You have finished recording, right? The chain stores, the distributors, the deadlines are tight, Brice. I want *Billboard* and *Rolling Stone* and the *L.A. Times* to be swooning. They do use 'swooning' in West Virginia?"

Brice scowled and bit back the retort. Truth was, he'd had writer's block for months. *Hard to write songs your fans expect instead of songs you want to write, songs that would lose you your entire audience.* "Almost done, I guess."

"You guess? That doesn't sound good. We need more than good. We need terrific." He heard Steve chewing; his agent might be the only man on God's green earth that chewed aspirin, though it wasn't for headaches but to keep his heart beating. His tiny Music Row heart.

"Being seen in public with that lovely wife of yours would help too. *People Magazine* took a bite out of your sales when they featured the separation. I need you to do something big, big, big for Valentine's Day. Get her one of those colored diamonds on a chain. One so large you don't need the Hubble to see it from space. Capiche?"

"Shelly's hardly speaking to me these days." *And if you knew why, you wouldn't be speaking to me either.*

"I don't need to tell you that every fan inside the Bible Belt likes their singers fine-looking, married, and covering some Christmas tunes to sing to their two grinning kids. Lose more weight and she'll come around. Women like abs. Ever see Brad Pitt wearing sweats? Never." Steve guffawed. "How'd last night's show go?"

"Last night?" Brice felt he ought to have more coffee before dredging up even a recent memory.

More crunching aspirin. "I know you didn't sell out."

I used to think that meant something else…and I still think I did sell out, only not by filling every seat in the house. "Naw. That's why this new Molasses Mount deal is so damn welcome. We gotta get my name back up there, Steve. And I gotta win that big award I'm up for. That'd make a big difference, don't you think? And we gotta get me back on the radio more often. We gotta—"

"I spoke to Buddy. He said you were a little unsteady on stage."

"Nothing to worry about, Steve. I swear."

"Were you on something? A little of the Bolivian marching powder?"

Brice limped up the stairs to the condo tower's patio, gritting his teeth. "Hold…on a minute." He hobbled over to a bench overlooking the water and sat heavily. *Damn that Buddy. I thought that if a guy did yoga and drank pulverized wheatgrass shakes he'd be too calm to be a little bitch and tattle on me. If he weren't such a great bass-player, I'd kick his ass.*

"Answer me, Brice. I need to know if we have to do the whole rehab spin. And Shelly would have to be on board about that. Two things a musician needs to make recovery from addiction a moneymaker: a loving, tearful wife and devotion to Jesus."

Brice groaned.

"If you fuck up, this new deal might go right down the toilet."

"I wasn't drunk. I had a few fingers of whiskey to lube my vocal cords. But my back's been giving me big trouble again. I take the pills the doctor *you sent me to* prescribed."

"All right, I'm already late for the big turkey dinner. My wife hired an Oriental cook last week and I bet turkey doesn't even translate in Korean or South Korean or wherever her Green Card says."

"Well, at least you have plans. Most of the band is headed home to Tennessee today. Buddy's over in Orlando, hanging out with some buddies of his. I'm just going to grab a bite here. Heading back to Nashville day after tomorrow. I'll check in next week to talk about—"

"Gotta go, Brice. 'Nother call."

Brice shoved the quieted phone into his shorts pocket. For a few minutes, he watched sunlight flash in the white collapse of waves and let his mind wander. He thought of Shelly and all he'd put her through. He thought of Zac, how the big man had wept when Brice, fearful of discovery, had broken it off and said goodbye. He thought of his childhood in the West Virginia mountains and the boys he'd loved from afar in high school and college. He thought of the summer when he was sixteen, when he'd helped his father pick such a surplus of strawberries that they'd sold them by the side of the road. Brice had made enough money to take the Greyhound to Daytona Beach to visit relatives. It was the first time he'd seen the ocean. There were so many exotic seashells, and the sand, in memory, was pure white, white as cane sugar, not at all like the dull dun stretching before him now. He was lean then, with a patchy beard, an agile frame, and lanky brown hair down to his shoulders. Already he'd been getting good on his guitar. Already he was writing songs and dreaming of Nashville and stardom. Already he was adept at hiding who he really was.

Brice watched a white egret fly by. He watched another patch of sea foam buffeted by wind sliding along the sand. The tracks left by the nearly naked runner remained on the beach. He remembered making love to Zac, the way the bushy-bearded man moaned as Brice took him from behind.

Bad back or not, I need me some strange. Grinning, he limped into the lobby, nodding at Billy, the guard on duty, a man he'd chatted with often during his three years of intermittent visits here. Despite his college degree and his annual income, Brice had never forgotten his roots. He felt much more comfortable with working-class and blue-collar folks than most of the music industry sophisticates he interacted with in Nashville.

"Hey, Billy, why ain't you home with your family?"

"I will be soon. I get off in an hour. And I could ask you the same. Why aren't you gallivanting in your native hills?"

Brice frowned. "Ah, I had that big show last night. Besides, not much family left. Shelly and I separated, remember? All I got's my sister and nephew in West Virginia. That fried clam place up in Ormond Beach still open?"

"Afraid not. Owner died." When the big man crooked his arm to run a hand over his bald scalp, his biceps bunched up.

"Ah, too bad. Any good delivery around here?" Brice said, studying Billy's big chest and lean hips. *Hell, I'm drooling over anything in pants. I gotta get laid tonight. It's been too damn long.*

"Stavros Pizza," Billy said. "It might give you bad heartburn later, but it sure is good going down."

"Thanks, man. I'll try 'em out. Happy holidays," Brice said, moving toward the bank of elevators. As much as he'd enjoyed all the attention last night, the sweet clamor of fans, he was ready for the silence and solitude of his comfortable condo. He was ready for good Kentucky bourbon, pain pills, delivery pizza, and an evening on the laptop spent cruising online sites that offered him what he craved.

CHAPTER TWO

ONE YOUNG MAN ONLINE, MOUTHWATERINGLY lean and hirsute, was simply rude: "Sorry, dude, you're too old. Not into Daddies." The rest just ignored Brice.

Fifteen years ago, when his career in country music had first taken off and he'd situated himself firmly in the closet, finding some discreet and hairy tail was pretty easy. At this age, it had become more difficult. Meanwhile, he'd grown tired of the pretense, tired of the sham marriage he'd shared with Shelly for nearly ten years, tired of sneaking around, tired of paying for sex, but what other options were there if he wanted to keep his career? That brief affair he'd conducted with his former lead guitarist, Zac—lots of furtive rendezvous in motel rooms in the countryside outside Nashville—had made him so fearful of being caught that he'd ended it after six months, despite Zac's teary protestations and his own deep regret.

After six slices of pizza, two pain pills, and three whiskey sours, Brice shifted to his computer and escort options at CallBoys. At first his strong preference for muscled Caucasians hindered his search, for most of the guys were Latinos, black men, or scrawny white boys. At last, however, he discovered Mike Dragon, a stud in his mid-thirties, a guy with the sort of country-boy looks Brice savored most.

"Ummm," Brice growled, squeezing his crotch and scanning the man's pics. "Looks like home." The guy did indeed resemble several trailer-park buddies and local garage mechanics that Brice had yearned after in his shy, suppressed youth.

In one picture, Mike stood facing the camera, shirtless, wearing a backward baseball cap and faded jeans full of rips and tears, flexing his brawny arms. His hair was shaggy and dirty blond, his face stubble-coated, his muscled chest and sculpted belly plastered with honey-colored hair. In a second shirtless image, he gave the photographer a side shot, flexing again—big swell of biceps—with a red dew-rag on his head and his jeans pushed down over his thighs, showing off a lean waist, curvy butt, and tan line. In a third, he stood with his tanned arms crossed, looking stern, tank top pulled up to expose the contours of a six-pack, the dark line of a thick treasure-trail, and a chunky Confederate-flag belt-buckle. When Brice switched to the guy's stats, he found more promising details: "Mild to wild, seven inches uncut, versatile, S&M, spankings, blow jobs, role playing, toys."

"Yeah, yeah, yeah," Brice sighed as he scanned the pictures again. He regretted what the years had done to him; staring at young men, even knowing he could *have* one, was a mixed blessing, a hot stew of emotions, chiefly regret and desire. "That's the one. Gotta love the rough redneck look." He grabbed his phone and punched in Mike's number, sat back, sipped his drink, and waited for the guy to pick up.

THE ESCORT APPRAISED THE SPACIOUS condo and the huge ocean view out sliding glass doors. His clothes matched the photos: backward baseball cap, tattered jeans, tight gray, ribbed tank top, and scuffed cowboy boots. "Fucking awesome place. You gotta be loaded."

Brice didn't like talking about money. "I do all right." Brice appraised the young man, gazing at the amber field of chest hair that Mike's low-cut top displayed. *Amber waves of grain*, Brice thought. "You want a drink? Whiskey sour?"

Mike nodded. "Sounds fancy." And then he crossed his arms. "Could I have my fee first?"

Brice kept hidden how the question made him bristle—after fifteen years of hiring rent boys, he anticipated the request yet always found it distasteful. *Makes me feel like I'm ordering fast food instead of a good meal; you pay for a real steak only after you eat it, but the sloppy burger is what's on the menu.*

"Here you go." Brice handed Mike a wad of bills before heading to the bar to mix the man a drink and refresh his own.

As Mike counted, Brice said, "The extra five hundred is an apology...in advance.

I'm in the mood to get a little wild tonight. So I might be rough."

"I ain't worried about that," Mike said as he slid the bills into his tight back pocket, where the denim kissed his fine ass. "For this much, I'm up for just about anything."

The two men sat at opposite ends of the couch. Brice's gaze was direct, Mike's shy. He kept grinning at Brice and looking away.

"So what's your name again?" Mike asked.

"Nick. Is yours really Mike?"

"Naw."

Brice chuckled. "Mine's not really Nick."

"I figured. That's cool. You play those?" Mike asked, nodding toward the Yamaha baby grand and Martin guitar at the far end of the room.

"I do." As much as Brice wanted to boast about his career, the thought of an ambitious hustler blackmailing him to keep quiet had no appeal, so he shrugged. "I've written a few songs."

"Let's hear one," said Mike.

"In a bit." Brice took a long sip of his drink. Between the pills and alcohol, his back was feeling almost back to normal. "First, why don't you take your shirt off? I wanna see those amazing tits of yours."

Mike blushed. "S-sure, man. Now that you've paid, I'm all yours."

"You bet your sweet ass you are." Brice leered as the hustler stripped to the waist. The big pecs, the cut abdominals, all that honey-hued fur...the deep voice and scruffy masculinity...the guy was glorious. Even the Confederate-flag belt buckle turned Brice on. It reminded him of the backwoods South he'd grown up in. A flag he felt in his heart wasn't about racism but regional pride; country music was a big working-class "Fuck you" to the snotty, over-refined Powers That Be, and country music was Southern and shouldn't be afraid to fly the Stars and Bars.

Brice resisted the urge to lick his lips like a starveling dog. How long had it been since he'd had a man so desirable? Probably that hugely hung porn star/escort Doug. Brice had spent several days in a fancy hotel room in Philadelphia last summer riding the buff brat raw.

"You haven't done this much before, have you? Hustling?"

"Not much. How can you tell?"

"I've hired a lot of guys before."

"Hey, I don't mean to look a gift horse in the mouth, but you're pretty handsome. Why hire guys when they'd line up to spend the night with you for free?"

Brice took off his ball cap and ran his hand over his receding hairline. "Dating's not my bag."

"Yeah." Mike frowned. "I get that. I have to stay in the closet 'cause of work."

"Where you work? Where you live?"

Mike stiffened. Nodding, Brice apologized.

"Sorry. Some guys aren't shy about their lives. And others want to stay quiet until the fun begins."

"I don't mind you asking. Just…you aren't what I expected. Most men that hire…." His voice trembled and he shook his head. "Not that I have any reason to be proud of where I live or work. It's a trailer court out toward DeLand. And I'm a slave to that Walmart near Orange City."

"You got no reason to feel ashamed. Not when I'm going to make you feel good." Brice leaned in close and took a firm hold of Mike's forearm, raising his arm high so he could breath in the man's pit-sweat. "Thanks for skipping the shower and the deodorant like I asked. You married?"

Mike blushed again. He brushed blond hair off his brow, then folded his arms behind his head, giving Brice a stronger whiff and a clearer view of his golden-fleeced pits. "Divorced. Child support, that's why I…do this."

Brice moved closer. He ran his hands over the man's chest and pinched a big brown nipple. Mike shuddered, smiled, and sighed.

"That feels great."

"Good to hear. You like big bearded men like me?"

"I do. A lot." Mike stretched out his legs, cocked a wooly eyebrow, and took a big gulp of his drink.

"You straight?" Brice said, bending to kiss Mike's right nipple. The bulge in Mike's jeans had grown considerably in the last couple of minutes.

"Ah, bi, I guess."

Brice moved closer still. He put his drink on the coffee table and wrapped his left arm around Mike's freckled shoulders. Cupping a thick pec in his right hand, he bent to kiss him. Mike grinned, rubbed his stubble against Brice's beard, pulled off his baseball cap, and opened his mouth, receiving Brice's tongue. The boy tasted of chaw tobacco and bourbon. *Wonderful*, Brice thought, lapping Mike's teeth, then pushing his tongue in deeper. Mike groaned and slipped his arms around Brice's back.

For a good ten minutes, the two men necked and kissed and drank and kneaded one another's stiff crotches. Brice refreshed their drinks and pulled off his own shirt, and then they kissed and caressed a little more. Brice flicked, tugged, and twisted Mike's nipples. Mike nodded, winced, and whimpered, kissing Brice even more hungrily.

"So you're liking this, right?" Brice whispered against Mike's stubbled cheek. "You're not just putting on a show 'cause of the money?"

"Yeah, I'm liking it. Ain't just the cash." Mike grinned, squeezing Brice's beefy, fur-coated pecs.

"So what do you like about me?" Brice said. "Gimme a little ego food for my money."

Mike chuckled. "I like your dark hair, and your beard, and your pretty blue eyes, and…and your lips, and this big chest of yours, and…it feels like you got a real big cock."

"Nice. You have an acting career in front of you, bud. Get naked now," Brice ordered, pulling away. Another advantage to hiring a hustler: Mike knew he'd been paid a lot of money to obey, and obedience turned Brice on.

"You bet," Mike said, pulling off his cowboy boots, unbuckling his belt, and shucking off his jeans and a very skimpy pair of camo briefs. He stood before Brice, hands on his hips, his erect cock swaying before him. The tip of it was already dewy with arousal.

"Damn, you're fine. The good Lord sure knew what He was doing when He made you," Brice said, ignoring the second's spasm of guilt that any reference to the divine caused to flare up in him. "You ready to give me what I want?"'"

"You just paid my rent for the next couple of months, so I'm up for anything, man. Whatever you're into. Just tell me what to do."

Brice smiled. He leaned back against the couch, unzipped his pants, and pulled his prick out. "That's what I wanted to hear. Get over here and suck my cock."

"You bet. I give great head, I promise." Mike fell to his knees before Brice, grinned up at him and winked, then buried his face in the older man's pubic hair. He breathed deep, licked his lips, and took Brice's hard-on into his mouth.

BRICE SAT NAKED AT THE piano, picking out slow chords and humming the tune under his breath. D to E to F-sharp minor, one of the progressions in "What's Always Missing," a mournful ballad included on his last CD, *Mountain Back Road*, the one he'd had such high hopes for, the one that won no awards and sold only moderately. Sea breeze filled the room, as did the distant sound of surf. Candles, the only illumination now, flickered around the room. Despite his penchant for paying for sex escorts, Brice still liked to fuck in a romantic atmosphere.

"You like that?" he asked, gazing across the room at the naked hustler sprawled on his couch. "I wrote that."

"Uuummmm huhh," Mike grunted. After five whiskey sours, Mike was shit-faced, which was fine by Brice.

Brice played another couple of bars in the treble clef, regarded his delectable guest, and stroked his own hard-on. Usually Brice's cock had problems working after so much booze, but not tonight, not with a man as delicious as Mike.

The hustler lay on the couch on his side, nodding along to the melody, his eyes glazed with drink.

Been too long. Been too long. Been too long, Brice thought, admiring Mike's powerful build. *God, I live for nights like this. I starve for 'em. He's just fucking beautiful.*

"You look good enough to eat." Brice let the final D chord fade. He stood, moving unsteadily toward the couch. He knelt beside Mike, stroked his shaggy hair, and fondled his half-hard cock. He bent, took the hustler's cock into his mouth, and sucked him softly till Mike got stiff and began to squirm.

"Ohhh, damn, that feels good. Oh, damn," Mike grunted, thrusting down Brice's throat.

Brice pulled off, licking his lips. "I'm going to fuck you now, buddy," Brice said, pinching Mike's nipples. "You ready for that? You want my dick up inside you?"

"Ohhh, yeah," Mike mumbled, his drunk, wide green eyes gazing up at Brice.

"Good boy. Here we go." Brice helped Mike sit up and then pushed him down into a kneeling position on the floor. Brice bent him over the couch seat and pushed KY up the hustler's compact butt. He finger-fucked him, gently at first, then more roughly.

"Open up now, pretty boy. Open up for me."

"Umm, that's good. Sure, man. Y'bet." Mike grunted low and writhed back against Brice's hand, clearly relishing the penetration.

"God, you're tight. This is going to feel so fine," Brice groaned, slipping on a condom and applying more lube. Without further foreplay, he pushed his cock up Mike's ass. Mike bucked, grunting with discomfort at the sudden invasion. Brice chuckled, gripping the rent boy's stubbly jaw.

"Does that hurt?" Brice asked, cock-probing Mike's butt with slow, shallow thrusts.

Mike whimpered and nodded but spread his thighs even wider. "Yeah, a little. But please don't stop."

"That's the right attitude." Brice pulled out long enough to give Mike's buttocks a few hard slaps and to add another dollop of lube to his hole. Then he wrapped an arm around Mike's chest, gripped his cock, slammed into him again, and began plowing him hard and fast.

Mike moaned and sobbed and gasped. Brice took his time, making the pleasure last, slowing his rhythm, speeding up, slowing, speeding up, slowing, speeding up. By the time Brice came, bourbon-soused Mike had already climaxed in Brice's hand and passed out.

Brice shucked off the semen-heavy condom and tossed it on the carpet. He tugged off the couch's afghan, pushed Mike's limp frame down onto the floor, stretched out beside him, and spread the blanket over them. Wrapping an arm around the unconscious boy, he snuggled close.

God, he's hot, Brice thought, running his sticky fingers through Mike's messy hair. God, he's so hot. God, his tits tasted good. God, his asshole was so fucking tight. Rapture. Man. Rapture. He's so warm. Why can't I hold a boy this hot more often? Why can't I have a guy like this in my life? Fuck. I'm tired of lonely and I'm tired of lies. I'm tired of having to pay for sex. I'm tired of living year after year with so little touch.

Listening to the waves and the wind, Brice pulled Mike closer and passed out.

CHAPTER THREE

MIKE ROUSED BRICE NEAR DAWN BY STROKING his nipples and cock. The two men kissed and cuddled. They both hit the bathroom to piss and to gulp aspirins and big glasses of water. Brice led Mike into the bedroom and shoved him backward onto the bed. Climbing onto him, Brice bit his pecs, sucking and chewing his nipples with such ferocity that Mike begged him to stop. Brice reluctantly rolled off, spooning the hustler from behind till both fell asleep.

Brice woke to the blaze of sunrise over the Atlantic. He rolled over, buried his face in Mike's hair, and fingered the boy's still-lubed hole. Mike grunted, nodded, and bucked back in welcome. Soon Brice was rubbing Mike's prostate and lubing up both their cocks, ready to take Mike again. He'd managed to wedge his cockhead up inside Mike and the hairy hustler was groaning against the hand Brice had clamped over his mouth when ringing began in the living room. It was Brice's cell phone.

"Screw it," Brice growled. "They can leave a message."

Mike nodded against Brice's hand and cocked a furry leg, giving Brice a better angle. Brice's prick slid home, and the two men began rocking together and groaning in unison.

"FUCK, MY HOLE'S SORE. THAT'S one fat dick you got there," Mike said, rubbing his bare ass.

"Your hole's a treasure, bud. A man-milker of the first order." Brice, dressed in nylon gym shorts, poured them both big mugs of coffee.

Earlier, Brice and his rent boy had indulged in

a long nap, one interrupted three times by the phone's repetitive buzzing. Brice had roused, pissed again, popped a few more back pills, then hoisted Mike's legs in the air and fucked him yet again, the pace of his cock-thrusts unhurried and leisurely.

Now it was nearly noon. Bright light flooded the kitchen; wind off the sea whistled around the windows. Brice was offering his buck-naked guest half and half for his coffee when Brice's phone rang yet again. He cursed and snatched up the thing.

So many messages from Steve? What the hell? I'll call him once this hot kid leaves. Irritably, Brice turned the phone off.

Mike leaned against the kitchen counter sipping coffee while Brice cooked up grits and relished the sight of his guest's continuing nakedness.

"You weren't kidding when you said you were gonna get rough," Mike said, fondling his swollen nipples. "My tits are just as raw as my butthole. Bruised-up, even."

"Sorry. It's been a while since I got laid. You're so sexy that I got carried away. Yep, you sure earned your fee. I wasn't too rough, was I?"

"Naw. I'm tough. I can take it," Mike said, scratching his balls. "Hey, you mind if I grab a shower? I got a late-afternoon shift at Walmart."

"Sure. Go on. You want some sausage patties to go with these grits?"

"That sounds great," Mike said, padding off toward the master bedroom. "Ain't often a john cooks for me."

Mike was still showering and Brice was browning sausage when the doorbell buzzed. "What the hell?" Brice snarled. When he peered through the peephole, he saw his bass player Buddy waiting in the corridor.

"Fuck, fuck, fuck," Brice muttered. *What the hell is he doing here?*

He darted down the hall and into the master bathroom. "Hey! Hey, Mike," he blurted, tearing the shower curtain aside. "You gotta hide."

"What? What's wrong?"

"My bass—a buddy of mine is at the door. He has no idea I fuck guys. Come on."

The buzzer sounded again. Brice tossed Mike a towel. "Hide in the...the bedroom closet."

"Closet. Appropriate," Mike sighed, toweling off and looking annoyed.

Brice pulled on a tank top before tearing back down the hall. He paused to compose himself, sharply aware of how fine a dissembler he'd become after decades in the closet. Then he cracked open the door.

"Hey, Buddy," Brice said, mustering a yawn. "What's up? I thought you were in Orlando."

Buddy, a bald, athletic man a few inches taller than Brice, just stared at him, as if he'd never seen him before. "I was. I just drove over here. I really need to talk to you," he said. This was not the usual laid-back Buddy, full of teasing wit. This man was tense in a way Brice had never seen him before.

"Sorry. Just got up. Hungover. Got a sore throat. You better not come in."

"Steve sent me. Why aren't you answering his calls? Something's happened. Something big." Buddy placed a hand against the door and nudged. "Brice, let me in. We have to talk."

Brice cleared his throat. "Okay, look. I got…a woman with me, okay? I'll call Steve in just a little bit."

"A woman?" Buddy's tone was sardonic. "Really? Guess this means you're finally over Shelly, huh? Well, why don't you introduce us?"

"Don't think so. She's shy. Look, man, how about we get together for dinner? Right now, I don't think—"

"Let me in, damn it," Buddy said, wedging his foot between the door and the wall.

"No, Buddy. Sorry. I—"

Buddy slammed his shoulder against the door, knocking Brice backward. "Hey, honey girl, come on out!" Buddy yelled. "I'm Brice's bass player, and I'm dying to meet you."

"Damn you, Buddy," Brice said, grabbing at his arm and missing by an inch. "Come back here."

Buddy ignored Brice. He stalked down the hall into the living room. Brice followed, stomach clenching.

In the living room, Buddy came to an abrupt stop. He scowled, surveying the evidence of last night's debauchery: piles of clothes, the tube of lube, the used condom.

"Looks like a shitload of fucking to me," Buddy said, crossing his arms and looking disgusted. "You hired yourself a whore?"

"Uh, just a bar pick-up. Look, let me get dressed, and you and I can head out and grab a beer and talk about whatever—"

"Your girl dresses like a man," Buddy said, swiping up Mike's camo briefs and one of his cowboy boots. "Got yourself a country girl? A cowgirl?" He examined the boot, then the underwear. "Size 11 boot? Sounds like an Amazon, man." He dropped both briefs and boot and snatched up the jeans. "Men's jeans. Size 32. What's going on, Brice? Wait! I think I know." With a grim grin, Buddy dropped the jeans and headed toward the master bedroom.

Brice followed him, mouth dry with anxiety. "Buddy, stop this shit. What the hell are you doing?"

"I'm confirming a suspicion. The big news Steve told me." When Brice grabbed his arm, Buddy shook him off. He strode into the bedroom. He stared at the mussed sheets. Grimacing, he picked up another tube of lube. He dropped it on the bed and stepped into the master bathroom.

"Okay. Mirror's still steamed. The vixen's been showering?" He gave the air an exaggerated sniff. "That isn't perfume. Smells like Old Spice to me."

"Okay, Sherlock. Enough of this," Brice snapped. Again, he gripped Buddy's arm, trying to drag him out. This time, the bigger man shoved Brice backward against the wall. Pain spasmed through Brice's lower back. Buddy threw open the bathroom closet.

"No?" Buddy stared at the roomy space full of shelves: folded towels, soap, shaving cream, and deodorant. "Honey girl? Where are you?" he yelled, re-entering the bedroom.

"Get out," Brice said, seizing Buddy by the elbow. Buddy responded by shoving Brice so hard that he fell backward onto the bed.

Buddy threw open the bedroom closet and stepped back, as if he were expecting a peevish anaconda to uncoil itself, reveal its rows of needle teeth, and lunge at them.

For a long moment, Buddy and Brice simply stared at the line of plaid shirts, T-shirts, and faded jeans on hangers. Then Buddy squatted, gazing past the row of Brice's expensive cowboy boots into the closet's far interior, and heaved a raspy chuckle.

"Damn, Brice, your girl needs to get herself one of those pretty, pink-handled razors. Look at those hairy calves." Buddy stood and parted the concealing veil of fabric.

Mike stood pressed against the far wall, a towel wrapped around his lithe waist. His face was very red. "Uh, hi, man?" he said, crossing his arms across his teeth-bruised chest.

"Well, howdy," Buddy said, extending his hand. "You can't be Brice's lady friend. Who're you?"

Mike's flushed face grew redder. "Uh, I'm Mike. We were just—"

When he gripped Buddy's hand, his towel slipped off, dropping down to swathe his feet. His dick, large even when limp, swayed in the morning light. He cursed, released Buddy's hand, and bent to snatch up the towel.

"Yeow! You can put that big thang away," Buddy said, jolting back. "Well, Brice?" he said, turning to his friend. "Who the hell is this?"

"Mike's a personal trainer I hire when I'm down here," Brice said. His capacity for composing quick, convenient lies had grown very deft over the years. "We were just working out."

"Really? This closet the door to your private gym? So where's the woman you mentioned?"

Brice got to his feet, willing his voice steady. To hide his shaking hands, he clasped them behind his back.

"She must have stepped out while I was brewing coffee. You know women, they—"

"I know women, yeah. But do you?"

Brice frowned. "What do you mean by that?"

"I mean you need to give Steve a call. Turns out you're in the headlines back in Nashville. Turns out you're not the man everybody thought you were. You're not the man *I* thought you were."

Buddy turned to sneer at Mike, who was edging toward the bedroom door, towel covering his groin. "You Brice's new boyfriend?"

"Boyfriend? Naw."

"You a whore?"

Mike gave both men a pained look. "Whore? Naw. Like he said, I'm just here 'cause—"

"You know who this guy is?" Buddy jutted a thumb toward Brice.

"Ah. Nick?"

Buddy guffawed. "Naw. This ain't Nick. This here's Brice Brown. Ever heard of him? Country music singer?"

Mike paused, adjusting the towel about his waist. "Uh. Yeah." He peered at Brice, rubbed his eyes, and grunted. "Well, hell. Wow. Yeah, I know a song of yours, I think. You look kinda different."

"He puts on a few pounds in between photo shoots. He loves the booze and the pork rinds. Yep, Brice here is famous. Well, he *was* famous. Lately, he's been *sorta* famous. But now he's *really* famous."

Something about the grim expression on Buddy's face made clear that "really famous" was not the kind of famous that Brice had been craving lately. He cleared his throat and glared at Buddy. "What are you talking about? You mentioned headlines. What headlines?"

Buddy crossed his arms and regarded Brice. Sadness flickered over his face, replaced by an expression of contempt.

"Zac outed you, man. He went to the press."

"What?"

"He told 'em you and him were lovers. Told 'em that's why he quit the band. 'Cause you dumped him."

"Oh, shit. Oh, holy shit," Brice said, sitting heavily on the bed. Disbelief made him dizzy. *Zac. Zac. Oh, man, why would you do such a thing?*

"Uh, damn, man, I better head out," Mike muttered. "Let you all talk."

"That'd be a good idea, kid," Buddy said, curling his lip as the hustler fled the room.

"Guess we do need to talk. You want a beer?" Brice said, getting to his feet. A cold numbness spread beneath his breastbone, as if the news about Zac had functioned as a long needle of Novocaine.

"Kinda early, but sure," Buddy said. Brice headed for the kitchen and Buddy followed him. In the living room, Mike was pulling on his clothes as fast as he could. "Bye," he blurted. Before Brice could respond, the hustler had scuttled down the hall and slammed the front door behind him.

Shit. He was fine. Guess I'll never see him again, Brice thought, pulling two beer cans from the fridge. He popped both, handed one to Buddy, and took a seat on the couch where Mike had sprawled, so prettily naked and submissive, just hours ago.

"So, was he a whore? Or are you dating him?" Buddy took an armchair. He didn't look at Brice. He looked out the plate-glass windows and over the sea.

Brice took a long pull on his beer, contemplating one lie after another and discarding them all as worthless and far too late. "You really want to know?"

"Yeah. Yeah, I do. I think the whole thing's hard to believe, but I wanna know. We've been friends for years, Brice. Or I thought we were. I couldn't believe what Steve said that Zac said, but then I come over here and...."

"And find a naked man in my closet. Yeah. Yeah, Mike's a hustler."

"Shit. You pay for sex?"

"Easier than having a real relationship. Safer. Easier to keep secret."

"So you've been lying to us all these years? You're really queer? Gay, I mean."

Brice licked beer off his upper lip. "I want other men, if that's what you mean. Yep. 'Fraid so."

"How long have you known?"

"Since high school. Since I looked at guys in the locker room after gym class and wanted them. Since I went to church alone and prayed that God would change me. But He never did."

"So, what about your marriage?"

"I thought I was in love with Shelly. I thought being with her would change things. But nothing really changed. And then last spring she figured things out. She found a few letters Zac'd sent me. That's when she asked me to move out. She's been real good at keeping my secret. I guess she likes being a star's wife, even if it's all a sham."

"So Zac's telling the truth? You and him...fucked?"

"We did more than fuck. We cared about one another."

Buddy snorted. "Really?"

"Really." Brice hung his head. He felt exhausted. He wanted nothing more than to down half a bottle of George Dickel, pop four or five back pills, and head back to bed.

"You and Zac? You both look like wrestlers. You both grew up hunting and fishing and splitting wood. You're cocksuckers?" He laughed and the sound hung like a secretive smog in the air around them. "Which one of you was the woman?"

Brice's mouth twisted. "Don't get nasty. I don't ask about whether or not you eat your wife's pussy, do I?"

"No, you don't. Yes, I do, as a matter of fact. Tastes like salmon fresh from Alaska." For a split-second, the Buddy that Brice knew appeared, only to be replaced by this cold man sitting across from him.

Buddy consumed the rest of his beer in a long gulp. Then he stood.

"You better call Steve. He's doesn't know whether to run, shit, or go blind. He says this news is going to ruin you."

Brice stood. For a split-second, he thought he might cry. "Yeah. I guess he's right. So will I see you back in Nashville?"

"Naw. I don't think so. Sorry, man. I don't want to be implicated, y'know? I mean, if folks believe that you were giving it to Zac, they might think...."

"What about next spring? Steve told me that Molasses Mount just offered us the deal. They'll want us to tour—"

Buddy rolled his eyes. "Are you crazy? Don't you get it? They're sure to cancel your contract now. The pop music folks might tolerate David Bowie and Elton John, but country music fans are wanting to hear about God and tradition. They're not gonna buy a gay guy's CDs."

Buddy crushed the beer can in one fist, then dropped it on the carpet. "Call Steve. I'm sorry this happened. Good luck, man. And goodbye." Buddy turned, strode down the hall, and left the condo, leaving the door open behind him.

Brice leaned back into the couch. He looked at the sun on the sea for a long time. Then he opened another beer, washed down a handful of pain pills and a couple of sleeping pills, and, back aching, went back to bed.

CHAPTER FOUR

IT WAS DARK WHEN BRICE DRIFTED TO THE surface of his chemical sleep. Rain was pattering on the windowsill. He rolled out of bed, took another round of pain pills, pissed, and took a long shower, savoring the way the hot water eased his lumbar region. Then he slumped naked on the couch, took a deep breath and a big slug of bourbon, and listened to the messages Steve had left on his phone.

"Brice, I have some bad news. I need to talk to you as soon as possible. Call me."

"Brice, call me, dammit."

"Brice, where the hell are you? We have a crisis on our hands. Call me!"

"Since you aren't returning my calls for some damned reason, I'm just going to have to break the bad news now. There's an interview with Zac Lanier coming out in tomorrow's *Nashville Banner* complete with a couple of photos. He claims that you and he were lovers, gay lovers, back when he played in your band. I've tried to squelch the article, but I've failed. What I need to know from you is…is this true? If it isn't, maybe we can salvage something. If it is, Brice…I don't know what we're going to do."

"Brice, if you've listened to my previous messages, you know you're in big trouble. Call me so we can do some damage control."

Brice peered at the clock—8:30 pm—and then dialed Steve's number.

"Where the hell have you been?" He had never heard Steve so angry before. He sounded rabid.

"Sorry, man. Had company. Drank too much. Passed out."

"You better have tickets back to Nashville?"

"Yep. Gonna leave tomorrow."

"Good. Right now I need to know one thing. Is it true? What Zac said. What you tell the rest of the world is one thing. What you tell me.... I need the truth. You owe me that much."

Brice took another swig of bourbon. "Yeah, I guess I do. It's true."

"Damn." Steve's breath resounded down the line as if he were hyperventilating. "Why the hell didn't you tell me? That way we could have headed off any possible.... Well, it's too late now. I did my best to keep the story out of the paper, but my efforts just seemed to make the bastards more determined to run it. You better fly first class and don't speak to a soul at the airport or on the plane, not even to ask for a damn pillow. Or a drink. You come by my office day after tomorrow early, say, nine am. By the time we meet, I'll have a better sense of where things stand."

"Thanks, Steve. I'm sorry I didn't—"

Brice stopped speaking. Steve had already hung up.

THE RAIN WAS WARM, BUT the Atlantic was cold. Brice, wearing nothing but gym shorts, stood ankle-deep in the surf. Addled on liquor and pills, he swayed from right to left, from left to right, like a cliff-side fern buffeted by high wind. To the north and south, the towering beachfront properties glowed, interrupting the autumn dark, illuminating a faint mist that hung over the sand. It was quiet except for the sound of breaking waves and low tide. The rain continued, tapping Brice's high brow and broad shoulders. He looked out to sea. Blackness of sky above the horizon; deeper blackness of ocean below. A few miles out, a pinprick light glowed, indicating a distant ship.

Brice tallied up the people he cared for as he waded farther into the sea, the chill climbing up his legs. Zac, who'd now matched Brice betrayal for betrayal. Shelly, his wife, who'd kept his secret so as to enjoy the occasional limelight and stay in their fine country estate. Steve, whose angry voice still resounded in his head. Buddy, the look of contempt on his face. Who else? His sister Leigh and her son Carden, whom he saw at best once or twice a year. Who else? His lead guitarist Tim. His drummer Jeff. His keyboardist Ken. The latter two religious types, likely to be horrified at the truth. And all their careers in country music derailed, if not ended entirely, by the public revelation of Brice's secret. How many of the folks in Brice's life would turn their backs on him now that they knew the truth?

Brice waded farther out till the cold water reached his thighs. So few kith and kin for a man who'd achieved so many of his professional ambitions, a man who'd lived forty years upon this planet. The things in his life were more abundant. The house near Franklin he'd shared with Shelly till she found Zac's letters and asked Brice to move out. The condo in Nashville where he'd lived since the separation. The house back in West Virginia, the place he'd grown up, inherited when his elderly father died. A collection of top-of-the-line guitars and pianos. The Daytona condo. His latest pickup truck, a slate-gray Dodge Ram 2500. His latest motorcycle, a black Honda Shadow. A slew of wildly expensive cowboy boots. A plethora of carefully hidden porn, both video and print. How many of those solid, substantial prizes he'd collected over the years of his success in the music business would he lose now that the world knew he'd slept with a man?

Brice strode out another yard, moving farther away from solidity and deeper into insubstantiality. The cold sea reached his genitals, dousing and shriveling them. He thought of Zac again, how furry and warm the man had been, how sweet he was to cuddle with during that one winter season they'd shared, so full of passion and kindness and need. He thought of Mike, grunting happily as Brice drove into him. He thought of Doug, that Philly call boy. He thought of faces and nipples and cocks and thighs and asses he'd briefly adored, briefly tasted and touched, most of the men's names long forgotten.

The water licked at Brice's plump belly, tickling his navel. He shuddered. *What'll be left if I live? Who'll mourn if I die?*

Nausea rose up in him. He turned his back on the sea, the horizon, and the sole ship's far flickering. He staggered up out of the water and onto the land. As soon as his bare feet hit dry sand, he fell to his knees and retched. Then he wiped his beard, fell over onto his side, pulled his knees to his chest, and began to sob.

Sunrise woke him, and the advancing tide lapping his toes. He rose on one elbow, a foul taste in his mouth. Before him, the Atlantic was a restless swarm of gold. He stared into the blinding light for a split-second, then closed his eyes.

Lord, the preachers back home would say that I'm an abomination in Your eyes. I don't think I believe that, though I'm not sure. Didn't You make me this way? I tried to change, but I can't. Help me, God. Ain't I Your child too? I need strength. Show me what to do.

Brice opened his eyes and staggered to his feet. His back ached, his knees ached, and his left eye seemed glazed, as if it were a window coated with ice. He shook his head, trying to throw off confusion, then shambled up the beach toward the condo tower, his belly growling. There was, he knew, a joint just north of Daytona on Highway A-1-A with strong coffee and top-notch biscuits and gravy. That would make a nice stop before the flight back to Nashville.

CHAPTER FIVE

THE SUN WAS BRIGHT AND THE BREEZE VERY COLD as Brice approached Steve's office building on the edge of Nashville's Music Row, the neighborhood that served as the business center of the country music industry. The chilly weather was well timed. It gave Brice an excuse to disguise himself as best he could, with a bulky rawhide jacket, a voluminous tartan scarf, and a brown fisherman's cap pulled low over his forehead. His in-between-CDs extra bulk served the same purpose. For future camouflage—if the consequences of Zac's newspaper interview proved to be as disastrous as Brice feared—he'd already decided to stop dyeing his beard and let it grow out into the thick bush he'd worn in college.

No fucking photographers, thank God, Brice thought, scanning the street. He loped down the sidewalk and slipped inside the building as fast as he could.

The hallway and flight of stairs leading to Steve's second-story office were blessedly free of spectators. When Brice entered the office, Carolyn, Steve's saggy-faced receptionist, was standing at a file cabinet, her back to him. She turned, regarding Brice over her spectacles. As he'd feared, the smile she had always given him in the past was not in evidence. Instead, her look was sour and accusatory.

Hardly a surprise, Brice thought, gazing at the devout Christian bric-a-brac displayed on her desk. *Anybody real religious is bound to be my natural enemy now.* He forced himself to meet her eyes and smile, determined to do his best to act as if nothing had changed. Maybe, if he put on the charm that had always swayed her in the past, her Southern politeness would conquer her judgmental piety.

"Howdy, Mizz Carolyn. That sure is a pretty blouse. How was your Thanksgiving? Lots of tasty turkey, I hope?"

"Mr. Brown," Carolyn said, her tone leaden. Glaring, she pursed her lips and looked him up and down, as if he were a rare specimen of zoological horror foreign to these parts, then took a seat behind her desk. "Mr. Morgan is waiting for you. Go on in."

"Mr. Brown?" It took me two years to convince her to call me "Brice." Shit. Brice's belly clenched up. This, he realized with a gray wash of despair, was the sort of reception he'd have to get used to in future, thanks to Zac, thanks to the secrets Brice had striven to keep since junior high school in his hometown of Hinton, West Virginia.

Brice muttered his thanks and hurried past her and into Steve's inner office.

Steve stood by the window, fingers tented, gazing down into the street. A short, stocky man with wavy gray hair, he turned as Brice entered. The hopelessness in his sharp-featured face made Brice's belly gripe him even more fiercely.

"Hey, Steve," Brice said, unzipping his jacket, loosening his scarf, and pulling off his hat. Apprehension and shame coated the back of his tongue with a bitter taste. "Carolyn out there was downright rude to me."

Steve sighed, ushering Brice to a seat before taking his own behind the desk. "You shouldn't be surprised. She told me this morning that she doesn't want to deal with you, that what you are is against her faith."

"Yeah, I figured. Well, screw her," Brice said, dropping his cap on a side table. "I don't care what she thinks. What do *you* think?"

"Did you encounter any reporters outside? They've been swarming down there."

"Not a one. Answer me, man. What do you think?"

"First of all, here's the interview," Steve said, handing Brice the previous day's issue of *The Nashville Banner.* "Have you seen it?"

"Naw. Spent all day yesterday traveling."

Steve cleared his throat. "Read it later. After a couple of stiff drinks. In any other context, the photos would be fairly innocuous, but combined with what Zac says in the interview, they're pretty damning." He shifted his gaze to the piles of papers on his desk and then to the bare branches trembling in November gusts beyond the window.

Reluctantly, Brice slipped the newspaper into his coat's inner pocket. *Feels like dropping a scorpion down my briefs. Bound to sting sooner or later.* "Steve, you're scaring me. So…how bad is it? What do we do now?"

"It's as bad as it can be. Other papers are taking up the story. I'm surprised that you weren't mobbed by reporters on the way here. Molasses Mount has canceled your contract. No new CD. No spring tour. You're without a label."

Brice cursed and moaned. He propped his elbows on his knees and cradled his head in his hands. His throat grew tight with the threat of tears, but he forced the feelings back. *I'm a country boy, goddamn it. My granddaddy fought in World War One, and his granddaddy fought for the Confederacy. No way I'm going to fucking cry in front of a witness.*

Brice sat in silence for a moment, gathering his composure. Then he looked Steve in the face. "So I'm without a label. Am I without a manager? Are you gonna drop me?"

Steve looked as if he might be sick. "Brice, I just don't think there's any way to repair the damage. I don't think there's anything left I can do for you. If you were in pop music, it might be a different matter. But country music? You know how folks in this town are. How country music fans are. So many are pious, old-fashioned, blue-collar, rural, or judgmental. They will never forget this. Most people are going to treat you just like Carolyn did. All those macho country-boy lyrics of yours…those love songs everyone assumed were directed to women, to your wife…. No one's going to take you or your music seriously. They're going to see you and hear you and think…."

"That I'm not a real man. That I'm a sinner and a pervert and a pansy. Do you think that?"

Steve shook his head and his glare softened to a sad expression "No, I don't. My nephew in New Jersey is gay. But it isn't my opinion that sells music. I don't think you and I…." Steve trailed off, gaze veering out the window again.

"Oh, God. Steve. Please. Don't drop me. Writing songs and singing them is all I know how to do. How am I gonna give all that up? What else can I do? I was dreaming about being a Nashville singer since I was a brat weeding my daddy's garden and plunking away at my grandmother's piano. I have bills, man. Mortgages. What'll I—"

Brice paused. The lump in his throat swelled. He choked up, again gulping back tears. He hung his head and managed to croak, "Please."

"If only you'd told me before." Steve shook his head. "Have you talked to Shelly since the article appeared? Is she freaking out?"

"Can't get hold of her. Yesterday, I called her on and off, but she won't pick up."

Brice rubbed at his receding hairline and sighed. "Shelly found out about me and Zac months ago. That's why we separated. I find it kinda hard to believe that she'll let me move back in now that the secret's out."

"She knew? Damn it. Who else knew? Other than Zac and whatever other guys you've…been intimate with."

"Just my sister Leigh back home."

"I still can't believe you didn't tell me. I had to find out with the rest of the world," Steve groused. "Keep trying to get hold of Shelly. Who knows? Maybe if she realizes that reconciliation could salvage your career, she'll agree to it. Or what if you got into one of those therapy programs that folks claim can turn you straight? I've already done a little research, and there's an organization like that here in Nashville. It's called Exodus International, and they employ several therapists. If you agree to do that, I could call them and see if they'd be willing to treat you."

"Oh, damn." Brice wiped his eyes and coughed. "Really? That sounds horrible. I've been looking at guys since I was, hell, thirteen or so. I can't believe that kinda evangelical shit would work."

"Maybe not. But maybe so. Maybe they could change you. Who knows? Either way, maybe your fans would be convinced that you're at least trying to change."

"Can't we just sue Zac for defamation of character or libel or slander or whatever the fuck it's called?"

"We could. But that would just extend the bad publicity into weeks or months of legal wrangling and possibly a trial. And you just told me that you're a homosexual. It's not libel if it's true. Zac's lawyer would dig up all the other men you've slept with. Have there been a lot?"

Brice blushed. "Uh, yeah. I, uh, got a pretty vigorous sex drive. And, uh, since I knew I needed to keep my homosexuality a secret if I was gonna go anywhere in Nashville, a lot of 'em were, uh, one-night stands. Hustlers, mainly."

"Hustlers? Oh, God." Steve rolled his eyes. "Are you a fool? It's a miracle one of them didn't blackmail you or expose you long ago."

"Hey, look! I'm horny, well, just about all the time. I have my needs, y'know? I had to have some kind of release. It was always safe sex, I swear. I just figured a steady relationship with one guy would be a bad idea. That's actually why I broke it off with Zac. I was afraid that us meeting one another on a regular basis would increase the possibility that we'd be found out."

"So you broke it off with him? In the article, he says he broke up with you."

"Naw, that's not how it happened. He was getting really serious, and...I cared about him, and, to be honest, I was pretty close to falling for him hard, but I knew that getting in any deeper was a bad idea for both of us, so I broke it off. He was really upset."

"Ironic. You broke up with Zac so as to reduce the risk of exposure, but that break-up seems to have embittered him so much that he was willing to expose both of you. What a massive mess. Does Zac have any other evidence he could use if we went to court?"

"Yeah." Brice rubbed at his tight temples. His back was throbbing again. "More photos...some of 'em pretty sexy. Quite a few letters, some of 'em explicit."

"Damn." Steve rose and began to pace. "Look, Brice, if Carolyn weren't holding my calls right now, this phone would be ringing off the hook. Reporters have been calling me constantly, asking for an interview with you. How about you and I handpick one who's likely to be, well, less vicious than most? You could repent. You could say that Zac exaggerated or lied outright. You could play up the Jesus thing. Tell folks that you have faith that God can transform you. Will you at least think about it?"

"Yeah. I guess, though I'm pretty damned tired of lying. Been lying about myself since I was in junior high."

"I hate to say this, but if you don't keep lying, you'll lose everything. And you'd better think about divesting yourself of some properties too. Your expenditures in the last few years have been pretty extreme. You've been spending as if you were still on top, and now...well, without the Molasses Mount deal.... I'll ask around, but I'm pretty sure no label will touch you. Maybe, in a year or two...."

"Jesus, a year or two? What the hell am I gonna—"

Brice jolted up out of his seat. "Okay, I can't stand any more of this. This is too hard. I'll call you in a few days, okay?"

"All right, Brice." Steve moved from around the desk and gave Brice a tentative squeeze of the shoulder. "I'd stay out of public spaces, if I were you. With a scandal like this, reporters are sure to be following you everywhere. And I know what a temper you have. For God's sake, don't punch any of them. You don't need an assault charge to make the mess we're in even bigger. Maybe you should get out of town for a while. Why don't you visit your family for the winter holidays?"

"Yeah. Might be a good idea. But Steve, one thing. Do you know why Zac did it? Why he told them? I know it must have been money, whatever big sum the newspaper offered him, but.... Surely he knew it'd ruin me. I mean, I dicked him over, but I didn't think he hated me so much that he'd do what he did."

"Actually, Zac called me this morning to apologize, because he knew my business would be taking a big hit. As you recall, he and I always got along very well while he was in your band, and I was really surprised when he quit. Seemed at the time like he didn't have a reason. Now I know he did."

"So you have his number? I want it. I wanna call the bastard and tell him exactly what—"

Steve shook his head. "He made me swear not to give you the number. He specifically said that he didn't want to talk to you, and he swore he'd get a restraining order against you if you start harassing him. You and I both know you don't need that kind of publicity on top of what's happened. 'Disgraced country star pursues and torments gay lover'? No, just leave him alone."

"Shit. Okay. So, did he tell you why? He's gotta have known that the story might end my career."

"Yes, he did." Steve grimaced. "Since he quit your band, he's been having problems getting work, and now his mother's suffering with advanced Alzheimer's, and he's been diagnosed...I hate to tell you this."

"What?" Brice grabbed Steve's elbow. "Tell me."

"Brice, he claimed that he ran sort of crazy after you two broke it off and he slept around a lot. Turns out he's HIV positive now, and with little health insurance."

"Oh, my God." Brice dropped Steve's arm and leaned back against the wall.

"Brice, I'm so sorry."

"I gotta get out of here," Brice gasped, snatching up his hat. "Gotta get some air, or I'm gonna puke."

"Call me," Steve urged. "Keep trying Shelly. And please consider doing an interview and visiting the Exodus International people."

Brice nodded. He tore out of the office, past a smugly smiling Carolyn. He pounded down the stairs, along the hallway, and out into the street.

"Brice! Brice Brown!"

A gathering of nearly twenty people, male and female, crowded the sidewalk before Steve's office building, shouting Brice's name. Several bore microphones; several bore video cameras. All bore faces fixed with avid journalistic determination.

"Oh, well, hell," Brice growled, scowling at them. "Get back, you fucking locusts. I ain't talking to any of you."

He tipped his cap over his eyes, turned up his coat collar, squared his shoulders, and began pushing through the noisy crowd and the click of cameras. *Where's a fucking cattle-catcher when I need it?* he thought. *Or a shit shovel like the one I used to muck out the horse stalls back home.*

Questions assailed him, some polite, some pointedly offensive.

"Brice, how long have you been a homosexual? Were you and Zac in love?"

"Brice, tell us your side of the story. What does your wife think of this? We thought you were a Christian. Don't you think homosexuality is a sin?"

"We hear your label's dropping you. What are you going to do now?"

"Was your marriage all a lie?"

"So you've been deceiving all of us all these years! Aren't you ashamed? Don't you think you've let down your fans?"

"Zac says he dumped you, and you cried like a baby. Are you sleeping with any other guys these days? Are you a top or bottom?"

"Fuck you. Get fucked. Fuck off. Move outta my way, you fucker," Brice snarled, deftly lobbing assorted versions of the F-word as he shouldered through the mob. He'd been a proud master of profanity ever since his high-school years hanging out with foul-mouthed hunting buddy Wayne Meador, an early role model with whom Brice had been futilely and furtively in love. He swatted away cameras, feinted left, then veered right, sprinting down a side street. A member of the track team at his high school, he was still fleet on his feet, despite midlife's extra weight and his stiff back. He zigzagged through a series of alleys, outdistancing the crowd. He'd just reached his Ram 2500 and was fumbling in his jeans pocket for his keys when one of the younger reporters caught up with him.

"Hey, Brice! Ever dressed in drag?" The lean, goateed man gave him a smile gleaming with derision. In any other circumstance, Brice would have found him attractive. "Or are you one of those gay boys into leather, whips, and chains?"

"You dick," Brice snarled. He shoved the reporter in the chest and threw him back against a brick wall. He had his fist cocked, preparing to punch the man in the face, when he remembered Steve's warning of only minutes before. Brice looked around—no witnesses in sight. Making the man a punching bag on which to wreak his rage was tempting, but the legal consequences, he knew, would be far greater than the brief pleasure of pummeling the man into unconsciousness.

"Go to hell, you worm," Brice spat, lowering his fist and stepping back. By now, a few of the other reporters had appeared at the end of the street and were once more shouting Brice's name. "Get the fuck out of here, and take your swarm of horseflies with you."

The man's response was predictable. Eyes wide, he gasped, "You manhandled me! I'll sue!"

"Right," Brice drawled. "Because you want all the world to hear about how scared you were that a burly faggot might kick your ass? Git!"

Brice stomped a foot and raised his fist again. The man yelped, jolted backward, spun around, and fled toward his compatriots. Brice leaped into the truck, started it up, and tire-squealed off, a waving middle finger in the Ram's rear window his form of farewell.

THE GYM IN BRICE'S CONDOMINIUM BUILDING was empty, much to his relief. After being harassed by reporters in Music Row, he was in no mood to tolerate the curious or hostile stares his fellow condo-dwellers might inflict on him. Following an angry workout—bench presses, lat work, and some much-needed time punishing the punching bag— Brice fled to his top-floor condo for a long shower. Afterwards, he sprawled in his briefs on the couch, watching rain clouds creep in over Nashville's skyline and getting up his courage to read Zac's interview. Remembering Steve's advice, he poured himself a tumbler of Glenlivet.

The article began on the front page, accompanied by a photo Zac had taken of Brice, despite his objections, after one of their last rough-sex sessions, an overnight rendezvous in a Knoxville motel. In the image, Brice lay in bed, grinning, hairy-chested, and sated. The sheet covered his legs and groin. His thick arms were folded behind his head, his furry armpits displayed, and a black Stetson that Zac had bought him was cocked over his forehead.

The photo made Brice anxious, ashamed, regretful, and nostalgic all at the same time. He well remembered that evening. He'd sucked Zac till he was close to climaxing, then ass-fucked him with his legs in the air. The feeling of having his cock buried deep inside Zac was pure rapture, so much better than the half-hearted, desultory sex Brice had shared with his wife during the first few years of their marriage, before their sex life had tapered off and faded entirely. Later, after Brice had come, he'd dragged Zac into the shower, dropped to his knees,

CHAPTER SIX

and finger-fucked him while sucking him off. The sex between them had always been glorious, as had the affectionate post-coital cuddling, and the photo served as a sharp reminder of how much Brice missed both.

He was in love with me. Why couldn't I just accept that and be thankful? Why couldn't I just go with my feelings for him and love him back? Why did I have to be a coward? Why did I have to close myself off and drive him away? If I hadn't, maybe none of this bullshit would have happened. Maybe he'd still be healthy and I wouldn't be square and fairly fucked.

The story continued on the fourth page. The photograph accompanying that segment was of Zac and Brice performing at a concert they'd given at the University of Georgia, a month after their affair had begun. Zac was playing his acoustic guitar while he and Brice sang into the same microphone, their bearded faces only inches apart. *Damn, he was so handsome. Damn, we made great music together. We were almost as good together on stage as we were in the sack.*

Brice scanned the article, wincing and groaning. Then he read the article more carefully, emitting little snorts of outrage. The contents entirely banished the razor-edged longing for Zac that the photos had evoked.

GAYS IN COUNTRY MUSIC?
A Chat with Zac Lanier,
Brice Brown's Ex-Guitarist

By Jerry Roberts

Country music has long been considered the bastion of traditionalism, old-fashioned religious faith, and family values, but now Zac Lanier, former guitarist for country star Brice Brown, has come forward with a shocking claim: he and the singer had a clandestine homosexual affair while Lanier was still a member of Brown's band. I spoke to Mr. Lanier in his apartment on the outskirts of Nashville.

JR: Mr. Lanier, when and how did your sexual relationship with Brice Brown begin?

ZL: Brice and I toured a lot together in 1995 and 1996. A mutual attraction developed, I guess you could say, but we were both reluctant to act on it. I tried to resist, because I've always been a real moral person and I knew feelings like that were wrong. Then one autumn night last year, it was mid-October 1996, after a lot of drinking at his fancy house in Williamson County—we'd had a party to celebrate the release of his latest CD—he and I ended up really intoxicated and stoned and in the hot tub together. He started stuff, touching, you know? One thing led to another. I tried to stop him, but then I was just so drunk that I gave in.

ZL: Are you saying he raped you?

ZL: No. I wouldn't say that. We were both adults. I just chose wrong.

JR. Had you been intimate in that way with a man before?

ZL: Oh, no. I was raised strict Southern Baptist. I had never even considered such a thing. The preachers back home in Georgia said it was an abomination.

JR: Do you think that Brown had been with other men before?

ZL: Oh, yeah. Lots. He seemed really experienced, if you know what I mean. Promiscuous.

JR: All this occurred at his house, you said? Was his wife there?

ZL: Not in the hot tub.

JR: I assumed that. I meant, was she in the house at the time?

ZL: Yes. She'd gone to bed hours before. I guess she'd gotten tired of all the carousing. You know how wild we country boys can get.

JR: I do indeed. How long have Brice and Shelly Brown been married?

ZL: Uhm, around ten years, I think.

JR: How did you feel, getting involved with Brown that way but knowing he had a wife?

ZL: I felt pretty bad, as you can imagine. Real guilty. As you probably know,

Brice and Shelly separated last May, and I feel kind of responsible for that. That's one of the reasons I'm coming forward now. That, and my faith. I just couldn't break God's rules anymore. I wish I could tell Shelly Brown how sorry I am and beg her forgiveness. She didn't deserve the lies we told.

JR: So how long did your affair with Brice Brown last?

ZL: Six months. Till April of this year. We used to meet in secret in motels here and there. That photo I gave you, of Brice naked in bed, I took that during one of those get-togethers. Brice got pretty attached to me. When I started to have second thoughts, he started buying me real expensive, real nice gifts, trying to convince me to stay in the relationship. But then I just couldn't take the secrets any more—every time I ran into Shelly, it nigh-about killed me, and the thought that we were lying to our fans was just awful—so I broke it off with Brice, though he cried a lot and begged me not to. Playing in his band got real uncomfortable after that—he'd harass me, you know?—get real feely—so that's when I quit.

JR: Have you had any contact with Brice Brown since?

ZL: No. I told him to stay away from me. I told him we were both sinners, and that I was tired of sinning. I stopped accepting his calls. So now I'm praying a lot and trying to get my life back on track and caring for my poor ill mother. Plus I'm dating a girl who's very spiritual and forgiving. She's helping to lead me toward the light.

JR: You're to be commended for your courage. What would you say to Brice Brown if you were ever to encounter him again?

ZL: I'd tell him to pray. Pray hard. Jesus loves him. And Jesus wants to heal him. He wants him to give up the life of a sinner and come to Him. Jesus will forgive him just like Jesus has forgiven me. I've forgiven Brice for leading me astray, so I know Jesus will too.

JR: That sounds like good advice. Thanks for speaking to me, Mr. Lanier. I know our readers will appreciate your honesty. All good luck in the future.

"Jesus fucking Christ," Brice spat. He briefly contemplated the destructive pleasure of throwing the tumbler of Scotch against the wall, but he dismissed the thought as wasteful. In West Virginia, farm boys learn early that waste is one of the cardinal crimes. Instead, Brice gulped down the rest of the glass in between bouts of muttered cussing.

"Honesty? The little bastard. The little prick. *I* broke it off with *him*, and he's been begging me to come back to him ever since. And he says *I* cried? God, I'd like to whip his ass. Greedy fucker. All that religious horseshit. He's ruined my entire life for money. For a bag of gold. Like goddamn Judas. I don't care if he's sick. He should never have—"

Brice's furious monologue was interrupted by the ringing of his cell phone. When he flipped it open, he saw Shelly's name displayed.

"Hey," Brice said. "I've been trying to get hold of you. We need to talk."

"We sure do." Shelly's voice was wry and weary. "Damn that Zac."

"You're telling me. So look, can I come by the house? I can be out there within the hour."

"I assure you, you don't want to come out here. This place has been surrounded by news crews ever since that article was published. They're like a pack of starving wolves."

"Well, sheeeee-ut! So can we meet somewhere else?"

"Yes. I have some things to say, and I want to do it in person."

Zac swallowed hard. The thought of what Shelly might say made his groin ice over. "Okay. So where?"

"Queenie's. For dinner. Say, six pm. I already talked to Lorrie. She's willing to close early so we won't be bothered by anyone. Okay?"

"Yep. Thanks, Shelly."

"See you then," she said curtly, hanging up.

"Ohhhh, fuck," Brice groaned. He bit his lower lip and ran his fingers through his thinning brown hair. Then, since his habit of running down to Jack's Bar-B-Que, his favorite downtown lunch spot, had been rendered impractical by all the bad publicity, he opened up a bag of pork rinds, stretched out on the couch beneath an afghan, and watched rain draw vertical bars of cold silver down the window glass.

QUEENIE'S WAS A ROADSIDE DINER just north of Nashville, managed since 1993 by Shelly's tart-mouthed distant cousin Lorrie Kershaw, a blonde vixen with enormous breasts and very short shorts she wore in all kinds of weather. The place specialized in hot chicken, a dish developed in Nashville: spicy chicken fried with lots of cayenne, served with white bread and pickles on the side. Brice was always hankering after hot chicken, and he and Shelly had been Queenie's regulars before the separation. In fact, there'd been a signed photo of Brice prominently displayed in the little restaurant. It was, Brice noticed as he pushed past the CLOSED sign on the door, still hung on the wall.

Brice hadn't seen Shelly's car in the rain-puddled parking lot, so he entered assuming she had yet to arrive. Lorrie sat behind the counter, cigarette in one hand and beer in the other. Instead of the outraged glare that Brice had been steeling himself against ever since Shelly suggested Queenie's as a meeting place, the look on Lorrie's face was perplexed concern.

Relief washed over Brice. *Maybe she ain't gonna tear me a new one after all,* he thought, giving Lorrie a weak wave.

"Hey, Lorrie," Brice said as he eased the door closed behind him. He knew that Lorrie hated it when folks made unnecessary noise. It was trashy, she had often declared. "Thanks for letting us meet here. It was real nice of you to close early so folks won't harass us."

"I don't mind, honey. I could do with an evening off. Shelly just called. She's stuck in traffic, but she said she'd be here soon. She said not to fix her any food—you know how her stomach gets when she's upset—but can I get you anything?"

"Right now, I'd kill for a beer," Brice said, taking a stool at the counter. "Once Shelly's here, I'd love a big plate of hot chicken, maybe a batch of fried pickles on the side."

"You got it." Lorrie ground out her cigarette and fetched a bottle of Sam Adams, a brew everyone knew Brice savored most. "So, you're in a peck of trouble, ain't you?" she said, opening the bottle and handing it to him.

"Yes, ma'am, I am," Brice said, taking a long swig of beer. It seemed to reduce the bitter taste that had filled his mouth ever since he'd heard that Zac had outed him. "I'm relieved that you're not cussing a blue streak. I figured you'd throw something at me as soon as I walked in here. I know what a temper you have and how protective you are of Shelly. And I know what a churchgoer you are. I figured you'd have taken my photo down already."

"Oh, honey, you've got me confused with the mean-spirited kind of Christian. Them's pit bulls. Christ was a shepherd of lambs, not pit bulls. I've committed too many sins myself to judge other folks. I must admit, a couple customers complained about your picture and told me I ought to take it down, but I told them that they ought to kiss my country ass. They flew right outta here in high dudgeon."

Lorrie snickered. Brice guffawed. He'd always relished Lorrie's crude sense of humor. She was as down-home as Shelly was sophisticated. "Well, thanks for that. I need all the support I can get."

"I know you do, sweetie pie. Shelly confided in me about you a long time ago, since I'm about the only family she's got, other than those stuck-up parents of hers. At first I was shocked, but then I prayed, and, well, there's this sweet little lesbian in my congregation, well, she ain't little, she's built like a linebacker, bless her heart, but her soul's pure gold, and she lives near me, and she and I have been making Mexican food together once a week for three years now—Taco Tuesdays, we call it—and I consider her a dear friend, so...I ain't judging you, Brice. You cain't help how you're made any more'n I can. Yes, you lied to Shelly, but I can see why...especially considering all that's happened to y'all in the last forty-eight hours. That haitful, haitful, *haitful* Zac Lanier. So destructive. So selfish. Hasn't he ever heard of 'Do unto others?'"

Lorrie popped open a Bud Light for herself and then lit another cigarette. "It's not like you and Shelly had a grand soap-opera love, and then you spurned her and broke her heart. I know my cousin. She grew up with money, and she was always determined to stay accustomed to that lifestyle. We both know that's why she married you, the handsome, wealthy, famous country star. She used you, honey."

"Yeah. I guess so. Guess I got what I deserved. I sure used her."

"Seems like y'all used one another. You got, what? A show of normality? And she got to pose in pretty dresses for *Country Weekly* and *People*, and she got to play the fine lady in that fancy house of yours. And she ain't been as lonely as you might think, if you know what I mean." Lorrie inhaled, grinned, and blew out a big smoke ring. "You ain't been the only one with secrets."

"Really?" A flicker of husbandly jealousy ran through Brice, then just as suddenly snuffed out. "That's good, I guess. Yeah, that's good. I've been feeling awfully guilty. We never really had...."

"A real marriage. I know, honey. She's told me. Hell, Harland hasn't pushed my lil' button for going on five years. Or licked it neither! Lots of folks past the craziness of youth are in the same boat. For most of us, marriage ain't exactly a fuck-a-minute. Was sex with Zac any good?"

Brice's face flared hot. He'd never discussed his man-on-man sex life with any woman before, much less his wife's cousin. "Lorrie, what a question!"

"Lord God, you look like you just gulped a whole bottle of Tabasco or a cup of cayenne pepper," Lorrie said. "Well, if it was good, count your blessings. I may be a Christian, but I ain't exactly a lady, and as far as I'm concerned, sometimes a prime piece of tail is worth the risk…though the price you're paying right now seems mighty steep to me. Oh, I think Shelly just drove up. I'll make myself scarce in the back. Got to start on those fried pickles and chicken." Lorrie stubbed out her cigarette and hurried off.

Brice took another swig of beer. *This ain't gonna be any fun atall.*

Shelly swept through the door, dressed in a purple raincoat, its hood sheltering her latest perm. Her smile was sad. "Well. Here we are," she said, shaking off her coat.

"Yep." Brice nodded, mouth tight. *Here at the end of things, I'll bet.* He stepped forward, helped her off with her coat, then pulled out a chair for her at the nearest table. Brice might have been a boisterous country redneck around men, but around women, thanks to his mother's coaching in manners, he was always a gentleman, more a creature of the nineteenth century than the twentieth.

"So, lots of reporters at the house, huh?"

"Yes. Swarming like gnats. Where's Lorrie?"

"In the back. She's cooking me up some hot chicken and some fried pickles."

"God, Brice. How can you think of food at a time like this?"

"You know me," Brice said. Sheepishly, he patted his belly. "Got to keep my strength up. Guess if my music career is over, I won't have to worry about dieting any more, huh?"

"That bastard. I'd like to put a bullet through Zac Lanier's head. And to think I used to be jealous of you two and prayed you'd part ways. Now I wish you'd stayed together, just so none of this would've happened. He wouldn't have outed you then, would he?"

"Probably not. Steve told me he did it for the money, of course, but also 'cause he's sick and has to cover a lot of big medical bills."

"Sick? I don't care if he's sick. He's ruined both of us."

"True enough. Though I sure played my part in said ruination. I'm so, so sorry, Shelly. I never meant…."

Fuck, Brice thought, swallowing hard and trailing off. *Seems like I'm on the verge of tears all the time now. Buck up, you pussy.*

"Brice, we had this talk last spring, after I found those letters. We both know this has been a marriage of convenience for a good while. But now it's over. It isn't convenient any longer."

Shelly paused to adjust her dark, wavy hair. She was a beauty, Brice knew, with her high cheekbones, green eyes, and coral lips. He'd always had a deep awe and appreciation for female beauty, though that appreciation had never translated into genital response. In some other world, where she loved him and he wanted her, he would have thought himself hugely fortunate, a bulky country boy from a hick town in Appalachia being married to a classy lady from the wealthy Atlanta suburb of Druid Hills. In this world, though, they were simply shipmates on a sinking craft, and while he bailed, she was eying the lifeboat. It was the duty of a gentleman, Brice knew, to help a lady step into the escape craft and then watch her recede into the distance while he went down with the ship.

Brice finished his beer and placed the bottle on the table. "You want a divorce," Brice said, trying to smile, trying to be calm and brave. All his adult life, his prayers in times of adversity had not been for this specific event or that specific thing, but for dignity and courage and the strength to do what was necessary. Encouraging his estranged wife to do what was best for her was necessary now.

"Yes. I'm sorry. I never really loved you, Brice, and I know you didn't love me."

"I did love you. Sort of. Not in a romantic way, but…. I still care about you, Shelly, so, look, do what you have to do," Brice muttered, suddenly wishing he had another beer, or, better still, a glass of good Kentucky bourbon with a twist of lemon.

"I hope you understand. I could live with our situation as long as no one else knew. But now…. It's humiliating. Who knows what folks are saying about me? I don't want their pity. I want the admiration I had before. Now Zac has ruined all of it. The only respectable thing for me to do is get a divorce. And reporters have been begging me for an interview."

Brice grimaced. Propping his elbows on the table, he cupped his brow in his hands. "I'm sure they're *real* eager. Are you going to give 'em one?"

"I think so. I'm going to tell them that I'm divorcing you. I'm going to tell them that I didn't know, that I'm as shocked as everyone else. If I told them the truth—that I found out about you and Zac but remained your wife—what would people think of me?"

Brice chuckled. "I guess they'd think you were a fruit fly?"

"Fruit fly?"

"It's gay slang. It means a straight woman who hangs out with gay men."

Shelly arched a shapely eyebrow. "Since when do you use gay slang?"

"Since I started sleeping with men back in college? What would people think of you? I guess they'd think what was true…that you stayed with me 'cause of the fame and the money, and I stayed with you to help hide my secret."

Brice rubbed his bearded jaw, then sat back in his chair, crossed his arms across his chest, and looked Shelly in the eye. "Look, honey, tell 'em what you want. My label's dropped me, which is no surprise. Steve says that if you and I make a show of reconciling, if you let me move back in, that might salvage my career, but I've thought about that, and it wouldn't be fair to you, so, like I said, do what you have to do. You're still young, Shelly. You're still beautiful. I'll bet you'll find another husband in no time."

"That's sweet of you to say. I'd like the house."

"Ah, here we go," Brice groaned. "Come to this, huh?"

"Half of marriages do, don't they? I want to put it on the market. I want to sell it and then move back to Georgia and buy a place near my parents. Daddy called and begged me to come home."

"I'll bet he did. Look, I ain't gonna argue with you," Brice said, extending his palms up and out in a gesture of surrender. "My parents may not have had a pot to piss in for most of my childhood, but they brought me up never to argue about money. All's I need's my truck and my old guitar. Let me come by and fetch the little bit of my stuff still there, and then you can do what you want with the house. The Florida condo I'll need to sell, I think, and the motorcycles. Some of the musical instruments too, since I doubt I'll be needing 'em. Might have to sell the Nashville condo too, just for spending money. The homeplace back in the mountains is paid for, thank God."

"That seems more than fair to me," Shelly said, smiling with visible satisfaction. "Our Williamson County estate is worth five times as much as all those properties put together."

"Yep," Brice said. "You always were good at math. To be honest, that place was always too big and fancy for me. I felt like a bearded version of Elvis with my own over-groomed Graceland."

"I know. I know. All you've ever wanted was a cabin way out in the woods somewhere." Shelly, relaxed with triumph, patted Brice's denimed knee.

"And a big audience. A big, big, big, big, big audience." Brice heaved a grim laugh. "So much for a sea of clamoring fans. None of 'em's gonna buy a faggot's CDs."

"Don't use that nasty word. So what are you going to do now?"

"Steve wants me to do an interview, issue a denial, some such thing. Maybe go into one of those ex-gay programs the evangelicals think can change guys like me. I'm not sure I'll be doing either of those, though. I'm going to head home to West Virginia for Christmas, I guess. Spend some time with my family, what's left of it, anyway. If they'll have me. Folks back home are even less likely to be understanding than folks in Nashville. Right now, though, I intend to gobble down a big plate of Lorrie's good food."

Brice rose and marched to the counter. "Lorrie, honey. We're about done talking. It's safe to come out. Those fried pickles ready yet?"

CHAPTER SEVEN

SHE'S A WOMAN. THAT MIGHT MAKE THINGS *easier*, Brice thought, regarding the stylish reporter sitting on Steve's office couch. Brice rarely felt any hostility toward the opposite sex. When his volcanic temper surged up, and the accompanying desire to kick ass—a tendency toward violence that he'd fought for decades—that ass was almost always a man's. *Fucking men's butts and kicking men's butts, the greatest suppressed urges of my life*, Brice thought, doing his best to look friendly and composed. *Between reining in lust and choking back rage, it's a goddamn miracle I haven't run amok ages ago.*

"Mr. Brown, I really appreciate your willingness to speak to me," said the smiling journalist. Karen Reed was in her early forties, around Brice's age, and from West Virginia. She was known as having left-wing views, and she wasn't overtly religious. Steve had chosen her for all those qualities. Furthermore, she worked for *The Tennesseean*, one of the more liberal newspapers in Nashville.

"Howdy, Mizz Reed. I'm pleased to meet you." Brice, good manners at the ready, rested his hands on his knees. Behind his desk, Steve studied the pair with anxious intensity.

"Shall we get started?" Steve said, clicking a pin.

"Yep. Sure. Fire away," Brice said. Years ago, he'd had a nonverbal communication class at West Virginia University, so he was deliberately arranging his body in such a way as to indicate relaxation. *Legs apart, back straight, look her in the eye.*

Ms. Reed pulled a miniature recorder from her purse and turned it on. "So, day before yesterday, the *Banner* reported that your wife Shelly had filed for divorce. Is that true?"

"Yes, ma'am. I'm afraid so."

"I see. How do you feel about that?"

"How do I feel? Like crap." Brice took off his ubiquitous baseball cap and rubbed at his close-cropped hair. Steve had advised him to be remorseful so as to impress the fans, but there was no need to fake the feeling. Remorse and shame of one form or another had hounded him since adolescence, since he'd recognized his desires for what they were and knew that the world around him would never tolerate the honest expression of them. The more you pretend to be someone you're not in order to spare or shield yourself, the more you wind up hurting others, he'd come to discover.

"I've made a big mess of things, and there's no reason a lady as fine as my Shelly should have to suffer for it. She'll be better off without me. I wish her the best, the very best. I'm just so sorry for everything."

"By everything, do you mean your affair with Zac Lanier? You are admitting that the two of you had a relationship?"

"Yeah. It wasn't really a relationship, though. I mean, he exaggerated a lot in that interview of his. He…well…."

"Go on, Brice," Steve urged.

God, another big shit-pot of lies. I wish I was dead. "Well, he started what happened between us, not me. I just shouldn't have gotten so damn drunk. And then he got out some pot, and, hell, after that, I didn't know what I was doing."

"Was this in the hot tub Mr. Lanier referred to?"

"Yes, ma'am." Brice folded his arms and sighed. Somehow his gaze had left the woman's face and was studying the arabesque design of the office carpet. "It only happened a couple of times. That ain't really a relationship, right? Just a couple of drunken mistakes. He got real attached, and I realized it was all wrong, so I ended it."

"But Mr. Lanier said you started it and he ended it."

"Yeah, I read the interview, but that ain't, uh, isn't true. I broke it off with him, and then he pressured me to get back together with him, uh, I mean, see him, meet with him, but I was afraid Shelly'd find out and it'd break her heart, so I told him to get lost. That's why he quit the band. That must be why he's trying to ruin me, claiming I'm a promiscuous homosexual. He's just bitter and vindictive."

"Have there been other men, Mr. Brown? Do you identify as a homosexual? As a member of the gay community?"

"Identify? Look, I don't know much of anything about 'the gay community.' Isn't that a bunch of skinny city boys all into fashion and shit?" No need to dissemble on this point either. Ever since Brice had started sleeping with guys in college, he'd never much related to open gays. Some of them had been fun to fuck, but most of them seemed too extreme and urban for his mountain-bred tastes.

"But have there been other men? Mr. Lanier indicated that you'd had a lot of experience in that regard."

Steve interrupted, his bunched brow a clear indication that he did not approve of the direction the conversation was taking. "Lanier is just trying to stir up scandal. Tell her about Exodus International, Brice. I'm sure your fans would want to know about that."

"Oh, yeah! So, Exodus International is a Christian group who can cure, uh, same-sex desire. I've made an appointment with a local reparative therapist in their organization, Dr. Adam Zucker. I don't think I'm gay, or even bisexual, but I'm planning on joining the Exodus program just to see if…well, maybe through them, God can…."

Brice trailed off, his throat tight, his voice husky with shame. Steve filled the conversational gap.

"Brice grew up in a God-fearing community in West Virginia, as you no doubt know, Ms. Reed. We both have faith that Christian therapists can put him on the right path. And we want his fans to know that. We're sure many of them have been very upset by the revelations of the last week, but we're confident that Brice's fans will forgive him. Please tell your readers that Brice will begin his therapy sessions with Dr. Zucker next week. After Brice has gotten the help he needs, he'll be taking some time off to get back to his country roots and work on a new album of songs. Right, Brice?"

"Uh, yep. Yep!" Brice forced another smile. "Been writing up a storm. Hard times can bring that out in an artist, y'know." Brice stood. "So, look, that's all I really have to say. I hope you have enough, ma'am. This has been awfully painful, as you might imagine, and so I'm going to go home now and pray. I hope you understand." *Pray and drink, drink and pray. I pity that bourbon bottle tonight.*

"Well, certainly." Ms. Reed rose. She clicked off the recorder and slipped it into her purse. "So where will you be going during this return to your roots?"

Reporters swarming around the Hinton house? I'm sure the locals would love that. I just hope I'm not tarred and feathered while I'm there. "Uhhh, not sure. Probably…."

Steve cut in. "We'd prefer not to say. After all he's been through, Brice needs his privacy."

"Certainly. One last thing. Any comments on that front-page photograph? The one Mr. Lanier says he took during one of your rendezvous? You must admit it looked a little incriminating, a little salacious. You bare-chested in bed, apparently naked, with that cowboy hat on."

"Hell, that was just me being silly. Some horseplay in a hotel room after a concert and some beers. I guess a camera brings out the fool in me."

"All right. Thanks, both of you. I'll see myself out." She moved toward the door, then paused.

"Mr. Brown, I honestly hope things improve for you. I've seen some pretty nasty headlines in the gossip rags since the *Banner* ran that interview with Mr. Lanier. "Homo Hot Tub," "Fairy Fornicator," and so on. Some of my compatriots are, well, ruthless and vulgar. Good luck, and happy holidays." With that, she left.

"Oh, fuck. Oh, fuck. Oh, fuck," Brice gasped, slumping back into the chair.

"What? Relax. It went tolerably well, I think."

"Thanks for pitching in. But, goddamn it, it's one lie after another. Feels like I'm sinking deeper into quicksand every time I open my mouth."

"Not that many lies," Steve said, patting Brice's shoulder. "You *are* going to see that Exodus therapist next week, aren't you?"

"Yeah. At least I have an appointment. Whether or not I have the guts to actually go, I don't know."

"Keep the appointment, for God's sake," Steve said, taking his seat behind the desk. "The folks I spoke to at Exodus seem very eager to work with someone as famous as you. We can stage a photo shoot, get some pics of you waving and smiling as you enter their facility. That might improve your public image and make you more sympathetic to your fans."

Brice heaved a hoarse groan. "Look, Steve, we both gotta face it. I want men, and I just don't think a Christian therapist is gonna change that. I may not give a damn about the gay community that Mizz Reed spoke about, a bunch of queens marching around and making a fuss, but I—"

"Have you ever fallen in love with a man?" Steve asked.

"It sure felt like I was in love with a buddy back in high school. Wayne Meador. He was only seventeen, but he could have been a porn star. And I was seriously infatuated with a few of my fraternity brothers at WVU. Even messed around with a couple."

Steve frowned and rolled his eyes. "You were a boy then. We all feel crazy things in our youth. What about Zac? Did you love him?"

"I could have, but I didn't let myself, I guess 'cause I knew it'd never work in my line of business. He was in love with me, though. He fell for me hard, and one of the reasons he's being so nasty is 'cause I spurned him and broke his heart. I cared a lot for him as a buddy, and…he was great in bed. But I wasn't in love with him." Even as he said it, Brice wondered if he were speaking the truth. *If you don't know the truth, how the hell can you tell it?*

"So you're saying that you've never been in love with a man. See?" Steve said with triumph. "You're not gay, Brice. You're not like any gay man I've ever met, and I met quite a few during my time in New York. You're just a horny redneck."

"You're saying I'd fuck a snake if I could hold its head still?" Brice gave Steve a sour grin. "'Gay' isn't a word I've ever related to…but I tell you, I want men, not women. I've never fallen in love with a woman either."

"What about Shelly?"

"I thought I loved her, but I was just fooling myself, trying to talk myself into normality since the alternative was so damn hard. I've been looking at men since I was a kid. Some of them I can hardly keep my eyes off of. I look at them, and everything in me downright aches to get them naked and touch them. I don't want to want them, and I know you don't want to believe I want them, but the truth's the truth."

"That kind of truth is a gallows, my friend, a gallows you might hang yourself on. Wanting men is the very thing you need to keep lying about. Otherwise, as I said before, you'll lose everything."

"I think I already have." Brice rose, pulled on his coat, and grabbed his cap. "I think it's too late. Maybe Kristofferson was right. Maybe 'freedom's just another word for nothing left to lose.'"

"Maybe. That's a terribly bitter form of freedom, though." Steve opened the door, and Brice prepared himself to ignore Carolyn's accusatory glare. "Call me once you've had your talk with Dr. Zucker. Maybe he and his Exodus cronies can pull your fat out of the fire."

"Maybe," said Brice, suppressing a shudder. Steve's wording made him think of Jews in a concentration camp or witches burnt at the stake.

CHAPTER EIGHT

DR. ZUCKER COULDN'T HAVE BEEN MORE THAN thirty years in age and one hundred and forty pounds in weight. He was dressed very professionally in a dark gray suit and tie—*the sort of get-up guys wear to funerals,* Brice thought—but his mannerisms reminded Brice of the fey boys he used to encounter in seedy gay bars he'd frequented in college.

"Quite the media circus outside," Dr. Zucker said, smoothing back his styled hair.

"You're telling me," Brice said, doffing his baseball cap and scratching his beard, which had grown gray-dusted and bushy over the last few weeks of his disgrace. "Sorry about that. I'd just as soon have kept things quiet, but my manager thought it would be good for my public image."

Dr. Zucker flashed Brice a very white smile. "No need for apologies. To be honest, it's good for our organization's image too. I'm a big fan of your music, Mr. Brown, and I'm really looking forward to working with someone so exceptional."

"Exceptional? Shit. I mean—sorry, I got a potty mouth—shoot. I'm just a country boy from West Virginia who got lucky. Though I guess my luck's run out, huh?"

"I think the Lord's hand was in what you've endured lately. Sometimes He brings us down and breaks us apart so we'll come to Him in our distress. Do you believe that, Mr. Brown?"

"Call me Brice, man. Yeah, maybe. I was brought up to believe that He works in mysterious ways."

"How were you brought up, Brice?" Dr. Zucker pulled out a notebook and opened it. "In terms of religious faith."

"Well, nothing strict. My hometown is southern Baptist pretty much through and through, but Daddy was sort of a Unitarian and Mommy was a Methodist. She used to sing in the choir. We all believed in God, and my Nanny read the Bible to me a lot when I was a kid, and we went to the Methodist church in Hinton sometimes, usually on holidays like Christmas and Easter, but most Sundays we were working in Daddy's garden instead of going to church. He always said that he felt closer to God in a garden or in the woods than in a church, and I'm liable to agree with him."

"Were you baptized?"

"No, sir." Manners dictated that Brice use "sir," but it felt absurd. *This boy's a prissy pup*, Brice thought. *Ain't any way he can help me, but might as well give it a try, if just to please Steve. God knows Steve's got a good bit to lose too, if I go down the shit-chute of ruination.*

"Let me confirm something. Did you have a sexual affair with Zac Lanier as he's claimed?"

"Yep. Everybody knows that now. Didn't you see my interview with that Reed lady in the paper?"

"I did indeed. Do you believe that what you did with Zac Lanier was a sin?"

"A sin? I honestly don't know. I guess you do."

Dr. Zucker gave Brice another gleaming smile. "Yes, I do. Yes, I do. Have you been with other men, Brice? Sexually?"

Brice squirmed in his seat. "This is all confidential, right?"

"Of course. I'm a professional therapist. I'm bound by the rules of my profession. Doctor/patient confidentiality is uppermost among those rules."

"Okay. Good. Yeah, I've been with guys other than Zac."

"How many?"

"Uh. Lost count."

"I see." Dr. Zucker retrieved a pencil from his desk drawer and scrawled in his notebook. "When did you first indulge in these desires?"

"Eighteen. Went to college. Ran across some guys willing to experiment."

"Have you slept with many women?"

"Other than my wife? Uhhhh, naw."

"I see." Dr. Zucker made another note. "Do you think this therapy can change you?"

Brice shrugged. "Don't know. My manager seems to think so. He seems to think that my whole career is hanging on this. So, before we get started, if you don't mind me asking a few questions…."

"Go right ahead."

"Well, how does all this work? Do I just meet with you? Do I go into some sort of clinic and stay there for a while? I mean, if I'm a homosexual, then—"

"You're not a homosexual," the doctor replied with yet another smile. "Any more than I'm a homosexual."

"But…I just told you I've slept with lots of guys."

"Let me explain. Christian therapists like me don't really believe in homosexuality per se. You're what we might call a struggler. Men like you are heterosexuals, but with, well, a homosexual problem."

"A homosexual problem?" *I'll say. I want to kiss and touch and suck and screw other men all the time, but now folks've found out, so now it's a problem. A big goddamn problem.*

"Yes. Your attraction to men is an anomaly. We here in Exodus International believe that such desires are caused by unhealthy family dynamics during childhood. What sort of relationship did you have with your father?"

"Oh, man, the parent thing? Should I be lying on a couch for this part?"

"That's not necessary." Dr. Zucker chuckled. "Were you and your father close?"

"Naw. We were too much alike. I can see that now. Both of us were selfish, strong-willed sorts who wanted our own way. Mommy was always refereeing our conversations. Him and me were always butting heads and fighting for attention."

"Did your mother dominate him?"

Brice laughed out loud. "*Hell*, no. He was one of the bossiest, most domineering men I've ever met. It was like my mother and sister and me were pathetic little planets orbiting around his sun."

"Really? A dominant mother is more typical of the childhood of strugglers. It was certainly that way in my family."

Brice stared at Dr. Zucker and grinned. "Your family? Are you a 'struggler' too?"

"I am. I thought I was gay for years. Now, thanks to lots of therapy and the love of Christ, I realize I'm not. That's why I'm in this profession. Now that God has healed me, I feel compelled to be a conduit for His love so that, through me, He might heal others like me."

"So you were gay, but now you're straight?" Brice tried to control his tone, but the words still came out sounding dubious.

"Yes. I've been married for five years, and I have three adorable children." The doctor brandished framed photos of a curly-headed blonde girl and two fat-faced toddlers. "Here's living proof of God's power."

"Hmm. So, if my attraction to men was caused by my parents...." Brice paused, suppressing a grin. He could still hear Bob, a hot Italian man he'd bedded in college, joking, "My mother made me a homosexual. And if you give her enough yarn, she'll make you one too!"

"That means that your feelings, your attractions, aren't chosen. But they become sinful when you choose to act on them. As you have."

"Yep. Again and again. I guess I can't help being a stud." Feeling defiant, Brice made a show of flexing his right biceps.

Dr. Zucker's eyes widened, but his thin lips pursed up. "'Stud' is not the word I'd use, and you *could* help it if you'd chosen to. I'd imagine a man with your looks, charisma, and talent could indeed be wildly promiscuous if he so chose. All that means is that you've used the many gifts that God has given you to break His commandments. And your use of humor is inappropriate in a serious setting like this, don't you think?"

"*Looks and charisma?*" *Ex-gay, my ass. I'll bet he likes my muscles.* "Yeah, maybe so. Sorry. I didn't mean to interrupt. You were saying? You were explaining where homo... uh, same-sex desires come from."

"Yes. Well, many strugglers like us lack healthy bonds with our fathers. Our relationships with them are sadly damaged, and so—"

"You did? Had a damaged relationship with your father?"

"Yes. And what that can mean is that, without a solid relationship with the father, we grow up without forms of healthy masculinity in our lives. Rather than having positive relationships with other men, rather than learning to embody masculinity in ourselves, we end up searching for masculinity in other men and eroticizing it. Does that make sense?"

Brice twisted up his mouth and coughed. "Yeah. But also no. Daddy and I didn't much get along, but I've had lots of buddies—good male friends—in my life. In high school and college. Guys in the music business. In my bands."

"Including Zac Lanier?"

"Yes. Including him. We were good friends for a long time before sex fucked things up. Sex fucks up friendships all the time, don't it? Between men and women too. And what you said about not embodying masculinity...."

Brice leaned back and interlaced his hands behind his head. "I gotta admit that I was kind of scrawny in middle school, but I started filling out in high school and ran track and played some football and started lifting weights. I feel pretty comfortable in my masculinity, if you wanna know. I'm not like those skinny, pretty gay guys I used to see in the bars in Morgantown. In fact, once I realized I wanted men and then met queeny gay guys like that, I was bound and determined *not* to be like them. I'm just a West Virginia redneck, Doctor." Brice cocked his baseball cap over his eyes, propped his right foot on his left knee, and stroked the brown leather of his cowboy boot. "I just happen to want other guys."

"I didn't mean to impugn your manhood, Brice," Dr. Zucker said, wrinkling his brow. "You are indeed a very masculine man, more so than many strugglers I've worked with. But is it manly to want other men? I think not. Please keep in mind that this therapy is not primarily about your gender expression. It's about helping you cast out your same-sex desires. Do you understand?"

"Yep. So enough of these theories. If I stay in this program, what happens?"

"You'll meet with me regularly. I suggest twice a week. If you do so, I have faith that we can free you of your same-sex attractions. With luck, we'll be able to heal your relationship with your wife Shelly. I'm sure she's suffering, and I'm sure you're suffering without her. I suspect that God wants the two of you to be together. If you continue your therapy with me, we can work toward you having the kind of marriage He wants you to have. Imagine! No more lies and shameful secrets. No more furtive desires. It's such a liberation, believe me. To stand in His Light and cast off the perverse affliction and feel clean and free."

"Okay. God knows I'm tired of lying, that's for sure. But I want you to know that— at this point, at least—I'm not entirely convinced this program is gonna do me any good. Right now, I'm just hoping, well, not to heal myself so much as my relationship with my fans. If I lose my career, I'll lose everything."

"That's a mercenary attitude, though it's understandable. I'm not talking about riches and fame, though. Those are things that thieves can steal and rust decay. I'm talking about spiritual health and a closer relationship to God."

"Well, spiritual health does sound like a right worthy goal. So what now?"

"Now you must take the first step. You must renounce your former self, the flawed and sinful man you were, and embrace the title of 'ex-gay.' Think of it as a sign of faith, your faith that God can heal your sexuality through me, through the teachings of Exodus International."

Brice scowled. "You don't mean some public thing? Like earlier today?"

"Yes. Exactly. We can schedule a press conference and make the announcement. Once people hear that you're adhering to our teachings, to our program…a man as famous as you…imagine the lost souls who will turn to us. You could be part of God's plan to save thousands of suffering, confused sinners."

Brice sat up straight and shook his head. "Uhhhh. Doctor Zucker, didn't you just say that I'd be free of lies? How can I tell the world that I'm 'ex-gay' if I still want men? Ain't that putting the cart before the horse?"

"It's a necessary step." Dr. Zucker pressed his thin lips together and tapped his pencil on his desk. "As I said, it's a sign of faith that our program can save you."

"But I just told you that I don't have that faith." Brice lowered his eyes and flicked a bit of mud off his boot. "I'm doing this to keep my fans and keep my manager. He's pretty much said that if I don't do this, that he'll drop me just like most of my fans have already. I know you don't wanna hear this, but I'm not here to save my soul but to save my career."

"This isn't a publicity firm, Brice. Don't you want your sexuality to be healed?"

"I ain't entirely convinced it needs healing. Why would God make me this way, put in my heart and head and, well, my dick, a desire for men, if He thought my feelings were wrong? I've been asking myself that since I first started looking at guys back in junior high."

"Brice, that just isn't the way to think. There's no question that the Lord disapproves of same-sex lust. Imagine all the fellow strugglers you could help in the process of helping yourself. I think we need to pray. If we pray together, God will convince you that this is the right course to take."

Dr. Zucker stood. He moved from around the desk, stood before Brice, and seized Brice's right hand in his. "Rise now," he urged, tugging at Brice. "Get up."

Holy shit. Stunned, Brice obeyed. *Holy shit. The crazy bastard is holding my hand.*

Dr. Zucker grasped Brice's left hand as well, then gazed into Brice's face with a sad smile. "You'll see," he said. "God will lead us. Let's close our eyes and speak to Him together."

"Yeah. Okay." Brice bowed his head.

"Lord, please hear us," Dr. Zucker began, closing his eyes.

Brice raised his head, studying the devout doctor's earnest expression and suppressing a grin. *Well, ain't this cozy? Except you ain't my type by a long shot. Never have been able to abide a scrawny guy.* Part of Brice wanted to punch Dr. Zucker in the nose. Part of him wanted to throw back his head and laugh. Part of him wanted to bolt out the office door and drive away as fast as he could. And part of him wanted to cry. *Yeah, Lord, hear us. Hear me. I need help bad.*

"Please help us, Lord," the doctor continued. "Please help this suffering man see that the path is open to him here. The path to healing. The way to escape the perverse lusts that have plagued him. Give him the strength to take the first crucial step on that path, the strength to announce himself publicly as one who has...."

Brice stopped listening. He closed his eyes, lowered his head again, and composed his own silent prayer.

I want to be close to You, Lord. I really do. But being in a church or here in this office just ain't the way, at least not for me. I've felt You close when I'm looking out to sea, or hiking the woods on the farm, or driving down a back road with the sugar maples burning in fall, or, yeah, when I've been lucky enough to hold a hot man in my arms. This guy's a nut, but he's right about one thing. I need to hear from You, 'cause I don't know what the fuck I'm doing, I don't know what the fuck I'm going to do now. Please don't let me lose everything. And if I do, if that's Your will, for some big reason I can't understand, then please give me strength to endure it like a man. If I'm about to lose the life I've had, please help me find a new one. I'm so sad and angry and lonely and scared. Bring me some kind of peace. Please? Please? Amen.

Brice raised his head. Dr. Zucker was just winding down.

"...I feel You here in this room. I feel the warmth of Your light upon us. Thank You, Lord. Thank You for the gift of Your Son. Amen."

The doctor opened his eyes and squeezed Brice's hands. "How do you feel?"

Really sad. Really lost. And you're even more lost than I am, you poor bastard.

Brice mustered a stiff smile. "I think that helped. I think I know what to do." He dropped the doctor's hands, then turned to grab up his jacket and cap. "Some things are clearer now. Look, I need to go home and think on all this. I need to pray some more. I hope you understand."

"That's fine." Dr. Zucker smiled. "We're about out of time anyway. Stop at the receptionist's desk, and she'll set you up with future appointments." He stepped forward and gripped Brice's hand. "I feel sure that you've come to the right place. I know the Lord sent you here, and I know that you and I will share many successful and enlightening sessions in the future."

"Yep. You bet." Brice gave the man's hand a hard squeeze, managed another smile, and then fled. *No reason to hurt somebody's feelings if you can help it. Best reason to fib I know.*

In the outer office, Brice gave the receptionist an awkward wave, then loped right past her desk and out the door into the bright December sunshine. In another minute, he was ensconced in his truck and punching in Steve's phone number.

Voicemail picked up. Brice sighed with relief, paused, and then spoke.

"Hey, Steve. I just got outta the therapist's office. Look, I wanted to tell you this in person, but I just don't have the guts to say it face to face. This ain't gonna work. This Exodus thing. These folks are lying to themselves, and I've been doing the same damn thing for a long time, and I just don't have the strength to do that anymore. I'm heading up to West Virginia tomorrow. Just leave me be for a while, okay? I know you're probably gonna drop me for sure now, and I'm real sorry about that, I'm real sorry about everything, but it just can't be helped. You were great, Steve. You were a real friend. I'm sorry I let you down."

Brice hung up. "Shit." He sat back in the sunlight for a few minutes, eyes closed, trying to concentrate on the comforting warmth that surrounded him. Then he dialed Shelly.

Voicemail again. He cleared his throat.

"Hey, honey. Look, I need to come by tomorrow and pick up those things of mine, if that's all right. I'm leaving town for a while. Don't figure there's anything left for me here, other than maybe Lorrie's hot chicken and a few more gossip-rag headlines. Call me, okay? Let me know what time'll work best for you. I still got a key, y'know, so you don't need to be there. Probably be best if you aren't. We've kind of already said our goodbyes, right?"

Brice hung up. He started his truck and pushed one of his own CDs into the stereo. "If I had her back," sang the baritone voice. "If I had her back, then for sure I'd—"

Who the hell is that? Brice thought, flipping the stereo off. "Her?" *Fucking hypocrite. Okay, first the liquor store. I'm in the mood for some rye. Then that take-out barbecue place down the road. With any luck, I can get outta there with some pulled pork before any ex-fans stone me to death.*

CHAPTER NINE

By late afternoon, the last lingering reporter had left the front gate of the Williamson County house. *Off after a hot new story. Guess I'm old news,* Brice thought, wedging the last of his possessions into the Ram's truck bed. For a few minutes, he gazed up at the edifice of white columns and brick, then out over the grounds, amazed that he'd ever come so far, that he'd ever been able to afford such a place.

Pool, hot tub, patios, fancy landscaping, horse barn. Long ways from Hinton, West Virginia. Well, folks back home always told me I'd come back, no matter where I roamed or how successful I got. Guess they were right. Guess I'll never see this place again. I hope Shelly gets a shitload for it.

Brice pulled on his camouflage hooded sweatshirt and denim jacket and climbed into his Ram. For another long moment, he stared at the house, saying his silent goodbyes to that era of his life. Then he pulled out his phone and dialed his sister Leigh.

A machine picked up. *Shit, it's Thursday. She's probably busy in her law office.*

"H-hey, Leigh. Sorry I haven't returned your calls. Things have been real rough here, as you can guess, with all the bad publicity. So, yeah, you're right, I think it's best if I come on home. Ain't that where every hillbilly who's feeling whipped wants to go? Driving back tonight, actually. I'm going to stay at the Ballengee Street house for a while and get my bearings. Think about what you and Carden would like for Christmas, okay? I sure am looking forward to getting some of your country cooking. See you tomorrow."

Heart heavy, Brice hung up. He drove off the estate, down the long lane lined with trimmed boxwoods and through the electric gate that had been keeping journalists at bay for the past two weeks.

At the main highway, Brice paused. Instead of turning right, toward I-65 North and Nashville, he turned left. In fifteen minutes, he'd reached the town of Franklin. Near the columned edifice of Carnton Plantation, a local historic site, he found what he'd come for: the McGavock Confederate Cemetery. He parked and clambered out, a bunch of Kroger-bought flowers in his fist. The graveyard was a flat, grassy space dotted with bare trees and full of rectangular granite tombstones only a few feet high, each marked with a man's initials.

Like a sea of stubby teeth, Brice thought. *Nearly 1,500 men.* He strolled between the markers till he found the grave he'd visited so many times since he'd moved to Tennessee.

Brice hunkered down, propped the flowers up against the stone, and scratched some matted lichen off the letters. *W.L.B. Great-great-granddaddy William Lucas Brown. Daddy used to talk about him all the time. Took a bullet in the head fighting beside Patrick Cleburne, the Stonewall of the West. Christ, only thirty years old.*

Brice fell to his knees beside the marker and ran his fingers over the letters. *Great-great-granddaddy...brother...I sure could use some advice right now, but you sure as hell ain't in any position to give it. One thing's for damn sure, and that's the fact that I ain't suffered a fraction of what you did, seeing all those men you cared about being slaughtered left and right, thirteen wild charges, heaps of corpses everywhere you looked, and then that goddamn Minié ball meant for you, and you bleeding out your life on the lawn of Carnton Plantation. Jesus, would I have stood and fought, or would I have turned and run?*

Brice shuddered, throat tight. He gulped back a spasm of tears and stood. *If you saw me now, wet-eyed, whipped and scared, worried about losing my fancy property and my fancy toys and my stadiums of fans, you'd probably spit in my face, and I wouldn't blame you one damn bit. I'm a cry-baby and a softie, but your blood's in me, so, by God, look over me, wherever you are, and lend me some of your soldier's spunk, 'cause I'm sure as hell gonna need it.*

Brice rose, knees twinging, and limped over to his truck. He sat back in the seat, rubbing the ache in his temples, and watched sunlight recede and shadows lengthen over the rows and rows of Rebel graves. When the setting sun slipped behind a bank of purple-gray clouds, he turned on the radio.

Country music started up. "Lucky bastards," he muttered, as a Tim McGraw song faded out and a Toby Keith song started up. "Handsome, hot, hetero bastards." He gobbled one of three Hardee's sausage biscuits he'd packed for the trip, then wiped crumbs from his beard, gulped coffee from his travel mug, and pulled out, ready for the long drive through the dark to his hometown in southern West Virginia.

PART
TWO

DAWN WAS BREAKING AS BRICE DROVE ALONG A high road carved into the shaly mountainside, far above the waters of the Bluestone Reservoir. Despite the several breaks he'd taken at rest stops to piss, snack, grab brief naps, or admire burly truckers, he was blurry-eyed and exhausted after so many hours of driving.

Just can't do road trips like I used to, he thought, massaging his brow. *One thing hasn't changed, though: these mountains are still the prettiest on earth. I've always loved the way they loom up against the sky, as if they were castle walls protecting their people. Why'd I ever leave? Oh, yeah, ambition. Wanted as many fans as I could get. Well, that's all come to shit, hasn't it? My life's a wreck, but these West-by-God-Virginia hills, they're just as solid and scenic as ever. At least some things stay the same.*

The reservoir in December was as he remembered it: broad and wintergreen, high with recent rains, lined with the lacy glint of ice. After a few miles' drive, Brice passed the Bluestone Dam and descended the hill. Two rivers converged at the bottom, the New and the Greenbrier. The road he took bridged the former, then the latter, then followed the railroad tracks into town. He passed gas stations, McDonald's, Kroger, and Magic Mart, then entered the suburb of Avis, a disparate array of little houses, some well kept, some dilapidated and dirty, a few in complete ruins. In Brice's youth, the town's economy was still healthy, but now the signs of poverty were everywhere.

Jobs on the railroad and in the state parks. That's about it, Brice thought, driving up the new bridge into Hinton proper. He turned left at the War Memorial—recalling the touch football he'd enjoyed in the lawn there, the bare chests of his Phys Ed classmates, and one amazing day when a slew of migrating Monarch butterflies had filled the air—and took a brief detour along the main street, Temple, counting the number of storefronts that had closed since he'd grown up.

Cato's was there, and there a men's clothing shop. And Murphy's, where I used to buy comic books and candy. And that big lot where the fire happened, I used to hang out at Bowling's with that hot-as-holy-hell Wayne Meador, drink coffee, and read the sports pages. Looks like this town and I are sharing hard times.

Brice turned up the bumpy cobblestones of Third, then turned right, the Methodist Church on one corner, the Presbyterian Church on the other. *How many churches are in this town? I doubt these small-town Christians are going to be particularly excited to see that I've come home. Bet they're having second thoughts about naming that bridge after me.*

Brice bumped down Ballengee Street, past the florist, past the post office, the crumbling bulk of the McCreery Hotel, and the red-brick towers of the monumental Summers County Courthouse. Before the street veered left, he pulled into a parking space and turned off the engine. The little park before him—three houses lining it to the left, four to the right—spread down a gentle slope and ended at a line of boxwood hedges. Beyond that, he knew, a sheer cliff dropped off. At its base ran the railroad, and, beyond that, a line of sycamores and willows edging the river. At least once during Brice's youth, a drunk from one of the Third Avenue bars had staggered into the park at night, probably to piss, and had unwisely pushed through the hedge and fallen over the cliff to his demise.

"Home," Brice sighed, watching the mountaintops across the river catch the first rays of sunrise. He cocked his baseball cap over his eyes, pulled up his hood, slipped on his sunglasses, and climbed out. To his relief, no one was on the streets at such an early hour. Free of observers, he looked around, remembering.

There, just down the street, was the Confederate monument Brice had always been awed by, a bearded, rifle-toting soldier atop a column. To its left was the Memorial Building, where Brice and his family used to attend suppers to raise money for the local Democratic Party. To the right was the firehouse, where he used to admire the firefighters in their tight, sweaty T-shirts as they washed their great red trucks. Beyond was the Central Baptist church, into which his grandmother once dragged him for a shape-note singing session.

And here, Brice thought, breaking into a faint grin, *in this very spot where I've parked, Robbie O'Neill gave me a blow-job in my truck one night that summer I came home from college and worked Recreation at Pipestem State Park and he and I got to flirting in the Bluestone Dining Room where he was working as a waiter. All that curly hair, and that tight mouth and talented tongue…and some cops shooting the shit just a few yards down the street, where the jail used to be. The good ole days, when I didn't have so damn much to lose.*

Brice pulled out his duffel bag and guitar case, locked the truck, and headed down the walk. The first of the three houses on the left, a turreted Victorian, housed his sister's law office, but the hour was far too early for it to be open. The third house, set nearest the cliff, was most likely empty at present, the retired couple who owned it having decamped to Florida, as they did every winter. The middle house, nearly a century old, as were all the houses edging the park, was painted a pale yellow with green awnings. In that house Brice had grown up. Now it was his, mortgage-free, something he might cling to if the revelations about his sexuality were to ruin his finances entirely.

He climbed the steps to the porch, back aching after the long drive, pulled out the key, fumbled open the door, and pushed inside. The house was as he'd left it nearly a year ago, when he'd visited his sister and nephew for the Christmas holidays. High ceilings, oak pocket doors. A front foyer. Stairs to the left. Kitchen straight ahead. To the right, front and back parlors, the former with a fireplace and an upright piano.

Groaning with relief, Brice locked the door behind him. He shambled slowly up the stairs and into the largest of the front bedrooms, which had once been his parents'. Painted a light gray with darker gray trim, it overlooked the park, with a view of the river far below and, farther off, the bridge that the town had named after Brice when he'd first achieved fame in Nashville. Outside the two front windows, someone—no doubt his sister Leigh—had hung green plastic Christmas wreaths in an attempt to bring a touch of holiday cheer to the house.

Brice dropped his duffel bag on the floor, stripped down to his socks and briefs, hit the bathroom, then drew the bedroom curtains, climbed into the big bed heaped with quilts his great-aunts had made, grunted happily at the feeling of clean flannel sheets, and almost immediately fell asleep.

BRICE WOKE THREE HOURS LATER to the sound of the doorbell. "Shit," he rasped, rolling out of bed. He dumped the contents of his duffel bag onto the dresser, tugged on a pair of gray fleece sweatpants, a white thermal undershirt, and a pair of moccasins, then thumped over the hardwood floors and down the stairs. Through the glass of the front door, he could see his sister, Leigh, waiting on the porch. She was bundled in a long gray coat and held a casserole dish. Beyond her, a light snow had begun to fall.

Brice flipped the lock and threw open the door. "Hey," he said. "Come on in!"

"The prodigal son," she sighed, heading straight to the kitchen. Leigh was five years younger than Brice, a very pretty woman with blue eyes, ash-blonde hair, a Rubenesque build, and a no-nonsense attitude. "Let me just put this down."

Brice followed her, sniffing. The aroma of food reminded him of how little he'd had to eat in the last twenty-four hours: those to-go sausage biscuits he'd gotten at Hardee's before he left Franklin, and, along the way, a burrito at a truck stop near Knoxville. "What's that?" he said, belly growling.

"Swedish meatballs," Leigh said. "I made them as soon as I got your message. Give me a hug."

"You bet."

The siblings hugged hard. They'd always been close, but Brice couldn't remember ever before being quite so pleased to see his little sister. "God, it's good to be back. The things I've been through since Thanksgiving…."

"I can imagine. I've seen several of the stories. It even made it to the local news out of Princeton. What a mess." Leigh shrugged off her coat, revealing one of the stylish Coldwater Creek outfits she wore in professional settings. "Mercy, it's chilly in here. I have a little while before I have to be in court. Let's have some coffee. Last night, I stocked up your kitchen with some basics. Coffee, sugar, flour, cornmeal, cereal, milk, Crisco, potatoes, cabbage. Some noodles to go with these meatballs. Some canned greens. Some pinto beans. Some chow-chow and bread-and-butter pickles and hot peppers I put up last summer. Buttermilk's in the fridge if you're feeling like biscuits. Jimmy Dean's in the freezer if you're feeling like sausage gravy. There's also some fried pies in there that my secretary Hope made. I know how much you love those."

"That all sounds great. You know me better'n anybody," Brice said, moving into the back parlor to turn up the heat. Despite his bleak career circumstances, happiness welled up in his chest. His little sister had always known how to improve his dark moods, mainly via simpatico commiseration and down-home victuals. "God knows I'm standing in need of some comfort food."

"I'll bet you are. I know all your favorites. Meatballs. Spaghetti. Meatloaf. Beef stew. Any kind of pie. Take a seat, Brice. I'll brew up the coffee," Leigh said, fetching filters from a cabinet. "Speaking of comfort food, you're heftier than you usually are, aren't you? And, mercy, your beard is so big. Getting salt-and-pepper too."

Brice sat by the kitchen table. "Since my music career's down the tubes, I don't have to go on another damn diet to look sexy for the next CD cover. Don't look like there's gonna be any more CDs. And I'm letting the beard grow out and go gray 'cause, well, it's kind of a disguise. So folks won't recognize me, so folks'll leave me the fuck alone. All kinds of asshole reporters were harassing me in Nashville."

"Did you kick any butts?"

"Anger management issues, me? Like I said, you know me better'n anyone. I was tempted. But no."

"Well, I'm glad you're home, 'cause that's where you ought to be in times of trouble, but...." Leigh paused to measure out the scoops of coffee. "You should know that the town...well, some folks here...."

"Ohhhhh, shit. I know what you're gonna say, and I ain't surprised. Everybody around here is backwoods devout. I know that already."

"You know it. But you've never lived in this town when.... Things are different now, Brice. When you lived here before, I was the only person who knew you were gay."

"Gay. Well. I don't know that I think of myself as—"

"Oh, please. Don't split hairs. You want men. You sleep with men."

"Yeah, okay. Sorry. Go on. A queer by any other name...."

Leigh poured water into the coffee machine and flipped it on. "Now everyone knows you're gay, Brice. It's not going to be easy living in this town. And I hate to tell you this, but the bridge...the one they named after you, they...."

"Oh, hell. Let me guess. Ain't the Brice Brown Bridge anymore, huh?"

"No. The town council, the week after that nasty Zac person spilled the beans about your all's affair, they voted to change the name to the Suzanne Matthews Bridge, after that little girl who's working up in Congress. They didn't get a chance to remove the sign, though, because some bastard had already torn it down the day after the local news carried that story about you."

"Shit."

"Well, I haven't told you the worst news." Leigh brushed hair out of her eyes, then fiddled with the diamond ring on her finger. "My husband, bless his heart, is being difficult. You and Jerry, I know y'all have always gotten along pretty well, but…."

Brice groaned. "Oh, no. I've been so wrapped up in the bullshit I've been going through that I didn't even think…."

"Yes. You know how much his faith means to him. Now that he knows the truth, he's been ranting and raving about having 'a faggot in the family,' as he puts it." Leigh made a face. "He and I have had several knock-down-drag-outs about you. He doesn't want Carden to see you now that everybody knows you're gay."

"Fuck him! Why not? Is he afraid I'll seduce my own nephew?"

"He hasn't come right out and said that. You know he's just downright narrow-minded and ignorant about some things."

"And he has the ambition of an ant. Hell, ants work more than he does. A lot more. The man can't seem to keep a job. You should have divorced him years ago."

"Don't start, Brice. I've told Jerry that he's just prejudiced and that you're the same man you've always been, but he won't listen. And his entire family feels the same."

"Well, Christ, of course they do. They're all Southern Baptists."

"Yes. Jerry's mommy, Mizz Mabel, well, the next time she says something snide about you, I just might cram one of those delicious dinner rolls she makes from scratch right down her throat."

"I'd like to see that. What does Carden think?"

Leigh smiled. "Carden's a lot like Daddy was. Doesn't much care what other folks think. He's actually cussed out a few kids at school who made fun of you in his hearing. And when Jerry starts on about you, Carden just rolls his eyes and leaves the room."

"Good for him. Wish I were more like that, not giving a shit. You know how I get. I sink down into one of those dark moods, and every little thing can knock me off balance. So do I get to see Carden or not?"

"I'll sneak him down here some day, I promise. And, by the way, I've asked everyone here around the park not to let on that you're back, so that reporters don't get wind of the fact that you're here. Some of the neighbors, especially the Wises, are a little dubious about you now, but they're all beholden to me in one way or another, or they just don't want to get on my bad side."

"That *is* inadvisable." Brice sniggered. "No one wants to piss off a lawyer, and we both inherited Mommy's streak of vindictiveness. But, hell, I can't stay hidden in this house all the time. I'll need to get groceries and liquor, at the very least."

"True. Fortunately, you're not one of those fashionably delicate big-city homosexuals I hear tell of. You look like you can take care of yourself. Actually, with that extra weight on, you look a little like a wrestler. How much do you weigh now?"

"230." Brice patted his belly, then stuck out his chest and flexed an arm. "It ain't all fat. Lot of it's muscle. I'm lifting heavier weights than I ever have, despite my back problems. Feel this here. Go on now. Give it a feel. Not bad for forty, huh?"

Leigh chuckled. She reached across the table and gave his bunched biceps a hesitant squeeze.

"Lord. Okay. That sets my mind to rest a little. You still know how to box?"

"Yep. Ever since that Phys Ed class at WVU all those years ago. And I intend to keep myself up, just in case I need to protect myself. That weight set still in the basement?"

"Yes. It's a little rusty, but it's still there." The coffeepot beeped; Leigh rose to pour them both cups. "Plus Daddy's guns are in the linen closet upstairs. So be honest. How are you doing?"

Brice cupped his brow in his hand and took a long breath. "Well, again, you know me. I'm a fucking wreck, Leigh. I've always fallen into black moods whenever I got a career setback or disappointment—all self-doubt and envy and resentment, y'know? If I didn't win an award, if a CD didn't sell the way I'd hoped. But this, this shit puts all those times to shame. This is about the worst thing's ever happened to me. Can't sleep. Angry as hell. Scared. Brooding. Drinking a lot. Wondering what I'm meant to learn from this. Wondering what's the point. Wondering what the hell do I do now?"

"You sound like Daddy. You sure get your depressions from him."

"Yep. Glad you didn't. It's hell."

"Well, don't do anything drastic, for God's sake. I'll take care of you as best I can. How long are you going to be here?"

Brice added sugar to his cup. "Don't know. Nothing for me back in Nashville but a bunch of reporters ready to swarm me like a pack of piranhas. Shelly's divorcing me and taking most of the property, which is fine by me, actually. She needs to get on with her life. She's wasted enough years on me. As you know, my label's dropped me. My manager was pushing me to get into one of those goddamn ex-gay programs, but I just couldn't bear to do it, so he's liable to drop me too, since he figured that was the one way I could possibly salvage my career."

"I'm so sorry, Brice." Leigh shook her head and sipped her coffee. "I know how much you fought to make it as far as you have. All those roadhouses you played in around here. The shitty little gigs in Beckley. The state fair. All those years living hand to mouth in Nashville, trying to break into the big time."

"And then I did. And now I'm here. Where I started. Except I'm not young. I'm not hopeful. And I feel like I've been kicked in the head, the belly, and the crotch."

Brice sat back, staring out the kitchen window. Wind had picked up; the snowflakes fell in crazy angles. "Financially, I'm fucked. Not much income is gonna be coming in, since I suspect most of my fans are now self-righteous *ex*-fans who'll stop buying my CDs, and there won't be any new CDs, and there won't be any tours or performances, except maybe at Hinton's latest in a long series of swank gay bars."

Both siblings snorted. Hell would freeze over, they knew, before a conservative little West Virginia town like Hinton would ever have a gay bar.

"Do you need money, Brice? I have a little in savings, but raising a child is pretty expensive."

"I know that, honey, and Lord knows I don't want your money. I've talked to a realtor about my Nashville condo, so it's on the market now, and she thinks she can unload it fast, and for quite a bit. Plus I have investments and savings I can fall back on. I can live on that for a while till I get my bearings and figure out what's next."

Brice yawned and took a big gulp of coffee. He hadn't gotten nearly enough sleep the previous night, or over the past few weeks, for that matter. "Shit, I used to be so poor, eating beans and canned soup in college, and then in Nashville, paying the bills with fast food jobs. And then all of a sudden I got famous and I owned a big fucking mansion and all sorts of other hoity-toity shit. And now here I am, with all that gone and with me just damned grateful you brought me some good food."

Leigh smiled. "I love to feed someone who appreciates it. For future reference, there's also Sam Adams in the fridge and a couple big bottles of George Dickel in the cupboard."

"Great! Thanks."

"Sure. I figured you'd need a little attitude-adjustment. Better than antidepressants, right?"

Again a round of shared laughter, though this one was anxious. "Have you considered antidepressants?" Leigh asked.

"Hell, no." Brice waved off the suggestion. "That shit's for the weak. Besides, they didn't help Daddy, did they? I'll stick to bourbon, and pain pills when my back's irking me."

"We both got a taste for booze from Daddy, though I prefer vodka these days," Leigh said, adjusting her blazer.

"With all the bullshit you have to deal with as a lawyer, vodka makes good sense. I'm damned glad you took up the family profession instead of me. So, speaking of Daddy, what do you think our parents would have felt about all this mess?"

"Oh, as long as you didn't swish and mince and get all citified, Daddy'd be all right with you. He'd tell you to live your life and tell folks to get fucked if they didn't like it. Mommy would wring her hands and worry about what the women in the lady's garden club might be saying, and then cuss them up one side and down the other if they got snippy."

"Yep, that sounds about right."

Leigh checked her watch and gulped her coffee. "Okay, I need to get back to the office. I'm due in court pretty soon. I'll check in with you at the end of the day. By the way, my secretary's son, Dakota, is coming by to fill up the woodshed out back. I bought a cord of wood like you asked. I told him to put a few armloads on the front porch too, for easier access."

"Great. That should keep the gas bill down. I'll write you a check right now."

"No rush. I'll pick it up later. Oh, and I forgot to tell you. An old friend of yours was in town for the Railroad Days street fair in October. He came by the office and asked about you."

"Really? Who's that?"

"Wayne Meador. Your old flame."

"I wish," Brice said, sitting upright. "I was crazy about him. I haven't seen him since high school. How's he look?"

"Well, he doesn't look the way he did in high school."

"In other words, like a male model or porn star?"

Leigh smiled. "Yes, he was pretty handsome. He even made a pass at me once."

"Yes, I remember. I should have been pissed, but instead I was jealous."

"He was too much of a rounder for me. At any rate, he's married, and he's working construction in North Carolina, and he looks pretty good. Chunkier. Grayer."

I can relate, Brice thought. "Did he leave a number?"

"No. But when he's in Hinton, he stays with his father and stepmother on Fifth Avenue. My secretary lives up that way. I can ask her to let us know when he's back in town. He told me he might come home for the holidays."

"Yeah, do that. It'd be super to see him again. He'd be more than welcome to drop by...if the Big Gay Scandal hasn't put him off. Considering the circumstances, I doubt that I'll be getting much else in the way of company."

"All right. I'll tell Hope." Leigh squeezed Brice's hand and rose. "I'm glad you're home. I might not be able to do anything about your career, but I can sure make certain that you're well-fed."

"Hell, yes. I'm going to get into those meatballs here in a little bit."

Brice saw his sister out. For a few minutes, he simply stood at the door, watching the snowfall through the glass. Then he entered the front parlor. Bending, he exposed the piano keys, picked out a few aimless notes, and abruptly stopped.

Nothing. Why the hell bother? There ain't any melody to be found in this frigging morass I'm in. He closed the piano, shook his head, and headed back upstairs to bed.

CHAPTER ELEVEN

Two days after Brice's return to Hinton, he and his nephew Carden sat side by side on a picnic table in the woods, sipping Cokes and munching carry-out hot dogs and fries they'd fetched at Kirk's, a roadside diner across the river from Hinton. Around them, the thick forest atop Sandstone Mountain was all gray trunks and fallen leaves, with the occasional drumming of a woodpecker or the quarreling of chickadees. Far, far below the little roadside park where they ate, Sandstone Falls tumbled its whitewater over river rock, a thundering faint but still audible at this distance.

"So what d'you want for Christmas?" Brice asked, in between straw-sips of pop. "It's coming up in just another week and a half, you know."

"I know. I can't wait. Maybe some Spider-Man stuff? Or some dinosaurs. I love T-Rex." Carden was ten, a sociable, handsome kid who seemed to have inherited the family willfulness but thankfully lacked the foul temper and dark moods that Brice tended toward.

"I think I can arrange that. I liked comic book heroes and dinosaurs just like you when I was your age. You enjoying school? Fifth grade, right?"

"Yep. I don't like math much, but science is cool, and so's English."

"I felt the same. Hated math. Speaking of school, your mother tells me that you've been defending my name. I appreciate that. Just don't get into any fights on my account."

"People have been talking about you a lot, saying mean things. They're just stupid, you know?

And when I think they're being stupid, I tell them. I tell them to shut their mouths. Daddy's sure being stupid about you."

Brice laughed. "And do you tell him to shut his mouth?"

"No. I was raised not to talk back, so I just try not to listen."

"Well, that's probably a good idea. I'm glad we could have lunch together up here. And thanks again for not mentioning this to your father."

Carden shrugged. "No problem. Sometimes Mom and I have to leave things out, you know? He's at church right now. He thinks I'm spending time with some buddies, and, like Mom says, what Daddy doesn't know won't hurt him."

Carden paused to take a big bite of hot dog. Brice sucked up more Coke.

"Flicker," Brice said, pointing at the flash of yellow veering between oak boughs high above. "See the white rump? I thought I heard one calling. Sounds like 'wik-wik-wik-wik-wik.'"

"That's neat. We see a pileated out back sometime, digging bugs out of a dead tree. Hey, Uncle Brice, are you really gay?"

Brice stiffened. For a split-second, he was poised to respond as he usually did to the word "gay" but then realized it would be pointless to argue semantics with a ten-year-old. "Yep. Yep, I am."

"Okay. That's cool. Some people just are, Mom says. How long you been gay?"

Brice chuckled. "You looking at girls yet?"

Carden flushed. "No!"

"Ah, c'mon. Your mother told me you've already had a few crushes. You can tell me. Ain't nothing to be ashamed of. Everybody gets crushes."

"Yeah, okay. Some girls can be pretty cool, I guess. Not as cool as Mom, but pretty cool."

"Well, I've been gay since about your age, I guess. But I didn't tell anybody 'cause I would have gotten into big trouble if they knew."

"So you lied."

"Yes, I lied. For a long time, it felt like I needed to lie, but I guess the truth's out, though I never had the guts to tell it."

"And now that the truth's been told, you're in big trouble, right?"

Brice laughed and patted Carden's shoulder. "Yeah, I guess so. But I'll survive. We mountain folks are tough, right?"

"Hell, yes."

Brice laughed louder. "Where'd you learn that, potty mouth?"

Carden grinned. "You say it, don't you?"

"Hell, yes, I say it. Just don't use it around your parents. Your father already thinks I'm a bad influence. Finish up there. Time to get you home before he gets out of church."

"Okay." Carden took the last bite of hot dog, then stuffed a few fries into his mouth. "Uncle Brice, you still gonna make music? CDs and stuff?" he mumbled.

Brice rose, dusting crumbs off his jeans. "I don't know. I don't think so. You need an audience to make music, and I'm pretty sure I don't have an audience any more."

"Why don't you make music for yourself then? Besides, you do still have an audience. Mom and I'll listen. Maybe next Sunday, while Daddy's in church. You brought your guitar with you, right?"

"Oh, sure. My guitar goes where I go."

"So why'd you bring your guitar all this way if you're not gonna play music?"

"Good question. Tell you what, you talk to your mother, and maybe y'all can sneak down some day while you're off school, and I'll make a fire and play you some songs off my last CD."

"It's a deal. Mom plays your music all the time in the car, when she drives me to school and back. She used to play it in the house, but…."

"Yeah, I get it. Your father's got his opinions. Come on now. I have a surprise in the truck. Two of those Hostess fruit pies with our names on 'em."

CHAPTER TWELVE

As Leigh had warned him, the sign was indeed gone. "The Brice Brown Bridge," it had proclaimed for years, and something in Brice's chest glowed whenever he was home to visit family and drove over the structure spanning the New. Now, the Saturday before Christmas, there was no warm glow in his chest, inspired by pride or the holiday spirit or any other agreeable emotion. Instead, he wanted to ass-kick the motherfucker who'd torn down the sign, punch every member of the town council who'd voted to rename the bridge, and slap upside the head that up-and-coming politico brat, Suzanne Matthews, whose name now graced, or, rather, defaced the bridge.

Brice drove past the new sign and over the river, snarling low in his throat. For nearly a week, afraid he might be recognized and harassed, he'd stayed inside the house, drinking beer or bourbon, watching junk TV and his library of action/adventure DVD's. When his scattered concentration allowed, he stretched out on the couch before the fireplace and reread tattered paperbacks he'd savored in his high school years: war novels, fantasy novels, and historical romances set in faraway countries and faraway times. His only exercise was desultory weight lifting in the musty basement a couple of times a week. Otherwise, he wallowed beneath comforters in aimless, restless, resentful sloth.

Brice's cell phone had buzzed every so often, but he'd refused to answer it unless it was Leigh. Shelly left a message saying she was sending him divorce papers to sign and that the Williamson County house was on the market. Lorrie left a message telling him she was worried about him. Steve left a message saying that the Exodus International people were very disappointed that Brice hadn't followed through with treatment and that Steve was seriously considering having to drop Brice as a client.

When Brice got hungry, which was often, eating being one of the few pleasures left to him, he'd gobbled either the food Leigh brought by on the way to her office, or delivery pizza, or mac and cheese from a box. He kept the heat low so as to save on the gas bill, so he rarely bathed, shuffling muskily around the house in moccasins, boot socks, thermal undershirt, fleece lounge pants, and his hooded camo sweatshirt. He slept late every morning, went to bed drunk around 9 pm, and woke in the dead of night to bouts of insomnia, grim thoughts of failure, public disgrace, and bankruptcy swirling around in his head.

Whenever Brice tried to compose new music on the piano or guitar, nothing came, leaving him even more despondent. Except for the one afternoon Leigh and Carden had managed to come by with a pot of beef stew and to visit for a surreptitious hour while queer-hating Jerry was off doing whatever the piddly-hell he was doing for a living, Brice refused to play his older tunes. Those songs—fifteen years' worth of CD hits— with their regular references to much-loved, much-desired country girls and beautiful women, seemed to him among the most egregious lies he'd ever composed.

That morning, though, he'd awakened late with the knowledge that he'd have to leave the house. Despite Leigh's best efforts to supply him with what he needed, he was out of beer, bourbon, and assorted groceries. For a long time, he'd simply lain in bed, listening to the distant sound of the river and boxcars rumbling on the rails below the cliff. He'd jacked off half-heartedly into his customary joy rag, a camo bandana, remembering how sweetly that Daytona hustler, Mike, had moaned and squirmed while Brice was pounding his fuzzy ass.

Near noon, Brice had crawled out of bed and showered for the first time in days, then stood before the mirror naked, feeling slovenly and overweight, studying his gray-streaked beard, widow's peak, and the beefy mounds of his hairy chest and belly, and cussing himself soundly. "You're so fucking fat, you're so fucking old, you're such a fucking failure. Idiot. Moron. Just pathetic. Who would want you?"

Grim-faced, he'd pulled on jeans, hiking boots, and sweatshirt, in the kitchen gulped a cup of coffee and snarfed a Pop-Tart, swathed his head in the customary concealment of a camo hood, this time atop a "Stars and Bars Forever" baseball cap,

tugged on his rawhide jacket, and tramped out into the light fall of snow. "Redneck wear,"
he'd always jokingly called his fashion sense, the sort of outfits most Summers County
men wore, but now that he'd been outed, Brice knew that his rough-edged country-boy
look was valuable camouflage against the possibility of being recognized. "An infamous
homosexual," Brice had muttered, starting up his truck. "Not exactly the career goal I'd
dreamed of."

Now he skirted the New River, driving through dusty swirls of snow, studying the
high green water to his left and the glistening mountainside icefalls to his right. Memory
after memory sideswiped him.

*There. KFC used to be there, where I went out on a date with that little Jennifer Wiley
my senior year, doing my best to be straight. And there's the Dairy Queen, where I fell off the
merry-go-round when I was in grade school. Where Daddy used to bring us for hot dogs and
fiesta sundaes. And there…Wayne…why were we there, that gravel turnout beside the water?
A summer night, it must have been. That was the last time I ever saw him. His plaid shirt
was unbuttoned. He bent down and picked up a stone and skipped it across the water, and his
shirt fell wide open as he lobbed it, and I could see how hairy his chest was, how flat his belly
was, and my dick got hard and my heart did a crazy flip. Damn. One of the best guys I've ever
known. Beautiful and brave and funny. A real buddy. Damn, I hope he gets back to town soon
and drops by. But why would anyone want to visit a has-been like me?*

Brice crossed the double bridge over the converging rivers, stopped for gas at the
Go Mart, then pulled into the Rite Aid parking lot. He pulled on his dark glasses, cocked
the brim of his cap over his eyes, and sucked in air. *Here we go,* he thought, clambering
out. *If I want more booze, I'm gonna have to risk the paparazzi.* Head down, he entered
the store.

To his immense relief, the place was nearly empty. A pretty blonde girl stood
behind the counter. She gave him a little wave. "How you?" she said.

"Just fine, ma'am," Brice said, giving her a crooked smile before grabbing a cart and
shuffling off toward the liquor aisles. He returned with four large bottles of Dickel, two
liters of Jameson Irish whiskey, and three six-packs of beer.

"Are y'havin' a Christmas party, sir?" the girl asked, as she rang him up.

"In a manner of speaking," Brice said. "Weather's so cold, I thought a toddy or two'd—"

Brice stopped in mid-sentence and swallowed hard. There at his elbow, in a metal
rack, was the latest issue of the *Star*, and there he was on the cover, juxtaposed with

a photo of Zac Lanier. The headline blared, "Brice Brown Disappears in Aftermath of Divorce Announcement!" A smaller photo in the lower right-hand corner showed Shelly leaving her lawyer's office, looking very stylish and very sad.

"Sir? Are you all right?"

"Yes, ma'am," Brice croaked, pulling his gaze away from the magazine. "Guess I'm just thirsty. Better get these bottles home and heat me up that toddy." He pulled out his credit card, realized his name was on it, tucked it back into his wallet, and counted his cash. He didn't have enough.

"Ohhh, hell," he murmured, biting his lower lip. "Credit card it is then."

"Sorry, sir, I'll need to see your driver's license, since your bill's over a hundred dollars."

Ohhh, hell, Part Two, Brice thought. Grimacing, he pulled out the laminated license and handed it to her.

"Tennessee. I have a cousin in Tennessee. She works at—"

Just as Brice feared, the pretty clerk paled. She looked at the license, and then she looked at Brice, and then she looked at the issue of the *Star*, and then she looked at Brice again.

"Oh, Lord. Mr. Brown. It's you," she said, blinking mascara-laden lashes.

"Yes, ma'am," Brice sighed, swiping his credit card. "In the flesh."

"Mommy told me you were from around here. What are you doing back? Oh, I'm sorry. I'm being rude. I didn't mean to be snoopy. Where are my manners?" With a jerky gesture, she handed him back his driver's license.

"Just back visiting family for the holidays," Brice said, voice husky. "Going to be writing a new album."

"Well, isn't that nice? That's just so nice to hear. Well, here you go," she said, handing him the receipt before bagging up his purchases.

Brice transferred the bags to the cart. "Merry Christmas," he rasped, tipping his cap before rolling the cart out into the parking lot. As he put the bags into the front seat of his truck, he could see the girl through the front window of the store. She was already on the phone, gesticulating wildly.

Brice pulled out fast, half-expecting the police, the fire department, and a van full of reporters and TV crews to materialize before he could leave the Rite Aid parking lot. "Shit, shit, shit," he murmured, driving only another block past the old folks' apartment building and parking in front of Kroger. "Let's make this fast."

Brice adjusted his cap and hood before hurrying into the grocery store. He grabbed a cart, bent his head as if he were a defensive back preparing to charge, and headed down the first aisle clutching a grocery list.

Okay, so I'm tired of eating junk food or relying on Leigh for meals. She's busy enough without having to cater to me. You're from a long line of country cooks, Brice. You can feed yourself. So. Canned collards. Barbeque sauce. Chips and dip. More brown beans. Eggs and bacon. Pork chops. Cube steak, since Leigh said she'd come over and make me country-fried steak with milk gravy and mashed potatoes sometime before Christmas. Chipped beef, 'cause I love SOS. Vienna sausages. Underwood deviled ham. Bread. Bologna. Cheddar cheese. And hell, yes, why the hell not? More Hostess pies and Pop-Tarts, and a German chocolate cake. No more damn diets for this ole boy.

After heaping his cart with goodies, Brice got into the shortest checkout line, behind a very old woman with purple-rimmed cat-eye spectacles who was chatting with the clerk, an acne-faced high-school girl, about a church supper they were both planning to attend.

Shit, hurry up, Brice thought, seeing the same issue of the *Star* displayed to his right and cursing beneath his breath. *Somebody figures out who I am, and I might just get stoned to death. Talk about an untimely end.*

The old lady pulled out her checkbook and began scrawling in it with agonizing slowness. Brice cleared his throat and scanned the other checkout lines. *Don't know any of these folks, thank God. Except…. Shit, is that Randy Doyle? We used to trade comic books back in junior high. Goddamn, it is him. We shot the shit in front of the courthouse the last time I was in town. He's liable to recognize me, despite my big beard and beer-gut, if I don't get out of here fast.*

"Hello, sir. Did you find everything you needed?" the checkout clerk asked.

"Yes, ma'am, I did." Throat dry, Brice turned his back on Doyle, gave the girl a curt smile and a nod, and stonily watched his purchases inching one by one down the automated runner. *Hurry up, hurry up. Surely she ain't gonna ask for an ID too,* Brice thought, gritting his teeth. *They never do here. My luck, she'll not only wanna see my driver's license, she'll announce my name to the whole damn store.*

The total came up and he swiped his card, then signed the receipt. The cashier gave his signature no notice. The young man bagging Brice's groceries was too busy looking at the clerk's breasts to give him much mind.

Great. Let's get outta here. "Thanks, man," he said to the mammary-mesmerized bag boy, pushing past him into the front of the store. He was nearly to the automatic door when he heard a loud voice behind him.

"Brice? Brice Brown? That you, Brice?"

Fuck! Brice was tempted to leave his groceries behind and simply dart out the door, but instead he turned and sighed. *Here we go. Bound to happen sooner or later, small as this town is. Maybe I should have stayed in Nashville.*

Randy Doyle stood there, looking Brice up and down with a sour grin. "Well, well, well. The big Nashville star. I hardly recognized you. What you doing back in town?" Thirty-some years ago, Randy had been an awkward kid who shared Brice's passion for *Superman, Batman, The X-Men,* and *The Avengers.* Now, Brice knew, he was a corpulent guidance counselor at the local high school, as well as a part-time minister out Wolf Creek.

"Howdy, Randy. I'm just back to see my kin," Brice said. He mustered a smile, trying to appear as if everything were normal. That was especially difficult, since Doyle's stentorian voice had broadcast Brice's name through half the store. To Brice's profound unease, just about everybody in sight was staring at him. Several folks were even pointing and whispering.

"So how you been?" Brice said, offering his hand. Doyle pointedly declined to shake, though his grin grew broader.

"Question is, how *you* been? That secret must have been an awful burden to carry all these years." Randy shook his head, wrinkled his nose, and pulled a copy of the *Star* from his grocery bag.

"Lord, you and I used to play football together. I just can't believe it. You? A big ole boy like you homosexual? When I think about how we used to take showers in the same locker room, it gives me the creeps. Now you've broke the heart of that pretty wife of yours and broke the laws of God too."

Doyle held up the magazine for all to see. The expression on his face was so aggrieved that he looked as if Brice had cheated on him instead of Shelly. "What a nasty scandal. You shouldn't have come back here. You don't belong here no more, after all that godless behavior we've all read about."

"Oh, hell, Randy," Brice groaned. "Really? You gotta kick a guy when he's down? Asshole." He shook his head, turned, and pushed his cart out through the electronic door.

"God help you," Randy shouted after him. "You're a hell-bound sinner, that's for sure. You're a blot on the good name of this town!"

"Fuck off!" Brice yelled back, barging past a trio of old ladies whose pursed lips indicated that they disapproved of his trashy speech. He hurried across the parking lot toward his truck, hoping that his masculine dignity wasn't entirely compromised by the speed of his retreat.

CHAPTER THIRTEEN

THAT NIGHT, SNUGLY DRESSED IN sweats and contentedly buzzed on the second whiskey sour, Brice was sliding a foil-covered baking dish full of pork chops, onions, and barbecue sauce into the oven when the doorbell rang.

His brow creased. *Who the hell could that be in this weather?* Night was falling. Sleet pecked the windows, and wind buffeted the eaves. It couldn't be Leigh, he knew. She had left the office next door hours ago, determined to get back to her Forest Hill house before the expected storm hit. *Probably Randy Doyle, come to deliver a sermon on the sins of Sodom. Or a goddamn reporter. Or a lynch mob.* Brice took a long sip of his drink, strolled to the front door, and flipped on the porch light.

A short, stocky man was standing on the porch, bundled in an army jacket and wearing a black toboggan. *By now, the news that I'm back must be all over town. Probably some asshole from* The Hinton Daily News, The Beckley Register-Herald, *or* The Charleston Gazette *wanting to interview the sad, disgraced faggot now that he's fled home with his tail between his legs.* Brice threw open the door, ready to lob a string of vulgarities at the stranger. "What the hell do you want?" he shouted.

"Hey! Hey, relax." The man pulled off his toboggan and stepped closer so that Brice could better see the features of his face. "It's me, man. Relax. I was in town and Hope Lily told me you were here."

The stranger's voice was rich and deep and somehow familiar. Dumbfounded, Brice studied the man's features. Short dark hair gone gray at the temples. Close-cropped black beard, as silver-stippled as Brice's own whiskers were.

"Jesus fucking Christ," Brice said. "Wayne Meador?"

"Yep. Guess we've both changed some. Can I come in?" He rubbed his upper arms and stamped his foot. "Cold as a witch's tit out here."

"Oh, shit. Sure!" Brice stepped aside and Wayne entered the foyer. "Nice place," he said, looking around. "Looks about the same as it did when we were in high school. Sweet fire you got going too."

"This place is about all I got left," Brice said, locking the door and flipping off the porch light. "I guess you've heard about all the Nashville bullshit, huh?"

"Sure have," Wayne replied, brushing sleet-wet off his shoulders. "My stepmother has most of the magazine and newspaper articles."

"Not the kind of celebrity I dreamed of, as you can imagine. So you know about all that and you come to say Hi anyway?"

"You bet I have." Wayne gave Brice one of those white catfish grins that used to make Brice's chest tighten up back in high school.

"Well, good." Brice offered his hand. "Thanks for dropping by then."

"Hell, man, I know we ain't laid eyes on each other for decades, but there's no need to be formal. Y'ain't gonna bite me, are you?" Wayne's grin broadened.

Brice grinned back. "Naw. Naw, I promise."

"Okay then." Wayne stepped forward, locking Brice in a bear hug so tight it was momentarily hard to breathe. To feel such warmth and affection from a man he'd been so passionately attached to, albeit decades ago, made Brice nearly choke up.

Wayne gave Brice's back a couple of hard pats before releasing him. "You've been through some shit, old friend."

"You're telling me," Brice said, studying the shorter man as Wayne peeled off his jacket and hung it on the hall tree. As Leigh had said, Wayne was broader and grayer, but his face was still handsome and his torso and arms still powerfully built. He was dressed in work boots, jeans, and a red plaid flannel shirt atop a black turtleneck.

"So how long you in town?" Brice asked.

"Till the day after Christmas. Staying with my folks on Fifth Avenue. Gail—that's my wife—she's back in Charlotte 'cause her mother's real sick, so I came up here alone. Ole Roy—my dad—he's really slowing down. In fact, I'm thinking this might be his last Christmas. So here I am."

"God, it's good to see you. Say, I'm making dinner. Can you stay?"

"You bet your sweet ass I can. I remember what good cooks your kin were. Smells great. Whatcha got cooking?"

Brice led the way into the kitchen. "Barbecued pork chops. Cole slaw. Cornbread. Canned collards. Plus a store-bought German chocolate cake."

"Sounds like a fine meal for an icy night. And whatcha got there?" Wayne nodded toward Brice's highball glass.

"Whiskey sour. You want one? Or a hot toddy?"

"Thought you'd never ask." Wayne wiped wet from his whiskers. "How about a hot toddy? I about froze my nuts off walking down here. The sidewalks are slippery as hell."

"Toddy sounds good. Two of 'em coming up."

Wayne took a seat at the kitchen table, watching as Brice heated water in the kettle, cut lemon wedges, and poured out bourbon and sugar. For a few minutes, the only sounds were the slosh of liquor and the tick of sleet on the windows.

"You're looking pretty good, Brice. Big arms, big beard. You were a skinny kid when we first met, way back in ninth grade. But now you're the solid kinda guy I wouldn't want to pick a fight with."

"Thanks. Years of weightlifting…and eating."

Wayne grinned again, pinching his gut. "I get that. Aging sucks."

Brice took a long look at Wayne. *You ain't the porn star you were in high school, but I'd still climb all over you.* "That's for damn sure. You're looking good yourself. I'd say we're both holding up pretty well for forty, huh?"

"Guess so. Gail says she likes the gray in my hair. Me, I ain't so sure."

Brice poured hot water into their mugs and stirred. "Remember when that massive bastard Billy Holt got wind of the fact that I'd asked his ex out on a date and punched me in the face in front of the hardware store? I would've gotten my ass whipped mighty bad if you hadn't shown up and driven him off. Even five inches shorter than me, you were more intimidating than I ever was."

Wayne shrugged. "I filled out early, I guess. Besides, you were my friend. I wasn't going to let that goddamn gorilla beat on my friend."

"Yeah. Well. I just wanted you to know that I've never forgotten that. It meant a lot that you stood up for me. It still does."

Wayne shrugged again. "You would have done the same for me."

"Yes. Yes, I would have. But I wouldn't have been half as effective. Here you go."
Brice handed Wayne his drink. They clinked mugs and both men took sips.

"Tasty," Wayne declared. "When'll dinner be ready?"

"A while. Chops cook another forty minutes, cornbread another thirty-five or so."

"Good. That means we got time for another one of these." Wayne winked and
grinned. When he rolled up the sleeves of his layered shirts, Brice could see the dark
hair coating his forearms.

God, you still got that smile. You still got those charms. "Count on it. How about we
head on in to the fire?"

"Sounds good." Wayne nodded, rising. Soon, the two old friends were sitting side
by side on the couch watching oak logs spark and flame behind the fireplace screen.

"I can't believe you got married," Brice said, angling a thumb at Wayne's wedding
band. "Congrats! I'm surprised, though. You always swore you weren't the marrying kind."

"Yeah, I was kind of a rounder in high school, huh?"

"Yep. Everybody called you 'Pooch,' remember?"

Wayne snickered. "'Cause I was such a pussyhound. Yep. Well, I continued in that
vein for quite a few years. Had some grand affairs with some gorgeous women. Paid
for some abortions. Caught the clap a few times. But that kind of life gets old, y'know?
Especially when you get old. Or older, at any rate."

"Yeah, I do kinda know that. So how'd you meet your wife?"

"She's an accountant at a construction firm I work for near Charlotte. We've only
been married a couple of years, but so far it's great. She's strong, beautiful, no-nonsense.
Won't tolerate my shit."

Brice grinned. "Sounds like you met your match, Pooch. 'Bout time. I'm glad you're
happy."

"Yeah. Took long enough. So how long you owned this place? It's real cozy," Wayne
said, settling back with a contented sigh.

"Since Daddy died in '94. Heart attack, just like his father."

"I heard about that. I still remember your mother. She was always so sweet to me."

Brice nodded. "I miss her. She died about ten years before Daddy. Damn cigarettes.
You still smoke?"

Wayne shook his head. "Naw. Quit while I was in Basic Training. They slowed me
down. With all that fucking exercise, climbing over things and hauling shit, I couldn't

afford to be hacking and wheezing and gasping for breath. So when's the last time we saw one another? Must have been...."

The night we stood by the river and your shirt fell open. "Summer of 1975. August, it must have been. I was about to head off to college, and you...."

"And I was heading off to the Marines, relieved as hell that the war in Vietnam had just ended."

"Yeah. We drove around some that night, had a few beers...."

"And a little pot, as I recall."

"Yeah." Brice nodded. "We pulled over by the river and you skipped stones."

"Really? You remember all that?"

"Oh, yes."

"Man, my memory's going fast. Seems like fucking forever since we drove these Summers County back roads in that broke-down ole Plymouth of mine. But now here we are." Wayne gave Brice's shoulder a gentle jab. "Man, it's good to see you. You've come a long way. I've been listening to your music since you first started recording."

"Really?"

"Shit, sure. I have all your CDs. I was always telling guys I worked with that I went to high school with Brice Brown, that we used to hunt and fish and drink together." Wayne paused, sipping on his mug. "So, Brice...."

"Uh, oh," Brice groaned. "That tone of voice. Let me guess. Are all the newspaper and magazine stories true? That's what you want to ask."

"Yeah. You got it. But you know me, man. We were real buddies back then. I know twenty years have come and gone, but that doesn't change anything, as far as I'm concerned. You can tell me anything."

Brice rose. He opened up the hearth screen long enough to add another log to the fire. Then he sat back beside Wayne, took a big drink of his toddy, and looked his friend in the face. "Yep. It's all true. More or less."

"Okay. Wow. Never would have guessed. How long have you known you're gay?"

"Well, I'm not exactly...." Brice began, but then he remembered Doctor Zucker and his insistence that Brice claim his identity as ex-gay and announce it to the world. "Oh, well, fuck it. Yeah. Gay. I've known since a few years before I met you."

"And you didn't tell me?" Wayne rubbed his whiskered jaw.

"Naw. Put yourself in my place. It was the mid-seventies. We were living in this little backwoods town in this little backwoods county with a damned preacher up every holler shouting about sin. You were…important to me, Wayne. Real important. And you were a big, macho, rough-edged stud and had girlfriends out the wazoo. I was afraid if I told you that you'd freak out. That you'd turn on me."

Brice stood up. He stepped over to the window and looked out into the park. In the gleam of the sole streetlight, the grass was going gray with ice.

"I'd never have done that, Brice. We were rabble-rousers and rule-breakers, remember? We were always talking about bucking the system and to hell with authority. Why would I have given a shit about what some retard preachers were saying?"

Brice rubbed his forehead hard, then resumed his seat.

"I was afraid you'd think I wasn't…a man. Wasn't worth running with."

"A man?" Wayne rolled his eyes. "You weren't a man. Neither was I. We were both boys. You're a man now. A big powerful man who's accomplished a lot. I was proud to call you my friend then, and despite all the years apart and all the media horseshit lately, I'm proud to call you my friend now. When guys at work who know you and me were friends start ragging on you, I tell them to kiss my lily-white ass."

Brice smiled despite himself. "Thanks, man. But you know what I mean, don't you? You know how we were raised. Fags were delicate, prissy little things, more like girls than boys. Fairies. Pansies. I mean, think about all the folks we went to school with. Imagine how they would've reacted to the truth. Hell, I ran across Randy Doyle in Kroger just this afternoon, and he told me I was a hell-bound blot on the good name of this town."

"Well, Randy Doyle looks like a tick left on a hound dog's ear too long. Bloated bastard. He can suck my dick. Oh, sorry." Wayne gave Brice a crooked grin. "Was that a homophobic comment?"

Brice laughed. "I ain't *that* sensitive. You heard they renamed the bridge, right?"

Wayne made a sour face. "Yep. My stepmother told me all about it. Her second cousin is on the town council."

"So…what was her reaction to all that? I'm sorta afraid to ask."

Wayne's expression achieved deeper depths of sour. "Well, she's a churchgoer, if you get my drift. To be honest, she and I have been arguing about you ever since I got to town. She demanded that I not come down here to visit you. As if that harpy can tell me what to do. She's so damn afraid of what the town might think if someone sees me down here hanging out with you. Fuck 'the town,' that's what I say. It's not like reporters are going to be out in this storm lurking around and trying to get shots of us."

"Shit. Sorry about that." Brice rose. "Yeah, I'm beginning to wonder if it was the smartest thing for me to come back here. I mean, when a guy's wounded or hurt, he just wants to go home, y'know? But what if home doesn't want you around? My sister and nephew are all I got left. Hell, even my brother-in-law objects to me. I have to sneak around to see my own nephew. Shit."

"Really? Jesus."

"Yep. He must think I'm some kinda pedophile, the moron. Another?" Brice peered into Wayne's nearly empty mug.

"You bet. Between Gail's mother being sick and Roy falling apart, and all the retards giving you crap, we could both do with a good buzz. Happy holidays, huh?"

"Right," Brice agreed, striding to the kitchen. In a few minutes, he'd mixed a second round of toddies. "Hold on," he said, placing the steamy mugs on the coffee table. "I need to get more firewood from the porch."

Outside, the sleet had shifted to snow, and a brisk wind was blowing. Brice loaded up his arms with five logs. He was bending down to grab one more when his back clenched up and a familiar pain surged through him. "Fuck!" he blurted, dropping the armload back into the wood box. Face distorted, he shuffled back into the foyer. Wayne stood there, body tense, face full of concern.

"What the hell happened? I heard a crash. Damn, Brice, what's wrong with you?" Wayne grabbed his unsteady friend by the shoulder.

"Frigging back. It goes out sometimes. Sacroiliac joint, they call it. Doctor says it's stress."

"You need to sit down," Wayne said.

"Good idea."

Wayne helped Brice hobble into the front parlor. Ever so slowly, face contorted and teeth clenched, Brice lowered himself onto the couch.

"Should you lie down and stretch out?" Wayne said.

"Naw. Sitting'll do for now." Stiffly, Brice propped pillows behind him, then leaned back and closed his eyes.

"Ohhhh, fuck, it hurts," Brice groaned. "Thanks, man. I'd be screwed if you weren't here."

"So what else can I do?" Wayne said, spreading an afghan over Brice's lap.

"Hand here that drink. Bourbon's bound to help."

"Here you go. What else?"

Brice took a big gulp of his toddy. "I got some pain pills upstairs in the bathroom cabinet over the sink. If you'd fetch those, I'd be mighty grateful."

"You bet." Wayne stomped up the stairs and was back under a minute with the medication and a glass of water.

"Thanks," Brice rasped, gulping down two pills. "I don't want to impose, man. I'm a mess. Y'ought to head home. Not only am I a big fat failure, I'm a broke-back geezer. Git on back to your family. I'll be fine."

"Fool. You just said you'd be screwed if I weren't around. I'm not gonna leave you here all crippled up. I'm staying the night, whether you like it or not. Besides, you promised me dinner." Wayne squeezed Brice's shoulder. "Right?"

"Okay, ornery," Brice said, a wash of gratitude hoarsening his voice. "Stay then. Seems like you're saving my butt again, just like back in high school. I got several guest beds upstairs." *I'd much prefer it if you got naked and slept with me, though with this goddamn back, I'm sure not in any position to seduce you, more's the pity,* Brice thought, massaging his spine. *And every time you touch me, I want to cry. God, I'm so starved for affection it's pathetic.*

"Lemme get more firewood, and then I'll check on the chops," Wayne said. "I'll take care of you, friend."

I need taken care of, considering what kinda wreck I've become, Brice thought. *In a better world, you and I'd be lovers, but, as it is, I'm damned grateful you're still my friend.* "Thanks, Pooch. Means a lot. Y'ought to let your kin know you're staying, or they'll worry. Phone's in the kitchen. Oh, and I should have offered sooner, but there's some cheese in the fridge and some crackers in the cupboard."

"Great! I'm starved," Wayne said. Soon, he had two big armloads of wood piled beside the hearth. Soon thereafter, he'd returned from the kitchen with a plate of Ritz crackers and Cheddar already sliced.

"Here you go. I have more water heating up. I want another of these toddies. You just sit back and snack while I check on dinner."

"Your wife's a lucky woman," Brice said, taking the plate.

Wayne chuckled. "I like to take care of my clan, man. That's the way we mountain men are, ain't we? Protect and provide?"

"Yep. Yep, I guess so. Glad you think I'm still part of your clan."

"You bet. Always. Be back in a minute. Those chops smell done."

Brice munched on cheese, massaged his lower back, and looked around the room. *Ain't lost quite everything yet. Cozy fire and solid house keeping out the winter. Good friend. Food to eat. Thank you, God, whoever You are, for all I got left.*

Wayne peered into the parlor. "Chop's are out. I mixed up the cornbread batter and stuck it in the oven. Used that cast-iron skillet and lots of bacon grease from that tin in the fridge. Right?"

"Right. Didn't know you could cook."

"Cain't. But I can read that cookbook on the counter."

Brice smirked. "I thought all us West Virginia hillbillies were illiterate."

"We are." Wayne smirked back. "You get that kinda shit in Nashville?"

"Occasionally."

"Yeah, I get it in Charlotte. They're just jealous. Those North Carolina flatlands ain't half as scenic as these hills of ours. Okay, let me call my folks."

Brice ate more cheese and sipped his drink. Between the bourbon and the pain pills, he was suddenly feeling very relaxed and content. *Ah, chemistry*, he mused. *Didn't much like the subject in high school, but I sure like what it's doing to my head right now.*

"Yeah. Hey," Wayne's voice sounded in the kitchen. "Look, Roy, I'm down at Brice's. Yeah, Brice Brown. Naw. Naw. I don't care. Look, his back's giving him fits, and it's coming down outside, and…. Naw, I don't wanna talk to her. I'm staying. It's no big deal. Naw. Ah, hell. Okay, okay."

Wayne heaved a husky groan. Long-corded phone in hand, he appeared in the parlor door. "Shit. Sorry, Brice. Here we go," he said before returning to the kitchen.

Oh, no. Brice put his head in his hands, his comfortable buzz dispersing. *His family's giving him grief, and it's all my fault.*

"Hey, Myrtle. Yep. Yep. Staying the night. Like I told Roy, Brice's back's gone out. Yep. Naw. Naw. Naw. Naw, I don't care if folks know I'm here. We're friends, Myrtle. Friends. Haven't seen him in years, but, yep…. Don't care about that. You should know me better'n—. What? Oh, please. Whoring? Really? No, I'm not worried. You're crazy. Seems to me it's my Christian duty to stay here and help—. What? No. Forget it. I'll see y'all tomorrow morning. I'm staying, and that's that. Good night."

Bang of phone into receiver. Muttered string of profanities.

Wayne strode in, black eyebrows bunched up. "Drink up, bud. Another's on the way."

Brice nodded. He swigged the last of the second toddy and handed his mug to Wayne. "Look, I don't want you to stay if—"

"I'm staying!" Wayne blurted. "You need me tonight. And I'm so fucking pissed at Myrtle I don't even wanna be under the same roof as her."

"So what'd she say?" Brice asked, once Wayne had come back with the third round.

"Oh, shit." Wayne wrinkled up his nose. "Do you really wanna—"

"Yes. Tell me."

"She...."

"Ain't nothing you gonna say gonna surprise me. I know the religious rhetoric as good as you do. We both grew up in this town, remember?"

Wayne sighed and rubbed his eyes. "Yeah. She said...you're an instrument of Satan, and you're bound to make a pass at me for sure. And she said that I have such a tendency toward sin—considering all the infamous whoring I indulged in in the past— I'd fall victim to your aggressive and notorious perversions, and then—"

"Aggressive and notorious perversions? Infamous whoring? She said that?"

"Sure did."

"Love it," Brice said, stroking his beard.

"Me too. When she gets her dander up, she can turn a phrase. As if I'd suddenly turn to cock-sucking after all these decades of chasing pussy."

"True." *Tragically true.* "Go on."

"She said if word gets around I'm here, word I spent the night, even word that we're still friends...ever'body'll say...."

"Go on."

"Folks'll say we got a thing going like you and that Zac guy had. Then we'll both be ridden out of town on a rail...."

Brice grinned. "Tarred and feathered too?"

The glower on Wayne's face lightened. "No doubt. Shit. You and me, bulky as you've gotten, we could take 'em all on."

"Sure we could. Especially with my back the way it is now."

"True. That might be a problem. Oh, and Myrtle said that Gail'll leave me for sure once the scandal gets out. And I'll be fired from my job. And I'll never be welcome in this town again. And she'll never, never, never be able to hold her head up at a church social again."

"Bless her heart." Brice shifted and stretched his back. The medication and the booze had herded off most of the pain, leaving him feeling warm and limp and only mildly uncomfortable. *Not that some of what Myrtle said ain't right. I'd love to make a pass at you, except that wouldn't do either of us any good. Ain't that a bitter truth? One of the bitterest. I think I met the love of my life in high school, and just my luck, the guy's straight.* "Myrtle's predictions are pretty dire. Sounds like high gay drama."

"True. Lemme go put those chops back in to warm up," Wayne said, standing. "Cornbread's smelling real good. Should be ready soon. You got any sorghum to go with it? Or wildflower honey?"

"Cabinet over the stove," Brice said. He wrapped his cold hands around the warmth of the toddy mug and admired the curves of Wayne's butt as he left the room. *Your wife is the luckiest woman on earth. Shit, I sure wish there was a pill to turn you queer. Shit, I wish I could meet some hot guy like you who wants me just as much as I want you.*

OH, MAN. I AM FLYING, Brice thought, drowsing on the parlor couch while Wayne, humming one of Brice's early tunes, washed dishes in the kitchen. *I haven't been this high since I butt-fucked that hot little hustler in Daytona.*

The two men had made short work of their suppers. Only one chop and a triangle of cornbread were left, tucked away in Tupperware in the fridge. Outside, a fine snow fell, driven along wild angles by increasingly blustery wind. Every few minutes, the windows went blizzard-blank, full of writhing white.

In the kitchen, the sound of splashing water ceased. In another minute, Wayne sauntered in, black bangs falling over his brow and two glasses of golden liquid in his hand.

"I'm drunk, and I feel like getting drunker," he announced. "Found this Jameson in your liquor cabinet. All right with you?"

"Oh, yes," Brice said. He knew only one Wayne was there, but he kept seeing two, both of them impressively broad-shouldered. "I'm pretty shit-faced right now, what with pills on top of toddies, but what the hell? It's a reunion."

"You bet it is." Wayne handed Brice a glass. "Gail's always scolding me about my booze habit, but—"

"But she ain't here tonight, right?" Clumsily, Brice bumped Wayne's drink with his. "To old friends."

"To old friends," Wayne repeated, taking a seat beside Brice. Both men drank, regarding one another with lopsided grins.

"Nice and toasty in here," Wayne said, unbuttoning and peeling off his flannel shirt. To Brice's drunken delight, the tight black turtleneck accentuated the brawny swell of Wayne's pecs and belly. *Wow, I can make out his nipples. Damn it*, Brice thought, trying not to stare. *It's a blessing and a torment, having him so close.*

"Thanks for cleaning up. Didn't know you liked Irish whiskey," Brice said, looking away. "Thought you were a Canadian whiskey kinda guy."

"Grew outta that. I love Jameson after a meal. How you feeling, broke-back?" To Brice's tacit pleasure, Wayne patted his thigh.

"Lots better. Again, 'cause I'm high as hell."

"Whatever works. Want me to lay another log down?"

"Naw. Getting late."

"Want some of that German chocolate cake?"

"Naw. Don't have room."

"Me neither." Wayne rubbed the curve of his belly. "Shouldn't have had that third piece of cornbread. Just cain't eat the way I used to."

"Me neither. Otherwise, I'd be twice as fat."

"You ain't fat. You're just burly."

"Tell my Nashville publicist that. Oh, wait. I don't have a Nashville publicist. Or a Nashville label. Or a Nashville wife."

"Shelly, right? Did she know about you?"

"Not for a long time. Then she found some letters Zac'd sent me. Kinda sexy letters. But she stayed with me anyway."

"'Cause she loved you?"

"Naw. 'Cause she liked the house and the fame. I don't think she ever loved me. She filed for divorce as soon as Zac spilled the beans about us."

"Did you love her?"

"Naw. I talked myself into thinking I did, but I didn't."

"Hmmm. If you think you're in love, aren't you in love?"

"Not necessarily. Are you in love with Gail?"

"Yeah. At least I think I am."

"Uh oh."

Brice giggled. Wayne guffawed. Both sipped whiskey, settled deeper into the couch, and stared into the fire. Wind noisily slammed the side of the house. In the distance, a train whistled.

"You ever been in love, Brice?"

Brice pursed up his lips and scratched his scalp. "Bastard. You gotta ask me that now?"

"What'd'ya mean? C'mon. Confess." Wayne nudged Brice in the side with his elbow. "I mean, guys like you love men like guys like me love women, right? Cain't be that much of a difference. You're forty, right? My age. Surely you've loved somebody."

"Shit, Wayne."

"Hey, we're friends. Friends talk about real stuff, right? Not just sports and the weather. We used to talk about real things in high school, right? Or did we? You kept so much from me then. Was all that talk just bullshit?"

"No. Not all of it."

"So? Talk. Look, buddy, I can tell you're real low, real down. You're bound to have been low ever since the news hit the papers about you and that Zac. Talk to me. Might help."

"Do you love Gail?"

"You already asked that. Yes, I do. First woman I ever loved, I think. The others, well, I was an asshole. I knew I was good-looking and I could get away with shit, so... well, I used 'em. I regret that. I was a young, horny guy, and I got all the pussy I could, and I broke a few hearts. Did...did you love that Zac guy?"

"I should have. I was afraid to, I guess. If I had, maybe I wouldn't be in this mess. He was a great guy, and he was so hungry to be loved, but every time he tried to make what we had more than sex, I pulled away. By then, I was married, and I had a career, and I knew if things got serious with him, and if the public found out, I'd lose everything. And then I lost everything anyway."

Brice cleared his throat and rubbed his jaw. "There were a few guys I really cared about before I got to Nashville. But when my career started taking off, when I was twenty-five, I made a deliberate decision to try to forget my feelings for other men, 'cause I knew there was no goddamn way I could get anywhere in country music unless everybody—managers, record executives, band members, and fans—thought I was straight. Then, at thirty, I married Shelly."

"Shit. Rough." Wayne shook his head and slurped whiskey. "So you give up any chance of a real personal life so you can make music?"

"Yep. Yep. I had to sacrifice any chance for love with another guy because of my love of music. And my ambition. At first it was all about the music, but then it became about the fame. Not even the money so much as the attention. I wanted to be famous, man. I wanted folks lining up at my concerts and screaming in the arena seats. I wanted to win awards. I wanted the music critics to go on and on and on about what a talent I was."

"Yeah, I remember how pumped up you were by the audience when you played at that little club up Pipestem that summer before we went our separate ways. Hell, Brice, you're a star. You deserve a big audience. I've always thought you were talented as all get-out, ever since you first sang some of your songs to me."

"Thanks, buddy. I guess you were one of the first folks to ever hear the stuff I wrote. Well, anyway, I lied and lied and lied, to everyone else and to myself, just to get into that spotlight and stay there. After a few year of trying to have a sex life with Shelly, we both gave that up. I tried to be celibate, but...."

"Celibate? Fuck! You'd have to institutionalize me. I gotta have my poontang. I'd blow my brains out otherwise."

"Yeah, that's one thing we've always had in common, though I guess you didn't know it. We're both oversexed hound dogs. It's just that you're a pussyhound and I'm an asshound."

"The Hound Brothers." Wayne snickered. "I had absolutely no earthly idea that you liked guys. You dated quite a few little girls back in high school, didn't you?"

"I learned to be a good actor."

"No need to act now, big man. Seems like you need a friend bad. Glad I'm in town when you need the company."

"Me too. You just keep saving my ass. My hero." Brice bumped Wayne with his shoulder.

"Somebody's gotta do it." Wayne bumped back. For a long minute, the two friends simply watched the fire and listened to the train rumbling along the tracks at the base of the mountain.

"So who'd you love?" Wayne said, eyes still on the fire.

"There was a frat brother. His name was Nathan. Short, muscular little guy a year younger'n me. Tanned skin, brown goatee. He was my first. We got drunk one night, started wrestling.... That was long before Nashville, long before I realized how much I'd have to give up to make it in the country music world, so I threw my whole heart into it.

When I got serious, he got scared, so that was the end of that."

"Yeah. Sounds like me. When a girl got serious, I was outta there. Tried that with Gail. Guess I didn't get away fast enough."

"I'm glad. I'm glad you're happy."

"Me too. Wish you were happier."

"Me too," Brice sighed. In the state of chemical relaxation he found himself, it was proving especially difficult not to wrap an arm around Wayne and kiss him hard on the mouth.

"Who else?" Wayne said.

"Another frat guy a year older. Gerry. Strong, beefy guy. About my height. Black beard, hairy body. God, did he look great in a pair of tighty-whities. He let me blow him every now and then, even though he had a girlfriend. When he graduated and left town, I thought I was gonna die."

"Yeah? I don't think I'd die if I lost Gail, but I sure as shit would be miserable. Don't know what I'd do without her."

They fell silent. Then Brice sat up, rubbed his bleary eyes, and said, "There was someone else. Someone when I was younger."

"Yeah?"

"Yeah." Brice swilled the rest of his whiskey. "Life is short, right?"

"Sure is. Roy and Gail's mother are reminding me of that. So?"

"So I'm real tired of lying. My manager wanted me to lie, and Dr. Zucker wanted me to lie, and—"

"Dr. Zucker? Who's that?"

"Ex-gay therapist in Nashville."

"Oh, hell, Brice. You didn't buy into that bullshit, did you?"

"No. Just couldn't bring myself to. Look, I told all those lies before 'cause I thought I'd lose everything, but I've lost just about everything anyway, so...."

"So you wanna tell the truth now. I get it." Wayne shrugged. "Ain't nothing you can say that's gonna make me run out that door."

"You swear?"

"Brice. Jesus. I swear."

"You," Brice said. "I was in love with you."

Wayne's face went blank. He shifted his gaze from Brice's face to the floor, then to the fire, then to the snow-blind windows, then back to Brice. "You little bastard. Really?" To Brice's relief, Wayne faintly smiled.

"You ain't gonna punch me?"

"Punch you? Are you brain-dead? Fuck, I'm flattered. So all those times we were hiking or hunting or shooting the shit by the lockers...."

"Yeah. I was wanting you. I thought about you a lot in college. Even wrote some songs about you. Most of the guys I've wanted over the years have reminded me of you in some way. Strong. Kind. Masculine. Loyal. I still think you're one of the best-looking men I've ever met, on top of what a great guy you are. I'm still a little in love with you, to be honest. This isn't creeping you out?"

"Naw." The faint smile broadened into the catfish grin. "Like I said, I'm flattered. Wait till I tell Myrtle that you threw yourself at me just like the twisted predator she said you'd be."

"Wayne! Don't you dare."

"I'm joshing you, stupid. But you ain't gonna make a pass, are you?"

"Do you want me to?"

"Naw. Sorry. I'm straight through and through."

"Yeah, I know that. In high school, I used to think about getting you real drunk and trying to take advantage of you. In fact, that first Christmas I came back from college, I was bound and determined to get you soused on some of that cheap Canadian whiskey you liked and then coax you into at least letting me give you a blow job. But you didn't come home for Christmas, dammit."

"Might have worked. A mouth's a mouth, right?"

Brice gaped. "Well, shit."

"Except I might have freaked out the next day. Who knows? And then we wouldn't be here tonight. Still buddies."

"So no blow job tonight, huh?"

Wayne gently bounced the side of his fist against Brice's shoulder. "Nope. Sorry. I'd have to tell Gail, and she'd machine-gun both of us. Besides, with that back of yours...."

"You might have to call for an ambulance, yeah," Brice said, feeling both disappointment and relief. "Okay. Guess I'll have to keep looking for a gay version of you. Meanwhile, we have this, right?" Brice offered his hand.

"You're damn right we do," Wayne said, taking Brice's hand and squeezing it. "I'm glad you told me. I do love you, man. Not the way you might want, but…. Okay, enough drinking and enough shocking revelations. It's late. Let's get you up to bed, gimp."

CHAPTER FOURTEEN

BRICE WOKE AT 3:30 AM WITH A VERY FULL bladder and hobbled to the bathroom, back hurting him again. He hadn't quite finished pissing when he remembered how much he'd told Wayne.

"Oh, hell," Brice murmured, rummaging through his booze-bleared memory. "Did I scare him to death? He didn't leave, did he?"

Anxiously, he trundled down the hallway in his boxers and undershirt to the small guest bedroom in the back of the house. To his relief, there he saw the lumpy silhouette of a man's form in the bed and heard the soft sound of a man's snores.

Still here, Brice thought. *Didn't run off. Fast asleep.*

Dim moonlight illuminated the room, faded, then grew bright. Brice sat on a chair beside the bed, rested his elbows on his knees, propped his chin in his hand, and watched Wayne sleep. He could see his friend's face against the pillow, the darkness of his mussed hair, thick eyebrows, and beard. He could see a bare shoulder rising just above the blankets. The urge to touch Wayne's face, to kiss his cheek, to climb into bed with him and hold him close was so great that Brice began to tremble.

No. No. Ain't gonna be the predator that the world expects. No. He's my friend. He trusts me. He's already made it clear that he doesn't want what I want.

Brice's left hand gripped his right, as if to prevent it from straying closer. He rose, throat dry and chest tight. He paused. On the floor at the foot of the bed, beside Wayne's hiking boots, lay the shapeless heap of his cast-off clothes. Stiffly, Brice hunkered down and ran a hand through the pile.

Jeans, flannel shirt, turtleneck. Underwear! Jesus,

he's entirely naked.

Lifting the white briefs, Brice pressed the crotch to his face, breathing the man-musk deep.

*Oh, Jesus. Oh, **Jesus**. The aroma of him. Oh, Jesus. Why the hell can't things be different? Lord, why'd You bring this beautiful man back to me? To comfort me or just to torture me further? Why do You make me want so bad someone I can never have?*

Heart pounding, Brice shook his head and returned the briefs to the pile of clothing. He stood up and shuffled silently through the chilly air back to his own room. There, he stood by the warmth of the radiator, by the window overlooking the snow-covered park, and listened to the faint sound of the river's whitewater rushing over its stony bed. There was the newly renamed bridge—*great big fat symbol of my great big fat fucking failure,* Brice thought—and the winter-whitened mountainside beyond. Moonlight illuminated the entire scene. Brice touched the window glass and chill filled his fingertips.

Cold snow. Cold river. Cold moon. Brice swallowed hard. *Damn, even with Wayne just down the hall, I feel so alone. Hell, especially with Wayne just down the hall, I feel alone. Or at least my body does.*

Brice sat on his bed, put his head in his hands, and closed his eyes. A few tears rolled down his cheeks. Another train moaned in the distance, its low call filling the valley. Brice cussed himself, wiped his face, popped another pain pill, took a big swig of water, and climbed back into bed. He lay there, listening to the train move closer, and thought of Wayne's naked body sprawled beneath blankets only yards away.

Seems like I never get what I want the most, but that sure don't make me unique. I guess that's true of most folks. I remember Wayne's body so well…in the showers after Phys Ed, and in the Greenbrier River, where we used to skinny-dip, or up at the Reservoir, him stretched out on the shore snoozing, wearing nothing but cut-off denim shorts, black hair covering his chest and belly. There's some gray there now, probably, like there is on me, this funny little patch of silver between my pecs. Damn, the fantasies I used to have about that boy! In high school and in college. I used to fill Kleenex after Kleenex, jacking off and thinking about him. In my head, he was so sweet and submissive. In my head, he did all the things he'd never do in real life, either then or now. Oh, damn….

Brice slid his hand over his hardening cock and stroked it. He looked out the window at the uncompromising winter night. Then he closed his eyes and constructed a warm alternative to the bitter facts that trammeled his life and hemmed in his heart.

CHAPTER FIFTEEN

WAYNE AND ME, WE'RE IN THE OLD TARPAPER-plastered garage behind the Meador house. Where Wayne and his father used to work on their carpentry projects. Where Wayne and me used to change the oil in his car and my beat-up Chevy truck. Where him and me used to sneak swigs of that bottle of Annie Green Springs Berry Frost hidden behind a pile of wood scraps.

Wayne's eighteen, just like me. It's a hot summer night. We're both barefoot and bare-chested, wearing nothing but jeans. We wrestle around for a while, laughing and getting sweaty, but I'm bigger and stronger, so I grab him by the wrists and I force him back against the wall. Wayne grins at me and squirms, his groin rubbing against mine, and starts cussing me.

"Lemme go, goddamn you, Brice Brown. What the hell do you think you're doing?"

"Don't give me that shit," I say, kissing his forehead. "You want this as bad as I do."

"Hell, no, I don't," he says, but the gleam in his eyes tells me otherwise. "Lemme loose now, or I'm gonna kick your ass."

"Shut up," I say. "This ain't about ass-kicking. This is about ass-fucking. You want me inside you, don't you, buddy?"

Wayne's eyes grow wide, and his mouth trembles. "Hell, no. Fuck you, Brice. Whatever gave you that idea? Lemme loose, or I'll yell for Dad."

"You'll so fulla shit," I say, gripping his wrists harder. "Fuck, you're so hot. You're the prettiest goddamn redneck boy I've ever laid eyes on," I say. I rub my face up against his, and I nuzzle his neck, and I say, "I got you now, don't I? You want this too, don't you?" and he looks at me, those dark brown eyes full of *need, and then he groans and nods and bows his head, and I say, "I got you. You ain't going nowhere. I want you so bad, you hot little fucker. And you want me just as bad. Don't you? Don't you?" and Wayne grunts, "Uh, huh. Uh, huh. Uh, huh," and he slumps against me and trembles, and I free his hands and squeeze a hairy pec and run my hand over his furry, flat belly, and I unbutton his jeans and reach down into his briefs and feel how hard he is, how much he's loving this, so young and strong, so willing to give himself to me.*

"You want me to make love to you now?" I whisper in his ear. He moans and nods. He wants it so bad. So I commence to pinching and tugging on his tits, and then I drop to my knees and unzip him and haul his hard cock out of his jeans and I take him in my mouth, and he's sweet and sour and salty and bitter all at once, and he grips my head and thrusts into me so far I'm ready to choke, but then we get our rhythm and pretty soon there's the taste of precum on my tongue and his legs are shaking and he's groaning low in his throat.

"Do you want me to stop?" I ask, pausing.

"Hell, no," Wayne whispers, shaking his head real fast back and forth, so I keep on, sucking harder and faster. He whimpers, and then he throws back his head and grunts, "Damn, Brice. Oh, damn, Brice. I'm so close. So close. Stop, man. Stop. I don't want to finish so fast, okay?"

"You bet," I say. I stand, and I wrap my arms around him, and he presses his face against my bare shoulder, and I can feel the wet of his tears as he says, "Brice, buddy. I've wanted this for so damn long. I love you, Brice, buddy. I love you."

"I love you too, Wayne," I say, pulling him even closer. He's wet with sweat, and he smells so good. I kiss him and kiss him and kiss him, and then I unbutton his pants and slide them off his hips and I run a hand over his ass—his butt-cheeks are so firm, and coated with soft, fine hair—and I say, "Do you wanna get fucked?" and he rubs his tear-stained face against mine and nods, so I wet my forefinger in my mouth and slip it between his butt-cheeks and I start fingering his hole....

Brice opened his eyes and took a deep breath. He was close to coming. The world created in his head was so much more appealing than reality that he didn't want it to end yet, so he stopped stroking himself till the crisis had passed.

Wayne would kill me if he knew about my jack-off fantasies. Or maybe not. He said he was flattered to know how I felt. Hell, if he knew the details, he'd probably elbow me in the ribs and call me a sick pervert and then ask me to mix him up another drink. Just another reason I love the guy.

So what would happen tonight, in a world where I got what I wanted? With Wayne naked in the next room? From the nightstand drawer, Brice pulled the camo bandana he'd used before for solitary sessions. The snow had resumed, batting at the windowpanes. With one hand, he stroked his cock. With the other, he pinched his left nipple, already stiff from cold and arousal.

"Hey, Brice? You awake?"

I rise on one elbow. Wayne's standing in the bedroom door, in a shaft of moonlight. He's naked, his brawny arms wrapped around himself. At forty, we're built much the same, still muscular but getting fleshy in the chest and belly, but that's just fine. I love the extra pounds that maturity has added to his frame.

"Yeah. Come on in. What's wrong?"

"I had a real, real bad dream. Scared the hell outta me. You and me were trapped on a hill—we were Rebel soldiers, I think, 'cause we were both dressed in gray—and a whole bunch of guys in blue were shooting at us and advancing up the hill…and then I got shot in the thigh, and you picked me up and were carrying me to safety, but then some of the bluecoats got between us and the woods, and they aimed their guns at us…and I woke up."

"Damn Yankees. They're always causing trouble. Hey, it's cold. Get on in here with me," I say, lifting the covers.

"You sure?"

"Hell, yes, I'm sure. C'mon."

Wayne hurries across the cold floor and dives into bed beside me. He scoots back against me, teeth chattering, and I wrap him in my arms and spoon him from behind. He's so much shorter than I am that my body cups his from head to toe.

"Oh, that's better. That feels good. You're so warm, Brice," he mumbles, taking my hand in his.

"You just sleep here with me. I'll take care of you, buddy," I say, rubbing my beard against his bare shoulders. When he cuddles closer, I cup the beefy swell of his right pec in my palm and knead it. I run my hand over the curve of his belly and feel the soft fur there. Then I cup his hairy pec again and start fingering the little nub of his nipple.

"Man, Brice," Wayne sighs. "That feels so good. Keep it up, okay?"

And so I do, fondling his nipples and kissing his shoulders and nuzzling the back of his neck. Then I lower my hand to his crotch and find the hardness there and start stroking him. His cock is just as I expected, medium in length but real thick.

Wayne grunts. He presses his head back against my chest and thrusts into my hand. "Oh, yeah. Mmmm. Oh, yeah."

"You want this, man?" I ask, fiddling with his piss-slit and finding it juicy.

"Oh, God, yes. I been wanting this for years, Brice. Touch me, man. Hold me and touch me any way you please."

We lie there for a long time, me jacking his cock and fondling his tits. Then he starts rubbing his butt up against my hard-on and that's when I know dreams can come true.

"Yeah?" I say, gripping an ass-cheek, caressing the soft fur there.

"Yeah. God, yeah. Please. I need...I need...."

Wayne pauses, grinding back against my groin and thrusting into my hand.

"Oh, man. I need...."

He pulls away, to my disappointment. But then he rolls over onto his back, and he takes my hand, and then he bows his handsome head and looks over at me, and the surrender and the love in his eyes make me want to just break down and cry.

"Do whatever you want. I need...I need you inside me, Brice. So damn bad. Please, buddy? Please? Take me, man. Screw me hard. Treat my butthole right."

"I'd love to. I'd love to. More than you know. I've been wanting to plow you for decades. But.... You ever been ass-fucked before?" I say, brushing aside a lock of dark hair and kissing his forehead.

"Naw, I ain't ever. But I want it bad. Real bad."

"You sure?"

"Hell, yes, I'm sure. I already told you, I been aching for this for years. I want you to be my first."

"Damn, Wayne. Okay, buddy. You got it," I say, kissing his furry cheek.

I climb up on top of Wayne and push my tongue into his mouth. His cock's super-hard, trapped against my belly. Wayne's eyes look moist, as if he's about to cry. I knead his meaty chest and arms, and he flexes inside my touch, his flesh so full of maturity and strength. I grip his thick right pec in both hands, and I squeeze it and pull at the thick silvery hair there, and then I nuzzle and suck and twist and tug his nipple, till he's squirming beneath me, mumbling baritone pleas for me to continue. Then I move my focus to his left pec and nipple and do the same, while his thighs stiffen and shake, and he rubs his hard-on against my belly.

I slide down the bed now. I bend Wayne double, spread his buttocks, and for a long time I eat his musky butt out, flicking my tongue over his hole and then delving into it while

Wayne whimpers and groans and wriggles against my mouth. His ass-crack and ass-cheeks and all the hair there are like a little gully full of brush between two wooded hills. Man, I love the smell—like forest loam and wild animals—and I love the taste—bitter like greens and pungent like black walnut and sweet like maple candy.

Now I hoist his calves onto my shoulders, lube up my forefinger and push a dollop of KY up his ass, and now I finger-fuck him while I suck his fat dick. I get him close again and again and again and again and again. He whines and squirms and cusses. "Let me come, man! I'm so close. Please let me come."

I pull off yet again, letting his cock slip out of my mouth's hungry suction with a pop. I work my finger in deeper so I can rub and poke his prostate.

Wayne's eyes grow wide. He jolts and gasps.

"Ohhh, fuck! What are you...? How...?"

"Feeling good, huh?"

"Shit, yes. Damn! That's amazing." My beautiful buddy heaves a low groan and rides my finger, trying to get me in even deeper. "That feels wonderful."

"You want something bigger up your ass now?" I say, grinning down at him.

"Believe so. Believe it's time." Wayne slides his calves off my shoulders, wraps his arms around his knees, pulls his thighs against his chest, and lifts his legs in the air. "Put it in me, man. Put that big thing up in me."

"You real sure?" I say, nibbling his cock-head and working a second finger up inside him.

Wayne glowers at me. "Hell, yes, I'm sure. Do it!"

"Let's hear you beg for it," I say, gently bending him double.

"Damn. You bossy bastard. Okay, okay. Please, Brice. Please, Brice. Please, buddy. I'm begging you. I'm begging you. Shove your big fat cock up my asshole. Now!"

"Here we go," I say. I lube us up, and then I kiss him hard on the mouth, and then I push my cockhead up against his tight ass-ring. Wayne heaves a sweet, heartbreaking little sob of surrender and then, slowly, gradually, his body opens up to me, and I slide my cock—steady and gentle, inch by tight, blissful inch—up his asshole.

"Like that?" I say, cupping a pec and giving his hole a few shallow thrusts.

"Uhhhhhh. Uhhhh huhhhh." Wayne nods and flinches and groans, crooks a leg around my waist, and bucks against me till my cock's slid all the way up his ass.

"Feel good?" I say, running my fingers over his hairy nipples and looking down into his dark eyes. Wayne huffs and grunts. "Ummmm mmm! Wow, you really fill me up. Wow."

"*Want more now? Want me to ride you, buddy? Fuck you hard? Fuck you deep?*"

Wayne nods. "*Hard as you want.*" *He squeezes my biceps and caresses my beard. His ass-channel constricts, gripping me from inside.* "*Plow me, big man. Split me in half. I can take it. I been wanting this as long as you have. Screw me cross-eyed. Screw me so hard I'll be walking crooked for a whole damn week.*"

"*You got it,*" *I growl. I shove into him as rough as I can. I start thrusting in and out like a wild man. He squirms and shakes and hollers, and I pinch his nipples and knead his pecs and spit in my palm and work his thick dick and kiss him and kiss him and kiss him, and I fuck my sweet, handsome friend harder than I think I've ever fucked any man before.*

Damn. Damn.... This is it. This is the paradise I've been hankering for all these decades. A strong, hairy, butch man, a man I love, all warm and naked in my arms, and my cock pushing in and out of him, and him panting and whining and begging me to ride him harder, and now I'm gripping his cock even tighter and working it even faster, and he's shouting "Oh, God, Brice! Yes! Oh, God!" and slamming his ass against my groin, and....

Brice tensed and shot, three big spurts into the bandana. He released a muffled moan and went limp. He lay there for a long time, heart slowing. Then he opened his eyes. He was alone again. He wiped off his hand, rolled onto his side, wrapped an arm around his pillow, released a shaky sigh, and fell asleep.

CHAPTER SIXTEEN

BRICE WOKE TO BRIGHT SUNLIGHT AND A scraping sound. He rolled onto his back and pulled his knees against his chest a few times to stretch out his lumbar region—a preventative exercise his former bass player Buddy had taught him—before slipping out of bed. 10:15, according to the clock on the nightstand. Outside, in the park, bright light reflected off snow. Bending carefully, fearful his back would start up again, Brice pulled on sweatpants and hooded sweatshirt, slipped on socks and moccasins, and trudged down the hall. The guest bed was empty.

Damn, where'd Wayne go? If I didn't know better, I'd say he read my mind last night while I was dreaming about giving it to him up the butt, and now he's run for the hills. Brice shrugged, used the bathroom, and descended the creaky stairs.

The scents of coffee and bacon filled the first floor of the house. There they were, four strips of bacon, nicely browned atop a paper towel on a plate. On the stove, a pot of hot water simmered. Beside it was a cylindrical box of grits. On the table sat the butter dish, two bowls, and two plates. On the counter, the coffee carafe was full.

Damn you, Gail Meador, wherever and whoever you are. Why can't I keep your husband? Brice poured himself a cup of coffee, added some half and half, then wandered through the parlors. He was alone.

Where the hell did he go? And what's that scraping? Brice moved to the front door and peered out.

There he is. My God. He's cleaning my walk.

Brice opened the door and stepped out into the frosty air. "Wayne! For God's sake! You don't need to do that!"

Wayne, bundled in jacket and toboggan, waved Brice off. "I ain't letting you do it with that bad back! Get back inside. I'll be done directly. Why don't you start up those grits?"

Brice limped back inside, muttering. "The ideal man. Goddamn it. The ideal man. And he's an inveterate pussyhound." Sighing, he turned the water up higher and measured out grits.

By the time Wayne entered the foyer, having shoveled the sidewalk all the way up to the top of the park, Brice had grits ready and church bells were ringing in the Central Baptist Church up the street. Wayne peeled off his coat and stomped snow off his feet, then took the mug of coffee Brice offered him.

"Thanks, man. It's still bitter out there, but the religious drones are swarming around the church anyway. It's their fault, you know. They're to blame."

"To blame? For what?"

Wayne sat heavily on a kitchen chair while Brice doled out grits. "For you being holed up here. For you losing your career. All that anti-gay shit, it's thanks to religion. Seems like every person I know who's gone on and on about what a monster you are is real religious, calling you not just a pervert but a sinner too. The guys I work with. Myrtle. Folks who ain't so devout generally ain't so judgmental."

"Like you?" Brice placed a steaming bowl of grits in front of Wayne.

"Yep. Like me." Wayne grinned. "And this tasty country breakfast is my reeeeward. Pass me that butter."

For a few minutes, the two friends ate in silence. Sunlight in the windows faded, and soon another light snow had commenced.

"So, speaking of religion, do you believe in God?" Brice asked, biting into a strip of bacon.

"Sure I do. Who wouldn't, growing up in these mountains, as pretty as they are? But I don't believe in some tight-assed bastard with a big beard looking down on us and just waiting for us to fuck up so he can snatch us up like ants and drop us into some kinda fiery pit. Do you?"

"Naw. But sometimes I still feel guilty. For feeling what I feel. About guys."

"Well, hell. Of course you do. Ain't you been told all your life that being queer is wrong? It's damned hard to feel something or think something that you know is right when all the rest of the world is telling you it's wrong. It's a lot easier to just assume that the majority is right and that you're fucked up somehow. Look, Brice, buddy, you have every right to feel what you feel about other guys. Stop caring so much about what the world thinks about you. What do you think about you?"

"I don't know. That's the problem. All my life I've tried to accomplish something so that folks would…well, love me. Treat me like someone special."

Wayne rolled his eyes. "Folks? What folks? The pious dickweeds in this town? Who named a bridge after you, and then turned on you when you were down? Why should you give a flying rat's ass what they think?"

"I don't know why." Brice shook his head and scraped the last bit of grits from his bowl. "I care about what you think about me. That's why I never told you I was gay."

"Yeah, you said that last night. I understand. I do. And, not that it'll do any good, but I'll tell you exactly what I think of you. You're a talented, kind, strong guy, and, like I said last night, I'm proud to be your buddy. And if I were different, if my dick worked like yours, I'd be glad to be your…lover? Honey? Husband? Whatever. As it is…."

Wayne reached across the table and gripped Brice's hand hard. "As it is, I'm your friend, and, by God, I say you need to get through this. This is probably the worst thing you've ever experienced, right?"

Brice looked Wayne in the eyes. *God, I love you. God, I want to kiss you. God, I'm thankful to have you in my life in any way possible.* "Yeah. It sure is. The life I've built is pretty much in ruins."

"I can see that. This is as low as you'll ever be, that's my guess."

Wayne released Brice's hand and took a big gulp of coffee. "You've lost a lot, absolutely. But don't lose yourself. Don't lose your music, what you do best. You gotta just say, 'Fuck all y'all,' and keep going. I know you get…grim. I never understood it myself, but Gail…sometimes…depression runs in her family too. You got to fight that, Brice. It's dangerous. Gail's aunt was on lithium. And her great-granddaddy killed himself. Don't you pull that kinda shit."

Brice stood. "More grits?"

"Naw. I've had enough, thanks. Brice, you hear me?"

"Yeah, I hear you. I just don't know where to go from here. I try to play my guitar, but nothing comes. And my old songs, most of 'em are just lies whipped up to please the Nashville executives."

"You'll get over that. The music'll come again."

"Maybe. Maybe not. Maybe I'm tapped out. And why keep writing music if there's no one who'll listen to it? Who'd care if I ever wrote a song again? Not my former fans. Not Nashville. Shit, Wayne, I'm nobody without my music and my fans. Who'd even care if I jumped off the frigging Suzanne Matthews Bridge? Who'd care if—"

"Brice, goddamn you. Stop talking that way." Wayne rose, scowling. "You keep that shit up, and I'll punch you in the jaw. Buck up, dammit."

"Okay, bossy. Bucking up right now," Brice grunted. "I'll do these dishes if you start up another fire. Looks like we're in for more snow."

Wayne was stretched out on the couch beneath the afghan when Brice, finished with his cleaning-up, entered the parlor. A fresh fire sputtered on the hearth.

"Ummm, feels good," Wayne said. "I could drowse here all day."

"Well, y'ought to," Brice said. *Because when you go, I'll be alone, and that's going to be even bitterer after time with you, being reminded of all I want and can't have.*

"Naw. Need to spend some time with ole Roy. And Myrtle. She's crazy as a shithouse rat, but she makes Roy happy." Wayne yawned and sat up.

"You need anything? There's more coffee."

"Yep." Wayne yawned again and stretched. "How about 'one more cuppa coffee for the road,' as Dylan would say? Then I better get on up the street."

Brice fetched them both cups and sat down beside Wayne. Brice studied the darkness of his friend's beard and the muscled heft of his chest. Remembering the fantasies he'd enjoyed the night before, he blushed. *How can I feel aroused and ashamed at the same time?* "So how'd you sleep?"

"Great. Like the dead. I love the sound of the trains. But then I had a bad dream about 4 am, and it took me a while to get back to sleep."

"Nightmare, huh? Yeah, I'm having those pretty often. Can't sleep real well either."

"Your nightmares aren't about a bunch of pissed-off country-music fans waving torches and a bunch of hill-holler preachers coming at you with pitchforks, are they?"

Brice grinned. "Pretty much. How about you? Your nightmare?"

"Uh, just Marine stuff. Fighting. Killing. Being killed." Wayne rubbed his brow and sighed.

"Weird coincidence. I dreamed last night that you and I were Rebel soldiers fighting in the Civil War together," Brice said, adjusting the truth. "Was it bad? The Marines?"

"Naw. Not really. I lucked out. If I'd been born just a few years earlier…."

"Yeah. I thought about that a lot after you enlisted. You would have ended up in Vietnam."

"Like so many other West Virginia boys. Cannon fodder. Like my cousin Joe."

"Yeah. That was the first funeral I ever went to. We were both ten, I guess."

"Yep. Aunt Sally never got over that. He was her only son."

Wayne stared at the fire. Brice stared at Wayne's handsome profile. "You could have ended up dead in some ditch in some godforsaken jungle."

"Yep. Like so many guys from around here."

"Guess that kind of loss helps put mine in perspective, huh? I was thinking about that the day I left Tennessee. I stopped by the cemetery where my Confederate ancestor is buried. That guy died at age thirty with a bullet in his head…and here I am, still alive and healthy and forty years old, whining about how I've lost my audience."

"We're both lucky, Brice, when you come to think of it. Okay, enough about nightmares and war and who lost how much. So I gotta ask…."

"What do two men do together?" Brice gave Wayne as sinister a leer as he could muster and moved an inch closer.

"I already know that, fool." Wayne scooted away from Brice and returned his mock-leer with a look of mock-fright. "You keep your hands off my butt now, you crazed pervert! Naw, what I wanna know is…last night you said that you'd written some songs about me back in college. Did you ever record any of 'em?"

"Ego!"

"What? I'm just curious."

"Well, you said you had all my CDs, right?"

"Sure do."

"Okay." Brice slipped off the couch, opened up the piano, slid out the seat, and sat down. "So what's this?" He picked out the melody in E minor.

"'Hard Gray Rain?' Title song of your first album. You wrote that about me?"

Brice grinned with pride. "Uh huh. Sure did. So what's this?"

Brice shifted keys, picking out a slow tune in C-sharp minor and humming softly along.

"That one too? 'Sad-Eyed Angel?'"

"Yep. I wrote it about that time we busted our butts on the football field but we still lost the championship to Liberty, and you and I went camping that night and we got drunk and you…."

"And I just about cried? Actually, I did cry, I was so frustrated and disappointed and angry."

"I cried too. I was just as disappointed as you."

"And the next morning, we both pretended not to remember how we'd lost it the night before." Wayne chuckled. "Amazing how you got such a pretty song out of such a silly evening. Fuck, it was just a football game."

"It was everything to us then, though, wasn't it? Okay, two more. Here's this one."

Brice played another melody, this one medium tempo in G major. *It feels good to have an audience again*, he thought. *Even if only for a few minutes.*

"'See the Storms as Baptism.' Hearken to your own words, Mr. Brown." In a low baritone, Wayne sang the lyrics.

> *See the storms as baptism.*
> *Stand out in the rain.*
> *Feel the heavens touch your cheek.*
> *There's learning in the pain.*

"Yeah, yeah. Easier sung than done. Last one. I recorded it on guitar, but here it is on piano." Brice shifted keys, slipping into a few rippling bars of another up-tempo tune, this one in E.

"'The Blood of Fire!' That's just about my favorite on that CD. C'mon, Brice. Sing it."

"Okay. Just a few lines. Here you go." Brice cleared his throat and sang.

> *Pale skin gleaming in the blood of fire,*
> *your youth holds mine this summer's night.*
> *Girl, your bare beauty's God's greatest gift,*
> *your black hair and eyes are all delight.*
> *My body's a bonfire,*
> *My body's alight.*
> *My body's a bonfire,*
> *burning upon your body's height.*

Brice ended with E major 9, letting the chord ring and die.

Wayne gave Brice a short round of enthusiastic claps. "Thanks! I always thought that was pretty amazingly poetical for a country music song. 'Girl,' huh?"

Brice nodded. "That was one of the first songs where I deliberately…well, wrote it to seem like I was singing a love song to a woman. Yeah."

"So what inspired that song?"

Brice blushed as he closed up the piano. "That last time we went camping up Madam's Creek, you and me and Thelma."

"Oh, yeah. Damn, I haven't thought about her in years."

"She was mighty big on you that summer, as I recall."

"Yeah. She cried when I left town for the Marines. I felt pretty shitty about leaving her."

"I think she was in love with you. I sure was. Anyway, we grilled hot dogs and drank a lot of cheap wine—Riunite—and it was August and hot and humid, so you—so proud of your body, you bastard—you spend the entire evening with your shirt off, with the flame flickering over your skin. Then you and her went to your tent, and I went to mine, and I could hear y'all, you know, doing it."

"Shit, Brice. Sorry."

"Well, anyway, the song's kind of a rewrite of that evening. With just you and me. I guess a lot of what I've written and what I've pretended to be has been an attempt at rewriting reality."

"Honesty sounds a lot simpler to me. But that's easy for me to say. It's gotta be so much easier being a straight guy."

"That's for damn sure," Brice said, twisting his mouth up.

"Okay, look," said Wayne, swigging down the last of his coffee. "I'd better get back home. I need to call Gail and—"

The doorbell rang. Both men jolted.

"Might be my sister," Brice said. "She said she had some extra work in the office and might bring me down some homemade rolls. Hold on a minute."

Brice shuffled to the door. When he opened it, he saw, to his deep distress, two portly strangers standing on the porch, flanked by a third, a tall, thin guy with a bulky camera.

"Who y'all?" Brice growled.

"I'm Leon Anderson from *Hinton Daily News*, Mr. Brown," said the broader of the men, waving a held-held audio-recorder. "Welcome home. I'd love to interview you for the paper."

"And I'm with the *Star*," said the other. "I'm Micah Jones, and this is my photographer, Curtis. We'd gotten word you were back in Hinton, and we thought we'd give you the opportunity to tell your side of the story."

"I ain't interested in talking to y'all," Brice said, torn between the polite manners with which he'd been raised and the bristling annoyance and sick anxiety he felt now that he knew the press had tracked him down.

"Please, Mr. Brown," said the Hinton reporter. "Don't you think local people, your fellow townsfolk, deserve to know the truth about—"

"What the *hell* do you all want?" Wayne's deep voice resounded behind Brice.

"Well, hello," said the *Star* reporter, grinning. "Who are you? Are you Brice's new lover? Are you two shacking up in there?"

He stepped aside, then nodded to the photographer behind him and said, "Get this, Curtis. This is great." Curtis, in response, started clicking his camera with eager rapidity.

"I think y'all need to get your fat asses off this porch," Wayne said, nudging Brice aside and barring the door. "You leave my buddy alone, or I'll tear each of you new buttholes right here and now."

"God, he's ferocious," said the photographer. Smirking, he trained his camera on Wayne and clicked wildly.

The Hinton reporter ignored Wayne. "Mr. Brown, it seems to me that you owe your many fans the courtesy of—"

"Give that here," Wayne snarled. Snatching the audio-recorder from the man's hand, he lobbed it over the side of the porch into the snow.

"Sir! How dare you? I'll have you know—"

"Shut the fuck up." Wayne pushed him aside and lunged at the photographer. The *Star* reporter had just enough time to squeal, "Watch out, Curtis! He's crazy!" before Wayne had wrenched the camera from the man's grasp and hurled it off the other side of the porch.

"Interview's over," Wayne said, stomping his foot and brandishing his fists. "Now git!" All three men stumbled back and cringed, as if a mad dog were about to go for their throats.

Recovering from his frozen surprise, Brice stepped out the door behind Wayne. He squared his shoulders, trying to look intimidating despite his ailing back, the weak link in his show of strength. "You heard the man. I have nothing to say to y'all. Now get off my property."

The reporters fled down the steps and into the snow in order to retrieve their devices. "We'll be back," the largest one shouted. "You have to live in this town now. You can't treat us like this! Word's out that you're here. There'll be all sorts of newsmen coming your way."

"Fuck off! Get out of here!" Wayne shouted, moving threateningly toward the edge of the porch. "Otherwise, all three of you are going be wearing your balls for earrings."

"Crazy faggot!" the photographer said, snatching up his camera and bolting up the sloped sidewalk. Brice and Wayne stood glaring at them till they'd reached their respective vehicles at the top of the park and driven off.

"Motherfuckers," Wayne said.

"You sure showed them. Now get back in here before more of 'em show up," Brice said, gripping Wayne's elbow. "That bastard's right. You know how fast news spreads in a town this size. Yesterday, between being recognized at Rite Aid, thanks to my damn driver's license, and then Randy Doyle shouting my name in front of everyone at Kroger's...."

Wayne nodded. "It's a miracle we managed to get down breakfast before they showed up."

The two friends stepped back inside and Brice locked the door. "You were my protector yet again, and thanks for that. But you need to get out of here, buddy. You heard them. 'Are you his new lover?' As much as I wish you were...."

"Flatterer. You're just talking sweet 'cause you think you can get in my pants," Wayne said, barking out tension in a raspy laugh.

"Yep. We homosexuals are a conniving bunch. Seriously, though, you need to head home. If you're seen with me...we're just lucky that Hinton reporter didn't know who you were...then folks'll be spreading the news that...."

"That I'm cheating on my wife, and that you and I are fucking. I get it. Yeah, I'd just as soon avoid that. Gail doesn't need to be dealing with that kinda crap, and, hell, Roy and Myrtle might up and have heart attacks from the sheer shame of it. But shit, Brice. I hate to leave you like this."

"Me, too, but it's for the best. Why don't you slip out the basement door?" Brice peered out the front windows. "No one's out there now. Leave before anyone else shows up. Just head out back, up the steps past the woodshed, and around the other side of the fire station."

"Shit. Okay. C'mere, friend."

Wayne grabbed Brice by the arm and pulled him into a brief bear hug. He stepped back and squeezed his hand. "Thanks for a great time. Please keep in touch, okay? Now I'm real, real worried about you."

"Okay. Here's my number." Brice scrawled on a notepad lying on the foyer table, tore the page off, and handed it to Wayne. "Call before you leave for North Carolina and give me your phone number and e-mail address. Now get out of here."

"I could come down for another visit before I head back to Charlotte. I ain't leaving till—"

Brice shook his head decisively. "Nope. Just another chance for reporters to see you and stoke up those flames of scandal they're so fond of. Sad as I am to say it, you should stay away from me. Now go."

"Okay. Listen, take care of yourself, brother. Don't let yourself get too down. Come down to Charlotte and visit Gail and me. She'd be cool with you, I swear. Just don't tell her you wrote those songs about me, 'cause I sure as hell ain't."

"Maybe I'll come visit. Now go." Brice cracked open the basement stairs. "Just pull the outside door closed behind you and make sure it locks. I don't want any of those news-rabid morons sneaking into the house."

"You bet." Wayne nodded, gripping Brice's hand a final time. "Bye, old friend. I'll be thinking about you."

Turning, Wayne clomped down the basement stairs. A few more moments, and Brice heard the outside basement door slam shut.

Brice pulled the front drapes closed and double-checked the lock on the front door. Then he put another log of wood on the fire, poured himself a big slug of Jameson, took a swallow, wrapped himself in the afghan, and closed his eyes. It was only a matter of time, he knew, before the doorbell would ring again.

CHAPTER SEVENTEEN

THREE DAYS LATER, ON THE MORNING OF Christmas Eve—three days that Brice had spent brooding, masturbating, over-drinking, over-eating, and shouting reporters off his property— Leigh, looking outraged and muttering obscenities beneath her breath, dropped off the latest issue of the *Star* on her way to the office. Scanning its cover, Brice discovered, to his profound regret, that tossing a camera off a porch into the snow does not always damage that camera's ability to preserve images.

Brice clutched the paper, belly tight with alarm, shaking his head as if that gesture might dismiss this latest wave of hostile reality. The photos of Brice and Wayne featured on the front cover were painfully crisp and clear. Wayne stood in the foreground, fists clenched, face contorted with anger. Brice, looming in the background, looked simply stunned.

Fuck, fuck, fuck. Damn, those Star *bastards are fast. I'll bet Wayne never speaks to me again,* Brice thought. He retreated to the back parlor, studying the photos, then skimmed anxiously over the short article.

APPALACHIAN LOVE NEST?

Brice Brown, disgraced country music singer, has returned to his hometown of Hinton, West Virginia. A local informant tipped off the Star *to his whereabouts.*

After the recent revelations in Nashville—his shocking homosexual affair and the tragic end of his marriage—he's holed up in the house where he grew up, near the Summers County courthouse and overlooking the New River.

When we attempted to interview him, Brown

answered the door looking like a hungover, overweight frat boy (one with a lot of premature gray in his beard) and he refused to speak to us, but then his companion revealed himself, a handsome man of about Brown's age, who grew very irate and attacked us, uttering vulgarities and making threats. He even snatched our camera and a local reporter's recorder and threw them into the snow.

Though Brown's immediate neighbors, including his sister, a Hinton attorney, refused to speak to us, several locals were more than willing.

"It's just so upsetting that he's come back here," said Charlotte Deeds. "I went to school with him, and I never imagined that he was the kind of man he was. He had us all fooled."

Another former classmate, Theresa Ferguson, said, "This is a God-fearing community. He should leave. And to think I bought his music. He's a liar and a pervert. He's betrayed the whole town. The whole nation, for that matter."

A third interviewee, Randy Doyle, a part-time pastor, was able to identify Brown's belligerent companion as Wayne Meador, a construction worker in Charlotte, North Carolina, and a married man.

"We three used to play football together. The thought of them leering at me when we were all naked in the locker room makes me want to throw up. I always thought there was something weird about them, and now I know what it is. I guess the two of them are old flames. They're going to hell, that's for sure."

Brown continues to cower inside his Hinton home. Meador could not be reached for comment.

Brice stood and paced. He picked up his phone, dialed half the digits of Wayne's home number, then put the phone down. In the kitchen, he toasted a brown-sugar/cinnamon Pop-Tart and ate it, swigging milk from the carton in between bites. He poured out more coffee, resisting the urge to add Irish whiskey to it and coast toward another bout of drunken oblivion. Then he sat down at his computer in the back parlor, and he composed an e-mail message to Wayne.

Hey, buddy.

Thanks for leaving your contact information on my phone. I'm sorry I missed your call. To be honest, I was passed out. I'm drinking too much, and I'm taking too many pills, and I know it. But I'm just so fucking miserable that it's a relief to be shit-faced or unconscious.

Your visit meant so much to me. I'm so glad and grateful that you didn't mind that I told you what I did (from what I can remember…man, I was drunk!). But now I'm guessing that you don't want anything to do with me at all. That article in the Star, they said you couldn't be reached for comment. They're all liars, so who knows if you know about this yet, or if they did even call you.

But, so, look, in case you don't know, the latest issue of the Star—which just came out this morning, from what I can tell—there's a picture of the two of us on the cover. That dildo photographer's camera wasn't broken, man! You should have thrown it harder! That prick Randy Doyle identifies you in the article as the guy who cussed them out so well on my porch.

You probably know all this, and it might be that asshole reporters are harassing you now too—about eight sets of them have come by here since I saw you last, and I've taken my lead from you and tried to scare them half to death, and, as big as I am, I've had pretty good success—but if they are hounding you, it could be that you're cursing my name and regretting ever being kind enough to come check on me, big old mess that I've become. So now you **definitely** need to stay away from me. I suspect your wife, if she knows about this, has already told you that.

If you come back to Hinton, buddy, for God's sake, don't come down here. There's no reason that all the dumb mistakes I've made should mess up your life, or your wife's (lucky lady that she is). I know your tendency is to say to everybody, "Fuck you! I'll do what I please, and I'll hang out with who I please!" but don't do that, okay? You've stood up for me and you've been brave and you've protected me again and again, and you mean so much to me, so now it's my turn to try and protect you. And that means, dammit, that as much as I hate this…I need to tell you to stay away from me. Okay? Please tell Gail that I'm so, so sorry. All this just makes me sick. Stay away, okay? I really care about you, and you've been mighty kind to me, and I want what's best for you. I love you, man. I love you, but stay away.

Big Hugs,
Your Buddy,
Brice

Brice sat there for a few minutes gauging the connotations of every word before he hit SEND. Then he pulled aside a curtain in the front parlor. Seeing no reporters lurking outside, he hurriedly bundled up, grabbed his grocery list, and headed out to his truck for a drive to Beaver, one county over in Raleigh, where, with luck, he might not be recognized.

BRICE WAS JUST BEGINNING TO unpack his haul of groceries and liquor when he heard a knock on the door, then heard the door opening. Before he could tense up with defense, he heard the welcome sound of his sister's voice.

"Hey, Brice. It's just me. I brought you some Christmas cheer."

"Hey! Come on in."

Leigh entered the kitchen with a big box. She put it on the kitchen table before brushing white flurry-dust off her coat and removing it. "I locked the door behind me. There was another batch of reporters coming down the walk, including that dullard Leon Anderson from the *Hinton Daily News*. What a horse's ass he is. I gave them all a sharp piece of my mind and threatened them with a harassment suit, so they scurried off. Where you been?"

"Didn't want to go to the Hinton Kroger's and be pestered, so I drove up Beech Run to Raleigh County to get liquor and groceries. I was lucky for once. I managed to load up and get home without running into any disgruntled ex-fans or pushy journalists."

"You're in a mess, all right," Leigh said. "Let me help you put this stuff up. I have a few minutes before I head up the road to Forest Hill."

"Thanks," said Brice, lugging big bottles of bourbon to the liquor cabinet. "Stay as long as you can. Be good to have some company."

"Other than Wayne Meador?"

"Yeah." Brice groaned. "I sent him an apology this morning on e-mail and told him to stay away from me."

"That's probably a good idea. Jerry's been saying even more obnoxious things about you at home. He and Carden had an argument about you this morning."

"An argument that ended with, 'Don't you sass me, boy!' right?"

"Pretty much," Leigh said, putting cheese and beer into the fridge. "Last week—I've been putting off telling you this—Carden even got into a fist fight with a kid at school who called you a faggot."

"Great. Now my ten-year-old nephew is defending my name."

"He wanted to come down here today to see you—he's off school this week—but Jerry wouldn't have it. Thus this morning's argument. But he sent you a present anyway. Here you go." Leigh handed Brice a festively wrapped package.

"Can I open it now?"

"You can do anything you want to. It's not like you have a Christmas tree to put it under. I thought about getting you a little one to go with those wreaths I hung upstairs, but...."

"But I ain't much in the mood for Christmas decorating, as you might imagine, with dildos from the *Star* and *People* and the *Globe* out on the lawn. Let's see here."

Brice ripped off the wrapping paper. "Oh, great! *X-Men Mutant Empire 3.* Fun!"

"You and Carden share several enthusiasms. It's odd how much he's like you, considering how little time you've spent together. So, see? You didn't need to get married and have a son. I had a little Brice for you."

"He sounds a lot braver than me, actually. Standing up for his pore ole queer—"

Footsteps thumped on the porch. Brice stiffened.

"Just the mailman," Leigh said, looking down the hall. "Relax."

"Good. Afraid it was more pestiferous gossip-rag types. So what you got in that box?" Brice said, rubbing his hands in an exaggerated show of excited expectation. "Christmas cheer, eh?"

"I figured this would be a pretty bleak holiday for you, so I brought you a bunch of tasty things."

"Good! Eating and drinking are about all I got left. Except for all those male prostitutes I keep hiring."

Brice's drawl was wry. He'd actually looked for local hustlers online only to give up when he discovered that the nearest were scrawny boys hours away in the state capital of Charleston. Upon further consideration, he'd realized that such boys might run off to the press afterward if they figured out who he was. He did not need a big *Star* story about "Brice Brown, Whoremonger and Pervert."

"Male prostitutes? Yeah, right. As if little Summers County is crawling with them.

Well, there's probably some crab-infested drunk down on Third Avenue who might be willing to trade sex for a big bottle of Mad Dog 20/20."

Brice guffawed. "No, thanks. Is that fruitcake?"

"Yes. Daddy's recipe. The only fruitcake I've ever had that isn't gummy and tasteless. And here's a container of chili I made the other day. And some corn muffins. And some ham biscuits. And some kale. It's real tender. And some sugar cookies. And here's a big bottle of attitude-adjustment."

"More Jameson. Good timing. Wayne and I put a dent in the bottle I had. Why don't you sneak Carden down here after school some day when he's back in classes, and I'll give him and you some belated Christmas gifts?"

"Don't get anything for me, brother. I know your finances are stretched. Just get Carden another WVU Mountaineers sweatshirt or something along those lines. Now I'd better get going," she said, pulling on her coat. "I promised Carden I'd get home in time to make more of those sugar cookies."

Brice walked Leigh to the door and saw her off. In his porch mailbox, two fat manila envelopes were wedged. Brice pulled them out and examined the return addresses. Both were from his agent, Steve Morgan.

"Uh, oh," Brice muttered. Back inside, he tossed the envelopes on the couch, then headed over to the desk in the back parlor and turned on his computer, both hoping for and fearing a return message from Wayne.

Nothing yet. It's only 4 pm. He's probably still at work.

Brice snacked on a few ham biscuits and sugar cookies in the kitchen and mixed up a hot toddy. *Shit, now this drink will always remind me of Wayne.* In the front parlor, he started up another fire. He lay back, watching the light outside fade and the night fall. He finished his drink, mixed another, and then, with a sigh of reluctance, turned on a corner lamp and opened the first of the two bulging manila envelopes. It was crammed with smaller envelopes.

Brice slid the contents out onto the couch. On a typed piece of Steve's business stationery was a note.

December 19, 1997

Dear Mr. Brown,

> *Since you left town, many of your no-doubt doting and admiring fans have sent you mail care of this office. I thought you might enjoy reading them*

and responding to them over the holidays.

Do have a glorious New Year.

Sincerely,

Carolyn Rood, Office Manager

Steve Morgan Management

Nashville, Tennessee

"Bitch," Brice growled. "I'll bet you're enjoying this something awful. I hope you end up dead in a ditch."

He took a couple swallows of his drink, waiting to feel a good, solid buzz. When, after another few minutes and another hearty swig, the warm, careless feeling filled his head, he tore open one of the letters.

Brice Brown,

You're a pervert. I thought you were a real man. I loved your music. But last night I threw all your CDs in the trash. To think that I've had a crush on you for years. Now I look at the pictures of you in the magazines and I'm disgusted. May Our Lord Jesus have mercy on your soul.

Candy King

"Shit. Just what I fucking need." Brice finished his drink and opened another letter at random.

Dear Sir,

Our church is praying for you. Your sin is one of the most grievous, an abomination hated by God. Surely you recall what happened to those cities on the plain, Sodom and Gomorrah? Repent, sinner, lest you be cast into the lake of fire, into the outer darkness, where there is much weeping and wailing and gnashing of teeth.

Yours,

The Congregation of the Millbrook Baptist Church

Danese, West Virginia

"Ack!" Brice grunted. *This is not the kind of attention from fans I've always craved.* He opened the second fat manila envelope and dumped its contents out onto the coffee table. The same thing: letters, letters, letters, almost all of them with the address handwritten.

The next one Brice ripped open was composed in all capital letters with a red pen.

FAGGOT! SOMEONE OUGHT TO SHOOT YOU IN THE HEAD AND PUT YOU OUT OF YOUR MISERY.

A sharp chill pulsed through Brice. *Okay, third time's the charm. Damn. You ain't even met me and you want to shoot me in the head? If the rest of these are anything like the first three, there's no damn way I'm going to get any sleep tonight.*

In the kitchen, Brice contemplated having a proper dinner, realized that he had little appetite after the haranguing messages he'd read, and settled for some pork rinds and a big glass of Jameson straight up. He trundled back into the front parlor, nudged another log onto the fire, closed up the fireplace, turned on the blower, clicked off the lamp, stretched out on the couch, and drank till he passed out.

Around midnight, Brice woke in need of a piss. Too tired to climb the stairs, he stumbled out into the winter chill and relieved himself off the edge of the porch. *Probably feeding that damn poison ivy that keeps coming up every year,* he thought, moving unsteadily back inside.

Oh, hell. Wayne.

Brice hurried to his desk chair and nudged his computer awake.

There it was, a message from Wayne in his in-box. Brice took a deep breath and opened it.

> *Hey, Brice,*
>
> *Thanks for the message, man. Those reporters <u>have</u> been calling here at all hours and showing up at the door too. I <u>have</u> been "reached for comment" several times, and every time the comment has been FUCK YOU.*
>
> *One guy at work today called me a faggot. If he does it again, I'm going to punch him in the face, sure as shooting, even if he is twice as big as me. Gail's real upset, and so are her parents, and, to be honest, my boss is giving me funny*

looks. If I lose this job, I'm fucked in a major way.

Look, Brice, Gail's pretty much told me what you told me: to stay away from you. I'll bet you never thought you'd see a day that Pooch Meador was so pussy-whipped that he'd do what a girl told him to do, but that day has come. I really love her, man, and, hell, her mother's dying, so, look, I'm going to keep my distance for a while. I sure hope you understand.

I love you like the brother I never had, Brice. You hang in there. Fight that dark shit inside you, man. Fight it. Stop caring so much about what other people think.

Wayne

Brice burst into tears. He staggered back into the front parlor, slumped down on the couch, and sobbed for a long time. Then, with great effort, he got to his feet, downed a glass of water in the kitchen, and trudged up the stairs to his empty bed.

CHAPTER EIGHTEEN

BRICE WOKE AT 3:30 AM. HE PISSED AND GULPED down another big glass of hangover-prevention water. He climbed back into bed and lay there, staring at the ceiling. Sleep refused to return. Not even the soothing susurrus of the river helped. He kept running over and over in his mind the words of Wayne's e-mail message. The time they'd so recently shared already seemed like long ago. He tried to summon another fantasy about Wayne—his friend naked and hairy and muscular and submissive, eager to give his body to Brice—but the gap between reality and erotic fiction was too great, so soon after reading Wayne's message. Brice's cock lay limp in his hand.

He rose, stood naked by the window, shivering, and looked out over the river, the bridge, and the mountains looming above the town. Now his mind veered back to the piles of scattered letters downstairs, letters yet unopened, hundreds of them, most of them probably as vicious as the first three. *All those people hate me, and all I wanted my music to do was make them love me. Ain't their God supposed to be about loving folks, not hating them?*

Sighing, Brice climbed back into bed, flipped on the bedside lamp, and tried to read a book of Civil War history. His attention refused to stay focused on the page. *All those soldier-boys just hoped to get home, but so many of them never did, and now here I am, I've made it home, but my battle's just begun. Hell, what kind of soldier would I be? I'm afraid to leave the house.*

The clock on the nightstand said 4:01. *Fuck it.* Brice slipped out of bed. He pulled on warm clothes and a pair of work boots with heavy tread, thumped downstairs, tugged on his camo hooded sweatshirt, rawhide jacket, and Stars and Bars cap, and stepped out into the night.

It was very cold. The light of a waning moon gleamed on hardened crusts of snow. *No assholes out here now, by God. Now I have the whole town to myself.* Brice stuffed his hands into his pockets and headed up the walk, taking deep breaths of air, feeling exhilarated, feeling free. There was no traffic whatsoever, and not a soul on the streets.

Brice's boots crunched on snow; his breath turned to vapor. In half a block, ice crystals edged his moustache. He walked slowly, and as he walked, the places he passed inundated him with memory. Almost every sight held significance.

The big ole courthouse, where Leigh spends so many hours of her days. The post office: I still remember when Daddy ordered that box of honeybees through the mail, and the postal clerk called him, all upset, and told him to get his ass up there, that some of 'em had gotten out, and here Daddy came down Ballengee Street, holding that box out with both hands, and three or four loose bees floating around his head, sticking close to their queen.

The florist where I bought that basket of daisies to take to the hospital for Nanny the day before she died. The theater. Watched The Great Gatsby *and* Jaws *and* Young Frankenstein *with Wayne. Gobbled popcorn and SweeTarts and wanted to hold his hand.*

The Presbyterian Church. How'd I get roped into that Christmas play? Played one of Herod's slaves who pissed him off and got dragged off to be executed. And the Methodist Church. Went to a few breakfasts in the basement there, just so I could look at Ronnie Burroughs' big chunky chest in those football jerseys he always wore.

Another block, and Brice stood before the high school. *Christ, the girls I pretended to get serious about. Jennifer and Patty and Joyce and TJ. I've been a liar from way back. Tenth grade, dissecting fetal pigs in biology, and eleventh grade, boiling test tubes in chemistry, the big explosion when Mr. Persinger mixed sodium and chloride. And the Senior Follies, when I played my guitar and sang one of the first songs I wrote and everybody applauded, and the sound of their clapping made me feel like I was worth something after all, was worth admiration and attention. I got the bug for applause that very night, and I've given up a real life for it, and here I am, standing on a snowy street, back in the town I'm from, the town that used to be so proud of me but now hates my guts, standing here at 4-fucking-30 on Christmas morning. Hell, I'm like a vampire, some sort of monster that can only come out at night, 'cause in the daytime I'd be hounded down the street by these fine Christian townsfolk.*

Brice turned back down Ballengee Street. The grumble of a car engine approached behind him. He pulled his cap down over his face as a salt-grimed pickup truck bounced past over the uneven cobblestones. *If that were full of the bad kind of good ole boy, as opposed to the good kind, like Wayne and me, and if they figured out who I was, I might get a serious ass-kicking right now and end up face-down in the snow.*

Brice picked up his pace. Soon, he'd entered the park. Instead of going inside, he snow-crunched down to the edge and looked out over the New River, at the detestable renamed bridge, at the wide black shushing flow and the lacy curlicues of whitewater foaming over rock midstream. *River sounds like applause,* Brice thought. *Reminds me of my first appearance on the Grand Ole Opry, there in the Ryman. Damn, I think that was the best night of my life. Knowing I'd made it. That I'd attained the company of the greats. All those people looking up at me, smiling, loving my music, loving me.*

He moved closer to the ragged boxwood hedge edging the park. There was a gap of about a foot toward the right end of the hedge. *Must have been where that drunk slipped through, the fool that staggered down here that night while I was still in high school and fell over the edge.*

Taking a long breath of winter air, Brice stepped sideways through the gap. *It's like a little door.* On the other side, two snowy feet of dead weeds shivered in a breeze, and after that, the land dropped off. Brice stepped even closer to the cliff-edge and looked down. Far below, perhaps a hundred feet down, railroad tracks gleamed in the sparse moonlight. Past the rails, a line of bare willows edged the New River.

He stood there for a long time looking down. For a few seconds, he ceased to think of anything. He forgot the past and the future. He felt his heart beating in his head and the cold on his face and in his toes. He listened to the eternal rushing of the river.

How can it get better? How can anything get better? How can I stop feeling this sick, black hopelessness? Everybody despises me. I've only allowed myself to care about a handful of men, and none of them could love me back. How can I live here? Where else can I go?

Brice took another step, his legs stiff, his hands clenched. The rough murmur of the river rose up to greet him, much like the sound of the surf at Daytona. *A fall so far'd do it. I guess. Maybe not. Maybe I'd end up a fucking pathetic cripple. And what would it do to them, the handful of folks who care about me? Wouldn't that be weak and cowardly as hell, to end myself and leave them to suffer? Leigh and Carden and Wayne.... Only three people? Jesus. Steve'd be sad, maybe feel a little guilty. Shelly'd get to play the grieving widow while she made the round of the wealthy folk's parties around Atlanta. Zac...shit, who knows how Zac would feel? I guess I don't care.*

Brice fell to his knees in the snow, only a foot from the edge, and bowed his head. *God, help me. God, help me. Please show me the way. Please help me climb out of this pit of tar. Give me the strength to keep going.*

Knees stiff, wet, and aching, Brice rose. He wiped ice crystals from his moustache. He trudged up through the park, into the house, and up to bed, praying that sleep's anesthesia might finally come.

CHAPTER NINETEEN

WAYNE STOOD BESIDE BRICE BEFORE THE ALTAR, before the minister with his big book. Both men were dressed in tuxedos. Both men were young, their beards still dark, their waists lean, their shoulders broad and unbowed. Stained-glass light poured over them. Wayne stepped forward. He lifted his hand to Brice's face and stroked his cheek. He pulled out a ring. "So how's about it, buddy?" Wayne said. "You ready to make an honest man of me?"

"Hell, yes," Brice said, pulling out a ring of his own and taking Wayne's hand. "Let's do it." Longing surged through Brice, a longing so vast and deep it threatened to burst him in half. Bending forward, Brice kissed Wayne on the mouth.

Brice woke, still feeling the softness of Wayne's whiskers against his lips. The room was gray with daybreak. He heaved a bereft groan as the dream dissolved. He rolled over onto his side, pulled a pillow to his chest, and, embracing it, fell back asleep.

When he woke again, it was nearly noon. He rolled out of bed, scratched his crotch, scratched an armpit, sniffed himself, found himself more than usually aromatic, contemplated a shower, then shrugged and pulled on sweats. *Ain't anybody coming by today. And I ain't going out. I've always liked the smell of my own pits anyway.*

Downstairs, he heated a couple of Leigh's ham biscuits to go with his coffee, then cut and ate a big slice of fruitcake. *Merry Fucking Christmas, country star!* he thought, stoking up another fire. He sifted through the letters, unable to bring himself to open another. *It's like there's a potential pit viper curled up and waiting in each one of those envelopes.* He sat at the piano and picked out a couple of the tunes he'd played Wayne. *He liked what I wrote about him. He was flattered.*

Brice let his fingers move into unfamiliar territory, trying to compose a new melody, but nothing came. *I'm too wrapped up in my self, dammit. My heart's crusted over, like the bark coating a hickory tree, and it won't let anything new in.*

Grumbling, he poured another cup of coffee and got out his guitar, fumbling with chords. He fingerpicked, slowly, solemnly. D A D A D E D E F-sharp minor. He strummed the minor and kept strumming, reaching for words, finding a shaky melody.

> *Black-bearded beauty, why you gotta stay away?*
> *Hairy-chested honey, why keep my love at bay?*
> *I cain't have you, this I gotta face.*
> *Life fulla loneliness, life fulla disgrace.*

Brice trailed off. *No one's gonna listen to a gay love song.* "Black-bearded beauty?" *Man, they'd love that in Nashville.* "Black-bearded beauty, why cain't you be gay?" He snorted and put his guitar away.

Brice spent Christmas afternoon in the back parlor watching action DVD's, reading his Civil War book, and watching a slow rain come down outside. At two pm, he drove off a new passel of reporters who seemed to have nothing better to do on the holiday than annoy him. At three pm, he started drinking consolatory toddies. At four pm, he put on a porn DVD, watched a bearded stud get it hard up the ass, and managed half-heartedly to jack off. At six pm, he had a bowl of chili, a corn muffin, a pain pill, and another toddy. At six-thirty pm, he started up a sword-and-sorcery DVD and passed out a quarter of the way through it.

Brice woke with a start at ten pm. He lumbered into the kitchen and gulped down an entire liter of sparkling water. He opened up a bottle of Glenfiddich he'd been saving for a special occasion and poured out a glass. Standing by the windows of the front parlor, he watched rain fall in the streetlamp's gleam. The fire had burnt down to mere embers. On the coffee table, the pile of letters still waited. He could almost hear their vicious whispering and their snaky hiss.

He sat heavily on the couch and reached for a letter. He paused. He sifted through them, as if trying to sense, by their look or weight or something more subtle, which few might be sympathetic, might even be uplifting. He settled on one in a pink envelope scattered with yellow flowers. *Looks like the kind of prissy stuff a seventh-grade girl would use*, he mused, thumbing it open. It was written in an immature scrawl that befitted the style of the stationery.

Mr. Brown.

In the past, I have so enjoyed your music, but I can't condone your perversion. My preacher has explained it all to me. I wish it were not so, but I know there's no hope for you. Now, when I hear your music, I can hear Satan's voice in it. The Last Days approach, and it sorrows me to know that you, because of your sexual crimes, will be left behind on the Day of Rapture, and you will suffer and writhe and rot with the rest of the sinners. I would pray that the Lord have mercy on you, but even the Lord, with a heart as vast as the universe, cannot pardon your insufferable sins…as Romans and Leviticus have made so clear.

Sincerely,

Rhonda Bennett

Columbus, Ohio

"You little cunt," Brice snarled. He tore the pink-and-yellow letter into pieces. He gulped the Scotch, fighting the urge to lob the glass against the far wall. Gathering up all the letters, he knelt by the hearth and fed them in twos and threes to the embers until the very last one was ash and smolder. He grabbed another bottle of sparkling water from the fridge and thudded up to bed.

Brice lay unsleeping for hours. He thought of his father's guns, hidden only yards away in the linen closet. He thought about the hideous mess a bullet through his brain might make, and how Leigh would most certainly be the one to find him. He thought about jumping off the Suzanne Matthews Bridge instead, launching himself off the concrete emblem of his failure and his fall, making that metaphoric fall literal at last, smashing down into frigid water and rock, where the molecules of his blood would merge with the New, run down into the Kanawha and the Ohio, and ride the Mississippi down past New Orleans and out into the sea.

He thought about the night his grandmother died in the hospital, the woman who loved him more than anyone ever had before or since, and how he sat by her bed until the end, and how, for a week after the funeral, he'd jolt awake at four am sharp and would sit in the darkness of the front parlor, rocking in a rocking chair and waiting for daybreak to come.

He thought about the night his mother died, in the very same hospital, and how he sat by that deathbed too, and the nurses put on soothing music, and he gritted his teeth, determined not to cry, and swabbed his mother's lips just as the nurses showed him, and how his father came by only long enough to sign some papers and then left, and how, when his mother was gone, he called his sister and walked out into the February cold and looked up at the moon, and a buck trotted across the end of the parking lot, as if it had shown up to give his mother's soul a ride home.

He thought of how his father had died suddenly while Brice was far away, on a concert tour in California, and how his father had never found anything Brice did of much interest, no matter how hard he strove to impress the man, and how poised Brice had been when he spoke at his father's funeral, and how much Brice had never said to him, about his anger and his resentments, because what would be the point of that kind of whining anyway?

He thought of past Christmases in this house, the red cedars he or his father always cut in a vale behind the farm where Leigh and her family lived now, and how the tree annoyed his mother's allergies but she tolerated it anyway, and Christmas dinner was either ham and scalloped potatoes and deviled eggs, with lots of eggnog spiked with bourbon, or exotic, fattening lasagna with garlic bread and a big green salad, and fruitcake, always fruitcake afterward.

The river. Always the sound of the river in this room. It used to be such a comfort, like the sound of the trains moving through the valley. How old is that river? Second oldest river in the world, after the Nile. Eternal, like God. Running through here when the Cherokee used these mountains as a hunting ground. Running between these same vast sky-stroking mountains when my ancestors got here, from England, and Scotland, and Ireland, and Germany. Running through here when the bluecoats and the graycoats battled it out and bled. Running here when I was still a gob of cells in my Mommy's womb. God, I'm so small. So brief. A spark off a campfire. A bug. Why the fuck think about blowing my brains out when my life'll be over soon enough? And what will I have done? What will I have achieved? Who will have loved me? Who will have touched my body with honest desire and welcomed me to do the same?

A roaring filled his ears. *Wind in the chimney. Deep and hollow.* A scratching started up. *What? Sounds like insect legs scrabbling at the walls and the windows. Hell, it's just those Christmas wreaths, they're shifting around on their wires in the wind. Sounds like water striders look, those funny long-legged bugs so light they can slide across the surface of a pool. So graceful and delicate, like birds gliding through air. God, I'm stuck. Stuck in this heavy, clumsy, creaky body. Stuck in this self. Stuck in this town. Stuck in this house. Fuck, what'll become of me?*

He rolled onto his side and cuddled with his pillow. He tried to pretend it was Wayne but couldn't. He tried to cry, just for the relief that might provide, but no tears came. Instead, he could feel a cold creeping over him, like the frozen glaze on snow he'd seen during his walk the previous night. An old numbness, one more profound than any he'd known before, had come to claim him, and he closed his eyes and nodded with recognition and thanks and let it take him.

CHAPTER TWENTY

ON THE LAST DAY OF THE YEAR, BRICE, RESTLESS and bored after days of being cooped up inside, took advantage of a midafternoon drizzle to leave the house. The streets were as deserted as he'd hoped, with no aggressive journalists surging toward him or pious townsfolk giving him surly looks. His face concealed by both sweatshirt hood and the cocked brim of his baseball cap, head down and hands crammed into his pockets, he walked briskly under slate-gray skies to the far side of town before turning back. He was nearly home when the light rain turned into a downpour. Cussing, he bounded up the steps of the Methodist church, a handsome, high-spired structure only two blocks from his house. When he found the door unlocked, he slipped inside.

In the vestibule, Brice pulled off his hood and shook rain off his cap, and then he stepped into the sanctuary. *Mommy used to sing here when I was a kid,* he thought, gazing down the central aisle to the choir stalls. *She had such a sweet soprano. "The Old Rugged Cross," that was my favorite. I never much enjoyed church—the sermons were boring as shit—but the church suppers…man, there was some good eating. Folks were welcoming then. They treated me as if I belonged, and that felt good.*

Unbuttoning his jacket, Brice looked around the dim, high-ceilinged room and at the huge stained-glass windows he remembered so well. *So quiet and warm in here, and no one else around.* Brice slipped into a pew, took a deep breath, propped his elbows on his knees, cupped his face in his hands, and closed his eyes, trying to remember the last time he'd attended services there.

Must have been Daddy's funeral. Damn, things were so simple then. I still had hope. What's left to hope for now? Man, I wish I were younger. I wish I were simple-minded enough to believe that faith could solve all my problems. I wish my parents were still alive. I wish I were straight, 'cause then I'd still have my career. Hell, okay, I take that back. I wish Wayne, or some butch country boy like Wayne, would be sharing my bed tonight. Damn, I'm just so tired.... I just can't seem to sleep through the night anymore....

Brice was well on his way into a drowse when a man's voice jolted him wide awake.

"Good afternoon. May I help you?"

Brice jumped to his feet, anxiety clotting his gut. A thin, middle-aged man with a receding hairline and a kind face was regarding him from the front of the church. He was dressed in a dark suit and wore a white clerical collar.

"Aw, I.... It got to pouring outside, so I ran in here. I...I used to attend services here as a kid. Before I moved away."

"Really? Then welcome back." The man smiled. "You're welcome here. Everyone is welcome."

"Th-thanks." Brice cleared his throat. "It's real nice in here. I've always really liked the stained glass. Are you the minister?"

"I am. I don't believe I've seen you at our services. Have you moved back to Hinton?" The man moved closer.

"Yeah. I.... Naw, not really." Brice bent to retrieve his ball cap from the pew. "I'm just back for a little while...for the holidays. To see family. I'm kinda in between jobs." He stepped out into the aisle as the minister moved closer still.

"Oh, you still have family here? Who are they? It's a very small town, you know. I might know them." The man gave Brice another benevolent smile.

Oh, shit. Brice took a step back, feeling panic creep up his spine. "Uh, maybe. But I don't think they attend this church. Look, I'd better get on home. Sorry to bother you."

"It might still be raining. You're welcome to stay until it lets up." The man offered his hand. "I'm Reverend Jim Jenkins."

Brice wanted to turn and run, but all his coaching in Southern manners denied him that easy option. Instead, he shook the man's hand, gave him a weak smile, and said, "I'm Brice."

"Good to meet you, Brice. You look troubled. Do you want to come to my office and—"

The reverend's voice came to an abrupt halt. He cocked his head and studied Brice intently. He dropped Brice's hand.

"You're Brice Brown, aren't you?" The man's mouth set in a grim line. He folded his arms across his chest and glared. "The disgraced singer? The infamous homosexual?"

The scorn in the man's voice made Brice want to punch him. His urge to flee vanished beneath a surge of belligerence. "Infamous homosexual? Yeah. Yeah, I guess I am." Brice clenched his fists and scowled. "You wanna make something of it? I'm fucking sick of everyone around here giving me grief. I grew up here. This is my town too. These are my mountains too. This is my home. When a guy's hurting, he just wants to come home. Right? Can't you understand that?"

The thin minister took a step back, as if suddenly noticing how dangerously brawny Brice was. "You don't belong here," he said. "You've violated God's laws. You've shamed our town. Please leave."

"You just said that everyone's welcome here." Brice shook his head in disgusted disbelief. "So you're gonna turn me out into the rain? Nice! I thought y'all were all about compassion. You said earlier that I looked troubled. Well, yes, I am. I am troubled. And I need help. I've been praying a lot lately, not for God to change me but for God to help me. Hell, it's the world God ought to change, not me. He ought to change hypocrites like you. You're a fucking preacher, man! Ain't you supposed to help the suffering? Jesus did. I just need a little compassion. Where's compassion, if not in a church? In a church my Mommy used to sing in!"

Reverend Jenkins flinched and squinted, as if buffeted by storm winds. "Don't shout! This is the house of the Lord. Have you repented? God and His followers can spare compassion only for those who want to change. Have you turned your back on your lusts? Have you prayed to be cleansed of your sins?"

"You mean the sin of loving men?" Brice rolled his eyes. "Y'know, I've thought a lot about all that since I lost my career and fled outta Nashville with my tail between my legs. My craving for other guys can't be a sin. Why would God make me that way, set that longing into my body, my heart, my groin—"

Brice thumped his chest and patted his crotch. The minister looked as if he might faint or vomit.

"Why would He make me what I am if what I am is what He hates? Is God a *retard*? Are you a *retard*?"

"Please leave! Please leave now!" The minister turned and backed up the aisle. "Or

I'll call the police!"

I've scared the shit out of him and it feels good. When Brice tapped his right fist into the cup of his left hand and made as if to follow him, the reverend bolted into an alcove and disappeared. A second later, a door slammed shut.

Guess I better get outta here in case he does call the cops. Snickering, Brice loped down the aisle and out the door. Outside, a cold breeze blew, but the rain had stopped. Feeling mildly triumphant after his outburst, Brice pulled on his cap and bounded down the steps, ready to get home to the solitary New Year's Eve meal he had planned: several rounds of hot toddies, a bottle of cheap champagne, a couple buttermilk biscuits slathered with butter and honey, and a big bowl of Crock-Pot-simmered beef stew.

CHAPTER TWENTY-ONE

SNOW FLURRIES POWDERED HIS WINDSHIELD as Brice drove back into Hinton. He'd spent most of New Year's Day at Pipestem State Park, hiking around Long Branch Lake, trying to walk off some of his holiday gut and his holiday blues in the leafless woods. He'd encountered very few fellow hikers, and none of them had seemed to recognize him. Now the sky over the town was purple-gray with late afternoon, and Brice's belly was rumbling. He was more than ready for a buzz, followed by some dinner beside the fire.

Weary after hours of exercise, Brice clambered out of his truck. He stood there for a moment, feeling peaceful, watching the snow falling about the towers of the courthouse. That's when a passing pickup truck much like his slowed to a crawl, only yards from him. The passenger, a scruffy-faced man he'd never seen before in his life, rolled down the window and shouted, "Faggot!"

Brice didn't hesitate. Cussing out the Methodist minister the day before had been a tipping point. He'd tolerated enough abuse. Now his hopelessness, loneliness, sadness, hurt, despair, and sense of defeat were entirely overshadowed by another emotion: rage. Turning, he squared his shoulders, clenched his fists, and shouted, "*Fuck* you!"

The truck jolted to a halt. The driver leaned across his passenger, eyes wide and glaring. "Fuck *you!* You goddamn queer! You need your ass beat!"

"You can *kiss* my ass, you shithead," Brice snarled. "You and your monkey-faced friend there."

"Goddamn you," the passenger said, opening the door. "We'll teach you to talk shit like that to us.

We're gonna beat the holy hell outta you, you stupid cocksucker."

The man stepped out of the car. So did the driver. Both were wiry, with features similar enough that they might be brothers, and both were shorter than Brice by a couple of inches.

I can take these assholes, Brice thought, chest and belly tight with tension. "Aint you a scrawny pair of little shits?" he said, giving them a menacing grin. "I think you need a big man like me to teach you a lesson."

In response, the driver drew out a hunting knife. "Don't matter how big you are, long as we got this."

"Oh, shit," Brice grunted, bracing himself.

"You shouldn'ta messed with us, faggot. We're gonna feed you your balls," the driver snarled. "Everyone around here knows better than to piss off—"

"Hey!" someone yelled to Brice's left. "You! Billy Ward! Bobby Ward! What the hell do you all think you're doing?"

All three men turned. Half a block away, before the courthouse, a man in a blue uniform stood beside a police car, hands on his hips. *He sure looks familiar*, Brice thought. *Do I know him? Damn good timing, whether I do or not.*

"Oh, well, hell," the driver said, sheathing his knife. "Looks like we'll have to finish this another day. Git in the car fast, Bobby. Let's git outta here."

It took the two men only a few seconds to disappear into their vehicle, careen down the street, run a stop sign by the Confederate monument, and disappear around the block.

The policeman approached, looking glum. He was a big, barrel-chested man, even thicker-built than Brice, with blue eyes, reddish-brown hair, and a jowly, flushed face. "Sorry so many folks around here are assholes. I bet you've been getting crap left and right since you got back to town, huh?" The cop offered his hand.

"You know who I am?" Brice said, as they exchanged a firm, fast handshake.

"Well, sure. Don't you recognize me? Guess I have put on a few pounds since high school."

"Me too," Brice said, studying the man's face. "Well, hell. You're Francine Bailey's big brother, right?"

"Yep. Frank Bailey. My sister and yours used to be fast friends."

"And now you're a cop?"

"Yep. And now you're...." Frank trailed off, looking pained.

"Disgraced?" Brice sighed, crossing his arms across his chest.

"That wasn't what I was going to say. I think you got a raw deal, Brice. I think you're super-talented. I'll bet nearly everybody in this county has some of your CDs."

"*Had* some of my CDs. Before they threw 'em in the fire." Brice pulled off his Rebel-flag ball cap and shook snow off it. "Or trampled 'em in the street. Like they'd like to do to me, apparently."

"Well, those folks are just plain dumb. Their religion's made 'em mean. That's pretty common around here. Look, you watch out for those Ward brothers. They've got tempers like rattlesnakes. If they bother you any—if anybody bothers you any—call down to the station and ask for me. Okay?"

"Yeah, I will. Thanks a lot. Look, I live just down there. You wanna come in and get some coffee? I'd like the company."

Frank frowned and looked away. "Can't. On duty. Got to get back to the station."

"Afraid you'll be fingered as my new boyfriend if we're seen together?" Brice coughed out a dry laugh.

Frank shrugged. "Well, that hadn't really occurred to me. Everybody knows I've been married twice and have six kids. Was that true about you and Wayne Meador, by the way?"

"That was bullshit. He's married too. We're just friends."

Frank shrugged again. "Okay, well.... Glad you have friends. Hard to get through without 'em. Happy New Year."

"Same to you. And thanks again for saving my ass. They might have cut me pretty bad."

"Yep. It's my job. Glad to help."

The two men shook hands and parted. Brice had trudged only a few feet toward the top of the park when Frank said, "Hey, Brice?"

"Yeah?" Brice turned.

Frank pursed his lips and scratched his cheek. "I hope you get it back. Your career. And I know you've got to be lonely. So I hope you find someone. I really do. It's a new year, right? Anything's possible."

"Right." Brice tried to smile. Finding someone to love in his ruined-outcast state seemed to him about as likely as renting a pleasure palace on Pluto. "A new year. Thanks,

Frank."

Frank waved and headed for his police car. Brice walked into the park, calves stiff from the hours of hiking. He stood in the grass for a few minutes, shivering while he watched the sun set over the notch Madam's Creek made in the mountains. On his porch, Brice stomped snow-dust off his boots. He was about to fetch in some kindling from the wood box when a flicker of color caught his eye. Something was waving by the door in the steady breeze and the dim light. He pulled it from between the screen door and its frame. It was a bright yellow piece of lined notepaper, folded in half. Brice unfolded it. In black Magic Marker letters were the words, "Repent, sinner. Or be damned."

Rage flickered through Brice again, but this time it subsided in seconds. Weary amusement took its place.

"Nice of these folks to be providing more fuel for my fire," he drawled. Brice crushed the note up into a ball and shoved it into his pocket before gathering up several handfuls of oak-twig kindling and entering the house.

CHAPTER TWENTY-TWO

THE SECOND GLASS OF IRISH WHISKEY HAD BRICE comfortably toasty. He'd just finished chopping up a head of cabbage and had it frying in a skillet with some bacon grease when the doorbell rang.

As usual, Brice tensed up, mind flashing through the possibilities. *Reporters? Leigh? Those fucking Ward brothers, come to finish what they started? Shit, I need to get some ammunition for Daddy's guns. Who knows if or when those Wards might show up here? They gotta know where I live. Screw courage. I don't plan to die under the knives of backwards bastards like them. Frank said to call the police station and ask for him, and that's exactly what I'm gonna do, if it's those assholes.*

Jaw set, Brice strode to the door and peered out through the glass. A man—tall and stocky, not at all familiar—was standing on the porch, faintly illuminated by the house lights. He was dressed in a WVU baseball cap, a black leather jacket, and a pair of jeans. His head was half-bowed, and the lower half of his face was covered by a thick beard. He carried a paper bag in his right hand.

Who the hell is that? Another damn scandal-rag journalist, no doubt. Well, I'll send the little prick packing.

Brice unlocked the door and threw it open wide. After the earlier encounter with the Wards, he was feeling hostile and on edge. "What the hell do you want?" Brice growled through the screen.

The startled stranger stepped back and stared at Brice, wide-eyed. "M-Mr. Brown? Uh. I…uh."

Lord, he's young. Mid-twenties? Handsome. Looks a little like me when I was that age. Could be my kid brother, if I had one. "Speak up, boy. What do you want?"

"Mr. Brown, I'm real sorry to bother you. I just—"

"Are you a reporter? Journalism major? If so, fuck off."

"Reporter? Aw, naw!" The boy shook his head, and shaggy hair swayed about his oval face. "I'm...I'm a fan. See? See here?"

He pulled a CD out of his jacket pocket—it was Brice's *Mountain Back Road*—and brandished it like a protective charm before slipping it back into his pocket. "Your music means so much to me, and what's happened to you lately...how mean people have been to you...well, I think you're brave. I think you're a hero. I'd love an autograph. And I brought you this. Kind of a Happy New Year present."

The boy offered Brice the bag. Brice opened the screen door and took it. Inside he found a fifth of rum, a quart of eggnog, and four fried pies in a Glad Bag.

"What kinda pies?" Brice asked.

"Apple. Homemade. I made them. My Nanny...my grandmother's recipe."

"Hm." Brice gave the boy the faintest of smiles. "So you're a fan, huh? What's your favorite song of mine?"

"Oh! It's hard to choose! Uh, maybe 'Sad-Eyed Angel?'"

"Yeah? So why is that your favorite?"

"Because it reminds me...of someone I knew." The boy cleared his throat and looked away, out over the porch and toward the muffled rushing of the river. "Somebody I loved. His name was Mike."

Brice's face broke into a wide grin. "You're gay?"

"Yes, sir." The boy met Brice's gaze and nodded. "That's kinda why I'm here."

"Well, hell, come on in. It's cold out there." Brice held the door open.

"Thank you, sir," the boy said, entering the house with a loping, long-legged stride. Brice closed the door and locked it. "Gimme that jacket and hat," he said. His visitor did so, after removing the CD and a square red envelope. Beneath his outer garment, he was wearing a black and red plaid flannel shirt with rolled-up sleeves atop a black T-shirt. *Nice build*, Brice thought, hanging the leather jacket on the hall tree before ushering his guest into the front parlor, where a small fire burned.

"So what's your name, son?" Brice said, offering his hand.

The two shook. "Travis, sir. Travis Ferrell. I've been wanting to meet you for a long time."

"Nice to meet you, Travis. It's sure good to meet someone who wants an autograph instead of an opportunity to beat me senseless. Two guys I ran into this very afternoon pulled a knife on me and were prepared to cut me up...before a cop arrived in the nick of time. Here now. Take a seat."

"Oh, wow, a knife? Really? Damn. Sure glad the cop appeared."

Travis set the CD and red envelope on the coffee table before plopping down on the couch. He stared up at Brice with a glassy-eyed, blissful fixation that Brice recognized. It was the stunned gaze of a fan in close proximity to an adored star, and it warmed Brice to his core. He hadn't been looked at like that for a long, long time. *Since that last concert in Daytona, I guess. Just before that poor bastard Zac outed me.*

"How old are you, Travis?"

"I'm twenty-four."

Twenty-four? A baby. Green eyes, auburn beard, solid build.... Good-looking kid. If I were a decade younger.... But my guess is he didn't come here to be seduced. Keep your paws to yourself, old man! "Old enough to drink, then. Do you drink?"

"Oh, sure!"

So wide-eyed. So enthusiastic. Just adorable. "Would you like to share a round or two with me?"

"Drink with Brice Brown? You bet! All the folks back at school will be crazy with jealousy."

"Good to hear I have a few fans left. I'm drinking Irish whiskey. Would you like some of that? Or some of that eggnog you brought?"

"Well, I have to drive home, so maybe a glass of eggnog with just a little bit of rum?"

"Sure. You got it." Brice tramped into the kitchen, calves still smarting from his long hike, and mixed them eggnogs, a jigger of rum for Travis's and two jiggers for his own.

"Thank again for this New Year cheer," Brice said, handing the young man his glass before settling down onto the opposite end of the couch. "By the way, I have dinner going. You want to stay around for that?"

"Really? Sure! That's mighty kind of you." Travis looked as if Brice had just offered him a thousand-dollar bill or a job as vice president of the planet. "I've never sat down to supper with a star before."

"Former star, I'm afraid. Your parents won't want you home for dinner? It *is* New Year's Day."

"Naw. They're overseas. Daddy travels a good bit on business. I came home for the holidays…just to be home, I guess. Just to get out of Morgantown for a few weeks. We live up Forest Hill, just a little ways from your sister, Miss Leigh, but there's no one waiting there for me tonight, so, sure, if you'd let me stay for dinner, I'd be real grateful. I haven't had much to eat today. Went by Kirk's for a couple of their hot dogs…."

Travis clasped his hands in his lap, and sadness filled his eyes. "They were closed for the holidays. Shoulda known."

Melancholy over the absence of hot dogs? This kid's more of a glutton than I am. "Well, I have black-eyed peas cooking, and fried cabbage too. And I'm going to make some cornbread. Got some sorghum to go with that. How's that sound?"

"That's exactly what my family fixes on New Year's Day. That sounds wonderful! Thank you so much!"

This boy is all exclamation marks, Brice thought, grinning. *I remember when I was that excitable and eager. Nice chest and arms. He must lift weights.* "So you mentioned Morgantown. You a student there?" Brice took a big swig of his spiked eggnog. *Strong and rich. Like I used to be.*

"Yes, sir. I'm in grad school at WVU. In English. I want to be a poet. Kinda like you."

"Like me?" Brice grinned and took another sip. *I like this kid a lot.*

"Yeah, sure. Your song lyrics are poetry, right?"

"Well, yeah, I guess so. At least I like to think so."

"I want to write poems like your songs, that get at the heart of emotions. That touch people and help 'em deal with suffering and sorrow. Your songs have sure done that for me. That's mainly why I came here tonight. To thank you for that. Your music has really helped get me through some hard times."

"Well, sure, kid. You're more than welcome. What hard times you talking about? If you don't mind my asking."

Travis shrugged and took a sip of eggnog. His eyes looked even sadder. "Oh, nothing like the stuff you've been going through. All that nasty publicity about you…I'd like to punch those people in the face!"

Brice chuckled. *Passionate and protective. He really is a younger version of me.* "Thanks. But as far as hard times go, this isn't a competition, son. Lots of folks suffer."

"Yeah, I know. Still…my gay and lesbian buddies and I, we all think the media's treated you something awful. Oh, and speaking of my buddies."

Travis picked up the square red envelope and proffered it to Brice. "They all signed this card. We're all members of the gay student group up at WVU."

"Yeah? Okay, thanks."

Brice tore open the envelope. "THANK YOU!" was printed in raised letters across the front of the card. Inside, someone had written in black letters, "We love you! Don't give up!" Around that swirled a messy storm of scrawled signatures, along with drawings of Lambdas and a little crayoned-in rainbow.

"Wow. Wow. Well, thanks, kid." Brice did his best to smile, but his throat was tight. "This…this means a lot. A great deal. Please thank all of 'em for me."

"We sure hope you put out more music. Will you?"

Brice laid card and envelope on the coffee table. "That's a damned good question." *Still haven't gotten a notice from Steve that he's dropped me, but I suspect it's only a matter of time.* "I'm not sure. So, do those hard times of yours have anything to do with that guy you mentioned before? Mike?"

For a split-second, Travis looked like he was going to burst into tears. Instead, he sat back, stared into the fire, and nodded. "Y-yeah. We were lovers once."

God, he looks miserable. I'd like to take this poor boy upstairs and get him naked and hold him all night and give him what comfort I can. "Once, huh? Was he a WVU student too? What happened?"

Travis shifted with discomfort and shook his head. "Mr. Brown, I didn't come here tonight to waste your time with my sad stories."

"Look, kid, you just started my year in a wonderful way. I've been pummeled and kicked and insulted and mocked for months now, ever since that damn story broke about me and Zac, and I've been depressed as fuck and looking for one good reason to keep on living and wondering what kinda hell might heap up on me next. But tonight you show up out of the snow, a perfect stranger, and you tell me you're a fan, and you bring me gifts, and you tell me that my music means a lot to you and that it's helped you through hard times, and you give me this sweet card. Can you imagine how much your visit means to me? You're a real gift from God, son. So sit back and share whatever you please with me."

"Well…okay." Travis brushed hair from his eyes. "So, Mike and I were lovers in high school, here in Hinton. But then he had to join the Army, and I went to college, and…."

"And you all broke up?"

"Yeah." Travis finished his drink. He put down his empty glass and rubbed at his eyes. "Shit. I'm sorry. Being back here just…makes me remember so much. The reason I wanted to get some hot dogs across the river today is 'cause Mike and I used to meet there…. I'm really sorry."

"No need to apologize," Brice said, fighting off the urge to hug the kid.

"Mike was bisexual, and being in the army, it was so hard to…. Well, I guess it got so hard—us being apart and all—well, after about a year, he ended up getting involved with a girl. I guess that was easier for him than being long-distance with me and pretending to be straight around all those butch guys who might have frailed the hell out of him if they'd found out about him and me."

Travis's voice shook. He wiped at his eyes again and cleared his throat. "My Nanny had died just before Mike sent me the letter telling me about that girl and how he felt he needed to end it with me, so that made all of it so much harder to take."

"I'm sorry, kid." Brice reached over and squeezed Travis's furry forearm. "That all sounds rough as hell."

"It was, sir. I guess I understand why Mike did what he did. I wish them well, I guess. Him and that girl. But, oh Lord, I loved him so much. So much. He was my first, and…I don't think I'll ever meet anyone I'll love like that again."

"Maybe. Maybe not. You can't tell about those things, Travis. You're a smart, handsome young man. My guess is you'll find a new boyfriend sooner or later."

"I hope so. Do I even dare to hope? I can't imagine feeling…." Travis trailed off, looking sheepish. "Can we change the subject, Mr. Brown? To be honest, I don't know you well enough to cry in front of you."

"Yeah, I don't want you crying. You might make me start off too, and what kind of New Year's celebration would that be?" Brice patted Travis's shoulder and stood. "You hang in there, kid, and I will too. Deal?"

Travis gave Brice a weak smile. "Deal."

"Good. Let me get that cornbread started, okay? I think we'll both feel better after a good meal."

"A good meal would be great, sir." Travis nodded, returning his gaze to the fire. "Food always makes me feel better. I really appreciate you letting me stay for dinner. And thanks for listening to me ramble on about my troubles."

"NOT HALF AS GOOD AS Nanny's, but it wasn't too bad," Travis said, scraping up the last bite of his fried apple pie.

"They're delicious. Would you like me to heat you up another?"

"Oh, no. I brought them for you. Thank you again for the wonderful dinner!" Travis wiped his mouth, checked his wristwatch, and sighed. "I should go here pretty soon, though. I just hope the roads aren't too slippery. I got a four-wheel drive but still, I hate to drive in snow. Will you sign my CD before I leave?"

"Sure." Brice fetched a pen from the desk in the back parlor and scrawled his name across the back of the liner notes. "Here you go."

"Thank you!" Travis blurted, sliding the liner notes back into the plastic CD case. "Oh, did you ever get my letter?

"Letter?"

"I sent you a letter weeks ago. Several of us in the gay student group did."

"Where'd you send it?"

"To your manager's office in Nashville."

"Oh, hell. What did the letter say?"

"Some of the stuff I've said tonight. I told you how much of a role model you'd been to me. How much I loved your music. How I was glad to know you were gay, even though I knew being outed was super-hard on you. How it was great to have an openly gay celebrity to look up to."

"Well, shit. I sure wish I'd read that letter. I burned them all. My manager's bitch of a secretary forwarded a whole bunch of letters to me, but the first few I read were so vicious and hateful and threatening that I couldn't bear to read any more of them."

"Oh. Okay." Travis stood. "Well, you didn't need to read my letter, 'cause I got to say my piece in person, which was lots better! I should get going now. I'll be back in town for Spring Break in March. Maybe I could come visit you then?"

Brice stood as well. He was already dreading the solitude that would descend on him as soon as this young man left the house. What a luxury it had been, having another gay person around, not to mention a handsome country boy who'd grown up in the same county. "Sure you can. If I'm still around. I'm thinking it may have been a mistake to come back here, since everybody knows me and knows where I live. Not only do most of them hate gays, but they're pissed as hell about me 'bringing shame to the town,' as a local minister put it yesterday. Guy up at the Methodist church."

Travis made a face. "That guy is a shithead. Nanny always used to say that he had the personality of toilet tissue. I heard about the town council changing the name of the bridge. Bastards. So where will you go, if not here?"

Brice shook his head. "I have no fucking idea. My wife got the house, and I'm selling some other properties just to have cash. My label dropped me, and my manager might drop me too. I have nowhere else to go. Any day now, I'm afraid I'll head outside to drive to the grocery store—in Beaver, mind you, where folks are a little less likely to recognize me than here in Hinton—and find my truck tires slit or my windshield smashed. After today's run-in with those assholes who pulled a knife on me.... Hell, I guess I should leave here, but I don't know where else to go. I can't really afford to go anywhere else."

"Mr. Brown, that's just awful. You want to spend some time in our Forest Hill house? My parents will be gone until the spring. They'd probably appreciate having someone watch the place once I go back to school."

"That's kind of you to offer, but anywhere still in Summers County—"

Travis's green eyes widened. "Oh, hell! Wait! I know!"

"What?"

"You need to meet Mr. Philip!"

Brice grinned. The boy was so excited he was practically doing a jig. "Mr. Philip?"

"Yeah! He's a graduate of WVU. He visits campus sometimes and comes to the student group meetings and takes us all out for dinners and down to the bar and always pays the tab. He's not trying to pick anybody up, he's just real generous and real rich. A philanthropist. He's donated lots of money to the group. He owns a kind of compound up in Randolph County, near Pickens and Helvetia. He even hosted a gay college-student conference last summer at his place. It's a bunch of cabins and a lodge. Used to be a guesthouse, I think. Real nice. Maybe he'd put you up for a while."

"For free? A stranger? I don't think so."

"But that's just it! You're not really a stranger. Not exactly. Mr. Philip attended our last meeting of the semester, back in early December, right after you'd been outed by that asshole Zac guy, and we were all talking about how much we loved your music, and how disgusted we were that the press was treating you the way it was. Mr. Philip was the one who suggested that we write you letters and that we sign that card I gave you earlier tonight. I was going to mail the card to your manager's office too, but then I heard that you'd moved back to Hinton, so I decided to try to give you the card myself when I came home for Christmas."

"I'm damned glad you gave it to me personally. Otherwise, I would have burnt it." Brice rolled his eyes. "Who knows how many supportive letters I destroyed? Stupid, stupid."

Travis snatched the card up off the coffee table and opened it. "Look here! Philip Rogers. He signed it himself. He's a huge fan of yours! I'll bet he'd love for you to visit for a while. The place is out in the middle of the woods, in the middle of nowhere. No one would bother you there. He has a little staff to keep things up for him. A cook and a handyman. I think you'd love the place!"

"Maybe, kid. I gotta admit that your enthusiasm is infectious, but—"

"You should try it! Mr. Philip could maybe help you get back on your feet. Restart your career! At least give you some breathing space where you won't be harassed by the ingrates and Bible-thumpers around here."

"Restart my career?" Brice gave a grim laugh. "That sounds too good to be true. It's hard to keep hoping that things could turn around. I'm afraid the rest of my life is going to be a long, slow, dark slide into—"

"You've got to hope!" To Brice's surprise, Travis seized his hand and squeezed it hard. "How can you not have hope? You're so talented! You're so handsome! You're Brice Brown! People know your name all over the country, even if lots of them have turned on you. Why, if I could write the songs you have.... I saw you in concert in Morgantown! And in Roanoke! You were amazing. And your music saved my life when Mike dumped me. You've got to hope! You've got to try!"

Brice laughed out loud. "Okay, okay. Calm down, kid. What's your e-mail address?"

Travis bent to the coffee table, grabbed up Brice's pen, and scribbled on the back of the red envelope. "There you go."

"Good. I'll drop you a line here in a day or so. Then you can give me this guy's contact information, and maybe I'll drop him a line too. All right?"

"You bet! You won't regret it!" Travis bounded into the foyer and pulled on his coat. Brice followed, missing the boy's energy already.

"Would you come back sometime?" Brice asked, handing Travis his ball cap. "We don't have to wait till Spring Break. I've really enjoyed your company."

"Sure. I'd *really* like that. I'm heading back up to Morgantown in another week or so, but I'll be around till then."

"Okay. Sounds good. Come back for another dinner."

"You bet!" Travis adjusted the cap on his shaggy head. He looked Brice up and down, and then he stepped forward and gave him a hard, quick hug. "You're great! Good night!" With that, the boy threw open the door and loped out into the darkness.

Brice locked the door. Outside, the flurries had ceased. In the kitchen, he poured himself another glass of Irish whiskey. He stretched out on the couch, watched the dying fire, and took a long sip.

"Hope," he muttered.

"To the young," he muttered.

Brice gulped the rest of his glass, rolled onto his side, dragged the afghan down on top of him, slipped a throw pillow beneath his head, and fell asleep.

PART
THREE

A FEW MILES NORTH OF PICKENS, BRICE PULLED his truck into the gravel lot beside a roadside general store and stepped out, belly rumbling and lower back smarting. The store's proprietors, he hoped, could tell him how to get to Mr. Philip's, a place seemingly as legendary and difficult to find as Brigadoon. He'd been driving up and down Randolph County roads for an hour now, but the directions Mr. Philip had e-mailed him were more poetic than specific, full of references to natural landmarks like tulip poplars, sway-back ridge-tops, roofless red barns, and silos painted with hex signs.

Brice looked around the high valley, savoring the quiet and remoteness despite his frustrations at feeling lost. It was the second of February. Fog made the pastures blurry, and the afternoon air was very cold. About the store, huge white oaks loomed, a few dead leaves clinging to their branches. To the back of the property, behind a rail fence, three shaggy ponies grazed. Across the road, a willow-skirted stream rushed, high and restless with winter rains. A red sign at the edge of the parking lot pointed to the rear of the store, announcing "This Way to Good Food."

"Just what I wanted to hear," Brunt grunted. He pulled his guitar case out of the extended cab, unwilling to leave his old Yamaha to suffer from the cold, then slammed the truck door and crunched over gravel toward the building. When he opened the back door, welcome warmth poured over him, and the scents of spicy meat and baking bread. The walls were lined with shelves full of wines and gourmet items in jars: relishes, pickles, olives, jams.

"Nice," he mumbled, moving up to the counter.

A sign on the wall, "Sandwich Special Today: Pulled Pork BBQ," made him briefly, intensely happy.

"Howdy," he said to the emptiness, peering at a door to the right that seemed to be the entrance to the kitchen. "Anyone here? Y'all open?"

Beyond that door sounded a rustling and then a voice. "We sure are. Welcome!"

A woman in her mid-forties appeared around the corner, rubbing her hands with a towel. She was solidly built and handsome, around five foot nine, with high cheekbones, her dark hair cut very short and graying at the temples. She wore black patent leather shoes, the shiny kind a cop might wear on duty, plus jeans, a white shirt, and a skinny black tie, the sort popular with men in the 1960's.

"Well, hey," Brice said, staring. For a split-second, he was taken aback by her masculine appearance. *Whoa. Not a lot of women in West Virginia dress like that. I do believe she's a ferocious bull-dagger.* But then he grinned, remembering butch lesbians he used to get shit-faced with in the gay bars of Morgantown back in his university days. *Maybe I'll fit right in here. I don't think she's as likely as some to throw me out into the fog if she figures out who I am.*

"Welcome to Radclyffe's Roost. You hungry?"

"I sure am." Brice had only stopped for gas during the lengthy drive from Hinton, afraid that he might be recognized and reviled if he stopped at any fast-food spots for lunch. "Starving. And I love barbecue. How about one of those sandwiches and a cup of coffee?"

"Coming right up." The woman might have been intimidating-looking but she had a friendly smile. "You want slaw on the sandwich?"

"Oh, yes." Brice deposited his guitar case in a corner and rubbed his still-chilled hands together. "Please."

"Potato salad or fries?"

"Umm. I'm plump enough." Brice perused the menu pasted to the top of the counter. *Long gone, the days I'd have to fucking diet for months to get lean for my latest album cover shots, but, hell, I can hardly get into any of my jeans after all that holiday eating.* "Could I have a side of the brown beans and chow-chow instead?"

"Sure." The woman poured out a big mug of coffee and handed it to Brice. "I've never seen you here before. What are you doing in our isolated little valley on such a cold and gloomy day?"

"Glad you asked, 'cause I was about to ask you for directions. The smell of your barbecue kinda distracted me. Do you know how to get to Mr. Philip's? Philip Rogers?"

The friendliness on the woman's face faded. Suspicion replaced it. She looked Brice up and down. "Why do you ask?"

"Uh, well, someone I met back in my hometown said that I should meet him. Mr. Philip and I, we corresponded, and he's asked me to visit him for a while."

The woman's mouth pursed. "I find that highly unlikely."

"Why?"

"You don't look like his kind of people."

"What do you mean?"

"Well, you look a little rough, to be honest. You look like you could be...hostile." The woman gestured vaguely to Brice's Stars and Bars cap. "Mr. Philip's is a safe place, and it needs to stay safe."

She doesn't know I'm gay. She thinks I'm some dangerous redneck. She's trying to protect him. Shit. Well, here goes. From the look of her, seems like honesty's the best thing here.

"Look, I need his help. Please? I really need to find his place. Look, what's your name?"

The woman folded her arms across her chest. "Grace Simmons."

"Well, hey, Miss Grace." Brice offered his hand. "Pleased to meet you. I'm Brice Brown."

Her face shifted yet again. She looked him up and down once more, as if trying to reinterpret a difficult mathematical formula or an opaque, experimental sonnet. "Brice Brown?"

"Yeah. The country singer? I've been in the news recently?"

That look of recognition Brice had seen so many times before—for years combined with adoration, more recently amalgamated with hate—flickered across her face.

"Well, shit!" Again came the friendly smile, this time broader.

"Welcome!" She reached across the counter and gave him a handshake so strong he winced. "I thought you were some nasty bubba who'd got wind of Mr. Philip's Rump-Ranger Ranch, as we call it, and wanted to bust up the place."

"I look like a bubba?"

"Haven't you checked out a mirror lately? You sure do. A big mean one. With those shoulders, that big beard, and that Rebel-flag cap? Is that the latest Nashville look? Well, Bubba Brice, lunch is on the house. After all the bullshit you've been through, it's the least I can do. I sure wish Amie were here. She's in Baltimore for a week, visiting her cousin. She loves your music."

"Amie's your...."

"Yep. My wife out of wedlock. Voluptuous little femme with a striking resemblance to Betty Page, the pin-up star. Ex-burlesque dancer. I'm crazy about her. We live in that white house with the Victorian gingerbread just down the road. Hey, you look around—we have some nice stuff here. Pick up some wine for Mr. Philip. He'd love that. I can show you which wines he likes. Then take a seat and I'll bring your lunch out to you here in a minute. After that, I'll drive you up the hill to Mr. Philip's myself."

Grace strode off into the kitchen. Brice picked up his coffee cup and sipped it. He wandered through a few shelves of this-and-that, noticing little, and then he sat heavily on a chair by a wooden table and leaned back, shoulders slumped with relief, staring out the big window into the fog. He'd found a place where he was welcome.

"You wouldn't be the first to seek shelter at Fairyland Ranch," Grace said. She sat across the table from Brice and drank black coffee while he snarfed up his food, which was even tastier than he'd expected. "It's mainly gay boys and gay men, but a few young lesbians have stayed there too, trying to get their heads together after their shithead families threw them out."

"When did he open the place?" Brice said, adding black pepper to his brown beans.

"Last spring. For a long time, it had been a guesthouse, but the new owners had the charm of water moccasins and snapping turtles, so a lot of former customers stopped coming, and the place went bust. Mr. Philip had been a successful corporate lawyer in DC for years, but then his wealthy daddy died—he was also a lawyer, with lots of coal company connections, and a nasty old bastard, from what I hear—and Mr. Philip inherited everything. He'd had enough of DC, so he bought this place as a sort of retreat for troubled queers who need somewhere to stay for a while. He's got loads of money now, so he does as he pleases. Sometimes he's up at Fairyland, or Rump-Ranger Ranch, or Sodomite Central, or Phagg Heights, or whatever he's calling it this week—the guy is a real wit, let me tell you—and other times he's down in his Florida condo. Right now, I'm pretty sure he's just up the hill, though I think he's leaving for Florida in a few weeks."

"Sodomite Central?" Brice snickered. "Sounds like just the kinda retreat I need. When everything went to hell in Nashville—"

"Yeah, Amie kept me abreast of all that. She's a huge fan of Dolly Parton, so she subscribes to lots of country-music magazines. We both felt really bad for all the crap you were going through. So you fled to your hometown, right? Hinton?"

"Yeah, it was a reflex action, I guess. Wounded critter scurrying back into its den." Brice stuffed the last bite of barbecue sandwich into his mouth. "Damn, that was delicious. Thank you. But everybody knows me there, and they treated me like a pariah. Once I'd been their cherished hero, the local boy who'd made it big, but then...."

Grace rose and moved toward the counter. "I get it. But then you sullied the town's good Christian reputation with your egregious sexual sin. Narrow-minded pricks. I grew up surrounded by that kind of nastiness in the coal towns of southwestern Pennsylvania."

Brice nodded. "People were downright vicious. I nearly got knifed by one pair of assholes. Last week, someone slit my tires, and someone else stole the wood out of my woodshed. And people kept leaving Christian pamphlets inside my screen door. I'm just glad the fuckers didn't heave rocks through the windows. So I closed up my house there—my sister will keep an eye on it—and I drove up here, hoping that Mr. Philip would put me up for a while."

"Oh, he will. Count on it. I bet a piece of Amie's pecan pie would lift your spirits. In fact, I'm going to have one myself. How about it?"

Brice grinned. "I ain't gonna argue."

Grace returned with two huge slices. "Dig in."

"Don't have to tell me twice."

A few moments of silence, five big bites, and Brice's plate was empty. "Goddamn. That woman of yours can cook."

"Why you think I married her? You got anyone in your life now that you're getting divorced?

"Like a boyfriend?" Brice snorted. "Naw. Thanks to my own ambition to become a huge star, and the conservative nature of Nashville, and my attempt at marriage... shit, I've never really had a love life to speak of. With a man, I mean. Well, other than furtive tricks. And the guy who outed me. I was too busy trying to be straight. Trying to convince folks I was straight."

"Trying to convince yourself you were straight? I did that some in high school. Then I fell in love with my female vocal coach. That ended my desperate attempts at heterosexuality. When my family found out about my affair with the female basketball star in college, there was hell to pay. I wish Mr. Philip's Homo Hideaway had been available then."

Grace collected their empty plates and cups. "Let me get these washed, and then let's drive up the hill. It's time you met Mr. Philip."

CHAPTER TWENTY-FOUR

BRICE'S PICKUP FOLLOWED GRACE'S HONDA. AT first, the road squeezed up the side of a narrow woodland gorge overhung with sharp rocks. Below, a splashing creek cascaded over a series of ledges. Then, as if one had just passed through a gateway, the land changed, opening out into yet another high valley spotted with clumps of forest and wide spreads of pastureland, the tops of the encircling hills all capped with milk-curd fog. After a couple of miles, they turned left at a roofless barn and climbed farther and farther up a dirt road. Where a gate made a gap in a long wooden fence fronting the road, they made a sharp right, drove through the middle of a wide meadow, and traversed a level quarter-mile between leafless forest trees. Brice could make out a scattering of cabins along the hillside and, farther on, a rustic-looking lodge built of rough wood and stone.

Grace parked in the circular driveway in front of the lodge and climbed out. Brice followed her lead, lugging out his guitar case and a colorful gift bag full of two bottles of wine. Grace led him up onto a wooden porch, past an array of rocking chairs, and into the lodge.

"Damn. Nice," Brice sighed, leaning his guitar case against the wall and strolling around. "Just the kinda cozy I like."

The place was built of dark logs, with a high, raftered ceiling. In the great room, a huge stone fireplace and chimney predominated. To the side was a well-stocked bar upon which Brice deposited the gift bag of wine. The furniture looked solid and comfortable: big brown leather couches, heavy coffee tables, baskets of magazines, green plants sprawling out of pottery, and huge armchairs in earth tones. The paintings on the walls were all Appalachian landscapes. To the far end, a screened-in porch gave Brice a wide view of the mountains above bare treetops.

"There's a pool for summer use and a hot tub," Grace said, pointing out a side window. "There's a grotto downstairs with a steam room and an indoor hot tub. The dining room's downstairs too, and the kitchen. I don't know how much of a staff Mr. Philip has on hand these days—or how many queer refugees he has staying here, for that matter—but a local Randolph County lady, Doris Ann, is usually the cook. She's as good as my Amie. In fact, she taught Amie how to cook. Let's see if she's around. Maybe she knows where Mr. Philip is."

Grace led the way down a flight of stairs, through a low-ceilinged dining room furnished with massive wooden tables, chairs, and antique sideboards and on into a long kitchen lined with windows. The big panes were spattered with rain. By one of the cluttered counters, an old woman with hollow cheeks and graying hair heaped up into a bun was peeling potatoes.

"Doris Ann," Grace said. "How are you?"

The woman dropped her paring knife, startled. Then she smiled.

"Mizz Grace! How you been?"

"Fine, fine," Grace said, ushering Brice around the counter. "This gentleman has come to see Mr. Philip. Is he around?"

"He's in Elkins today, getting supplies, but he should be back in another half-hour or so." Doris Ann wiped her hands on a towel before turning to Brice. "You're welcome to wait for him upstairs. Are y'all hungry? I could heat you up some vegetable soup and biscuits or—" She paused, staring.

Here it comes, thought Brice. *Daddy always said, "Be careful what you wish for, or you might get it." I wanted to be famous....*

"Lord God!" she blurted. "Brice Brown! What are you doing here?"

She shuffled forward and seized his hand. Her finger-joints might have been gnarled, but her skin felt soft. "Oh, what a stupid question. I know what you've been through. I'm so glad you found us. Mr. Philip said we'd be having a special guest."

"Thank you, ma'am. I'm very glad to be here. Should I move my truck? It's parked just out front."

"It'll be fine right there. How about I have Lucas start a fire for you upstairs and you can wait there till Mr. Philip gets back."

"Who's Lucas?" Brice asked.

"Our handyman. He can do just about anything. I'll call up to his cabin and have him come down. I can heat up some nice apple cider for you too. It's getting on to five, so I'll doctor it, if you'd like. I know you like your bourbon."

"Sounds great. How do you know I like bourbon?"

"Lord, son, half your songs make that clear. All that lovesick driving down back roads and 'sucking up Dickel from a flask,' as you put it. Mizz Grace, will you stay for cocktails? Mr. Philip is always home for cocktails at five."

"No, thank you. I need to get back to the store. Some folks are due in about half an hour from now for an early dinner. Jeff and Brendan? That couple from Roanoke that bought that little place down the road? It's their anniversary."

Grace turned to Brice and gave him another wincingly powerful handshake. "Okay, Bubba. You mind if I call you that?" She cocked a dark eyebrow and smiled.

Brice chortled. "Not at all. Just remember that I'm a good bubba, not a bad bubba."

"I'll keep that in mind. Tell Mr. Philip he ought to come down for Sunday dinner sometime soon. You come along too. Amie will make her famous fried chicken."

"You bet. Hey, *thank* you. It meant a lot to me that you made me feel welcome. That hasn't happened much in the last few months."

"It'll happen a lot around here. Right, Doris Ann?"

The elderly lady nodded. "Oh, yes. We here in Brantley Valley know how to take care of our fugitives. And feed 'em too."

Brice wandered around the lodge, cupping a mug of spiked cider in his hands, waiting for the handyman to show up to start the fire. In the high-raftered great room, he found an upright piano, which he tested, finding it fairly well in tune. In one side room, he found a pool table and an elegantly appointed bathroom. In another, an especially cozy space with big windows looking out over the covered pool, he found more overstuffed leather furniture, a computer atop a dark-wood desk, and shelves stuffed with books built into the walls. *I love this place*, he thought. *Country-masculine, like a hunting lodge, just the way I like it. This Mr. Philip must be very cool.*

Brice took a sip of cider, rubbed at a twinge in his lower back, and looked out over the pool. Night was falling. Winter rain continued, running down the glass, and mist floated in patches over the pool deck. Beneath his breath, Brice murmured a brief prayer of thanks, to have found a place in which he might feel safe.

A blue gleaming on one windowsill caught his eye. It was an enormous point of quartz crystal, at least a foot long and half a foot wide, embedded in a wooden stand. An electric light inside the stand shone up through the milky mineral, illuminating it, making it resemble frozen flame. Awed, Brice stepped over to it and stroked it.

So beautiful. How old is it? Where was it found? How did it get here? It was probably on this planet before the first human being ever evolved.

Brice leaned his brow against the cold glass, suddenly exhausted, and stared out into the rain. *Hell, it might have been buried in a cave when the dinosaurs breathed their last, gleaming on a hillside when the mastodon....*

Brice's stream of thought snagged and stopped. A man had appeared in the mist on the far side of the pool. He paused beneath a clump of bare trees, then skirted the pool, heading toward the lodge. Something about the purposeful way he moved fascinated Brice, a cross between a youth's self-conscious swagger and a warrior's long stride toward the front lines of battle. As he strode nearer, he looked up and saw Brice standing at the window.

The stranger paused again. Through the storm-stippled glass, their eyes met. The man nodded and then disappeared around the corner.

A moment later, a door opened elsewhere in the lodge. Boots stamped off wet. The stranger appeared in the door of the library. He nodded at Brice, unsmiling.

"Doris Ann said you wanted a fire?" His voice was husky, his accent country-thick.

Holy shit, he's handsome, Brice thought, trying not to stare but taking in every detail nonetheless. The stranger looked younger than Brice by over a decade and shorter than him by several inches. His face was striking: big blue-gray eyes, luxuriously long eyelashes, a close-cut reddish-brown beard framing an oval face, and thick black metal hoops in his ears. Everything he wore was black: black denim jacket, black ball cap, black jeans, and black work boots.

"Hey. You must be Lucas."

"Yep." The boy's face reminded impassive.

"Lucas was my great-great-grandfather's middle name. He was a Rebel soldier. Died at the Battle of Franklin in Tennessee."

"Yeah?" Lucas shrugged. "Got a Confederate ancestor myself. So, did you want that fire?"

"A fire would be great," Brice said, offering his hand. "I'm Brice Brown."

"Uh, huh." Lucas shrugged again. "Uncle Phil told me you'd be coming."

"Mr. Philip is your uncle?"

"Yep." Lucas hesitated a long moment before shaking Brice's hand. He stepped back, looking Brice over. The glow of transfixed fandom that Brice had hoped for, especially coming from a young guy this hot, was nowhere to be seen. Instead, the boy seemed vaguely disappointed, as if Brice in Person contrasted unfavorably with Brice the Legendary Star. *Well, I am about twenty pounds heavier than the last CD cover, damn it,* Brice thought. *Was I ever as sexy as this boy? Not in my best years. Shit.*

"Okay, well, lemme start that fire," Lucas said, pulling off his wet jacket. Beneath, he was wearing a tight slate-gray T-shirt beneath a closely tailored, unbuttoned leather vest. Metal-studded leather bands adorned his wrists; tattoos streaked his furry forearms; metal chains glinted around his neck.

Everything about him made Brice ache. He followed Lucas into the great room, full of an erotic fascination he hadn't felt since he'd met Zac so long ago. *Boy, this kid is built. Big shoulders, small waist. Look at those biceps. Shit, shit, shit. And that butt…. Is he gay? Maybe. Maybe not. Shit!*

Brice took a big swig of his cider, nearly choking on it. "Need some help?" he said. *Any excuse to move a little closer to you.*

"Naw." Lucas bent by the hearth, arranging kindling and twisting up strips of newspaper. "I got this."

Brice settled into an armchair, watching the boy's broad shoulders move. When Lucas bent over, his back to Brice, and lit the paper, Brice stared at the kid's compact little rump and suppressed a groan. He settled back into the soft chair and closed his eyes. *God, he's hard to look at. To look but not to touch? It's torture. I'd rather not see him at all….*

"Hey, you asleep?"

Brice jolted out of a drowse. Lucas stood over him, brushing wood-dust off his hands, his brow creased with what could have been concern or could have been bemused disapproval. Behind him, the fire was already beginning a busy blaze. "Sorry. Just resting my eyes. Tired. Long drive. Long day."

"Whatever," Lucas mumbled with deep disinterest. He removed his hat, shook off the wet, and ran his fingers over his chestnut-colored buzz cut. "So you do country, right? I mainly listen to industrial stuff."

Brice nodded. "I guess lots of younger guys are into that." *Ummm, those pretty lips. It's been so long since I've kissed a boy as desirable as that.* "Say, I'm about done with this cider Doris Ann gave me. Would Mr. Philip mind if…." Brice gestured toward the bar.

"Help yourself." Lucas picked up his coat and hat. "Uncle Phil should be back any minute now. I'd better head back up the hill."

Hell, don't go, Brice thought. "You want a drink too?"

"Naw. I got too much to do. Studying and shit."

"Studying? You in college? Grad school?"

Lucas dipped his head and looked away. "Naw. Studying for the GED."

"Oh. Okay."

Lucas jerked on his jacket, his back to Brice. "I dropped out of high school. My mommy needed me to work. A man's gotta provide for his family, right? Nothing to be ashamed of," he said, voice tight, even deeper, defensive.

"N-no. Not at all," Brice stammered. *Shit, I've pissed him off.* He slipped behind the bar and examined the Scotch, looking for single malt. Discovering a bottle of Glenlivet, he poured out a healthy dram.

Lucas pulled on his hat and turned around. "You go to college?" It sounded like an accusation.

"Yeah. WVU. A long time ago," Brice said, feeling faintly guilty.

"You're damn lucky. Must have been nice." Lucas scowled. "When I was a kid, I wanted to study biology and become a forest ranger. Didn't get far with that big dream. Daddy died and I had to help Mommy—"

"YOOOOO HOO!"

Both men jumped. A door slammed downstairs and a heavy tread ascended the steps.

"Here comes Uncle Phil." Lucas stuffed his hands into the pockets of his jeans and rocked back on his heels. The sour expression on his face had melted into a broad grin. "Prepare to be entertained. He's a hoot."

CHAPTER TWENTY-FIVE

A PLUMP, BALD MAN IN HIS SIXTIES ACHIEVED THE top of the stairs. Lucas's height, he wore a short gray beard, tan dress slacks, and a many-hued Hawaiian shirt full of fern fronds and parrots. He put his hands on his hips, regarded the two of them, arched his eyebrows, and said, "Y'all drunk yet?"

Lucas sniggered, pulled his cap off, and rubbed at his right temple. "Oh, Lord. Here we go."

"What y'all waiting on? It's cocktail time." Phil gave Lucas a fond hug before heading for the bar. "You'd better watch this one, Mr. Brown. He can be ferocious trouble."

Lucas's face reddened. "Well, hell, Uncle Phil. Why'd you have to say that?"

"I'm just teasing you, boy." Mr. Philip threw himself at Brice, giving him a big bear hug. "Mr. Brice Brown! My favorite country star! Welcome to Phagg Heights! That's 'Phagg' with a 'P H,' by the way. More sophisticated. I'm so glad you could visit. You're looking healthy." To Brice's chagrin, Philip gave his waist a pinch. "Let's have us some drinks to celebrate."

"I've already gotten into your Scotch," Brice said, sloshing the golden liquid in his glass. "Lucas here said it would be all right. Should I start a tab?"

"A tab? Certainly not."

"Well, depending on how long I stay, I should give you some kinda rent or grocery money or something. I don't want to be a freeloader."

Philip waved the offer away. "What sort of mercenary heathens do you think we are? No spare-changing here. *Mi casa es su casa.* You're our guest. Besides, thanks to my frightful ogre of a father and his timely demise, I'm fabulously wealthy. About godddamn time. What would you like to drink, little Lucas?"

Lucas blushed again. He bent briefly to toss another log on the fire, and again Brice did his best not to openly ogle the solid curves of his ass. "I told you to stop calling me that. I ain't so little anymore. I can't get all wild and drunk with y'all. I got studying to do. Ain't you always telling me I need to buckle down and make something of myself? See you later, Mr. Brown."

Brice took in the boy's broad expanse of shoulders and smiled. "You're welcome to call me Brice."

"Naw." Lucas grimaced. "I wudn't brought up to call my elders by their first names. That's bad manners."

Philip laughed. "Since when did you care about the niceties of etiquette? You can study some other night, boy. We have here a famous star."

"Yeah? Then *you* entertain him." Lucas shook his head. "I got more important things to do." Eyes averted, Lucas strode out of the room.

"See you at breakfast?" Philip called after him.

There was no answer, just the slamming of a door.

"God love him," Philip said, scanning the bar. "He knows that Doris Ann's making biscuits and sausage gravy tomorrow morning. He'll be back down here, come hell or high water, salivating like a rabid coyote. That boy will heap his plate so high it'll look like the veritable Tower of Babel. Now what shall I sip to toast to your new membership in our Homo Hideaway? We needed a bear to complete our little zoo."

"Bear? I guess so." Ruefully, Brice patted his belly. "Since my tragic fall from grace, I've been pretty good at consoling myself with lots of food and drink."

"I hope you intend to do the same here. Doris Ann is a grand cook, and so is lil' Lucas."

"Why not? I won't be posing for any publicity shots anytime soon. Oh, I brought you some wine." Brice indicated the beribboned gift bag. "I stopped at Radcliffe's Roost down the hill to ask for directions, and Grace told me you'd like these. They're still chilled, I suspect."

"Bless her inverted Amazonian heart! We members of the Third Sex have got to stick together." Philip pulled the dew-moist bottles out and smacked his lips. "Chardonnay and Gewürztraminer. Excellent."

He opened the latter and poured out a big glass. "Take a seat, Mr. Brown. Let's drink. Let's drink and gossip up a storm, just up a storm! You must tell me all about your travails."

Brice groaned, settling into the armchair. "How about we talk about that after I have another couple of these?"

"Whatever you prefer." Philip patted Brice's knee before taking a seat in a matching armchair. "Let's focus on the positive. It's beastly out, cold rain coming down, and Lost Creek close to flooding, and patches of fog in the fields, and here we are, all cozy and safe. Lucas has made us a nice little fire. Do you need anything to eat?"

"Ah, naw. I had some of Grace's great barbecue." Brice gulped Scotch, feeling the welcome wash of an alcohol buzz, and looked around the big room. "This is a wonderful place you have, and I'm real grateful to be invited for a visit. As you know after that e-mail back-and-forth, things have been pretty hard for me."

"Yes! Those jackals in Nashville, and those troglodytes in your hometown. I'd like to take a bullwhip to each and every one of them. Wouldn't that be fun? Or we could tie them to anthills. Or toss them into a seething sea of hungry Chihuahuas! Or, worse, into a swarm of rabid drag queens whose long red talons would shred them posthaste."

Brice grinned. *This is the kind of outrageous gay guy that used to intimidate the hell out of me back in college, but now I'm damned thankful to know someone so funny and kind. This sort of place and his sort of wit are just what I need at this grim, lowdown place in my life.* "Actually, yeah. I *would* enjoy that. I like how you think."

"Revenge. Almost as delicious as this Gewürztraminer." Philip swirled the wine around. "Such a pretty color. Thank you. You stay here as long as you want, Mr. Brown."

"Brice, okay?"

"Brice. Yes. Call me Phil. That sweet Travis Ferrell was so excited to meet you and recommend you to me. I think if he weren't still so torn up over his grand break-up with that Army ruffian, he'd have a little crush on you. As it is, he's nearly the mess that Lucas is."

"A mess, huh? Lucas does seem like a guy with some issues. I've only known him for a few minutes, but.... So he's your nephew?"

"Yes." Phil's face darkened. He sighed. "Lucas is the reason I bought this place, actually."

"Really? How so?"

"Bless his heart, he's the poster child for Troubled Gay Youth."

Brice gaped. "Lucas is gay too?"

"Yes, indeed. Gay as a goose. And this compound—I call it many names, among them Sodomite Central, Phagg Heights, and Fairyland Ranch—is meant to be a retreat for troubled gay youth. And older folks like you, once in a while."

"Glad to be included." Brice lifted his glass. "Real, real glad. How old is Lucas?"

"He's twenty-seven. My apologies for his brusqueness earlier. He's always aloof around strangers."

Brice scratched his jaw and shifted in his seat, trying to ignore the throb in his back. "No problem. I was afraid I'd made him angry somehow."

Phil waved away the idea. "I doubt it was anything you did. Lucas is always angry, I fear."

"Why is that?"

"That's a long, sad story. He's terribly shy. He pretends not to care in order to keep his distance, especially from strangers. He might warm up to you eventually. Introverts like him take time. They need to get to know people before they open up."

"He's an introvert? He sure has a cocky walk and a rough-and-tough look for an introvert."

"All defense mechanisms. He comes across like a street-hellion, the quintessential bad boy—well, he once was one—but he's very bashful. His muscles may be hard as rocks—the boy works out frequently in our little gym—but his feelings are as delicate as lace. You should know that if you're going to live here for a while. Lucas was far too sensitive for his own good even before…."

"Before?"

Phil took a long sip of wine. "Lucas has a complicated history. An unfortunate one. As much as I love to gossip, I think it's his place to tell you, not mine."

"Sure. I'm not trying to pry. I just met you all. I'm just a guest here."

"I think you two might get along eventually. After all, you've been through some unfortunate times as well."

"Yeah." Brice sighed. "That's why I'm here."

"Yes. And it's for folks like you that I created this place. If Lucas does allow you to get closer, if he decides to tell you what he's endured, I suspect that'll encourage you to give him the empathy he needs."

Brice suppressed the urge to blurt, "I'll take any opportunity to get closer. The guy's a walking porn star. A walking sex-god. I'll give him empathy, all right. Empathy right up his tight little ass! Besides, how much shit could he have gone through, as young as he is?" Instead, he said, "You don't need to tell me anything. It's none of my business, obviously."

"I'll tell you this much." Standing, Phil walked to the fire and poked at it a bit before turning to Brice and taking another sip of wine. "Lucas is very smart. He was doing so well in high school. But then, when he'd just turned seventeen, his father died in a mining accident, so his mother, my only sibling, Kim, needed Lucas at home. Or, rather, she begged him not to quit school, but he did anyway, despite the money I offered to send to support them. Kim and Lucas can both be too prideful for their own good."

"So your sister is poor? I thought your family had a lot of money. You said your father had left you a huge inheritance."

"He left *me* a huge inheritance. Kim didn't get a penny. Daddy was a fearsome snob and disinherited her when she married a coal miner. Odd how he found my homosexuality infinitely less offensive than her choice of a mate. Well, at any rate, Lucas took to working at the Walmart in Elkins, but it turns out he was involved in...."

"Uh-oh. Drugs?"

Phil shook his head. "No. I've said enough. Lucas will tell you the rest, if he decides that he wants you to know. Let's just say that he got himself into serious trouble. Certain illegalities."

"Illegalities? Damn."

"Damn, indeed." Grimacing, Phil shook his head. "More recently, he and his mother have had a horrible falling out, thanks to her backward fundamentalism. I'm really the only person he's willing to interact with. Well, me, and Doris Ann, and Grace and Amie down at the store. I'm hoping that having you here might help. I don't know what would become of him if something happened to me. He's turned into a total recluse. Hates to leave the compound. At least he's studying for his GED. That shows some hope."

"Yeah, sounds like evidence that he's thinking about the future. I'll do the best I can with him. Least I can do to repay your hospitality."

"Thank you. He badly needs a friend. Be careful with him, please."

"I will. I promise."

"I believe you. You've suffered. You're not likely to cause further suffering, especially with a boy as fragile and wounded as Lucas. Reminds me of what Mr. Oscar Wilde said, something about only being interested in those who know beauty and those who've known suffering. Well." Phil drained his glass. "I assume your luggage is in your truck out front?"

"Yep. I didn't bring all that much."

"Let's get you settled in Laurel Cottage. It's not far. King-size bed and bathroom upstairs. Kitchenette, fireplace, living room and half-bath downstairs. Big porch with a view over the valley. You'll love it here at Rump-Ranger Ranch."

"Sounds wonderful. Sounds god-sent." Brice finished his drink as well. "Lead on," he said, pulling on his cap and jacket and picking up his guitar case.

In half an hour, having unpacked, settled in, and promised to show up for the breakfast bell, Brice was alone in his new home. Beyond the bedroom window, fresh snow was falling. It was only eight pm, but Brice, exhausted, back aching, took a pain pill, stripped, climbed beneath the quilts, and switched off the light. He rolled onto his side, grabbed a pillow, and hugged it to his chest, as was his wont.

Already, Brice knew, he was smitten by Lucas's good looks and eager to discover the details of the boy's mysterious history. Already, in his mind's eye, Brice was removing Lucas's clothing, holding him tenderly, and kissing away whatever dark years of damage he might have suffered.

Fragile and wounded, Phil called him. Brice hugged the pillow closer. *Hell, maybe focusing on Lucas's wounds will distract me from my own.* He fell asleep to the mournful sound of winter wind soughing around the cabin's high eaves.

CHAPTER TWENTY-SIX

BRICE WOKE TO THE THOUGHT OF LUCAS AND THE sound of rain on the roof.

I wonder if his chest is hairy. Or his ass. I hope so. Just how many tattoos does he have? I'll see him today, for sure, and get to look into those long-lashed eyes. It's amazing, to have something big to look forward to for the first time in months.

Brice's memory of Lucas's compact body soon shifted into erotic imagination: Lucas naked, arranged in an assortment of sexually submissive angles. Brice was well into a self-stroke session when a distant bell started clanging in the direction of the lodge.

"Breakfast," Brice muttered, dropping his dick and climbing out of bed. "Maybe breakfast with Lucas." He pulled on clothes and boots, stomped down the stairs, donned jacket and cap, and headed out.

A light coating of snow covered the shrub-lined walkway. A cardinal, bright shot of intense crimson, flew overhead. All about the cabin, tree limbs were lined with white powder. Shivering, Brice zipped up his jacket, his breath clouding before him, and walked briskly toward the lodge.

As soon as he stepped inside, his stomach growled, responding to the delicious scents. When he descended to the dining room, he found two places set but no one around. On the sideboard sat coffee cups and a carafe. On the sound system, peaceful space music played.

Shit. No Lucas. Brice hung his jacket and cap on a wall hook before knocking at the half-open door to the kitchen. "Hey, anyone here?"

"Good morning, honey!" Doris Ann appeared.

"You pour yourself some coffee, and I'll fetch you a plate. You like buttermilk biscuits and sausage gravy?"

"Oh, yes, ma'am. That's one of my favorite breakfasts."

"Good. Give me another minute, and I'll scramble you some eggs too."

Soon a contented Brice was gobbling. When he finished the first helping, Doris Ann set him up with a second, which he downed just as rapidly.

"That was wonderful. Thank you." Brice scraped his plate bare. "Where's everyone else?"

"Mr. Philip ate early and drove down the hill. Lucas don't always eat breakfast, though I'm surprised he isn't here for this one, since he loves my biscuits."

"Are there any other folks staying here?"

Doris Ann shook her head. "Not now. We've had passels of poor kids here, on and off…and me run off my feet trying to feed 'em. But since that sweet Lisa reconciled with her family and went back home to Cincinnati in November, it's just been Mr. Philip, Lucas, and me. And now you. Can I get you anything else?"

"No, ma'am. I'm stuffed. I'm just going to sit here and finish this cup of coffee."

Doris Ann nodded, turning toward the kitchen. "If Lucas shows up, tell him to come on in and help himself. They's lots left. If you need any lunch later, come back by."

"No need for lunch," Brice said, rubbing his belly. "Not after all that."

"Well, dinner then. I'm off tonight, but Lucas is making chicken and dumplings. They usually eat at seven, but Mr. Philip will be mixing drinks and setting out crackers with his favorite fancy cheeses at five sharp."

"That all sounds great. I won't miss it. Thank you again. It was all just delicious."

"You're welcome, honey. I love to cook for folks. It's my one true talent. That, and quilting." With a wave, Doris Ann disappeared into the kitchen.

Brice sat back with a sated sigh and let his mind wander. *If I stay here very long, I'm going to balloon. Where the hell is Lucas? I wonder if they have Internet here. They must, 'cause Phil exchanged e-mail with me. I'm afraid to check my messages, though. If Steve drops me, I'm fucked forever. If he doesn't, though, maybe he can find me a new label. Then maybe I can start writing again. Been over a year since I wrote a new song. I'm nothing without an audience.*

Brice rose. He was about to pull on his coat when footsteps sounded upstairs. *Lucas?* He hung his coat back up, poured himself another cup of coffee, and hastily took a seat.

The stairs thumped, and then Lucas appeared in the doorway. He paused, staring at Brice as if he were an unwelcome intruder.

"Oh. Hey. You're here." Lucas entered, averting his eyes, and poured himself coffee. To Brice's disappointment, the boy's shapely arms and torso were swathed in a baggy sweatshirt, though tight camo pants displayed his delectable rump.

"Hey, Lucas. Good morning to you." Brice mustered the sort of smile he'd so often flashed at fans from onstage. "Doris Ann said to come fetch your breakfast in the kitchen. Sausage gravy and biscuits. They're great. She said you favored them."

"Yeah, I do." Lucas hesitated, scanning the tables in the room and frowning. The only place already set was right across the table from Brice. "Guess I'll sit here then," he said, putting down his cup. In another minute, he'd fetched a piled-up plate and was digging into his breakfast as if he hadn't had a decent meal in days.

"Good, huh?" Brice grinned. "You seem pretty hungry."

Lucas looked up and scowled. "I am. I have a big appetite. You making fun of me?"

"No, I'm not." *God, he's prickly.* "I have a big appetite too. So what are you up to today?"

"Chopping wood." Lucas wiped his mouth. "Then I'm gonna make dinner."

"That's what I hear. Chicken and dumplings, Doris Ann said."

"Yeah. So? Nothing girly about cooking. All the guys in my family are good cooks."

"You're a real thorn bush, ain't you? I'm just trying to make conversation." Brice sat back with a sigh. "I think it's great that you can cook. I'm a decent cook myself, when I put my hand to it. A man should be self-sufficient, right?"

Lucas glared at Brice for a split-second, then dropped his eyes.

"Thorn bush, huh? Maybe so. I ain't the best for social skills. Seems like a waste of time."

"How about I save you some time by helping with the wood?"

"Help?" Lucas cocked his head, as if the concept confused him.

"Help." *Jesus, what pretty blue-gray eyes.* "I'm not bad with an axe. I used to gather wood with my Daddy all the time."

"Why d'you wanna help?"

"Simple enough. If I don't pitch in here and there, I'm going to feel like a great big parasite. I don't want to wear out my welcome, right?"

Lucas stuffed another bite into his mouth. "I get by all right by myself. I'm used to doing things on my own."

"You sure? I'd appreciate the company. I've been alone a lot lately."

"I like being alone." Lucas sopped up the last of the gravy with the last of a biscuit. "Especially out here in the country."

"Me too. But only so much. Don't you get tired of it?"

Lucas shrugged. "Not really." He gulped the last of his coffee, wiped his mouth with the back of his hand, and stood. "Look, Mr. Brown, I don't need no help with the wood, though it's kind of you to offer."

"You sure? I—"

"I'm sure. See you around."

Lucas turned and stomped back up the stairs. Brice sat back, dull disappointment heavy inside him, sipped his coffee, and heard a door slam. After a few minutes, he rose, carried the dirty plates into the kitchen, and headed back to his cabin, with no idea whatsoever of how to spend the day.

CHAPTER TWENTY-SEVEN

THAT EVENING, BRICE AND PHIL MET IN THE great room for drinks and snacks before dinner. To Brice's great regret, Lucas did not join them.

"Sometime he gets in a nasty mood and simply doesn't show up," Phil said, mixing a pitcher of whiskey sours. "The boy's probably up at his cabin drinking and brooding and listening to that abominable industrial music he savors. It sounds like the mating music at a marriage of baboons, if you ask me. So, give me more of the hideous details of your Nashville trauma. Those trashy periodicals gave you a tarring and feathering, didn't they? And do you ever hear from that loose-lipped Judas, Zac Lanier? That man needs a thrashing of the first order."

They had several rounds of drinks as Brice shared the humiliating details of his ruined career. They enjoyed a big meal of chicken and dumplings in the downstairs dining room, and then bowls of bread pudding, also the product of Lucas's culinary skills. Still the boy didn't show up. At evening's end, Brice bade Phil a good night and trudged back to his cabin. He fell asleep convinced that Lucas was avoiding him.

Brice slept fitfully and woke late. In the lodge's dining room, no one was about, though Doris Ann had left a note saying that oatmeal was ready in a pot on the stove. Brice had a bowl, along with a cup of coffee, then headed upstairs to check his e-mail in the cozy library that overlooked the pool.

"No more bad news yet," Brice muttered, shutting off the computer. He was examining the shelves for a book to browse through when Lucas appeared outside, a heavy-looking tool belt buckled around his lean waist. Brice raised his hand and gave the boy a smile, but Lucas ignored him, shifting his gaze to the pool deck and walking away.

"Man, do I have ageless charm or what?" Brice muttered to himself, watching the boy's fetching form disappear around a corner of the lodge. "Always attracted to the ones I can't have. It's an unerring gift. It's my mutant power." He pulled a book with an interesting title—*Greek Homosexuality*—off a shelf, slumped into a leather armchair, and flipped through black and white photos of erotic images adorning Greek pottery.

"'Men courting youths.' Shit. Just reminds me of what I'm missing," Brice groused, slamming the book onto a side table. "I need a long hike. Or a cold shower." Pulling on his coat and hat, he stepped out into the chilly air, determined to walk himself into exhaustion.

AFTER A LONG WALK ALONG the valley road and back, followed by a short nap, Brice returned to the lodge, expecting the cocktail-hour company of Phil at least, if not of Lucas. Instead he found another note, this one from Phil, who explained that he was spending the evening with his bridge club at Radclyffe's Roost and encouraged Brice to help himself to the vegetable beef soup Doris Ann had left in the fridge.

Brice did so. Feeling grim, he also helped himself to four bottled beers, some leftover bread pudding, and, back in the great room, a big glass of Scotch. He was sitting on one end of the big couch, staring numbly at the black ashes of the fireplace and heartily wishing that the last several years had never happened, when a door slammed behind him and Lucas entered the room.

"Hey," said Brice, watching the boy's unsteady movement toward the bar. *Been drinking. Boy that lean can't handle his booze as well as a big guy like me.* "What's up?"

Lucas said nothing. His back to Brice, he sloshed out bourbon into a glass and took a long sip before turning to regard Brice.

"Nothing's up. Still here, huh?" He squinted at Brice, as if the few yards between them had been quadrupled.

"Still here, yes. Do you mind?"

"Why should I mind?" Lucas gave his customary shrug. "I don't give a shit. Go or stay, I don't care."

"I'll stay then." Brice scratched his jaw. "Have a seat. I'd appreciate the company."

"Hell, why not?" Lucas sat heavily on the opposite end of the couch. "So, let's have a talk, Mr. Brown. I want to know how much Uncle Phil told you about me."

"He didn't—"

"Look, be honest. I hate liars. I can generally tell when folks are lying."

"Okay." Brice rested his chin in his hands. "He told me you'd dropped out of high school, started working at Walmart, and then got into some kind of trouble. 'Illegalities.' That's all he said."

"So discreet. 'Illegalities.'" Lucas sipped his drink and snickered. "So well-spoken. Such a gentleman, unlike my own redneck self. I was in prison, Mr. Brown." Lucas glared at Brice. "For several years. Are you shocked?"

Brice looked Lucas in the eye. "Not really. A couple of hunting buddies from my high school years went to prison. Two for dealing pot. One for beating his wife. Honestly, as hot as my temper is, I'm lucky not to have ended up there myself."

"So you still want my company?"

"Yes."

"Why?" Lucas cupped his hands behind his head. "Why would a celebrity like you want to spend time with an ex-con piece of poor white trash like me?"

"You're not trash."

"I'll take your word for it. So why?"

Brice shrugged, trying to look nonchalant. Even through the baggy sweatshirt, he could make out the kid's biceps-bulge. "I told you. I've been alone a lot."

"I don't think that's the real reason."

"Oh? What's the real reason then?"

"I think it's because you want me. Do you want me?"

Brice flinched. "Damn. Does making folks uncomfortable give you a thrill?"

Lucas grinned with triumph. "Yeah, it does. Answer the question."

"Why are you trying to put me on the spot?"

"What are you afraid of? Be brave, big man. Answer the question."

"Yeah, I want you." Brice fumbled with his Scotch and stared at a landscape painting on the wall to Lucas's left. "Who wouldn't? Anyone with eyes would, you cocky little shit."

"True. Have you paid for sex?"

Brice bit his lip and shifted uneasily. "We only met a couple days ago, and you're asking me that?"

"Yep. You said you want my company? Well, let's get to know one another then. Now you know one of my secrets. Only fair that you give up a few secrets in return, right?"

"Right. Okay. Yes, I have paid for sex." Brice forced himself to meet Lucas's amused gaze. "Many times. I was married, I was trying to act straight, but I wasn't straight, so I got horny as hell for other men. Easiest way to get sex on the sly was hustlers."

"Would you pay me? Only a hundred bucks, since you're a friend of Uncle Phil's."

"Jesus, Lucas!"

"That's my last question." Lucas grinned, obviously enjoying himself. "I promise."

"I would have at one time. I don't want to now."

"Why?"

"You said 'Last question.'"

"This is the same question, just follow-up." Lucas stretched out and propped his muddy work boots on the coffee table.

"Damn, boy. Were you raised in a barn? Get your feet off the table."

"Ain't your table. Well?"

"Because, as much as I—"

"As much as you want to fuck me?"

Brice stood up. "You're a real prick, aren't you? You think you're God's gift to everybody?"

Lucas rubbed his beard. "Yeah, some have called me that. They've handled my prick and called me God's gift, yes, indeed. Answer the question, and tomorrow we can split some wood together. I would appreciate your help. I would appreciate your company, big country star."

God, what a grin. Acting like a devil but smiling like an angel. Just my luck. "What was the question?"

Lucas snickered. "You are so fucking flustered right now, Daddy."

Brice moaned. "Daddy?"

"Don't you like that?"

"Not really," Brice lied. Having a boy this beautiful call him "Daddy" made his dick twitch.

"Uh huh. How old are you anyway? Wait. I know, 'cause I looked you up online when Uncle Phil told me you were coming. Your fan page has been taken down—I used to check that out every now and then—but I found info elsewhere."

"Scandal sheets online?"

"Yep. Nasty ones. You been raked over the coals, that's for damn sure. You turned forty last August. I'm twenty-seven. So I guess 'Daddy' is appropriate. The question was, 'Why won't you pay me?' If you say you've paid hustlers and you think I'm hot."

Brice rolled his eyes. "I didn't say you were hot."

"You said you wanted me. Same difference. If you answer the question, tomorrow, after we chop wood, we can take a hike together. There's a great overlook I'd like to show you. It's called Lee's Knob."

Brice kneaded his forehead. His skin felt hot, feverish. "I don't want to pay you because...because I'm trying to get away from my past and all my failures and mistakes. I'm tired of using and being used. I haven't ever been in a real relationship with another man...except for Zac."

"He's the asshole who outed you, right?"

"Yeah. And he did it because he's sick and he needed the money. And because I broke his heart because I was too much of a coward to be myself."

"So now?"

"So now I'm trying to figure out how to live a new life. It's hard."

Lucas dropped his feet to the floor and folded his arms across his chest. He stared at the cold hearth. "Yeah. It's hard for sure."

"I don't want to pay you because I don't want to use you. Look, yeah, I think you're a handsome guy, and we have some things in common. We've both had hard times. So, yeah, I want to get to know you. I know we just met, but, if we're going to be here together, maybe we should—"

"Yeah, yeah." Lucas abruptly stood. "I'll see you tomorrow. Let's grab some breakfast, say around ten. Then we can hit the woodyard." With that, the boy stumbled to the door and out into the night.

CHAPTER TWENTY-EIGHT

THE NEXT MORNING, BRICE WOKE EARLY AND HE woke hard, his head full of nebulous, fragmented images left behind by erotic dreams of Lucas. When he entered the lodge kitchen, he found the boy chopping parsley on the counter. By his elbow sat a paper-towel-covered plate of fried sausage patties. When Lucas gave Brice a curt nod, Brice noticed a shadow of weariness in his young face.

"Good morning," Brice said, mustering his cheeriest tone. "Nice and sunny today."

"Uh-huh. Coffee's in the carafe over there."

"Thanks." Brice poured a cup and seated himself at the table. For a few moments, silence prevailed, while Lucas broke eggs into a bowl and Brice appreciated his compact frame and purposeful movements.

"How'd you sleep?" Brice asked, trying to imagine the boy naked and slumbering.

Lucas stared intently into the bowl and beat the eggs hard. "So-so. Bad dreams. I have 'em a lot. Seems like every other night I'm beating up on someone. Sound sleep and me, we ain't exactly best buddies these days."

Brice chuckled. "Yeah, I get you. I have dreams like that every so often. I guess that's what comes of lots of hostile male hormones mixed with being perpetually pissed off. How you feeling? Seemed like you downed quite a bit of booze last night."

Lucas scowled into the eggs, then turned that scowl on Brice. "I'm an adult. I can drink as much as I damn well please."

I should have known he'd take that as a criticism. I've got to learn to watch my words around him, Brice thought. "Yep, we're both adults. I was just thinking that I'd be a little hung-over the morning after, if I were you."

"Yeah? Well, you ain't me." Lucas pulled a bacon-grease container from the fridge and spooned out a dollop into a cast-iron skillet heating on the stove, where it sizzled and popped. "Actually, I woke up with a headache, so I swallowed me some aspirins."

"Are you still up for chopping wood today?" Brice couldn't resist a mischievous grin. "Or do you even remember saying that? Do you remember anything you said last night?"

"Yep. I do. I remember everything." Lucas sighed and fell silent. He poured the eggs into the skillet, added salt, pepper, and chopped parsley, and stirred everything with a big wooden spoon. In another moment, he'd doled out the scrambled eggs and sausage patties. The two men took seats at opposite ends of the table, kept their eyes on their food, and ate without speaking.

This boy hates my guts, Brice thought with a flicker of despair. *The first guy I've met in ages that I feel a sort of savage tenderness toward, and he can't stand me. Why am I even here?* He wolfed down his food, barely registering the rich tastes. Standing, he carried his emptied plate to the sink, then turned, trying to appear nonchalant.

"So, hey, thanks. That was real tasty. I'm gonna check my e-mail now, so if you wanna get to that wood, just—"

"We'll get to that here in a bit." Lucas looked up at Brice with an expression that he couldn't read. "First, uh, I wanna talk to you about something. That all right? You got the time?"

Now you're mannerly? "I got all the time in the world." *Especially for a boy as handsome as you.* Brice leaned back against the counter and crossed his arms. "What's up?"

Lucas took a sip of coffee and fidgeted with his dirty napkin. "So, yeah, I do remember last night. How I acted. All flirty and, well, mean. Putting you on the spot and all. Asking you if you wanted me, if you'd pay me. I wudn't brought up to act like that, being nasty and vulgar to people who are trying to be nice to me. I was just real drunk… and, honestly, I've been pissed as hell ever since…."

Lucas paused. He looked up at Brice and furrowed his brow, as if he were trying to make up his mind.

"So you got the time, and I got stuff to say. Have another cup of coffee, man. Take a seat."

"Okay." Brice, curious and relieved, did as he was told. "So what d'you want to talk about?"

"Look, I.... Last night, you said that we'd both gone through rough times, that we had that in common. You're right. I know a good bit about the shit you've been dealing with, since it's been in the news and the tabloids and all. You got a raw deal, for sure. So, if you're gonna hang around here a while, I guess I oughta be straight with you. About why I went to prison. 'Cause I got a helluva raw deal too."

"You don't need to tell me if—"

"I'm not ashamed of what happened. Are you thinking I should be ashamed?" Lucas's face took on an expression of flushed defiance.

"Lord, calm down. Don't get all riled up. Tell me whatever you'd like."

"Okay. Shit. Sorry. Seems like every goddamn little thing sets me off and gets me breathing smoke and fire. So...."

Lucas leaned back in his chair, wrapped his arms around himself, and dropped his gaze to the tabletop.

"So, Uncle Phil always used to say that my looks would be my undoing, and I guess he was right. To tell you the truth...when the job at Walmart didn't pay enough, and it was looking like Mommy might lose the house, I.... Well, not to be indelicate, to use Uncle Phil's kinda phrasing, but I took to rampant whoring in truck stops along I-81."

"Damn. Really?" Brice wiped his mouth. The thought was vaguely exciting.

"Yep. Giving blowjobs in truck cabs and sleeper cabins. I made a decent amount of money, too."

"Well, I don't mean to be indelicate either, but as, uh, handsome as you are, I can see how men would be willing to pay you." *Just like I've been paying hustlers for years. Just the thought of you blowing another guy makes me want to shoot.*

"I was a damn fool. It's a mercy and a miracle—another of Uncle Phil's expressions—that I didn't end up with some nasty disease, though I did get crabs a few times. But then that little whoring hobby of mine led to prison."

"What happened?"

Lucas scratched at his buzz cut and slurped at his coffee. "Well, I only offered guys oral sex. But one day I ran across a man a lot bigger'n me who was determined to take more."

"Oh, no. And then what?"

"We were in his sleeper cabin. I fought him hard, but the bastard knocked me out. When I came to, he had me roped up and was about to rape me. But I managed to wiggle loose before that happened. I pulled a knife from my jacket pocket and stabbed the fucker in the thigh. That caused enough of a hullabaloo that other folks at the truck stop came running."

"What happened then?"

"The asshole claimed that he'd caught me trying to rob him, so I got arrested, which led to a big trial. Mr. Would-Be Rapist got on the stand and made a big fuss about being straight and married and a devout Christian. Then two other truckers testified that I'd propositioned them for sex at the same truck stop, which was true. The jury was loaded with tight-assed homo-haters. So I was convicted of prostitution and malicious assault. I spent six years in prison. Six goddamn years. Just before I got out, Uncle Phil bought this place. To give me a home, and other fucked-up queer kids the world's run over. So, are you horrified?"

"Horrifed?" Brice rubbed his brow and frowned. "Hell, no. Seems like your raw deal was a helluva lot worse than mine. Puts all my whiny career complaints in perspective."

"Pain's pain. We've both endured some major shit, that's for sure." Lucas finished his coffee and stood. "So, enougha the soul-baring. You wanna get to that wood?"

"Sure. I need to work off some breakfast. I'm not exactly in tip-top shape these days. Been eating and drinking too much since all that happened last fall."

"You look fine to me," Lucas said. "You were too damn skinny on that last CD cover."

"You know my CDs?"

Lucas ignored the question. "C'mon, Paul Bunyan. Let's get some work done." Grabbing his ball cap off the sideboard, he headed up the stairs. Brice happily followed, admiring Lucas from behind.

CHAPTER TWENTY-NINE

By the time they got to the top of the wooded slope, Brice was panting but trying to hide it. The contrast between his beer-gut trudge and Lucas's lean lope was not flattering. Several hours of splitting and stacking wood had about worn him out. His fingers ached, as did his lower back.

"Here we are. Lee's Knob," Lucas said, leading Brice out onto a rocky ledge set high above Brantley Valley. Above them, the sky had cleared, an icy azure. The wind was cold and brisk, convincing both men to turn their collars up. Late afternoon sun slanted over Lucas's face as he pointed out landmarks.

"Out there's Helvetia. It's a sweet little town settled by Swiss immigrants. Some damn good eating in the restaurant there. And a great ramp feed, come April. That way's Pickens. Highest rainfall in the state. That way's Elkins. Down there—can you see it?—is Grace and Amie's store."

"It's all beautiful," Brice said, moving in a slow circle to take in all 360 degrees of gray-blue mountains receding into winter sky. "Why did I spend all that time in Nashville? Hell, it's called *country* music for a reason. Did you grow up in this county?"

Lucas nudged a rock over the edge with his boot. "Yep. Grew up in Mabie. Little piss-ant shack, but we were happy there. Last time I was happy, I guess."

"Happy's hard," Brice said, studying Lucas's downcast face.

"Ain't that the fucking truth? Helps to be ignorant of the world, and I sure was. Then Daddy died in that mine accident." Lucas took his ball cap off and rubbed his scalp.

"That's when you quit school, right?"

"Yep. I was a busy boy. Working Walmart during the day, hustling truck stops at night. Man, what was I thinking?" Lucas shook his head. "A few of those guys were hot. Most of 'em…not. Still, the horny way they all fawned on me and pawed me made me feel…important, I guess. It felt good to be desired, y'know?"

"Yeah, I'd imagine so. Not that I've felt desired much lately."

"You're shitting me. Your fans must have been all over you."

"My *female* fans were all over me. That felt good, but it wasn't like being wanted by another man. Now that everybody knows I'm a faggot, no one wants me. Talk about love turning to hate. You should have read some of the hate mail I've received."

Lucas grimaced. "Hate mail? Assholes."

"Enough about me. You were talking about those truckers."

"Yeah. The ego food felt as good as being paid, especially if they were handsome." Lucas kicked another pebble over the edge. "That trucker I stabbed was one of the best-looking men I'd ever seen. If we'd met in other circumstances, if he hadn't tried to force me, hell, I might have let him do what he wanted to do."

"Really?" *Damn, you look sad. I wish I could hug you right now.*

"As it was," Lucas continued, "when I resisted him, he punched me in the face so hard I passed out. Came to with my hands tied behind my back and a nasty rag taped in my mouth, and him with his prick out, greasing it up and rarin' to go."

"I'm glad you got loose. If I were you, I'd have stabbed him too."

"You know what that got me. Shit, I should have just rolled over and let him screw me. Wouldn't have hurt half as much as what came next. Six years of my life down the fucking toilet." Lucas hawked and spat over the ledge, then stuffed his hands into his pockets.

"Was that terrible? Prison?"

Lucas spat again. He took a step back and glowered at Brice. "That, I ain't gonna talk about. Just 'cause I told you all that other stuff don't mean we're bosom buddies or anything."

Brice put up his hands in a conciliatory gesture. "Hey, I'm sorry. Didn't mean to pry. How about we head back and I help you make dinner?"

"Do as you please." Lucas hunched his shoulders and stalked down the hill the way they'd come. Brice followed, cursing himself for bringing up a conversation-derailing question and looking forward to the back-medicine anesthetic of a stiff drink.

"Lucas, honey, those pants are so tight they're like a cheap hotel."

Downstairs in the kitchen, the cabbage rolls Brice and Lucas had collaborated on were simmering. Upstairs in the great room, the cocktail hour had begun. Phil had set out a plate of cheeses: Brie, Cheddar, and Maytag blue. All three men were drinking, Phil in an armchair with a glass of white wine, Lucas at one end of the couch with a bottle of IPA, and Brice at the other end with a tumbler of Scotch neat. Before them, another fire Lucas had set up flickered and popped.

"And how are they like a cheap hotel, Uncle Phil?" Lucas twisted his mouth in amused expectation.

"There's no ball room!" Phil howled.

"I told you he was a hoot," Lucas said. He leaned back into the corner of the couch, spread his legs a little wider, and yawned. Brice took a furtive look at the boy's crotch and mentally agreed with Phil's assessment.

"Did you two have a nice day together?"

"We did," Brice replied. "Had a good breakfast, got some wood chopped, took a hike. I'm gonna sleep well tonight."

Lucas nodded. "Mr. Brown and I had a talk or two. He even helped me make dinner."

"You talked to someone? You, my misfit nephew? Lucas Bryan, the brooding and asocial misanthrope? The weightlifting recluse?"

"Yep. Hard to believe, I know. I talk too little and you talk too much. Why don't you tell Mr. Brown about what happened by that baggage carousel the last time you flew to Florida?"

"Oh, yes! Well, there I was, minding my own business and waiting for my bag to show up at the Fort Lauderdale Airport when this little old lady came up to me—I guess she was looking for a representative of her cruise line—and she looked up at me and said, in this itty-bitty voice, "Are you Princess?"

"And what did you do then, Uncle Phil?"

"Well, then I put my hands on my hips and I said, 'No, ma'am! I'm no princess! I'm a queen!' I mean, I wasn't going to be demoted right there by the baggage carousel!"

Lucas guffawed. "That is so fucking funny. I love that story."

"What did she say?" Brice gasped.

"Oh, she just laughed and patted me on the arm and tottered off, God love her. I hope she had a fine cruise."

"I better check on those cabbage rolls." Lucas stood. "By the way, when you leaving for Florida? Real soon, right?"

"Day after tomorrow. I'll be gone for about six weeks. And I'm giving Doris Ann a couple of months off, since she wants to visit her sick sister up in Moorefield. So it'll just be you two. What y'all planning to do for Valentine's Day? It's coming up soon."

Lucas and Brice exchanged glances. Lucas made a wry face, and Brice shrugged. *Six weeks alone with him? If he doesn't warm up to me pretty soon, I'm going to lose my mind. Maybe coming here wasn't the best idea after all.*

"Hell, I don't know. Eat chocolate till we throw up?" Lucas knocked back the rest of his beer before tramping off to the kitchen.

"Little monster," Phil said, watching his nephew go. "He could do with a few sessions of Charm School. He was much more mannerly before...those troubles I've referred to."

"Before prison?"

"He told you?" Phil blurted, then lowered his voice. "I'm amazed."

Brice lowered his voice as well. "Yep, he told me. About the hustling, about the trucker who tried to rape him, about the trial. I can't believe that stupid-as-fuck jury sent him to prison instead of his assailant."

"Never underestimate the power of rural homophobia. I'm floored that he's shared all that with you. He must be coming to trust you already."

"Not so sure about that. One minute, he's civil, and the next, he's acting like he wishes I'd drop dead. Every conversation with him feels like I'm walking on eggshells. I really pissed him off today when I asked what his prison time was like."

Phil bit his lip. "I know it was deeply unpleasant. He's never told me about it in any detail. A boy as handsome as he is...I figure that what he narrowly managed to prevent in that truck he had to endure quite a bit in there, though he assures me that he's still free of disease. I do know that he was attacked, because his mother and I visited him in the prison hospital a few months before he was released. His torso was all bandaged up."

"Shit. How bad was the attack?"

"I'm not sure. He refused to give us the details." Phil nodded in the direction of the pool. "When he swims here in the summer, I can see his scars, but when I ask him about them, he just shakes his head and walks away. As you can imagine, when he came out of prison, he was much different from the boy he was when he'd gone in. All the angers and resentments and insecurities he'd already had were intensified."

"I'll bet they were. It makes me feel a little sick when I think of all he's likely been through."

"I feel the same. You two ought to do something nice for Valentine's Day. Just to have a reason to celebrate, to do something different, to get off the compound for a while. Maybe have a nice dinner in Elkins. There's an elegant mansion there with a fine restaurant."

"Valentine's Day," Brice murmured. "I guess that meant something to me once, during those first few years of marriage when I'd just about convinced myself that Shelly and I had something real. She sure insisted that I make a big fuss out of the holiday. Roses, candy, fancy dinner out...."

"You've never celebrated Valentine's Day with another man?"

"Naw. Never got that chance. Never gave myself that chance."

"Lucas hates the holiday for that very reason. The only love he's received from men has been in the form of rampant genitals and cold cash."

"He's never been involved with another guy romantically?"

"Not that I'm aware of. Who knows what went on in prison? I quail to think of it. Well, tomorrow is another day, as Miss Scarlett famously declared. As for Valentine's Day, you two tortured wrecks ought to keep each another company. It'll be like *Wuthering Heights* set in West Virginia. God knows Lucas needs—"

"This stuff's ready!" Lucas shouted up the stairs.

Phil drained his wine and stood. "Would you be kind enough to escort my faded glory down to dinner? I'm hungry enough to eat a bear's butt."

DURING THE MEAL, PHIL REGALED them with an assortment of outrageous travel stories that had Brice aching with laughter. Afterward, Phil pled exhaustion and retired to his quarters in a wing of the lodge. Brice helped Lucas clean up, trying and failing to start up a conversation with the boy, who seemed as distant as ever, despite their frank chats earlier in the day.

Chores done, Lucas gave Brice a brusque "Good night" and, without waiting for a reply, slipped out the back door of the kitchen. Through the window, Brice watched him climb a circular staircase to the pool deck and fade into the darkness.

Shit, I thought we'd found some kinda rapport today, Brice thought, wiping down the counters a final time. *What do I do with this longing? Is desire always pointless? Always destructive? Not for some folks, but certainly for me. Wanting other men has wrecked everything. What kind of mass-murdering son of a bitch was I in my last life?*

Restless, Brice climbed the stairs to the bar, poured himself another Scotch, and wandered around the rest of the lodge. He shot a solitary game of pool. He sat on the dark screened-in porch, rocking in a rocking chair, listening to a fine rain on the tin roof and enjoying the invigorating cold that nipped him out of postprandial sluggishness.

Downstairs, he found a tiny massage room, a shower, a steam room, a dry sauna, and, in a sort of dim grotto, a hot tub steaming beneath a padded covering. For a moment, he contemplated a long soak in the jets to ease his sore back but decided to put that off for another evening, perhaps one during which he could convince Lucas to join him in the tub. *I want to study his scars. I want to memorize his every tattoo,* Brice thought. *And now I'm thinking like some kind of lovesick schoolboy. At age forty. Pathetic.*

Brice returned to the great room. He stood by the piano, picking at it, a few chords from the last set of songs he'd written, composed well over a year ago. The first few notes of a new melody drifted through his mind, but when he tried to follow it with his fingers, he lost it.

"Played out," he sighed. "No point. You fucking has-been. You fucking washed-up loser."

Brice slumped into an armchair. He watched the fire fading into embers behind its grate, sipped his Scotch, and sifted through memories of what Lucas had said to him earlier, trying to pinpoint some certain and solid clue that might reveal how the beautiful boy regarded him. Did Lucas despise him, did Lucas like him, did Lucas pity him, did Lucas hold him in complete and utter contempt? Brice was unable to marshal enough evidence to support any theory save for one: that the young man was as much of a contradictory, confused, emotional mess as he was, if not more so.

"Bad, bad combo," he sighed, knocking back the last of his drink as the familiar feeling of dull despair spread like tar in the pit of his stomach.

Brice tugged on his jacket and cap and lumbered out onto the pool deck. There, he lifted his face to the night sky and felt the cold rain misting his liquor-flushed face. In a line of empty guest rooms overlooking the pool, Brice found a small gym, furnished with a few weightlifting machines and racked free weights.

I'd like to watch him work out. While he's shirtless. Maybe he'd let me work out with him? God knows I could stand to firm up. Where does he live anyway? The first time I saw him, he came out of the woods on the far side of the pool.

On a whim, Brice returned to the pool deck. *There. He was standing beneath that little grove of trees over there. Redbuds, looks like. And there's a flight of stairs heading up the hill.*

Brice crossed the deck and started up the wooden steps. They were slick, so he gripped the railing as he climbed. The steps ended in a small graveled space—parking for the rooms above the pool, Brice assumed. He peered up the hill. *There. A light among the trees. And here's a gravel driveway.*

Brice followed the gravel path into the woods and up the slope. Soon he was standing beside a cabin much like his own, set against the slope of the mountain, with an elevated porch in front and a Ford pickup truck parked in back. He could hear faint music playing inside. Around him, the drizzle thickened, moistening the shoulders of his jacket and dripping off the brim of his cap.

Brice stepped onto the back porch and moved toward the nearest window. *Don't get caught, Brice. Being revealed as a stalker or peeping Tom is not going to endear you to that sullen boy.* The music paused. He stood to one side of the lit pane and peered inside.

What he saw was the cabin's living room. Lucas lay sleeping on a couch near the window into which Brice gazed. He was sprawled on his side, facing the embers of a hearth-fire. His head, on the far end of the couch, rested on a cushion. An afghan covered him, except for the pale skin of his bare right shoulder.

Is he naked under there? Jesus. Brice stood, transfixed, one hand gripping the other. Then the music began again, and Brice nearly gasped out loud. He knew that series of chords in E minor better than anyone in the world.

*My God. I don't believe it. I don't **believe** it. "Hard Gray Rain." Title song of my first album! The kid is playing one of my CDs. The little bastard has been giving me the cold shoulder, and he's up here listening to **my** music.*

A flicker of joy burst in Brice's throat. He swallowed hard, took one last look at the exposed skin of Lucas's shoulder, then backed away from the window, padded off the edge of the porch, and made his way over crunching gravel back down the hill toward the lodge.

CHAPTER THIRTY

"Long drive to the Charleston airport," Lucas said. "But Florida will be good for him. The winters are harder and harder on him lately. Only reason he stayed here as long as he did this season was 'cause he knew you were coming."

On a gray February dawn, Lucas and Brice stood before the lodge, watching Phil's car bump down the hill. As soon as it disappeared around the corner, Lucas turned his back on Brice. "See you around."

"Hey," Brice said. "Are you lifting weights today? I'm thinking I could do with some exercise. Maybe we could lift together? I haven't gotten to a gym in months."

Lucas shook his head and kept walking. "Ain't lifting weights today."

"Do you want to meet for dinner at least?" Brice followed Lucas into the lodge.

"Nope. Gotta study. There's some beef stew in the fridge. Help yourself to that any time you want."

"How about a hike later, if you want a break? Or a drive? You could show me more of this county. I'd love to see that Swiss town you mentioned."

Lucas turned, scowling. "I ain't here to entertain you, Mr. Brown. I know you were used to the high life before, and the attention of lots of fans and minions, but you ain't gonna find that here."

"Fine." Brice shook off a wave of hot anger mingled with sick disappointment. "I realize that. Good luck with your studies." Face flushed and set, Brice tramped back to his cabin.

Later that day, Brice sat in the library of the lodge, staring at the desktop computer screen. He reread the e-mail message with numb disbelief. When his eyes teared up, he wiped at them.

> *Dear Brice,*
>
> *This morning, I was having breakfast with a representative of the Country Music Museum and Hall of Fame. He mentioned in passing that, due to the recent revelations about your sexuality, they had dismantled the exhibit about you. Last month, apparently.*
>
> *This conversation led to a long-delayed revelation of my own.*
>
> *I've put this off long enough. I haven't wanted to hurt you, but today I realized that my silence must be inflicting a terrible kind of hurt on you already.*
>
> *I'm afraid that it's time for our professional connection to end. After all that's happened, I see no way that your career can be resuscitated and no way that I can help you.*
>
> *None of this is your fault. I understand why you kept such an enormous secret from me. You can't control being the kind of man you are. Unfortunately, we also cannot control the kind of society we live in, and the conservatism of country music fans is such that I can't imagine that you have any hope of a future career in Nashville.*
>
> *I'm so, so sorry. Wherever you are, please take care.*
>
> *Regretfully,*
> *Your friend,*
> *Steve Morgan*

Brice turned off the computer. He walked out of the library and into the great room. There, he took a half-full pint bottle of Ezra Brooks from the bar, opened it, and put it to his mouth. He gulped a big mouthful, then another, then another, and then another, till the bottle was empty. He sat on the couch and put his head in his hands, waiting for the welcome numbness inebriation brings. Soon enough, it came.

Ahhhh, yeah. Like wading waist-deep in dark, warm water. Relieved, he stretched out on the couch and closed his eyes.

When Brice came to, it was late afternoon. He lay there for a few minutes, drowsy, still drunk, staring at the ceiling and trying not to think of anything. For a few seconds, he succeeded. Then it was all there again, surrounding him and hemming him in: his great ambitions, the grand lies of his past, his humiliating exposure, the forwarded letters from former fans full of hate, Wayne's abrupt reappearance and just as abrupt disappearance, Steve's e-mail message, hard-faced and handsome Lucas turning from him and walking away. And tomorrow, nothing but grim gray, every breath a pointless effort, every day off key, a sour flat, dragging himself around in his heavy, aging, loveless body.

Brice sat up and nausea flooded him. He rose, ready to dash to the toilet to vomit, when the urge just as quickly faded. He grabbed a bottle of Perrier from the fridge beneath the bar and gulped down every drop. Then, leaving his hat and coat behind, he opened the door and staggered out onto the pool deck.

To the west, the winter sun was close to setting. Snowmelt dripped from the eaves. In the redbud grove, a flock of chickadees was chattering. Somewhere, incongruous, a bass guitar thumped dance music.

What the fuck is that? Obnoxious. I drive all the way out here to get me some sweet country silence, and now this? Sounds like a fucking gay bar.

Brice followed the sound toward the line of rooms overlooking the pool. There, through the wide floor-to-ceiling windows of the gym, he could see Lucas. The boy was bareheaded, dressed in a snug black A-shirt, baggy gray nylon shorts, and black running shoes. Several silver chains hung about his neck. He sat on a padded bench, working his way through a set of biceps concentration curls with a metal dumbbell.

Brice's first reaction was awe. *Those pale shoulders. Those thorny tattoos. Man, look at those arms bulge. Yep, that's a decent dusting of chest hair, all right. Pretty, pretty curves, those pecs beneath his undershirt. And those furry calves. Holy Jesus, he's just as sexy as I imagined he'd be.*

Brice's second reaction was rage. He threw open the door and stepped inside, glaring. "Hey, Lucas. How's that workout going?"

Lucas looked up, startled. He dropped the dumbbell with a thud. "Shit, you scared me."

"I thought you said you weren't going to work out today, but here you are."

Guilt flashed across Lucas's face, then annoyed defiance.

"Yeah. So? I changed my mind. I got more work done this afternoon than I thought. I needed a break."

"I told you I wanted to work out with you. Did you forget that?"

Lucas moved to the incline bench. "I got more things on my mind than what you want, Mr. Brown. Did you expect me to send you an engraved invitation? You're welcome to work out in here any time you want." Hooking his feet beneath the rounded pad, he began a set of sit-ups.

Brice leaned back against the wall. Between the aftermath of so much bourbon and his present blaze of anger, his head was spinning. "Jesus. You don't want any goddamn thing to do with me at all, do you?"

"I sure don't right now, the way you're acting," Lucas said. Hands folded behind his head, he arced upward, touching his elbows to his knees.

"You act like you hate my guts. You act like I've done you some wrong. Why is that?"

"You're imagining things. Leave me alone, goddamn it."

"Answer me, boy," Brice growled. "Look at me when I'm talking to you."

Lucas did another sit-up and then another. He lay back on the pad, head slanted downward, and rolled his eyes up at Brice. "Don't talk to me like I'm a child. I ain't no boy. I ain't your son. I ain't here to cater to you. You, you, you. It ain't all about you. It ain't all about you and your satisfaction."

"Thank you for that helpful reminder." Brice pushed himself away from the wall, swaying. "As if the whole *fucking world* for the last few *fucking months* hasn't already made that crystal clear. You're an arrogant little bastard. Someone should kick your ass."

"Yeah, right." Lucas slipped off the incline bench and righted himself. "You? Try it, Mr. Brown." He clenched his right fist and rubbed it in his cupped left palm.

Brice snorted. "You scrawny little shit. Big as I am, I could wipe up the floor with you."

"Maybe." Lucas was clenching both fists now. "Except I probably know a lot more about taking a guy down than you. While you were strutting across the stage of the Grand Ole Opry, or living in that big mansion with your pretty wife and fucking hustler boys like me on the side, or driving around on your fancy bikes or in your fancy sports cars, I was learning how to fight dirty in prison."

"You little prick," Brice snarled, stepping forward, hands clenched. For a split-second, he contemplated punching the kid in the face. Then he thought of what had happened to Lucas in that truck, and what most likely had happened to the boy behind bars, and his anger flared up, deflated, and died.

Jesus. So young and handsome. So wounded and angry. What the fuck am I doing? He's gone through far more shit than I have. Brice swayed and stumbled backward. He rubbed his face, staring down at Lucas, who stood tense, still poised to offer him a fistfight.

"You're all defense, ain't you? What's the use? Why should I give a fuck how you…. First Steve, and now…."

"Steve? Who's Steve? Hey, are you drunk?" Lucas said, lowering his fists.

"Look, I'm sorry. I shouldn't have come here." Brice coughed and took a step back. "I'm going home now. I don't belong here. You sure as hell don't want me here. I don't want to be here. Tell Phil I appreciated the break."

"Hey! What d'you mean, you're going home?"

"Home. Hinton."

"Now? You're driving to Hinton now?"

"Yes, I am. Me being here ain't helping anybody."

Brice turned, bumping into the doorframe. Lucas grabbed him by the arm.

"You ain't driving to Hinton now, you moron! It's nearly dark, and you're drunk. Plus it's supposed to snow tonight. What kinda fucking fool are you? You'll end up driving into a tree or over the side of the road."

"Leave me be," Brice said, shaking Lucas's hand off. "Why should you care? I can't stand to be here now."

"Why? Why the rush?"

"You being plumb hateful is one damn reason. I think I wore out my welcome with you the day I got here. Why the shit should any man stay in a place where he isn't wanted?"

"You ain't driving anywhere tonight," Lucas said, grabbing Brice by the arm yet again.

"Get off, kid," Brice growled, trying and failing to pull his arm from Lucas's insistent grip.

"No," Lucas said. "You listen to me now—"

"Shut up and let go of me." The more Brice pulled away, the harder Lucas held him.

"Listen to me, Brice," Lucas hissed between gritted teeth. "You don't want—"

"Don't tell me what I fucking want."

For another furious moment, the two men grappled and swayed. "Get OFF!" Brice yelled, slamming his palm hard against Lucas's chest.

Lucas staggered backward, wide-eyed. He tripped over the leg of a weight bench, spun sideways, and fell, slamming face first into the side of a Nautilus machine.

"Damn!" he wailed, dropping to his knees and holding his head.

"Oh, holy shit," Brice groaned. In a second, sober with shock, he was kneeling beside Lucas.

"I'm so sorry. I'm so sorry." He wrapped an arm around the boy. "Here now. Let me help."

"You big, dumb, drunk bastard," Lucas snarled. "Don't touch me."

"Let me see," Brice insisted, cupping the boy's chin.

"No." Lucas twisted away. "Ain't you done enough damage?"

"I didn't mean to hurt you. Let me see. Keep still," Brice said. His hands were trembling, with shock and guilt and the feeling of Lucas's hard body against his.

Lucas resisted for a moment more before letting Brice examine him. The boy's right eye was bruising up, but his cheekbones and nose seemed undamaged.

"Come on," Brice said, helping Lucas to his feet.

"Whoa. Dizzy," Lucas moaned, swaying.

Brice clasped the boy's tattoo-sleeved left arm. "Easy now. You're gonna be all right, I think. But maybe I should take you to the emergency room anyway. Where's the nearest hospital?"

"Elkins. Shit, no. No hospital. I'm fine."

"You sure?"

"Hell, yes. I just need to lie down for a while."

"Okay. Come on. I got you. Come on now."

Brice wrapped an arm around Lucas's waist. The boy's scent was strong. *Damn, what a fuck-up I am. Damn, but you smell good.* "Let's get you…where? To your cabin or the lodge?"

"Cabin. Just up the hill." Lucas leaned against Brice. "Damn. So dizzy. You asshole. You asshole."

"Yep, asshole. I claim that. I got you. Let's go." Brice took a deep breath, inhaling Lucas's rich aroma, before helping the dazed boy out the door and up the hill into the forest.

"Lemme just rest here a minute, okay?" Lucas leaned against the back of his couch with a groan. He fingered his swollen eye. "Damn, that hurts. How's it look?"

"Like hell. I truly apologize. Can I get you anything?" Brice asked.

"A bottle of whiskey, a glass of water, and a couple aspirin? Liquor's in the cupboard across from the stove. Pills are in the bathroom cabinet over the sink."

After Lucas had gulped his pills and taken a few swigs of Tullamore Dew, Brice helped him up the stairs to the bedroom. Lucas sat on the bed, bent forward, and fumbled with his shoelaces.

"Ummm," he grunted, cupping his head in his hands. "Too shaky. Shit."

"Hey, hey. Lemme do that." Brice knelt by the bed, unlaced and pulled off Lucas's shoes, then helped him stretch out on the bed and pulled the covers over him. Lucas sighed and stared up at the ceiling.

"Thanks."

"I'm so sorry, kid. I shouldn't have.... I really, really, really didn't mean to hurt you."

"You big dumb fuck. I know that." Lucas gave Brice a pained grin. "Shit just got outta hand. Happens with guys all the time. Why were you so damn drunk anyway?"

"I got a couple pieces of real bad news today. I'll tell you about it later."

"Okay." Lucas closed his eyes.

Brice interlocked his fingers and studied the boy's bruised face. *God, what have I done? You could have been hurt bad, even killed, if you'd fallen the wrong way. I want to stroke your face so bad. I want to climb into bed with you and beg your forgiveness and hold you all night. Brice, you are the biggest fucking fool God ever had the deep regret of creating.*

"So you need anything else?"

Lucas opened his eyes. He looked very, very tired.

"Naw. Thanks."

"Okay. Well, I better leave you to sleep."

"Yeah, I could do with some shut-eye. But, hey? Don't go, okay? I don't want you to go."

Brice cocked his head. "Do you mean....?"

Grimacing, Lucas shifted, pulling the blankets higher. He blinked up at Brice. "I mean, don't you fucking dare drive to Hinton tonight. I mean, I want you to stay here with us at Homo Central, Phagg Heights, whatever Uncle Phil's calling it these days. I mean, I want you to stay here tonight. I've been awful to you, I know. But would you please stay anyway? On the couch? There's lots of extra blankets in the closet over there."

Brice smiled. "Sure, kid. Be glad to. Least I can do."

"Great. Good night."

"Good night."

Brice rummaged in the closet. He found a woolen blanket and a quilt. When he turned toward the bed again, Lucas had rolled over, his back to Brice.

Brice wanted to sit by the bed and watch Lucas sleep. Instead, he turned off the bedside lamp and descended the narrow steps to the living room. He drank a big glass of water and pissed. Then he sat back on the couch in the dark, wrapped in blankets, and stared at the cold hearth.

Mommy used to talk about grace. God's love for the undeserving. Well, there you go. Here it is. It does exist.

CHAPTER THIRTY-ONE

BRICE ROLLED ONTO HIS BACK, GRUNTING AT THE hungover throbbing in his head. Bright sunlight and thick silence filled the cabin. He lay on the couch, remembering the previous evening's scuffle, quailing at the possible futures that sheer luck and chance had permitted him to escape.

I've got to stop drinking so damn much. Lucas could have ended up in the hospital, or, worse, the morgue. But he asked me to stay here anyway. Amazing. I can't believe it. How will he act today, though? Like a little shit? Or different? I never know what to expect from the beautiful bastard. If he's surly again, I should just leave, no matter what he said last night. He was probably so stunned he didn't know what he was saying. Probably didn't matter whether it was me who stayed over or not. Could have been anybody, I suspect. He just didn't want to be alone. Why should I hang around here, hankering after a boy I want so damn bad but can't have?

Brice's confused cogitations were interrupted by footsteps upstairs, then the noisy gurgle of a piss-stream in the toilet, then the commode's flush, and then, after a rustling pause, the thud of Lucas descending the stairs. *Here we go,* thought Brice. *Congenial or crabby, it's anyone's guess. Mercurial brat.*

"Hey, brawler. How'd you sleep?" Lucas rounded the couch by Brice's head. He was fully dressed, in jeans, blue plaid flannel shirt, and heavy boots. He crossed his arms and gave Brice a smile as warm as the sunlight flooding the room. The brightness of his expression contrasted dramatically with the bruised black of his right eye.

Thank God. He's in a good mood despite that

shiner I gave him, Brice thought, tossing off his blankets, heaving himself into a sitting position, and wincing at renewed pain in his back. *Damn couch. Damn aging joints. Ain't the boy I used to be.*

"I slept fine, though I got a headache after all that damn bourbon I sucked down. That's a helluva black eye you got. Again, I'm really sorry that—"

"Forget it. You apologized already." Lucas gave Brice's guilt a dismissive wave. "Let's just not get into a stupid scrape like that again, okay?"

Brice nodded. "Deal."

"Great." Lucas peered out the window. "It snowed real big last night, just as predicted. You hungry?"

"Yeah. Yeah, I am. Didn't eat any dinner yesterday."

"As I recall, you drank dinner. How about some breakfast?"

"Sure. Here or down the hill at Grace's store?"

"Here. The lodge, that is."

"Great." Brice tried to rise and flinched. "Shit."

"What's wrong?" Lucas raised an eyebrow.

"Bad back. Thanks to all the stress I've been dealing with, all the shit that's on my mind. Runs in the family. Daddy used to be damn near incapacitated sometimes."

Lucas offered Brice a hand. "Here. Last night, you helped me. Now I help you."

Brice took Lucas's warm hand and rose with a pained grunt. "Thanks. You feeling all right?"

"Just fine." Lucas shrugged, gingerly touching his swollen eye. "Though I ain't gonna be posing for no spreads in gay porn mags any time soon. Not the first time a big, good-looking guy has blackened my eye. I reckon I've made a career of it."

"Good-looking? Did you just give me a compliment? Did they just set up a snow-cone stand in Hell?"

Lucas grinned. "Don't let your head get all swole up."

Brice grinned back. "I doubt you'd let that happen. You're talking about that trucker punching you, huh?"

"Yeah. Plus guys in prison. Eric did it regular, to keep me in line. Where's your coat?"

"Down at the lodge. Eric?"

Lucas's expression grew melancholy. He lifted his black denim jacket off a hook, pulled it on, and cocked his black ball cap over his eyes. "Story for another time. After a few stiff drinks. You like buckwheat cakes and bacon? With sorghum and maple syrup?"

"Hell, sure. Most mountain boys do. You cooking?"

"I am, Mr. Brown. It's your belated 'Ex-Con-Welcomes-Country-Star-to-Phagg-Heights' breakfast."

"Sounds great. You gonna call me 'Brice' now?"

"Whatever you want. C'mon, Big Brice. Help me shovel out some, and then I'll mix up the batter and heat up the griddle."

Lucas hesitated, surveying Brice and slipping on a pair of sunglasses. "On second thought, with that bad back of yours, how about I shovel us out and you can fry the bacon?"

"Yep. Sorry to be of so little help." *Great. Now he thinks of me as old, broke-down, and weak.*

"Pore ole man." Lucas gave Brice a gentle clap on the back. "Needs a young buck to take care of him."

Grabbing a snow shovel by the door, Lucas stepped out onto the snow-heaped back deck. Astounded, Brice followed, feeling more smitten than ever.

BRICE FLIPPED THE BACON AND watched Lucas's lean frame cross to the fridge for buttermilk. *Damn. That butt looks like something Michelangelo sculpted.* "I love buckwheat cakes. Y'ever been to the Buckwheat Festival in Kingwood? I went every September when I was in college at WVU."

"Yep. Fun." Lucas measured out buttermilk, poured it into a zinc bowl, added eggs and buckwheat flour, and mixed up the ingredients with a wooden spoon. "I used to get a kick outta the livestock and ag exhibits. Biggest goddamn pumpkin I ever saw was there. One year, I won a raffle and the prize was a colt. After a couple of weeks, Daddy made me sell it, though. Said we didn't have the money to feed it. I'd already named it Bucephalus, 'cause we'd been hearing about Alexander the Great in school." Lucas shook his head. "I cried for a week."

"Tough little swaggering shit like you?" Brice blurted before he knew what he was saying. "I can't imagine you crying."

Lucas turned, his face solemn. "I've shed a few tears in my life. I s'pect we're all a little deeper and more complicated than we appear."

"Sorry. That was a stupid thing to say."

For a few minutes, both men were silent, backs to each other. Brice tonged up the bacon onto a plate lined with paper towels.

"This done enough for you?" he said, lifting the plate.

"Looks like. Bring it on over here. Gimme a taste."

"Well, sure."

Brice crossed the kitchen, broke off a piece of bacon, and held it up. Rather than reaching for it, Lucas looked Brice in the eye and nibbled it from his fingers.

Brice gave a low laugh. "You're a fucking tease, y'know that? You're like a completely different person today. Did that blow to the head give you brain damage?"

Lucas licked his lips and wiped his mouth. "I know I've been a prick." He stepped over to the stove, drained a little of the bacon grease into a tin, then placed the griddle back on the stovetop and turned up the heat. "So let's start over. Let's pretend we just met."

"All right. That would be a pleasure and a relief. I'm Brice Brown. Would you like more coffee?"

"I'm Lucas Bryan," Lucas said, stirring the batter. "Yes, please, I'd like more coffee, sir."

Brice poured them both fresh cups. Lucas took his and smiled up at Brice, blue-gray eyes free of the guarded caution Brice was so used to discerning in them. Lucas turned and poured dollops of batter onto the griddle. "So you wanna tell me about Steve? The guy you mentioned last night before...."

"Before a big drunk redneck attacked you? Yeah." Brice sat on a stool by the kitchen counter, studying Lucas's broad shoulders, lean hips, and plump butt from behind. "Steve Morgan was my manager. The important word there is 'was.'"

"Uh-oh. So.... Uncle Phil told me some things, and I've read a buncha shit in gossip rags and country-music magazines and stuff online, but I have no fucking idea how much of it all is true. You wanna fill me in on the real story? From the horse's mouth?"

"Hmmm. Maybe after a few shots of bourbon. A little early for that, though. Especially after all I drank last night."

"Story's that painful, huh? Well, how about mimosas? Uncle Phil likes me to mix those every now and then. Nice cheery drink for a cold winter's day."

"Champagne?" Dubious, Brice furrowed his brow. "What's to celebrate?"

"Hell, I'm outta prison, after six frigging years. You're far away from those assholes who've been persecuting you. We're in this big, comfy lodge all nestled up in pretty, snowy mountains. We're here together, and we're about to have a helluva hillbilly breakfast."

"Together, huh? You *really* want me here?"

"Yep. Don't make me repeat myself. Long as you don't shove me around any more. I've had enough of that in my life."

"No more shoving around, I swear. And you're not gonna act like a chilly bastard any more?"

Lucas sniggered. "I'll do my best. The chilly-bastard act was starting to wear me out, to be honest. Guess it's easier to be nice."

"Hear, hear. All right. Mimosas it is. Sounds great. Mix away."

"Okay. You keep an eye on the pancakes. This batch is about ready."

Brice complied, flipping the cakes while Lucas popped open a bottle of Freixenet and fetched orange juice. He waited till Brice had plated the browned pancakes before handing him a champagne flute filled nearly to the brim.

"Healthy serving," Brice observed.

"Might help your head. Big serving for a big guy. Here's to a better future," Lucas said, lifting his glass. "For both of us."

"Well said."

They clinked glasses. Brice slurped up a sip. "Tasty."

"So, do tell," Lucas said, taking a big swallow from his own glass before pouring more gray batter onto the griddle. "If it ain't too unpleasant."

Brice took his seat on the stool and stared out the window into the snow. A cardinal was munching on black sunflower seeds at a bird feeder just beyond the glass.

"Okay. To be brief…I've wanted other men since I was about thirteen. I grew up in a little town where everyone thought that being gay was the thing God hates most, where acting on my desires would have gotten me killed."

Nodding, Lucas fiddled with his left ear hoop. "I get ya there. Same in Mabie."

"No surprise. So I did my best to convince myself I was straight. Had some one-night stands with guys in college anyway, a few heavy infatuations. Then got serious about my music and knew to make it in Nashville—"

"You'd have to play the lady's man." Lucas flipped more pancakes.

"Yep. Dated a lot, was seen in public with some starlets. Even had kind of a reputation as a rounder. Then I met Shelly. Thought I could love her. Married her. You know how that went."

"I think. I've read stuff. What really happened?"

"What really happened is that I faked it for years. Pretty soon, my marriage had turned into a sham, a habit, a convenient disguise. When I was horny, as I've already admitted to you, I hired hustlers on the side. Then Zac—he was a guitarist in my band—he and I got involved. I could've loved him if I'd let myself, but I was just too afraid of what would happen if I…."

"If you let yourself feel too much. Oh, yeah. I know about that too."

"Then Shelly found some letters Zac wrote me. There was a big scene. She broke a bunch of stuff. Cheap stuff. Even in the middle of a rage like that, she was careful to leave the pricy pieces alone. So I moved out. But she agreed to keep my secret 'cause she enjoyed the…I guess you'd call it the social prestige of being married to a star. I *was* a star back then."

Lucas looked over at Brice. For a split-second, Brice thought, the expression in his eyes was simple, frank desire. "That's for damn sure. You were great."

"So you know my music?"

"Yeah." Lucas turned away. "I got some of your CDs. Well, okay, all of 'em. So get on with your story."

"Okay. I'm nearly done. I broke it off with Zac. It tore him up. He dropped out of my band, ran crazy, and slept around a lot. He caught HIV. He went to the tabloids so he could make money for treatments. And to hurt me, I suppose."

"Shit! Are you…?"

"Healthy? Yeah. Zac caught the virus a few months after we went our separate ways, and I've been real careful with the hustlers I've hired. Anyway, when the big homosexual scandal hit, my wife started divorce proceedings. She's taken a lot of what I owned—I feel too damn guilty to bicker with her—and the rest I've sold just to have some money to fall back on. From feast to famine, right? My label dumped me as soon as Zac's story came out, and yesterday I heard that…."

Brice paused. He dug his fingers into his scalp and scowled. "Goddamn it. God *damn* it."

"What? What did you hear?"

"It turns out the Country Music Museum and Hall of Fame took down the little exhibit they had about me. But that's not the worst news. The worst news I got was that my manager, Steve, is dumping me too."

"So what does that mean exactly?"

"It means that…without his help, without his connections, ain't no way I have a chance of salvaging my career. No way in hell."

"How about some other manager? There've gotta be scads of 'em in Nashville, right?"

Brice shook his head. "After all the bad publicity I've gotten, there's no way another manager would touch me with a ten-foot pole. An openly gay country music singer? Impossible. Just ain't gonna happen."

Brice fooled with his glass and took a long drink. "My career was going downhill anyway. I was getting older, and lots of young up-and-comers were beginning to crowd me out. Being with Zac had made me real sick of lying, so writing love songs to imaginary women—which is what my label wanted me to write, of course—started to feel like, well, mercenary hypocrisy. So I stopped writing songs. 'Cause I couldn't write the songs I wanted to write. Who would want to hear a country song about a man loving another man? Plus, well, other than my feelings for Zac, which I nipped in the bud, I've never really loved…. I've never shared…."

"Hold on." Lucas removed the last of the buckwheat cakes from the griddle and slid the heaped platter into the microwave. "We can heat these up in a little bit. Go on now. I think I know what you're gonna say, and I could say the same thing, and it's a hard thing to say. But say it anyway, all right?"

"Shit, what's the point?"

Lucas took a sip of his mimosa and slid onto a stool beside Brice. "'Cause sometimes it helps to tell a friend about painful things. Talking to Uncle Phil has sure helped me. I think I might have blown my brains out by now if I hadn't had him to talk to."

"Friends? Are we friends?" Brice cleared his throat. "This is the first day you've been decent to me."

Lucas nodded, staring at the floor. "Yeah, you're right. And I'm sorry about that. Things'll be different now, I swear. I think we're gonna be friends, yeah. I think having talks like this is what makes a friendship."

Brice studied Lucas for a long moment. "I think you're right. God knows I could do with a friend."

"Me too. Real bad. Real, real bad." Lucas met his eye, then returned his gaze to the linoleum. "Go on."

"What I'm trying to say is that…I was sort of in love with a straight buddy in high school, and then I had some confused, conflicted infatuations with a few guys in college, and God knows I've sneaked sex with as many men as my closeted state and married status allowed, but, other than the thing with Zac, which scared the hell out of me and sent me running for the hills, I've never had a real relationship with another man. I'm fucking forty. My life's half over, and I've never let myself love another man and had that feeling returned. Pathetic, ain't it?"

Lucas stood. He strode over to the fridge to fetch butter and maple syrup, then over to the cupboard to fetch sorghum. "If you're pathetic, I'm pathetic," Lucas said. "I've lost count of the strangers who paid me to suck their dicks, but the only guy I've ever halfway loved was Eric, and he used to beat me up about every week. You want pathetic, *that's* pathetic."

"Shit. Really? He beat you?"

"Afraid so. He liked to beat me up before he fucked me. It turned him on. Didn't turn me on, but…small price to pay. He protected me from worse sorts. Way worse. Like I said earlier, story for another day, after a few big glasses of booze."

"Christ," Brice groaned. "We're a pair, that's for sure. So what do we do now?"

"That's easy." Lucas chuckled. "I got us a rigorous agenda. Now we gobble buckwheat cakes till we can't eat anymore. This afternoon, we work breakfast off with a long walk in the snow. Come nightfall, we have a few drinks and heat up that beef stew and some of Doris Ann's biscuits. Then we stretch out on those couches in the great room and relax and listen to music and talk some more. If there's one thing that's helped me get through shit—other than talking to Uncle Phil—it's the little things in life. Bourbon, beer, down-home cooking, wood fires, and long walks in the hills."

"Yeah, I know exactly what you mean." Brice thought of the copious comfort food his sister had brought over again and again during those lonely, harassed weeks in Hinton. "Take those sweetenings on into the dining room and I'll bring in the buckwheat cakes."

CHAPTER THIRTY-TWO

OTHER THAN POINTING OUT FEATURES OF THE natural landscape—a few remaining bright-red hawthorn berries not yet plucked by hungry birds, snow-dusted heads of dead goldenrod, and a nuthatch crawling upside down over the trunk of a locust tree—Lucas was silent during their walk. The silence was, Brice sensed, not of the sullen and prickly variety encountered before but a sort of contemplative withdrawal, as if Lucas wanted to spend time with Brice but needed time to think, to turn within. *Fine with me, just as long as I can look at you and be close to you,* Brice thought, watching Lucas's breath stream out in curlicues of fog, his beard-framed pink lips purse as he bent to examine the bright feather a blue jay had shed.

They parted for a few hours, Lucas to study for his GED and Brice to nap a bit and check e-mail in the lodge library. Shelly gleefully proclaimed the divorce nearly final, Leigh told him that she and Ferrell missed him and that she was still driving reporters away from his Hinton house, and his ex-label informed him that a small check had accrued from the next-to-nothing sales of his CDs and would he please send them a forwarding address so that they might mail it? Another request for a forwarding address came from Steve Morgan's venomous secretary, who wanted to send along another "package of praise from your adoring fans," as she put it. Brice resisted the urge to tell her to stuff the letters up her prissy, judgmental twat. Instead, he didn't respond. More hate mail was not what he needed.

Brice had just sent off an update to Leigh when

Lucas appeared in the library doorway. "It's cocktail time, as Uncle Phil would say. What you feel like, drink-wise?"

Brice rubbed his head and yawned. "Something with bourbon?"

"How about something sweet and strong?"

"Like me, huh?"

Lucas rolled his eyes. "Just what I was gonna say. You know how to make mint juleps? I know they're a summer drink, but Doris Ann bought some mint at the store the other day to put in some fancy salad, and I don't want the rest to go off. Plus Uncle Phil has some fancy silver glasses he uses for juleps. I figured you'd like 'em, being from southern West Virginia and all."

"Yeah, I know how to make 'em. Sounds good." Brice turned off the desktop computer and rose.

"Okay, you mix 'em up—fancy glasses are on a shelf above the bar, mint's in the kitchen—and I'll start us a fire."

The hearth in the great room was flickering by the time Brice had prepared the drinks, but Lucas was nowhere to be seen. Here and there, candles were lit around the room. *Yesterday, he's treating me like shit and tonight he's arranging a romantic atmosphere? I don't think I've ever met anyone as unpredictable, but at least things are changing for the better. At least right now. Who knows how he'll act tomorrow?*

Brice settled onto one end of the leather couch and gazed into the fire. *So quiet here. God, the silence is wonderful. Why did I ever want to live in a city? The people, the traffic, the noise. Ugh.*

The door opened and Lucas stepped in, hefting an armload of wood. He stomped his boots on the welcome mat. "It's snowing again. Glad we got some provisions stored. For a few days, it's gonna be hard to get out."

"I ain't going anywhere," Brice replied. "It's not like folks are clamoring for my presence any longer. I was just sitting here thinking about what a great place this is. How quiet, compared to cities like Nashville."

"That's one reason I'm here. Can't stand noise. And, man, was prison noisy. Jesus." Lucas deposited the wood in the wood box by the hearth, wiped shards of bark and dust off the front of his shirt, unlaced and removed his boots, and plopped down at the other end of the couch. "Hand here that drink."

Brice obliged. Lucas sipped. "Oh, yeah. That's nice. Haven't had one of these since last summer."

"So how long have you lived here?" Brice asked.

"Since last spring. Right after I was released." Lucas leaned back onto the pillows cradled in the arm of the couch, stretched, and yawned. Lifting his legs, he nudged his sock-covered feet into Brice's lap. "You mind?"

"No, I don't mind." Brice took a foot in his hand and squeezed, more than happy to share such unexpected, albeit minor, intimacy. "Now you're getting all cozy and snuggly with me? I never know what you're gonna do next."

"I like to keep guys guessing." Lucas gave Brice a wink. "Keeps the tension up. So look, I wanna explain some things."

My God, he is just so fucking fine. The most beautiful boy I've ever met just winked at me. "All right. Go for it."

"I said it before, and I'll say it again: I'm sorry I've been such a bastard. Sometimes I do shit, and even I don't know why I'm doing it. Uncle Phil calls me 'irredeemably and charmingly neurotic.'"

Brice snickered. "Nice phrase. Join the crowd. I think we're all pretty damned neurotic. God knows I am."

"You seem pretty together, considering all the crap that's been thrown at you lately. Anyway, you've been real nice to me ever since you got here, and you didn't deserve the cold shoulder I gave you. I mean, hell, you're a guest. I was raised better than to be rude to a guest. Getting my eye busted up…it's what I deserved for acting like such a jerk."

"Naw, that was my fault, acting like a drunk douche." Brice kneaded the sole of Lucas's foot. "You have been pretty cold to me, though. I thought I'd insulted you somehow."

"Naw. I'm just…a fucking mess. When I'm scared or insecure, I get chilly and nasty just to drive people away, 'cause it's easier for me to be alone. Look, I think you're amazing. That's part of the problem. I mean, I love your music. You're so talented. You've achieved so much."

"All that's great to hear, especially the fact that you love my music…but I've lost just about everything I've achieved." Brice rubbed his thumb hard along the arch of Lucas's foot. "Feel good?"

"Hell, yes. Thanks. Well, the reason you've lost so much is just total bullshit. It's 'cause so many folks are backwards, narrow-minded assholes. The fact remains that you're amazing. Man, the songs you've written…so beautiful. So beautiful."

"Well…thank you," Brice said, feeling profoundly touched. "I had no idea you felt that way."

"Sure. Just speaking the truth." Lucas rubbed his undamaged eye and sighed. Brice took up Lucas's other foot and massaged it. The fire spit sparks. In the corner, a grandfather clock ticked.

"You just intimidate the hell outta me. It's hard to be around you." Lucas's voice had dropped to a whisper. "That's why I've been so distant, so downright rude. I'm really sorry."

Brice chuckled. He dug the ball of his thumb into Lucas's heel. "I intimidate you? You've got to be kidding."

"Naw, I ain't kidding. You're a star, no matter what shit's been said in the press, no matter what's happened in the last few months. You followed your dream. You've put out bunches of CDs and toured and performed. You've created. Your music has moved who knows how many people?"

"But all that's over."

Lucas folded his hands behind his head, arched his back, and groaned. "You sure know how to rub a foot. Well, maybe it's all over, and maybe it's not. Who knows? The fact remains that you've accomplished a helluva lot. Me, I ain't done jack shit. Why would you want to spend time with me? I'm the biggest goddamn loser you'll ever meet."

"I don't think of you as a loser, Lucas."

"You don't know me very well. I ain't done nothing with my life. I've worked at Walmart, sucked cock in truck stops, and got to be Eric's butt-bitch for five years. That's it."

The image of little Lucas getting his ass pounded by a huge convict was arousing, but Brice dismissed the flicker of lust as untimely, something to be savored when he was next alone in bed with a Kleenex handy. "You're twenty-seven, and you're from a rough background. You haven't had much opportunity to do things. And you ending up in prison is as much a crock of unjust bullshit, far as I'm concerned, as me losing my career 'cause I was outed."

"Yeah. No justice anywhere." Lucas sipped his julep and sighed. "Yum. This is good. You can make me one of these any time. Well, I'm glad you like it here, but… there's gotta be some place you'd rather be. Somebody you'd rather spend time with."

"Nope. I don't have much of anyone left. Just my sister and nephew back in Hinton, and I want to stay away from my hometown for a while, because most folks there hate me and think I've shamed the town, and the damn reporters were knocking on my door day and night. Thank God they don't know I'm here, or the same thing would happen. Funny. When I was on top, people couldn't get enough of me. I always had a passel of hangers-on. Now...no one wants anything to do with a disgraced old bastard like me. So, no, there's no one else I'd rather be spending time with."

"So here we are." Lucas wore a tired smile. "Together at the ends of the earth. The snowy wilds of Randolph County."

"Yep. I'm glad we met. Not only do I think that you're, well, really good-looking, but, what you said about friendship earlier, I think that could happen. Like I said at breakfast the other day, you and me have some things in common. We're both kind of at the same place in our lives."

"True enough. Damaged. Outcast. Hiding from the world. Wondering what's next. What's coming up next. God, I've felt so completely outta control of my life."

"Like there's nothing to look forward to and no choices left? I get that. But here's a choice." Brice stroked his bearded chin, feeling nervous. "Valentine's Day is coming up in a couple of days. I think we should celebrate it."

"Together?" Lucas toed Brice in the belly.

"Yeah, together. Let's go out. Interested?"

"Out, like on a date, right?"

"Uhhh, right." Brice squeezed Lucas's big toe.

"Where to?"

"Up to you. These are your stomping grounds, not mine."

Lucas slipped his feet off Brice's lap. "I know a place."

"Where?"

Lucas stood. "It'll be a surprise."

"So that's a yes? You're agreeing to go out on a Valentine's Day date with me?"

"That's a yes. I figured you wouldn't have the guts to ask."

"I wasn't planning to, since you were so consistently surly. But today...."

Lucas gave Brice a crooked grin. "Guess that weight machine knocked some sense into me. About time, huh? You ready for some dinner?"

Brice drained his drink. "You bet. I'm starved."

Lucas grabbed Brice's hand and pulled him to his feet. "Come on, ole broke-back Daddy. Let's get you fed."

"Is that thing tuned?" Lucas asked, nodding at the upright piano against the wall.

The two men, full with a big dinner, sprawled side by side on the couch, sipping some of Phil's stash of Frangelico and watching the fire die. Lucas had arranged a knitted blanket over the both of them. The proximity of Lucas's body made Brice ache, but he feared that Lucas would turn cold again if he made any kind of move.

Gotta wait, Brice thought. *Gotta be patient. He's willing to go out on a date, so at least that means he likes me some. Settle for that for now. Don't scare this skittish kid away. Let him take the lead. Let him let me know if he wants more. Damn, it's hard not to lunge.*

"Yeah, it's tuned," Brice said. "I fiddled with it the first day I got here."

"So are you ever gonna play for me? On that, or on your guitar? Uncle Phil said you brought your guitar with you."

"I did. I don't know why. Like I told you, I haven't written anything in months and months. Major writer's block."

"So play me something old. Off one of your albums."

"Ahhhh, I don't know. I've lost my chops. I'm thinking music's done with me."

"Bullshit." To Brice's surprise, Lucas reached over and tweaked his chin. "You're a singer and a songwriter. What are you if you're not that? Worthless. Worthless like me."

"Stop that shit. You ain't worthless. You're smart, and you're intense, and you're handsome. You have potential in spades. You just need a break."

"*You* stop *that* shit about music being done with you. A gift like that don't just shrivel up and disappear. So you're going through a dry spell. That'll change. Mark my words."

Brice rubbed his jaw. "I sure hope you're right. 'Cause, honestly, when I'm not writing, I feel rudderless. Like time's a'wasting. Like there's no real point to anything. I've been at kind of a loss for around a year."

"You'll get it back. You'll get it back." Lucas leaned over, bumping Brice's shoulder with his own. "You're fucking Brice Brown! Things are gonna turn around, you just wait and see. Meanwhile…you expect me to be snowed in with a major country music star and—"

"*Former* major country music star."

"Whatever. The point is, I've been listening to your music for years. Hearing it in prison…."

Lucas bowed his head and dug his knuckles into his brow. "God, it felt like a blessing, like the walls and the bars disappeared and the ceiling vanished and all those loud, mean, brutal assholes faded away for a few minutes…and the sky opened up, and I was driving down a country road all by myself, with maple leaves falling, leaves the color of those wood-embers there, or I was walking down by a riverbank in spring, watching the sycamores and the willows leaf out, or…a big man was holding me in his arms and telling me I was tough, telling me things'd turn out fine, that we could survive anything long as we were together, and…."

Lucas trailed off. He wiped at his eyes and coughed. "Shit. Sorry. Got carried away. Anyway, I been listening to your music for years. So now that you're here, how the hell can you expect me not to ask you to play?"

"Wow, kid." Brice shook his head. "I'm glad my music helped." Reaching over, he squeezed Lucas's shoulder. "Okay. I'll play. What do you want to hear?"

BRICE PLAYED FOR OVER AN hour, with Lucas stretched out beneath the blanket, making request after request. By the time Brice plead weariness, the fire had died down and the room was chilly.

Lucas swung his feet off the couch. "That was wonderful. Just wonderful. Thank you so much."

Brice closed up the piano. "Sure, kid. It means a lot to me that you like my stuff. I guess you're my last fan."

Lucas smirked. "Oh, please. I kinda doubt it. Can you imagine all the queer folks across the nation—shit, the world—who are so happy to find out that a gifted guy like you is one of us?"

"That's what Travis said. That kid who came to visit me in Hinton."

"Yeah, I met him last summer. Cute, scruffy guy. Came here with a bunch of other queer kids from WVU. So, you wanna lift weights with me tomorrow?"

"That would be great."

"Okay. Get back here around nine, and I'll cook us up some grits and sausage." Lucas turned abruptly and headed for the door.

"Good night." Brice rose, watching Lucas don his jacket and leave. An ache was building in his belly, a mingling of longing and regret. He closed up the fireplace and snuffed all the candles. He pulled his cap and coat off the hall tree, slipped them on, and stepped out onto the snowy deck. Above, gaps in snow clouds torn apart by wind revealed patches of night sky jeweled with constellations.

Brice pulled a scarf out of his jacket pocket and arranged it around his neck. He was about to head up the path toward his cabin when he heard a shout behind him.

"Hey!"

Brice turned. Lucas stood beneath the redbud grove. He lifted a hand.

"Wait."

Lucas loped over the snowy deck to stand before Brice.

"Sorry. Forgot something."

Wrapping his sinewy arms around Brice, Lucas craned upward and kissed him softly on the mouth.

Brice stood stunned, heart commencing to race, mind swamped with disbelief.

"Thanks for the music," Lucas said, kissing Brice again, this time on the cheek. "See you tomorrow." He released Brice and stepped backward before Brice could return the embrace. Then the boy turned and disappeared into the darkness.

Brice stood for a long moment, looking after him. He shifted his eyes to the stars. Amazement and thankfulness welled up in his heart. He shoved his hands into his pockets, drew in a long breath of cold air, then tucked his chin against his chest and started along the path to Laurel Cottage, filled with the sudden conviction that Lucas was right, that things might turn around, that anything was possible.

CHAPTER THIRTY-THREE

THE DIGITAL ALARM CLOCK BY THE BED SAID 3:33. Brice rose, pissed, climbed back into bed, and stared up into the dark. He thought of Lucas's unexpected and astounding kiss. He thought of the way Lucas moved, the color of his eyes, the color of his beard, the way his chest and biceps and butt bulged, filling out his clothes. He tried to imagine what Lucas must have suffered, a smart, sensitive, desirable introvert of a boy trapped in a big cage for six years with who knows what kind of hardened, brutal men?

"And I'm feeling hopeless 'cause I lost my audience and had to give up my fancy condos and shiny toys," Brice muttered, tossing off the covers. "Christ, what a big baby. What a spoiled narcissist."

Brice climbed out of bed and dressed. He pulled on his jacket and cap and left Laurel Cottage. The snow had stopped; the skies were clear. He walked for an hour, around the compound, where he circled Lucas's dark cabin, and then down the road into Brantley Valley. He trudged over hard-packed snow, breathing in bitterly cold air, taking in glimpses of the Milky Way. "I'm a small man. I'm a small, sad man," he murmured again and again, looking up at the forested hills, the drifting clouds, the gleaming angles of the Big Bear and Orion.

Face, toes, and fingers chilled, Brice returned to his cabin. He stripped down to his underwear, sat on the edge of his bed, and cradled his face in his hands. Sleep, he sensed, was still far, far away. He thought of Lucas sleeping soundly in his own bed, several hundred yards distant. Lucas naked, his well-defined, lightly hairy chest rising and falling, his left arm covered with tattoos. His cock limp, nestled in pubic hair the color of his beard. His armpits full of the same ruddy hair, smelling of youth's virile musk. The same fine, gingery moss in the cleft between his plump, pale buttocks.

"Okay, by God," Brice groaned, rising. From the corner of the bedroom, he hauled out his guitar case and opened it. "No help for me but this."

Brice sat on the edge of the bed and tuned up his guitar, remembering the first guitar he'd learned to play, a miniature one his grandmother had bought at Sears and given him for Christmas when he was thirteen. He remembered the guitar he'd played on the Grand Ole Opry, a sleek Martin, and the Washburn that Zac smashed over a chair when Brice told him that they were through. This old guitar was his favorite, a Yamaha FG-345, the only brand he could afford back in college when he first started getting serious about songwriting.

He picked through a few bars of "Hard Gray Rain," the song he'd heard Lucas playing in his cabin, a tune that Brice's feelings for Wayne had fueled. He fooled with "Sad-Eyed Angel," another Wayne-inspired song.

"The past. That's the past." Brice sighed. He slipped the guitar off his knee, poised to case it up again, and then he paused, and then he thought again of Lucas kissing him, the feeling of the boy's lips on his, the soft brushing of his moustache.

"I need something new," Brice muttered. He propped the instrument back on his knee and retuned it, searching for something fresh, something beyond the strictures of standard tuning. In a few minutes, he'd dropped into G-tuning—DGDGBD. He piddled with that for a few minutes, remembering chords by Joni Mitchell and Nanci Griffith, tunes of theirs he'd covered on his second album. "Newer," he said, dropping the B string to A and then the bass string to C.

Brice strummed the open chord—CGDGAD—and grinned. "There you go." For long minutes, he forgot about everything else—his disgrace, his hopelessness, even his smoldering desire for Lucas—as his fingers moved up and down the strings, stumbling over dissonance, slipping into chords, patterns of suspension and resolution.

"Now then, Lucas Tuning, give me a song," Brice whispered. "Give me a reason to keep breathing."

In fifteen minutes, a tune had surfaced inside the flow of new chords. It stumbled, backed up, started over again, took a minor path, wavered through uncertainties and irresolutions, shouldered into a series of majors, swayed across a hanging bridge of major sevens, then tapered off into a minor nine, and ceased.

He ran through his new discovery a second time, then a third time, writing down the progression in a notebook he carried with him everywhere. The last notation, the last new song, according to the scribbled date of the final entry—October 3, 1996—was one he'd written about his desire for Zac, the lyrics carefully sidestepping any use of revelatory pronouns. He'd never recorded it.

Brice put away both guitar and notebook, sipped some water, used the bathroom, and climbed back into bed. He lay there in the dark, listening to wind soughing in the eaves.

Sounds like death trying to get in, Brice thought. *Death cold as the space between the stars. But I got an answer for that. At least for now.*

Closing his eyes, he hummed the melody he'd created, music that would capture a little of how he had come to feel about Lucas.

CHAPTER THIRTY-FOUR

"Helvetia," Lucas said, steering his Ford down the wooded valley. They passed an assortment of alpine-themed buildings set along an ice-edged, rocky brook. "A bunch of Swiss immigrants settled here in the 1870s. It's downright adorable, ain't it?"

"It sure is," Brice said, admiring the quaint, pitch-roofed structures, some clapboard, some log, some covered with dark-wood shingles. "And out in the middle of nowhere."

"Exactly," Lucas said, slowing his truck. "Out in the middle of nowhere is just where I wanna be. Any place that has more trees than people, that's my kinda place. I felt that way even before I spent six years in a little cell, and I feel even more that way now."

Brice almost asked Lucas if he'd ever tell him about his prison experience but decided that Valentine's Day was definitely not the right time.

"So there's a restaurant here?"

"A great one. The Hutte. Here we are." Lucas pulled into a gravel lot and parked beside a long, low wooden building with dormer windows and an open porch. The two men climbed out.

"Glad I made reservations," Lucas said, surveying the many parked cars. "Lots of folks out on dates."

"Uhhh. Lots of people?" Brice flipped his jacket collar up and pulled his ball cap down over his eyes.

"Afraid of being recognized? Hey, I'm the local boy turned violent criminal and faggot whore, remember? The food'll be worth it, I promise."

Brice nodded. *I don't want to look like a coward in front of him.*

Lucas led the way up onto the porch. "People

around here have been pretty decent to me since I got out, though it's not like I leave the Phagg Heights compound all that often. The folks that do recognize me will be too polite to say anything, since I'm one of their own, a Randolph County boy. I don't think you have anything to worry about. Your beard has bushed out so much since your last album cover, and it's gotten way grayer—plus you're a lot heavier. I'll be real surprised if anyone figures out who you are."

Brice patted his gut. "Do you like the big, salt-and-pepper beard and the extra weight? I stopped dieting and dyeing my beard when I lost my contract."

"Would I be having a Valentine's Day date with you if I didn't?" Lucas held the door open for Brice and winked. His right eye was still faintly bruised. "I asked Eleanor for a quiet, kinda isolated table near the rear. That'll help."

Brice stepped inside and began hungrily snuffling the scents. Several people looked up as they entered, but no one responded, except a rangy young guy near the door who shared a table with what were presumably his wife and toddler daughter. "Hey, Lucas," the man said, raising his hand. "How you doin'?"

Lucas strode over and shook the guy's hand. "Hey, Ray. Just hungry for some of that Swiss sausage. Hey, Marion. Hey, little one." The wife smiled; the child hid her head behind her mother's back.

"How'd you get that shiner?"

"Ah, just brawlin'. You know me."

"Yep. A wild man to the end. Who we got here?" Ray asked, looking up at Brice.

"This is Ken," Lucas said, without missing a beat. "He hails from the southern part of the state. He's my date."

Though Marion squirmed at the word "date" and pulled her child closer, as if they were in the presence of a threat, Ray seemed unfazed. He gave Brice a quick, firm handshake.

"Welcome to Helvetia. You all have a great evening. Lil' Lucas here deserves some good times. Save some room for the peach cobbler. It's super."

"You bet," Brice said. "Nice to meet y'all."

"See y'all around." Lucas gave Marion a defiant grin before leading the way on into the restaurant. Soon they were seated at a little table in the back, relatively private, as Lucas had promised.

"Ray and I went to high school together," Lucas said, shedding his denim jacket.

He was dressed in black jeans and a slate-gray button-down chamois shirt. Much to Brice's delight, it was unbuttoned far enough to show off rusty chest hair and a couple of silver chains above the scoop of an A-shirt.

Brice sloughed off his coat as well. He'd worn a pair of gray chinos and a WVU sweatshirt. Taking off his ball cap, he ran a hand over his scalp. Feeling exposed, he placed the cap back on his head. "How'd you know my middle name was Kenneth?"

"I've done some Internet stalking, Mr. Brown." Lucas winked and grinned.

"Lucas!" A thin, middle-aged woman with short, wavy brown hair and sharp features bustled up to them. "I'm so pleased to see you out and about."

"Howdy, Miss Eleanor. This is Ken. We were wanting to enjoy a nice Valentine's meal together, and I couldn't think of a better place for a romantic evening than your restaurant."

"Hello, Ken," Eleanor said, handing them menus. She too seemed to be unbothered by the concept of two men sharing a Valentine's Day date. "Welcome to Helvetia. Where you from?"

"Hinton, ma'am." Brice gave her an anxious smile and then dropped his gaze to the menu.

"He's staying with us for a few weeks up at the compound," Lucas said.

"Mercy, you do look familiar," Eleanor said, studying Brice's features. "Have you been here before?"

"No'm," Brice mumbled. "First time here."

"Well, again, welcome. Do you have any idea what you'd like?"

"Mind if I order for us?" Beneath the table, Lucas nudged Brice's calf with his foot. Brice nearly jumped out of his chair.

"Oh, uh, yeah. Go for it," Brice muttered. All of a sudden, he wanted to cover his head with his coat.

"We'll both have the lemonade. I'll have the bratwurst with sauerkraut, and Ken here'll have your all's homemade sausage with the *rösti*. And please save two pieces of cobbler for us."

"You got it. Coming right up." Eleanor smiled, took their menus, gave Brice another quizzical look, and hurried off.

"Oh, Lord," Brice groaned. "She's gonna figure out who I am, for sure."

"Relax, big Daddy." Lucas nudged Brice's calf again.

"How can I relax when you keep doing that? Don't you get tired of teasing me?"

"I'm only a tease if I don't intend to follow through." Lucas's grin was broad and impish.

My God, am I hearing things? "Do you intend to follow through?" Brice bumped Lucas's thigh with his knee.

"You want more than a kiss?" Lucas pretended shock. "The last few days, we've lifted weights together, gathered wood together, hiked together, cooked some good meals together, got a couple buzzes on together, watched—what?—three or four action films together. Greedy! What more do you want?"

"I want—"

Brice fell silent as Eleanor appeared with their lemonades. "Food'll be out in about five minutes," she said, before hurrying off.

"You were saying?" Lucas took a long pull on his glass.

"I want more of the same. I want to spend time with you. I want to get to know you better. I want...." Brice took a gulp of lemonade. He lowered his voice. "What do you think I want? I want you. You know I want you. I've told you that. I want us to kiss again. I want to hold you."

"You want one of my truck-stop-special white-trash blow-jobs, huh?" Lucas bit his lip and looked away.

"Stop that shit. Stop trying to push me away. I don't care what you did at those truck stops. You don't care that I hired who knows how many hustlers in the past, do you?"

Lucas shook his head. "No, I don't care. Sorry. It's some fucking reflex action of mine, pushing folks away. I think you're...really cool, and I still...I still can't believe that you...that you want...a fucked-up nobody like me."

"If we were alone, I'd take your hand right now."

"So do it."

"What?"

"Be brave, big man. No one's looking at us. Mean and muscly as I am and big and burly as you are, we could kick the ass of any other man in this place. If you feel like doing it, do it."

Brice hesitated. He looked around the little room. Two tables had already emptied, and the elderly couple to their left seemed thoroughly engrossed in their meals.

Brice took a deep breath—*feels like standing on the edge of a cliff*—reached over, and took Lucas's hand. He squeezed it. Lucas squeezed back.

"Hey, Miss Eleanor," Lucas said, looking over Brice's shoulder. Brice jumped, releasing Lucas's hand.

Eleanor stepped around Brice with a heaped platter. "You two make a real cute couple," she whispered, as she set the plates before them. "I hope you enjoy your time in our county, Ken. It's served as a refuge for all sorts of folks in dire need of shelter. And if you'd just sign these real quick, I'd be grateful forever."

From the deep pockets of her apron, Eleanor pulled out four of Brice's CDs. She offered him a pen. "Don't you worry, honey," she said, patting his hand. "I'm not telling a soul."

Brice took a deep breath and exhaled. He signed the CDs so fast that he almost blurred his autograph.

"I appreciate your discretion, ma'am. If folks knew who I was—"

"Lord, I don't want any trashy reporters in here." Eleanor pursed her lips and slipped the CDs back into her apron pockets. "Then I'd have to pull out my shotgun, and *that* surely wouldn't be good for business. I hope you enjoy our food, and happy Valentine's Day. God bless you."

Lucas and Brice watched her go. "Sometimes Christians can surprise you," Lucas said. "Dig in, big man. Let me know how you like that *rösti*. In fact, if you give me a few bites of that, I'll share some of this here tasty sauerkraut."

"So, I HAVE KIND OF a little Valentine's Day surprise for you," Lucas said, as they entered the lodge at kitchen level. "Two, actually."

"Yeah? Well, I actually have something for you."

Both men shed coats and stomped dead leaves and mud off boots. The weather outside had shifted at nightfall from a cloudless calm to a blustery drizzle.

"Here you go," Lucas said, pointing to the counter. On it sat a potted amaryllis in full bloom.

"Wow." Brice stroked the plant's long leaves and the ruby-hued explosion of its lush petals. "Thank you! It's beautiful."

"Yeah, they're cool. You never can tell when they're gonna bloom. That lump of a bulb just sits there for months and months, like it's dead, like it might as well be a chunk'a rock. And then one day, bam! It comes alive. Like Christ striding outta that cave. Like some kinda dormant volcano. And here's the second surprise."

Lucas pulled a bottle from the fridge. "Uncle Phil left it for us, for tonight. It's some fancy pink champagne. Prosecco. Want some now?"

"Sure. But first, here's your gift." Brice pulled a small package from his jacket pocket and handed it to Lucas. "I hope you don't think it's inappropriate."

"Hmm." Lucas tore it open and pulled out a pair of skimpily cut black Speedos. "Not a lot to it," he said. "Tiny little thang."

"I figured you might wear it this evening, in case you felt like heading down to that grotto and hitting the hot tub with me. It's a nasty, cold night. Taking a warm soak might feel just right."

Lucas arched an eyebrow. "You've had this all planned out, haven't you? Trying to get me naked?"

"What do you think?" Brice took the risk of reaching over and stroking the boy's cheek. *Don't bolt! Don't bolt!* he prayed. "Besides, you won't be naked. You'll be wearing those stylish briefs."

"How about you? What'll you be wearing?"

"I, my handsome friend, *will* be naked. I didn't bring any swim trunks. That all right with you?"

Lucas looked Brice up and down, his face unreadable. "Sure. We're all just guys here, right? I'll fetch us some towels, then head down and get the tub ready. How about you grab a couple glasses and bring the champagne?"

CHAPTER THIRTY-FIVE

WHEN BRICE GOT TO THE GROTTO, HE FOUND it dark and toasty, illuminated by a single stocky candle burning on a sconce. The floating plastic cover had been removed from the hot tub, the bubbles were on full blast, and steam rose from the water, but Lucas was nowhere to be seen.

"Hey, here I am!" Brice yelled, placing the champagne bottle and glasses on a little table in the corner. He sat on a bench lining the wall and tugged off his boots and socks. He stood and peeled off his sweatshirt and undershirt. Bare-chested, he was unbuckling his belt when, across the humid room, the door to the bathroom opened.

Lucas stepped out. He wore nothing but his silver neck-chains and the Speedos Brice had bought him. He hesitated in the dim light, eyes lowered, sinewy arms wrapped around himself. He took a deep breath, raised his eyes, and gave Brice the faintest trace of a smile. "Hey. How do I look?"

Brice stared. As he'd expected, the tiny garment highlighted the leanness of Lucas's hips and the flatness of his midriff. Even in light so dim, Brice could make out the prominent crotch-bulge and the trail of belly hair disappearing beneath the black Spandex.

"Uhhh. Beautiful. They, uh, fit you just right." *Oh, Christ, I'm getting hard already.*

"Ready for that dip?"

Brice nodded. He studied the boy with awe. *That pale skin. Those dark tattoos. Those shoulders, those arms, those hips, those thighs. He's like a little sex-god, a country porn star. I want to hold him so bad. I want to shove him up against the wall and kiss him till our mouths bruise up.*

"Let me just get these pants off." Awkward and excited, seized with sudden self-consciousness, Brice turned his back to Lucas as he stripped. *He's perfect, so young and slender, and I'm so old and fat. God, please let him like the way I look. Please don't let me be too old or too heavy or too hairy for him.* Naked, heart pounding, Brice turned. To his chagrin, his cock had risen to half-mast. Blushing, he covered his crotch with his hands.

Lucas's faint smile widened as he looked Brice up and down. "I can tell you approve of these briefs you bought me. Would you pour the champagne?" Lucas said, stepping down into the water.

Brice popped the bottle and poured them generous amounts. Carefully, he climbed into the bubbling tub, sat on a submerged ledge beside Lucas, and handed him a glass.

"Happy Valentine's Day," Lucas said, lifting his drink.

"Same to you," Brice said.

The two men tapped glasses and drank. For a long moment, neither said anything, each studying the other in feeble candlelight.

"Tasty stuff," Lucas said, taking another sip.

"It is. Plus this hot water feels great on my back." Brice rubbed at his lumbar region and groaned.

"Good. You should take advantage of this tub more often. Good therapy for you. Plus I give a pretty damn good massage."

"Yeah? Would you give me a massage sometime? I'd sure appreciate it. Might help me get rid of some of the outed-as-a-scandalous-homosexual stress, you know?"

"How about right now?" Placing his glass beside the tub, Lucas scooted closer to Brice. "Come sit here between my legs."

"Gladly," Brice said, attempting to sound calm rather than emitting the "Yee-Haw!" of happiness that filled him at such an invitation to touch. He set his glass down too, then slipped over and sat on the lip of the ledge between Lucas's spread thighs.

Lucas ran his fingers lightly over Brice's shoulders and then down Brice's back. "Man, you're built. I wish I had half the bulk you do." Lucas gave Brice's shoulders a firm kneading before working the balls of his thumbs down either side of Brice's spine. "I like a guy with some heft on him. You were just too skinny on those CD covers of yours."

"Hell, I wish I could get rid of some of this bulk. I've always run to fat. I was always having to diet to look good for photo shoots or concerts. I got so fucking tired of protein shakes and rice cakes and salads. My publicist and my manager were constantly nagging me about how I had to fit the Nashville look."

"I think you look great, man," Lucas murmured, resting his bearded chin on Brice's bare shoulder. Brice trembled, choking back a gasp of incredulous gratitude. "I've always liked bigger, older guys, and you ain't no exception."

Lucas's strong hands begin to rub Brice's lats. "Maturity is a huge turn-on. Most guys my age are fucking flakes who don't jack shit about anything. You, you've done and seen so much. You're so burly and handsome."

I can't fucking believe this! "Y-you think I'm handsome?" Brice murmured.

"I sure do."

"Well, that's pretty sweet news. Most guys your age don't feel the same, I assure you."

"I ain't most guys my age. Take a fucking compliment, will you?"

"Yeah, okay. Thanks, Lucas. I think you…I think you have the perfect body. Strong and compact. And, damn, your hands feel really good."

"Thanks, man." Lucas moved his fingers down to Brice's lower back and began to probe. "You feel damn good too. It's been a long time since…."

Lucas trailed off. He found the troublesome joint in Brice's lower back and kneaded it with increasing pressure.

"Oh, yeah. Oh, yeah," Brice groaned. "That's it. Oh, yeah, please keep that up."

Long minutes passed, Lucas humming and Brice grunting and sighing. Finally, Lucas ceased.

"Hands getting sore. I'm out of practice," he said.

"Thank you. That felt just wonderful." Brice rested his elbows on his knees. "I needed that real, real bad."

"Good." Lucas wrapped his arms around Brice's waist, pressed his chest against his back, and kissed him on the nape of the neck. "Brice?"

"Yeah?" Brice said, quietly exultant. *God, such precious touch. So long yearned for. A boy so beautiful, nearly naked, his arms around me. Unbelievable. It all seems too good to be true.* Against his lower back, he could feel the hard pressure of Lucas's erection.

"I…. It feels so good to touch you like this. I haven't touched anyone since Eric back in prison. I…I've been…."

"Yeah?" Brice took Lucas's small hands in his and leaned back against him.

"I've been hankering to hold you, to…be with you…."

Brice squeezed Lucas's hands. "So…you're saying my desire for you is…that you… reciprocate those feelings?"

"Y-yep. That's what I'm saying."

"Wow. Well…I'm delighted, but I'm mighty surprised. After—"

"After me being so distant? Yeah. Well, that act's over. But…could we please take it slow? Like I told you, after all the shit that happened in prison, I'm real confused, real fucked up. Kinda fragile. I hate to admit it, since you know we country boys are raised to be all strong and stuff, but…sometimes I hurt so bad to be touched. I fucking *ache* for some strong guy to care for me and to love me and to hold me down and…top me hard…screw me stupid. But then the next minute I think if that were to happen, I'd shake so much I'd shiver into a million pieces. That's why I fought so hard to keep you at a distance."

"Ah, kid…."

A hot rush of compassion filled Brice's throat and edged his eyes with tears. He slipped off the ledge, turned, and knelt waist-deep in the steaming water. He took Lucas's left hand and kissed it. He reached up and stroked Lucas's bearded cheek. He ran his fingers over the boy's moist hair.

"I understand. At least I think I do. Of course we can take it slow. As slow as you want."

"You won't get impatient? You won't get tired of waiting and leave for greener pastures?" Voice hoarse, Lucas squeezed Brice's hand. "I know you said you want me, and I want you too, but it might take a little time for me to…to be ready for more than… kissing and cuddling. After how I was treated in prison…those groups of guys…before Eric took me under his wing…. And even then, the way Eric beat me all the damn time…. God, I'm so ashamed."

"Hey!" Brice rose, sat beside the boy, and wrapped an arm around him. "You don't have any goddamn reason to be ashamed. What could you do? No matter how strong a man is, there's always gonna be someone stronger. And no matter how strong a man is, he's no match for a gang, right?"

"Yeah, I guess." Lucas, trembling, slipped an arm around Brice's waist and leaned his head on the bigger man's shoulder.

"As for me leaving, honestly, I can't imagine greener pastures." Brice fondled the metal hoop in Lucas's left ear. "I think you're one of the most desirable men I've ever met, and the fact that you've gone through so much, that you've suffered and that we're both at dark, lonely times in our lives, all that just makes me feel closer to you, even though we haven't spent all that much time together."

Again Brice took Lucas's hand and kissed it. "Look, I'm not a patient man by nature. Honestly, I've been fighting the urge ever since I got here to grab you up and carry you to bed like some kind of crazy caveman. I'd like to make love to you till we're both sweat-soaked and sore."

"I'd...I'd like that too. I really would. Eventually."

"Eventually sounds good to me. You're more than worth the wait." Brice shook his head and laughed low in his throat. "I still can't believe that we met, that we're here together. To have been through all the bullshit of the last few months, then to come to this beautiful place and to meet a handsome guy like you...it's like God's answered my prayers."

"Thanks," Lucas said, grinning weakly. "I've been praying too. I've been praying for years, in and out of prison, that I'd meet a strong man who'd—"

"Who'd take care of you and cherish you?"

"Yeah. Something like that. Does that sound silly?"

"No, it doesn't. It's probably kinda premature to say this, but I think you've met that man, Lucas. I've gotten real fond of you already, dangerously fond, and I intend to stay here as long as you want me to and to spend as much time with you as possible... and see what happens between us. Okay?"

Lucas nodded slowly. "Yeah. That sounds good."

"Going slow will be frustrating for me, but it'll be good for me too. It's about damn time I lived my life differently. In the past, as I told you the other day, most of my experiences with men were quick, meaningless, anonymous fucks with guys I'd just met, didn't know, and would most likely never see again. With Zac, it was more than that, but I wasn't ready for more. I'm ready for more now. Yep, let's take it slow and see if what we're feeling for each other is something real, something that'll last, something...."

Lucas kissed Brice on the cheek and ran a hand over his furry chest. "Something to...something to maybe found some kinda future on?"

"Yeah. Exactly. Lucas?"

"Yeah?"

"I know you need to feel safe with me. Safe and in control. You're welcome to initiate anything at any time, 'cause I'm ready for anything, hot as you are. There's probably nothing you could ask of me that I wouldn't be willing to give. But me…I'm going to ask your permission before I start any kind of intimacy. All right?"

Lucas sighed. "That sounds great. That sounds just right. Thank you."

"You're welcome. So, may I kiss you now? A real kiss? A deep kiss?"

"Yeah. I'm ready for that."

"C'mere then."

Brice pulled Lucas close. Lucas took a deep breath and smiled. Brice kissed him lightly, then harder, slipping his tongue into the younger man's mouth and probing gently. Lucas groaned and nodded, opening his lips to Brice's eager tongue. Brice ran his hands over the boy's lean sides, up over his smooth back, across his fuzzy chest. As much as he yearned to take the boy's prick in his fist or his ass-cheeks in his hands, he limited his explorations to above the waist.

"That feels so good," Lucas sighed against Brice's lips. "You're so gentle. I need gentle real bad." Lucas stroked Brice's thick beard and squeezed his beefy biceps.

"Then gentle's what you're gonna get." Brice tugged at Lucas's neck-chains and fooled with Lucas's chest hair. It was as he was sliding a palm across Lucas's ribs that he felt the low, thin ridges of coarse skin.

Lucas stiffened and pulled away. "That's enough. Let's take a break, okay?"

"Sure," Brice said, concealing his disappointment and alarm.

Lucas scooted back a few inches along the seat. He filled up their champagne flutes, handed Brice his glass, and took a swig from his own. He avoided Brice's eyes, gazing into the bubbling water of the tub.

Brice took a tart gulp of Prosecco, doing his best to act casual. "I'm sorry. Did I do something wrong?"

"My scars. You touched 'em." Lucas grimaced. "I got 'em in prison. They're ugly."

"There isn't anything ugly about you, Lucas. Scars aren't ugly. Hell, we're all scarred, past a certain point in life, either inside or out. Scars are just evidence of history, of how hard life can be. They're proof that we've survived. Still, I'm sorry if I upset you."

"No problem. Not your fault. I just…." Lucas drained his glass. "I overreacted, as usual. You see what kinda mess you're dealing with? Sure you're not having second thoughts about getting involved with me?"

"No second thoughts. And I don't see any kind of mess. I see a super-handsome young man who's damaged by the hard times he's had to endure, just like most of us. You're stubborn and strong and resilient, far as I'm concerned. Sorta heroic, to have survived what you have."

"Heroic? I sure don't feel heroic." Lucas slipped off the ledge and submerged himself to the neck. "The scars are just reminders I carry around and can't get away from. They take me back to prison. I got waylaid a few months before I was released. Six of the bastards. With shivs. Damn scars still ache sometimes. When it rains, when it's cold out. Eric, he...."

"Oh, fuck it." Lucas submerged completely. He burst back up with a gasp. He shook wet off his head, grabbed Brice's hands, and pulled him to his feet.

"Used to be, Mr. Brown, these scars were like little jagged mouths. They'd whisper to me in the dead of night, when bad dreams woke me up and I couldn't sleep. They'd tell me I wasn't worth shit, that nothing would get better, that I didn't deserve nothing better, that I couldn't do nothing right, that I was a piece of ignorant white trash with no reason to hope for anything, that no one would ever feel anything for me, except for bastards who might want to use my mouth or my asshole as their tight pussy for the night, that I might as well find myself a nice, scenic mountain ledge and throw myself right off the edge and break my worthless neck. But you know what?"

"What?"

"I'm tired of that shit. Tired to death. Those voices can shut the fuck up. I got better things to do now than listen to them. You said I could initiate anything, right?"

"Yes. Yes, I did. I'm up for whatever you are."

"Will you...?" Lucas paused, shook his head, and grinned. "This is kinda hard. Will you...will you come back to my cabin and sleep with me? No sex yet. Just snuggling good and close. Will you? It's not real late, so we could climb in bed and watch a movie, if you want. I even got a jar of moonshine we could sample. How's that sound?"

The thankfulness that Brice had felt so often since the first evening he'd seen Lucas's solemn face pulsed up in him again. He finished his champagne. He bent forward and planted a kiss on Lucas's brow. "You bet, kid. I've been waiting for weeks for you to ask me something like that."

"Good. If you can rein in those horndog lusts of yours till I'm ready for more, we might just make sharing a bed a regular thing."

"Whatever you say," Brice said. *I'll do anything necessary to hold you.* "I'll be on my best behavior, I promise."

The two men climbed out of the hot tub, covered it, dried off, and dressed. Lucas snuffed the candle. As they left the grotto and climbed the spiral steps to the pool, a light drizzle falling on their shoulders and faces, a sudden realization hit Brice: he couldn't recall ever being happier.

Happiness? My God, happiness. How long has it been since I've felt this way? I don't think I've ever really felt this way before. Savor it, Brice buddy. Savor it while it's here. Who knows how long it might last or when, if ever, it might come again?

"Thanks for a wonderful Valentine's Day," Brice said, taking Lucas's hand.

"Thank you," Lucas said. "You're one sweet Daddy, that's for sure. As much as I liked the Speedos, I'm thinking a cuddle-fest with you is gonna be the best Valentine's Day gift of all. Furry as you are, snuggling's gonna feel great."

CHAPTER THIRTY-SIX

"I'M THINKIN' UNDERWEAR IS BEST," LUCAS SAID, smiling shyly. Standing in the low lamplight of his bedroom, he peeled off his clothes, giving Brice a glorious show. Brice watched, full of a profound ache, an ache composed of equal parts erotic desire and aesthetic awe, admiring the boy's well-defined muscles as they were exposed, admiring the contrast between white skin and chestnut-colored body hair.

"Me too," Brice said with a sigh. *Damn, those sweet little nipples. I'd like to suck on 'em till the sun comes up.* Slowly, he stripped as well. "That'll make it easier for me to keep my hands off that prominent crotch of yours, or that magnificent butt."

Lucas face flushed. "I'm thinkin' all those are gonna be yours to handle sooner or later."

"Promise?"

"Uh, yeah. I feel safe in promising that."

The two men stood face to face, a few feet apart, Lucas in his tighty-whities, Brice in his gray boxer briefs. Both of them gazed with greedy fascination at the other's exposed body, both of their cocks discernibly hard.

"This is crazy. We're both stiff as boards. I really don't mean to be a tease." Lucas moved over to Brice, wrapped his arms around his waist, stood on tiptoe, and kissed his whiskered cheek. "You sure you can do this? Give me just a little time to…to feel safe and adjust and get over my hang-ups?"

Brice hesitated. The crotch-swell in the front of Lucas's white briefs and the buttock-swell in the back were more than sufficient to make him suffer. "I think so." Brice stroked Lucas's bearded jaw and looked into his sad blue-gray eyes. "Yes. Yes, I can do this. For you, Mr. Lucas, I can do anything. Including resisting the violent urges I'm feeling right now."

"Thanks, Daddy. That means a lot. Your patience will be rewarded, I swear. Okay, let's get to this movie. It's one of my favorites. Lotsa stuff gets blown up."

Lucas fetched the jar of moonshine, and they climbed into bed together. For the next few hours, they took turns sipping the liquor, watching *The Rock* on Lucas's VHS machine, and cuddling together beneath a heap of blankets in the high, chilly room.

Both men were half- or fully hard all evening, but Brice behaved as promised, holding Lucas close but resisting the temptation to initiate anything sexual for fear of the boy's negative response. Sometimes, Lucas rested his head on Brice's torso or shoulder and fooled with Brice's belly hair or navel. Sometimes Brice curled against Lucas from behind, fondling the boy's soft chest hair but avoiding his nipples. Brice desperately wanted to stroke, pinch, lick, suck, and bite them, for he'd always found men's chests in general and men's nipples in particular especially appealing. Even a glimpse of Lucas's fur-swathed little nubs brought out the rough and raging Top in him. Still, he controlled himself, determined to make the boy feel safe and comfortable no matter what, as if a magnificent but thoroughly skittish wild animal had been given into his care and keeping.

They fell into kissing bouts with regularity, beards brushing beards, tongues softly wrangling, Lucas's strong arms tight around Brice's big shoulders. When the movie ended and Lucas turned out the light with a whispered, "This is wonderful. Thanks for staying with me. Good night, Daddy," Brice spooned him close from behind, stroking the boy's cheek and kissing his shoulders till Lucas began to snore.

Brice studied his face in the dimness, stunned yet again at his remarkable good fortune and the universe's sudden and thoroughly unexpected generosity. Already, he sensed, the loss of this fuzzy human warmth he held in his arms would be greater than any loss he'd ever experienced, and he fell asleep praying that such a bleak eventuality might be delayed as long as mortality might permit.

BRICE OPENED HIS EYES TO the sight of Lucas, still in white briefs, sitting on the bed's edge and holding two steaming mugs. "Good morning, Daddy," Lucas said. "Sun's out, snow's meltin'. How'd you sleep?" Warm light streamed through the window, glinting off his silver necklaces, illuminating the curves of his fuzzy torso and the scrawls of his tattoo sleeve.

"Great. More than great. You?"

"Great too. Felt damned good, those beefy arms wrapped around me. None of the usual nightmares neither. Coffee?"

"You bet. Thanks. Let me hit the toilet first."

When Brice returned, he found the pillows arranged in a heap against the headboard and Lucas back in bed. The two reclined side by side, blankets pulled up to their bellies, and sipped their mugs.

"You have such a beautiful physique," Brice said, running a finger over Lucas's biceps. "That weightlifting you do really pays off."

"You too, brawny. That fur all over your chest and belly gets me pretty het up."

"Good to hear. I gotta admit that being, uh, chaste last night was—"

"Hard? Yeah, I agree. You were hard, I was hard." Lucas snickered. "Like I said, just give me a little time."

"I will." Brice put down his mug and cupped Lucas's cheek. "Pretty eyes. Pretty beard. Everything about you is just so fine."

"Even these?" Lucas gingerly fingered his scars. In the bright light of morning, they were glaringly obvious, ragged pink lines etched across his ribs on both left and right sides. Another scar, a puckered oval one, gleamed beneath the dusting of his ruddy belly hair.

Brice gripped Lucas's arm and bent over. When he kissed the scars over Lucas's left ribs, the boy tensed and gasped.

"Even these, kid." Brice kissed the scars over his right ribs next, then the one upon his belly. "They only make me...."

Brice paused, swallowing hard. *Love. Already I want to say "love." My God, how has all this happened so fast? And what will I do if his feelings aren't as deep as mine?* "They only make me care for you more."

Lucas fell silent. He sipped at his mug, then put it down on the bedside table, stretched out, and folded his arms behind his head, displaying red-brown thickets of armpit hair.

"I want to tell you about them," he said, staring at the ceiling. "My scars. How I got them. It happened exactly two years ago today. February 15, 1996."

"Really?" Brice was torn between surprise and a desire to bury his face in Lucas's armpits. He took a deep breath, savoring the boy's rich scent. "You sure you wanna talk about it?"

"Yep. I want to tell you about prison. You wanna hear? It ain't pleasant."

"I figured that." Brice settled back into the pillows, half-afraid of what he was about to discover. "Yeah, I do want to hear. I'd like you to tell me."

"Okay." Lucas paused. "Then we can head down to the lodge and I'll cook us up some sausage and fried apples and a cheesy grits casserole."

"That sounds great."

"So...." Lucas closed his eyes. "I wudn't in prison but a week before four guys ambushed me in the shower. They crammed a washrag in my mouth, and they held me down, and they took turns with me. I'd fought so hard to keep that fuckin' trucker's dick outta my ass, yet there I was, on the tiled floor of that shower, those bastards on top of me, one after another, pounding away. I hollered and I fought, but it didn't do no damn good."

Brice groaned. "Jesus, Lucas. I'm so sorry. As good-looking as you are, I figured that something like that might have happened."

"Yeah. Bad combo: they liked my looks and they were all a lot bigger'n me. God, I wish I'd been your size. I might have had a chance."

"Like I said before, no matter how big a man is, if he's outnumbered...."

"He's screwed. Literally, in this case. What made it worse is that I hadn't been fucked before." Lucas rubbed his forehead and grimaced, the ghost of past pain darkening his face. "Ever. Old-fashioned fool that I was, I was saving my cherry for some guy I really cared about." Lucas shot Brice a glance and then closed his eyes again. "Someone like you."

"Like me? Really?"

"Yeah. Really." Lucas rolled over onto his side, his back to Brice. "There's a kindness in you that...well, ain't no use to talk about might-have-beens, right?"

"How old were you when all this happened?"

"I was twenty." Lucas pulled the blankets up to his shoulders. "All the lube they used was soap and spit. I bled some afterwards. And that was only the first time. About every two weeks, those guys would get me somehow, somewhere. Brett, and Rick, and Greg, and Matt. Fuckers."

"You reported them, right?"

"Oh, sure. I told the guards, begged 'em to do something, but they just snickered and rolled their eyes like it was some kinda big joke to them. After a while, when those bastards grabbed me, I stopped fighting and just tried to relax. It didn't hurt as much then. And they were less likely to slam my head against the floor or punch me in the side, if I just lay there, bit down on that washcloth, and took it. They were always tellin' me to 'take it like a man.' So I guess I learned to do that."

"Lucas?"

"Yeah?"

"I'm asking permission to hold you. Would that be all right?"

For a long moment, Lucas said nothing.

"Yeah. Please."

Brice scooted across the bed. When he wrapped an arm around Lucas and pulled him close, the boy emitted a low whimper and curled into a ball.

"Is this all right?"

"Yeah. You make me feel safe. You made me feel safe last night, when you held me close in bed. I cain't recall when I ever felt safe before. When I was a kid, I guess. Before Dad died."

"I'm real glad I make you feel safe. Do you want to go on with your story? Or have you had enough?"

"Naw, I want to finish it."

"Okay. So they just kept on…raping you all those years?"

"Naw. That shit went on about six months. Then Eric showed up. And things changed."

"Eric. You've mentioned him. You two were lovers?"

"Yeah. I guess you could call it that. The only lover I've ever had. He was six foot three, built like a brick shit-house. Messy red hair. Big red beard. Blue eyes. Pale, freckled skin. Thick hairy legs, smooth chest, arms like oak limbs, shoulders so damn broad he'd have to shift sideways to get through some doorframes. He was like some kinda thunder god outta Norse mythology."

A faint tremor shook Lucas's frame. Brice kissed the boy's shoulders. "Go on."

"I hated Eric sometimes, the way he beat me, but, man, he was a goddamn glory. He'd only been there two weeks when he caught those guys giving it to me—one of 'em with a dick up my ass and another with a dick down my throat, both of 'em pumping away to beat the band. I'd pretty much given up any kind of fight by then, after half a year of that routine, so I just let 'em do what they pleased."

Lucas coughed and chuckled. "Well, Eric lunged into that room and beat the ever-living hell out of all of 'em. Then he—God, this sounds like some kinda romantic movie—he threw me over his shoulder and carried me back to his cell, like I was some kinda prize he'd won. I guess I was. Of course, then he beat me up and raped me himself, which weren't all that romantic...but the funny thing was, after he'd blackened both of my eyes and bruised my ribs up, when he threw me down on the bed and clamped a hand over my mouth and fucked me...he was so tender."

Lucas shuddered. "It was crazy. Those big fists pounding into me, and then him on top of me, holding me down and kissing me and riding my ass, just as slow and gentle as if he were a groom and I was some kinda delicate virgin bride on her wedding night."

Lucas shook his head and huddled even closer to Brice, his back pressed against the older man's chest. "Just fucking crazy. He'd grip my jaw and thrust in and out, that huge body of his crushing me into the sheets, and he'd whisper, "Does that feel good, boy? I want you to feel good, boy. Tell me that feels good, boy.' And I'd nod and mumble into his palm, and after a while, I wudn't lying, 'cause he did make it feel good. Damn, was I insane?"

"Naw. Folks are complicated critters, and our sex drives are probably the most complicated and irrational elements of all. So...what happened with Eric, that got to be a regular thing?"

"Yep. He pulled some strings, and suddenly we were cellmates. I was his bitch, his boy, and everyone knew it. No one dared to touch me then. And God, I was so grateful. Getting beat up by him every now and then...his moods were erratic as hell, and the slightest little thing could piss him off...being bruised up all the time was worth not being gang-banged by those skanky pricks. So, yeah, that went on for years. Eric slapping me or punching me or whacking my ass red as fire, and then him gripping my head and fucking my face till I was drooling and choking and close to puking, and then him on top of me, hand tight over my mouth, screwing me slow and deep and sweet...and me crying...I think every goddamn time he fucked me, I broke down and cried like a baby, I don't know why...'cause it hurt my hole some, 'cause no matter how slow he went, his dick was huge...and 'cause I was in pain, face and belly and sides red with the marks of his knuckles...and 'cause I was thankful that God had sent him to protect me from everyone else…and 'cause I was pretty sure he loved me…a love just as strong and deep as it was brutal and fucking nuts…and 'cause I guess I grew to love him too…and 'cause every time he fucked me, my dick was as hard as the bars on the door and the window of our cell, and I always, I *always* came, he always insisted I come before him…."

Lucas's voice broke. He fell silent, trembling violently.

Brice rocked him and soothed him. "Hey. Hey. It's all right. It's all right. I got you." When he caressed the boy's face, his fingers encountered hot tears.

"Ah, Lucas. Ah, sweet boy." Brice kissed his shoulders and hugged him hard. "That's enough. That's enough. Let's get some breakfast."

"Naw." Lucas shook his head, wiping his face with a balled-up fist. "I want to finish. I'm almost done."

"You sure?"

"Yep." Lucas took a deep breath. He gripped Brice's hand. "You holding me helps. So…."

Lucas cleared his throat. "So Eric owned me, and I guess I owned Eric, for over five years. He'd hold me at night, and he'd tell me about how hard his life had been…crazy, abusive, drunken parents…the drugs he'd been on…the shit he'd stole…the woman who broke his heart…the older guy who took him in, used him as a boy-toy for a year, then threw him out…the years on the streets…the gang he joined…the armed robbery he got busted for. Hearing all that, I could forgive him for his meanness. Man, he clung to me at night. Sometimes it was hard to pry his arms off me long enough to piss. There was something desperate in the way he held me. He told me he adored me—something he'd say while he beat me up and when he screwed me so slow and gentle right after—and I got to believe him. I got to thinking I couldn't live him without him. But then I had to."

"He got out of prison? He was paroled?"

"Naw. Eric died. He was murdered."

"Jesus. Really? What happened?"

"Well, this conversation got started when I said I was gonna tell you how I got these scars. So now we're around to that topic. Just a few months before I got out of prison—two years ago today—some new guys in our cell block decided that they wanted my ass and that Eric's monopoly of me was done. They cornered us in the bathroom. Six of 'em. With shivs, knives they'd made. Two of 'em grabbed me and four ganged up on Eric. Two of the four were as big as Eric was. They had him pinned to the wall with a shiv to his throat. The other two—strong, nasty fuckers—subdued me pretty easy. I mean, I can fight with the best of 'em, but once again, my smaller size was a big handicap. One of 'em jerked down my pants, and the leader said that everyone was gonna have a go at me and that all Eric could do was watch. Well, Eric wasn't gonna tolerate that, shivs or no shivs, and he went fucking crazy, and I followed his lead, and I went crazy too. To make a long story short, in a few seconds, Eric had stabbed one of 'em to death, one of 'em had cut me across my ribs real deep, and another had stabbed me in the belly. So that's how I got the scars. Eric...."

Lucas rolled over, his face gleaming with tears. He pressed his face into Brice's chest hair and choked up a strangled sob.

"Hey, buddy, go ahead and cry if you want to." Brice hugged him close.

"Naw. If I get started, I'll go on all goddamn morning. Eric.... By the time it was over, Eric was on the floor, looking up at me, a knife in his chest and his throat half-cut open. I stumbled over to him, and he grabbed my hand, and he smiled up at me, and he coughed up about a fucking bucket of blood, and he closed his eyes and died."

"Christ. What happened then?"

"Then the powers-that-be covered it up. They told me they'd fuck up my parole if I made a fuss. Eric had no family left to miss him, and neither did the son of a bitch he killed. I had only three months till my release—early release for good behavior—and Eric was gone, so...the warden told me that he'd arrange for my protection during the little time I had left inside, so no more rapes. My Mommy and Phil came to visit me while I was healing up, but I didn't tell 'em what happened. No point. You're the first person I've told."

"It means a lot to me that you trust me enough to tell me. Your mother's still alive, right? You never mention her."

"Oh, she's alive. She's still living in the house in Mabie. But she's so ashamed of having a 'queer whore,' as she puts it, for a son that we don't see one another very often. Holidays like Christmas or Thanksgiving, Uncle Phil has invited her up here, but let's just say the conversation is as awkward as the food is fantastic. Speaking of food...." Lucas wiped his face yet again. "I'm tired of being all sad and pathetic. Thank for listening. Your reward is gonna be another big country breakfast."

Lucas gave Brice a quick kiss on the mouth and slipped out of bed. "By the way, for future reference, I got tested when I got out of prison, and I'm glad to say none of those bastards gave me any kinda disease. Kind of a miracle, really."

"Thank God for that. Well, for future reference, I'm clean too. I got tested before I left Nashville."

"Damned fine news." Lucas poked Brice's shoulder. "Get dressed, Daddy Bear. I'm famished, and it's gonna take a while for that cheesy grits casserole to bake."

CHAPTER THIRTY-SEVEN

LUCAS HAD THE SAUSAGE AND APPLES FRIED, the casserole in the oven, and a warm fire going in the great room. Both men, dressed in thermal undershirts, jeans, and thick wool socks, were sipping Bloody Mary's, and Brice was fooling around on his guitar, picking out a new melody surfacing inside his head and beneath his fingers, when the phone rang.

"Odd. No one ever calls up here," Lucas said. He bounded up off the couch and answered.

"Yeah? Hey, Grace. Yeah, Brice is here. What's going—" Lucas frowned. "What? What? You've got to be fucking kidding me. Yep. Yep. Okay. We'll be here."

Lucas hung up. The look on his face was flushed fury. "I'll be goddamned. You're not going to believe this."

"What?" Brice lowered his guitar into its case and stood, on the alert.

"There's some fucking reporter down at Grace's store, asking about you. How the hell could they have found out where you are?"

"I don't know. Dammit!"

"Grace just sent him on a wild goose chase. She's gonna keep an eye on the store, since he said that other reporters were on their way. But Amie, she's coming up here to tell us what the bastard looks like, what gossip rag he works for. Plus she's bringing up some of her potato soup. She always sends some up when something bad's happened or someone's sick. Maybe we should hide your truck. It's got Tennessee tags, right?"

"Yeah. We can do that. But…. Shit, I think I know how those assholes found out I was here."

"How?"

"Just a couple of days ago, I heard from my label—well, my ex-label—asking for an address to send the piss-ant amount of money my CDs have earned recently. I gave them your all's post office box number. They're the only folks who would know where I am, other than my sister and that Travis Ferrell boy. I'll be damned."

"Travis would never give you away. He thinks you're a hero. Some sneaky bastard who works at the record company sold the information?"

"Exactly."

"That motherfucker. Okay, let's hide your Ram. There's a shed that'll do just fine."

BRICE AND LUCAS HAD THE telltale vehicle safely stashed and were nervously finishing their drinks by the fire when steps sounded on the porch and there was a knock at the front door.

Lucas jumped up and peered out the front window. "It's just Miss Amie." He loped over and opened the door with a smile.

"Howdy, ma'am!" Lucas said, throwing his arms around their visitor before escorting her into the great room. As Grace had said on Brice's first day in Brantley Valley, Amie did indeed resemble the glamorous pin-up model Betty Page, with long ink-black hair, thick bangs, voluptuous hips and breasts, and dramatic make-up. She was wearing black stockings, a low-cut dress in a flowery print, a black woolen shawl, and high heels. A string of pearls gleamed around her neck, and jeweled rings flashed on her thin fingers. She carried a scarlet clutch purse that matched her lips. Behind red cat-eye glasses, her long-lashed eyes were a friendly dark brown.

Amie smiled at Brice and offered her hand. "There you are! One of my favorite singers. I can't believe you've been up here for weeks, and we're only now meeting. Grace told me to give you your privacy, and I have. But now…I had an excuse to come visit."

"Great to meet you, Miss Amie," Brice said, taking her hand. On a whim, he gave it a light kiss.

"Oh, you Southern men are always so gallant," she said. "We don't get that too often up in Pennsylvania, where Grace and I grew up. I wish we were meeting under better circumstances, Mr. Brown."

"Please call me Brice, ma'am. You come bearing unpleasant tidings, I gather."

"Yes. A reporter from *Country Weekly*. A tall, gangly, ill-favored man who's the spitting image of Ichabod Crane. He came into the store, claiming that he knew that you were 'holed up,' as he put it, in Brantley Valley. Grace and I pretended ignorance, so then he offered us money. Grace told him you were staying in the lodge up at Canaan Valley State Park, so off he went, the little ferret."

"Good job, Grace!" Lucas enthused. "Hey, you wanna stay for breakfast? Or, at this hour, I guess it's brunch. Sausage, fried apples, cheesy grits? You want a Bloody Mary?"

"I'd love one. Do you mind if I stay for brunch, Mr. Brown?"

"It's 'Brice,' and I don't mind at all. I may be a notorious homosexual, thanks to the scandal sheets, but I've always enjoyed the company of elegant ladies like yourself."

"And I may be a high-femme lesbian, but I've always relished handsome gay men with immaculate manners. Oh! I forgot the potato soup in the car. There's a loaf of cranberry and orange nut bread too."

"I'll fetch 'em," Lucas said, grabbing his black denim jacket and black ball cap off the coat rack. "Car unlocked?"

"Yes, indeed."

"Be right back." Lucas jogged out the door, slamming it behind him.

"That boy's a treasure," Amie sighed, slipping off her shawl. "He looks like a tough little redneck, but he can be sweet as pie. Awful, the things he's been through. He's alone too much. I'm so glad you're here to keep him company, since Mr. Philip is in Florida."

"Me too. I haven't been here very long, but I've already gotten mighty fond of him."

Amie batted her eyes. "Oh? Have you managed to break through his considerable defenses? He can be downright glacial to strangers."

"Lucas was pretty rude at first, but I'm glad to say he's opening up to me. Hey, where are those manners you were talking about? Have a seat and let me make you that drink."

"Thank you. That would be lovely."

Brice was pouring chilled vodka at the bar when Lucas entered, carrying a paper bag. The young man looked perturbed, with set mouth and furrowed forehead. "Uh, oh," Brice murmured, regarding him.

"What's wrong, honey?" Amie asked, rising from the armchair.

"There's a car coming up the hill. I don't recognize it." Lucas placed the bag on the bar. "Brice, buddy, you better hide. Just in case."

"Hide? Like a criminal? I don't want to hide."

Lucas scowled. "Brice, dammit. Just do it. If it's reporters, if they see you up here, they won't leave."

Amie nodded, pulling on her shawl. "Lucas is right. If it's a journalist, we can send him packing."

"Makes me feel like a coward," Brice groused. "Why should y'all have to stand up for me?"

"Just do it, man! Go down to the kitchen and check on that casserole, will you?"

"All right, all right."

Brice headed down the stairs, just far enough to let Lucas and Amie step out onto the porch and close the door behind them. Then he retraced his steps. He stood in shadow beside the front window, opened it a crack, and peered out.

The car, a boxy green thing, was parking in the driveway below the porch. The man who climbed out was clearly not the gangly journalist Amie had described as appearing at Radclyffe's Roost earlier that day. Dressed in a travel-rumpled gray suit, he was built much like Brice, with a strong-looking torso and arms and a moderately plump midriff. His features were sharp, his graying hair short, his eyes keen. A camera hung around his thick neck.

"Hello!" he said, lifting a hand. "Is this Philip Rogers' place?"

Lucas shoved his hands into his pockets. "Yep. He's in Florida. Who're you?"

The man flashed them a friendly smile. "I'm Robert West. I'm a reporter for the *Star*. Who're you?"

"I'm Lucas, Philip Rogers' nephew. What d'you want?"

"I got a tip that country music star Brice Brown was staying up here, and I'd like to interview him."

"Brice Brown? Up this valley? Ain't he in Nashville?"

"No, he 'ain't.' He's getting mail at a post office box a few miles from here, in Pickens. The lady down at the store told a colleague of mine that Brown was in Canaan Valley, so he went to check that lead out, but right after that, this lady drove up here in a big hurry, so I figured I'd follow her."

Amie pulled her shawl more tightly around her. "You followed me?"

The man's smile was vaguely apologetic. "Yes, I did. And damned if you didn't lead me here. This is the place where a big pickup truck with a Tennessee license plate has been parked, according to a local down the valley who's scraped your road after the last snowfalls. A slate-gray Dodge Ram 2500, which, last I heard, was the kind of vehicle

Brice Brown was driving when he fled Nashville for his hometown."

"You see any such truck here?" Lucas said, folding his arms across his chest.

"No, I don't. But I see some mighty big tire tracks in the mud over there. I'd like to take a look around anyway. If you don't mind."

"I do mind," Lucas growled. "Brice Brown ain't here. This is private property. My uncle left me in charge of this place. I'm thinking you should leave now."

"It'll just take a few minutes. Hey, did you say your name was Lucas?"

"Yeah? So?"

"Lucas Bryan?"

"Yep. So?"

The man's smile widened. He took a few steps forward. "Some folks in Pickens told me about you. You're the kid who got sent to prison for prostitution and stabbing a man. You're gay. So's Brice Brown. This is all looking even better than I'd thought. Are you two sharing some sort of homosexual love nest up here? Maybe I should interview you, if Brown isn't around."

Lucas spat off the side of the porch rail. "You ain't interviewing nobody today. Git on outta here."

"Ah, come on." The man took two steps up the porch stairs. "I could pay you well. This kind of story is worth a lot of money to the *Star*. Are you Brown's new lover now that his old guitarist has dumped him? How old are you anyway?"

"You need to get the fuck off my uncle's land, buddy. Now." Lucas clenched his fists.

"You're sure you won't give me an interview? I'd love to hear about your time in prison. Did that experience make you a homosexual? A good-looking boy of such small stature would surely have been popular in there."

"Goddamn you. Shut the fuck up," Lucas rasped.

"Are you normally this hateful, Mr. West?" Aimee said, shifting her clutch purse from her right hand to her left. "Leave us alone, or you'll regret it."

"You heard the lady. Get outta here, or I'll kick your ass over into the next county."

The reporter snickered, though he took a step back. "I don't think you're in any position to do that, Mr. Bryan."

"And why the fuck not? Just 'cause you're bigger'n me? I've taken down bigger guys than you."

"I'm sure you learned some fighting skills in prison. No, I'm not talking about your size or strength. I'm talking about the fact that you're probably still on parole. You probably have a parole officer somewhere. You brawl with me, and you'll get sent back to prison. Is that right?"

"*Damn* you," Lucas snarled. "Just leave us the fuck alone."

"That's what I thought," West said. "I think I'll just look around the property a bit before I go. You sure you don't want to tell me about prison? About being a truck-stop prostitute? Our readers would love the nasty details about how many men you serviced with that pretty mouth of yours. You're a manly little guy. Who ever would have guessed that you were slinking from truck cab to truck cab, head bobbing up and down on—"

Brice had had enough. He threw open the door and stormed out onto the porch. "Hey! Asshole! Leave the boy alone!"

"Brice, you retard," Lucas said, but his blue-gray eyes were full of thanks. "You shoulda stayed inside."

Brice gave Lucas's shoulder a quick squeeze. "I wasn't going to let that prick talk to you that way."

West's face gleamed. "Brice Brown! So you *are* here! Surely you'll give me an interview."

"What the hell do you think? No, I'm not going to give you an interview. I'm going to give you something else, something a lot more memorable. I'm going to give you the ass-kicking of your life if you don't get in your car and get the fuck out of here now."

West moved backward, still smiling. "Just a few pics before I go. This is priceless. The infamous gay singer who's lost everything but his new lover, who happens to be a white-trash truck-stop hustler young enough to be his son. Just beautiful. Just beautiful." He aimed his camera and began snapping photos. "Say cheese."

"Okay, that does it." Brice stomped toward the edge of the porch. "I'm gonna feed you your front teeth."

Amie placed a soft, bejeweled hand on Brice's forearm. "I'm sorry. I abhor violence. Let me handle this loathsome person."

Brice paused. "What? How?"

"Like this." Amie opened her purse and drew out a small pistol. It was a delicate thing, with a pearl handle and leafy etchings all along the barrel.

Brice and West both gasped. Lucas guffawed. Amie aimed and fired into the snow a mere foot from West's right shoe.

"Holy shit! You crazy bitch!"

West ducked and fled. In a few seconds, he'd scrambled into his car. He sped away. Amie aimed again, nicking the left edge of his rear bumper. A score of seconds later, the vehicle had raced out of the compound and disappeared around the corner.

"My God," Brice breathed. "That was amazing."

"You're a frigging goddess!" Lucas exclaimed. "I forgot you carry that thang around."

"After a girl's almost raped by a predatory, porcine businessman in an alley following her first burlesque performance, she learns to protect herself. And her friends. I've been a crack shot since I was twenty-three."

Amie slipped the pistol back into her purse and took Brice's arm. "Well, that's enough excitement for today. How about we go in to brunch? I haven't savored Lucas's cooking in many a month."

CHAPTER THIRTY-EIGHT

"This should scare away some of 'em," Lucas said, wielding the hammer.

One by one, he mounted a series of homemade signs along the wooden fence that fronted the Phagg Heights compound. Made of old boards, the signs announced, "Trespass at Your Own Risk!" "Don't Piss With Us!" and "Our Friends Are Cops!" Lucas had even drawn skulls sporting exaggerated fangs on some of them.

"You really think the local police will help?" Brice stared down the dirt road and up the leafless hillsides, feeling profoundly paranoid, as if a reporter might materialize from any direction at any time, even parachute out of the clouds.

"Considering how much money Uncle Phil donates to their department, yep, they'd damn well better. I don't know that they're all that much into defending queers, but they sure are into protecting locals of whatever stripe from pushy, intrusive outsiders. 'You all may be gays, but you're our gays,' as Doris Ann likes to put it. Our family's lived in Brantley Valley for generations, and that kinda thing counts for something around here. All we need to do is call the cops if one of those reporters trespasses, and Chief Willey said he'd send someone up to drive 'em off."

"That would be great. As much fun as it was to see Amie pull her pistol this morning and send that shithead packing—"

"Yeah! Wudn't that a fucking thrill?"

"It was, but.... So, that asshole was right about your parole? They can send you back to prison?"

"Yep." Lucas frowned, hammering up the last sign. "'Fraid so. I'll be on parole for a little while yet.

If I violate it, it's back to being some convict's boy-toy."

"Well, we sure as shit don't want to do anything that might risk that."

"You're telling me," Lucas muttered, slipping the hammer into a loop on the side of his workpants. "Only guy whose boy-toy I hope to be any time soon is a famous country star." He winked at Brice. "I dream of becoming a star fucker. Or star fuckee."

"Fuckee, I hope." Brice licked his lips. "A prospect I'm eagerly awaiting."

"Me too. Okay, this job's done. If these signs don't keep 'em off, Phil says we can put up a gate. You want to work off some of that big brunch and help me split wood? After the snows we've had lately, we're running a little low."

"Sure, kid. Got a question first."

"Yep?"

"Sleeping with you last night was probably the sweetest thing that's happened to me in months. Well, okay, years. Could we…do that again?"

Lucas gave Brice a soft punch in the shoulder. "Greedy Daddy! Hell, yes. I'm thinking every night."

"Sounds like heaven, but…Lucas, I gotta be honest. It's gonna be hell too. I want so much more with you."

"I know. I want it too, I swear."

"Good. Good. Look, I've had a ferocious sex drive since I was fourteen. It's gonna get hard to behave, as you put it. To control myself."

Lucas nodded. "I get it. I honestly don't know when I'll be ready for more. Could be tonight, could be tomorrow, could be next week, could be next month. I don't wanna be a cock-tease. Would it be better if we slept apart?"

"No. Absolutely not."

"Then let's take it as it comes, okay? Let's just stay honest with each other. You asking me if doing something is all right with me before you do it makes all the difference."

"Good to hear. I promise to keep doing that, rather than lunging, which is my usual erotic modus operandi."

"Yeah, no lunging yet, mad dawg." Lucas patted Brice on the back. "Let's get to that wood."

Two hours went by, the weak February sun over Brantley Valley moving in and out of scudding clouds, as Lucas split chestnut oak and Brice stacked it. The grace with which Lucas handled the axe, the way his strong shoulders and slender hips shifted, caused Brice to pause often in his labors just to soak up the sight.

Youth and beauty in action, Brice thought. *And I'm the blessed witness. Tonight— what a miracle!—I'll hold him in my arms again. Is this my reward for suffering so much shit in the last six months? Hell, to hold him, I'd endure fifty times as much. Look at that sweet little butt. Look at that boy move.*

They were taking a break in the kitchen—gulping down water, then sampling some mulled cider Lucas had heated up—when a loud series of knocks resounded on the door of the great room upstairs.

"Son of a bitch. That better not be...." Lucas growled.

Lucas took the steps two at a time. By the time Brice joined him, Lucas had the door thrown open and was shouting at a new intruder. On the porch stood the Ichabod Crane lookalike that Amie had described as appearing at Radclyffe's Roost. He seemed very familiar to Brice.

"Get outta here!"

"Mr. Bryan, I assume? Look, all I want is a story. I've got to do my job. Mr. Brown, hello! I'm Larry Johnson from *Country Weekly.* I've done several articles about you before, including a couple of interviews. Remember?"

Brice paused, recalling his past experiences with Johnson. The man had been polite and understanding, with a sense of humor Brice had enjoyed. At Brice's request, the man had even deep-sixed an article about Brice's separation from Shelly, though the *Star* had run with its own article instead.

"Larry, yeah. Sure, I remember you."

"Good! Won't you please talk to me?"

"Naw, not now. Naw."

"Fuck this. I'm calling the cops," Lucas said.

"Hold on, Lucas," Brice said. "No need for that, I think."

"No need, indeed. I'm just about to leave. But let me ask you this first, Brice. Hasn't there been enough scandal? Hasn't enough been taken from you? Here you are, hiding way up this remote valley like some sort of outlaw. Isn't it time you told us all your side of the story? Don't you want an opportunity to tell your version of the truth?"

Brice shook his head and jammed his hands into the pockets of his pants. "I'm not ready to do that. Not yet. Right now I just want to be left alone."

"I understand that. But—"

Brice sighed. "Ain't I old news by now? That damned article outing me was back in November. It's nearly March."

"You're about to be fresh news again. My colleague at the *Star* got some photos he plans to do a lot with."

"Well, shit. I was afraid of that. Look, Larry, you have a card? If I change my mind, I'll give you a call."

"Promise?" With a hopeful smile, Johnson pulled a business card from his jacket pocket and handed it to Brice.

"Yep. If you promise to leave me alone. And keep those other bastards away from here while you're at it."

"I can promise the first. I can't promise the second. Some of my journalistic colleagues are—"

"Horse's asses?" Lucas said. "Pit bulls? Rattlesnakes?"

"Yes, I'm afraid so. Brice, can you answer just one question?"

Brice shrugged. "Maybe. Depends on the question."

"Have you retired from country music?"

Brice hesitated. "I-I don't—"

Lucas stepped forward, his face only a foot from Johnson's. "Hell, *no*, he ain't retired! He's got more songs in him than a field of July corn has kernels. Just wait. Just you wait. This man has a glorious future. His comeback is gonna be like nothing nobody's ever seen before. It's gonna be like a goddamn supernova!"

"I hope so." Johnson stepped back in the face of Lucas's loud onslaught. "I hope so, truly. Brice has amazing talent. Good luck to both of you. Brice, I'll wait to hear from you."

Johnson offered his hand. Brice hesitated, then shook it. Soon, the journalist's tan SUV had disappeared out the front gate. The sound of it descending the valley diminished and died, leaving only the sough of rising wind in the woods.

"Storm's a-comin'." Lucas nudged Brice inside, then closed the door and locked it. "You shoulda told that guy to get screwed."

"He was pretty considerate in the past. Who knows? Maybe one of these days, I might be willing to give him that interview."

Lucas frowned. "Don't seem too wise to me. Who knows how they'd twist your words? Look, I need to split more wood. Since I cain't split heads."

"Sure. Lead the way. I could work off some anxiety too."

IN THE WOODYARD BEHIND THE lodge, Lucas made an axe-slit in the top of a big cross-section of oak, then set in a wedge and fetched a maul. Hands sliding expertly along the handle, he brought the maul down once, then twice, with resounding metallic clangs.

The round of wood creaked and cracked. On the third blow, it began to divide. Another three blows upon the wedge, and the cross-section split cleanly in half. Lucas wedge-split the halves into quarters before taking up his axe again. Soon he'd made stove-lengths of one quarter.

"Damn, you're good at that."

"Practice. Daddy was better." The boy took off his ball cap, looked up at the sky, and wiped his cheek. "Fixing to rain. I'll get all this covered with a tarp before it gets wet, if you'll stack all that there in the shed."

Brice complied. By the time they were done with their respective chores, Brice's back was panging him and a soft rain had begun. For a long moment, they stood under the eaves by the back door, watching the woodyard's dove-gray and beige hues darken to slate-gray and burnt sienna.

Lucas wrapped an arm around Brice's waist and rested his cheek on Brice's shoulder. "So pretty soon my picture's gonna be on the cover of some scandal sheet?"

"I'm afraid so. Those guys at the *Star* have no concept of personal privacy."

"Shit. The good folks around here are gonna love that. As if I don't have enough of a bad reputation. Well, we've both been through worse, right?"

"Yes. You…a lot worse."

"True. Screw 'em. Never wanted to be famous, but here it comes, huh?"

Brice bent to kiss Lucas on the brow. "Yep. You and me, together in infamy."

"Together sounds good. Infamy, who cares? I think it's time for a long shower and a few stiff drinks by the fire."

"Sounds great." Brice was tempted to ask if they could shower together but feared the suggestion might be regarded as unduly lecherous.

Inside, they shucked off their jackets and ball caps. "Will you play your guitar for me later?" Lucas asked. "Or the piano? It'd relax me. As pissed off as I am by our series of uninvited visitors today, I could do with some relaxing."

"Sure. I've actually been fooling with a new song. I have the melody, but I don't have any of the words yet."

"New music? And I thought you said that music was done with you."

"Yeah, well. I guess you were right about gifts not disappearing entirely. The new music's thanks to you, by the way."

"Yeah? How so?"

"Well, the music's inspired by you. By my feelings for you."

"Really?" Lucas face gleamed.

"Yeah. You're my new muse, kid."

"Wow. Talk about flattering. I've got to hear this music later. As for now, time for that shower."

"Yeah, sure." Brice moved to the bar. "Enjoy. What you want to drink afterwards?"

"Drinks later. Shower now. You coming?"

Brice froze, afraid to hope. "You mean together? Take a shower together?"

"Yep, I mean together."

"Naked? Both of us?"

"Naw, in fucking evening gowns. Yes, naked. Least I can do is to share a shower with the man who defended what little's left of my honor. I loved how you bolted out onto the porch when that motherfucker was making fun of me, calling me a truck-stop cocksucker. That meant a lot."

"I wasn't gonna let that slime-ball insult you." Brice draped an arm over Lucas's shoulders. "Lead the way. First shower together it is."

They were heading downstairs to the grotto when the phone rang. "Amie again?" Lucas said. "More asshole journalists down at the store? Uncle Phil?"

"Or my sister. I gave her this number when I told her that we're too remote up here to get cellphone service."

Lucas snatched up the phone. "Hello?"

Brice's stomach sank, watching Lucas's brows bunch up and his pretty lips curl into a snarl.

"How the hell did you get this number? How? Fuck, no, you can't talk to Brice Brown. Get fucked. Get *fucked*! You call here again, and I'll track you down. I'll tie your testicles into a bowtie and hang the itty-bitty thangs around your neck and then feed the whole goddamn pathetic packet to the pigs. Get **fucked**!"

Lucas slammed the phone back into the cradle. Even in the dim light of late afternoon, Brice could see his small hands shaking.

"More of 'em. *Damn* it. We're gonna have to change the number." Bending, Lucas unplugged the phone. "How could they have gotten this number?"

Brice rubbed at his tight temples. His lower back smarted. "I don't know. I gave it to my sister. That's it. I didn't give it to the record company. Wait, I gave it to my manager too. My ex-manager. Oh, no. Surely Steve didn't sell it to the bastards? Maybe that bitch of a secretary came upon it in his messages or papers? Shit, I don't know."

"Harm's done. We'll fix it. Later tonight, I'll e-mail a note to Phil. C'mon. Now I need a shower more than ever. After dealing with those shitheads today, I'm feeling dirty."

Downstairs in the grotto, the two men began to undress. Brice pulled his upper garments off, then sat back on the bench to savor the sight of Lucas slowly stripping.

"You could make a living at this," Brice said, grinning up at the boy. "Head to some big city, gyrate on top of some bar, make some big money."

"I don't dance well enough for that," Lucas said, dropping his jeans and then hanging them on a wall hook. For a moment, he simply stood there, hands on his hips, wearing nothing but his customary neck-chains and a small pair of crotch-bulge black briefs, looking Brice in the eye. Brice could detect pride in his features, pride in his young body, and amusement, and just the smallest trace of hesitant nervousness and shame. Just when Brice began to fear that Lucas would draw the line and demur, the boy turned to the side and slipped off his briefs.

"Oh, Lucas," Brice groaned. "You're just glorious."

Lucas bowed his head. "It turns me on when you watch me," he whispered. He turned to Brice, displaying a large, erect cock standing up in a thicket of ruddy pubic hair. "Go on and get naked, Daddy."

Brice stared, absorbing every detail: the small nipples, the rusty body hair, the shapely lyre of Lucas's hips and lower abdomen, the impressive prick.

"Damn, Lucas. You're just…."

"Go on now. I wanna see you naked too."

Brice shook himself from his erotic trance. He bent over with a jolt to unlace his boots. When he did so, a savage pain stabbed him in the lumbar, one greater and more pervasive than any he'd ever felt.

"Oh! Damn!" Brice slipped off the bench and fell to his knees. Another wave of pain hit him, and with a choked shout, he fell forward onto the floor. Tears sprang to his eyes.

"Fuck!" he gasped. "Oh, damn."

"Brice!" Lucas was beside him in a second. "What is it?"

"My back. Oh, man. Hurts worse than it ever has. Oh, oh, *man*."

"Oh, Brice." Lucas grabbed his hand. "Poor guy. What can I do?"

"Just…. I…."

"What? Tell me!"

"Just…. Let me lie here for a while. Oh, *damn*."

"Okay. Okay. Here, let me…."

Lucas slipped astride Brice's waist. Brice could feel Lucas's genitals resting against him but was in no shape to savor that fact. He squinted his eyes shut as another spasm shook him. "Uhhhh!"

"Easy." Lucas pushed his thumbs into Brice's lower back and commenced a firm kneading. "How does that feel?"

"Good. Good. A little better. Ah, damn…."

"Relax, buddy. Just relax." Lucas concentrated on the troublesome sacroiliac joint, massaging Brice for long minutes, the room silent save for the older man's grunts and whimpers.

"Okay." Lucas climbed off Brice. "Can you get up? We should get you to bed."

Brice tried. He winced violently, slumping back onto the floor. *Get up, damn you*, he upbraided himself. *You get this delicious young guy naked at last, and your geezer back goes out? Pathetic! Idiot! Moron! Get up, you miserable old wreck.*

Brice tried again. This time, gulping back a sob, he managed to make it to his hands and knees. He swayed there, trembling with agony, gritting his teeth. "Ohhhhh, man. Oh, *man*, it hurts."

Lucas offered Brice a hand. "Damn, you're really bad off. I think we should get you into the hot tub. The warm water will help your back. Let's get those clothes off, okay?"

"O-okay." When Brice took Lucas's hand and attempted to stand, another flare of pain paralyzed him. "Uhhhh! Naw. N-naw."

"Okay, buddy. Hold on."

Lucas hurried over to the hot tub controls and fumbled with them. "Okay, bubbles on. It's gonna get good and hot soon. Lemme get those boots and pants off you."

For long moments, Lucas fumbled with bootlaces, boots, socks, jeans, and boxer briefs, stripping Brice with care and patience as the older man mumbled, winced, and cussed.

"Not exactly the scene I had in mind, you stripping me all slow and seductive."

"Best laid schemes of mousies and men, right? Get in there and lean back against the water pulse. Let it massage you, okay?"

"Yeah." Wincing, Brice crept across the floor. *Crawling like a fucking cockroach,* he thought. *Like a frigging centipede. Like a feeble cripple. So much for being a big, butch Daddy about to bed a hot young stud.* With Lucas's help, he clambered down into the tub, propped himself on the submerged seat, and closed his eyes. The hot water brought, almost instantly, some modicum of relief.

"How's that feel?" Lucas squeezed Brice's bare shoulder.

"Uhhhhhhhhh. Good. Good. Lucas?"

"Yeah, buddy?"

"Would you…? In my cabin. In my backpack. Bottle of pills. For this kinda pain. Would you fetch 'em? Them, and a glass of water? Please? Please?"

"Oh, sure. Oh, sure."

Lucas leapt up. In another minute, he'd pulled on his pants, stuffed his feet into unlaced work boots, and rushed off, still shirtless, into the rainy night.

CHAPTER THIRTY-NINE

DROWSY ON MEDICATION AND TWO BIG GLASSES of Irish whiskey, Brice lay beneath the covers of Lucas's bed. The pain had subsided somewhat, but it still hurt even to roll over.

It had taken Lucas a long time to help Brice get dressed. It had taken even longer to help him out of the lodge and up the drizzle-wet hill to Lucas's cabin. "I'm walking like an old man over ice," Brice had snarled, taking small, wincing step by small, wincing step. He'd napped away the remainder of the rainy afternoon. Now, nightfall descended on Brantley Valley and the sky had cleared. It filled the bedroom window with velvety petunia-purple, centered by the glistening white pinprick of the evening star.

"Hey." Lucas entered the room with a tray of food. "Are you hungry?"

Brice rubbed sleep from his face. "I am. What you got there?"

"Two mugs of Amie's potato soup. And sausage biscuits." Lucas placed the tray on the dresser. "And beers. That Yuengling stuff."

"Sounds great. Thank you." Brice rolled onto his side and tried to sit up. "Sheeee-ut. Whoa."

"Need some help?" Lucas strode over and gripped Brice's hand.

"Afraid so."

Brice strained and Lucas hauled. Soon, the bigger man was sitting unsteadily on the edge of the bed, taking deep breaths and trying to ignore new waves of pain. Lucas slid the tray onto Brice's lap.

"Want me to feed you, pore ole Daddy?"

Brice chuckled. "Fuck you, kid. Now you're making fun of me?"

Lucas kissed Brice's brow before taking his portion of the meal and seating himself at the desk. "Figured a little humor wouldn't hurt."

"True. It is funny in an absurd, pathetic way. I can bench-press and preacher-curl a decent amount of weight, but…talk about a chain only being as strong as its weakest link. One lumbar joint goes out and, hell, if all the homophobes in Nashville were to show up tonight, crippled up as I am right now, they could beat me to death with the greatest of ease."

"They'd have to go through me first," Lucas said, flexing his biceps. "Parole or not, ain't no one gonna mess with you long as I'm around. Plus Amie isn't the only one around here with a gun."

"Really?"

"Really. What my parole officer don't know won't hurt him. We country folks like our guns. Who knows what kinda crazy asshole might show up on the doorstep, way out here in the boonies? Ain't you noticed that shotgun I have there in the corner behind the bed?"

Brice turned stiffly to regard the weapon. "No, I hadn't noticed that. When I'm here, all I notice is you."

Lucas guffawed. "Listen to that sweet talk. Eat your soup before it gets cold. Amie puts lots of carrot, bacon, pepper, and parsley in it to jazz it up."

Brice nodded. The two men fell silent, savoring their meals, murmuring with pleasure. When they were done, Lucas piled the dirty dishes on the tray and took them to the kitchen. He returned, carrying two more bottles of beer and another round of pain pills.

"Looks like you're in no shape to play me your guitar, so how about another movie?" Lucas handed Brice a Yuengling before pulling the curtains against the cold and lighting a stubby candle on the bookshelf by the bed.

"Yep. Sounds fun." Brice gulped down the pills with a chaser of beer.

Lucas tugged at the shoulder of Brice's sweatshirt. "Want some help getting those clothes off, ole crip?"

"You cocky little prick." Brice smiled, pushing back the pain and the weariness. He grunted and huffed with discomfort as Lucas tugged off first his sweatshirt and T-shirt and then his jeans. Lucas helped Brice stretch out on the bed and arranged a supportive pile of pillows behind his back.

"Cold in here," Lucas muttered, stripping down to his black briefs. He popped a DVD into the player before diving into bed. "Warm me up, Daddy."

"I'd be damned glad to." Brice wrapped an arm around the shivering boy.

"Ummm, feels great. Don't you worry, man. I'll take good care of you." Snuggling closer, he nuzzled Brice's neck. "So here we go. *From Dusk Till Dawn.* I love vampires. Word is we even got some near here."

Brice cocked an eyebrow.

"For years, there've been rumors about guys over in Pendleton County found drained of blood. Round about Seneca Rocks, Spruce Knob, and German Valley."

"Creepy."

"Local bullshit. Those are real pretty areas. We could hike around there come spring, if you'd like. Unless you're afraid of bloodsuckers."

"Yeah, right. I guess we West Virginians have some pretty crazy folklore."

Lucas bumped Brice's side with his shoulder. "Crazy? Don't you believe in the Mothman and the Snarly Yow and the Flatwoods Monster? They're the stuff of mountain men's nightmares."

Brice took a swig of beer before pulling Lucas closer. "After today, the stuff of this mountain man's nightmares is reporters, scads of 'em, dropping from the trees and slithering out from behind bushes. Like diamondbacks or stinging caterpillars."

"Yeah, that's a pretty horrible vision. How long you think before that *Star* issue is out?"

"They work pretty fast. A matter of days."

"Mommy's gonna love that. Her neighbors picking up that rag and reading it and waving it in her face...." Lucas's face fell. "Shit. As if she ain't ashamed of me enough already."

"It's my fault. I'm so sorry. You were just trying to—"

"I was trying to protect you." Lucas's voice was firm with defiance. "Because I care about you a lot. Because, ever since you got here, despite me being a mean little icy—frigid!—bastard, you've been nicer to me than just about anyone other'n Uncle Phil, and Grace, and Amie, and Doris Ann. Mommy's been downright rattlesnake-mean since I come outta prison. So much for being a compassionate Christian."

"Oh, hell. Enougha this." Lucas rolled over and grabbed up the remote. "Let's get to those vampires. I sure like the looks of that George Clooney. He could nip my neck any time."

Brice woke to find the closing credits scrolling over the TV screen and the sound muted. He was lying on his side, with Lucas curled in his arms.

"Uhhhh. Man. I fell asleep?"

Lucas took Brice's hand. "You sure did. After the first twenty minutes or so. You were snoring up a storm."

"Beer and pain pills.... Sorry about that."

"No problem. You were my own private furry furnace while I helped Mr. Clooney kill off those fanged bastards. They sorta did remind me of the reporters that've been snooping around here." Lucas switched off the TV and rolled onto his back. "How you feeling?"

Brice risked an exploratory stretch. "Better. Those pills always help. The pain's moved from agony to dull ache, which is definitely an improvement."

"You want another back rub before we hit the hay? Might do you some good. I could work in some Bengay."

"God, yes. That would be wonderful."

Lucas slid off the bed. He opened the bedside table and pulled out a tube of the heat rub. "On your belly then."

Grunting, Brice repositioned himself.

"Underwear off this time."

"Yeah? Really?"

"Yeah, really. I'm gonna concentrate on your lower back, but I'm gonna rub your glutes too."

Brice shifted about, trying to slide down his boxer briefs.

"Here. Lemme do it."

Lucas's fingers slipped under the waistband of Brice's underwear. "Lift up your hips. Yep. Yep. There you go."

The garment slipped down Brice's legs and off. "Oh, yeah," Lucas said softly. "Just the kind of big, chunky, hairy butt I'd imagined."

Brice laughed. The cool air of the room goose-pimpled his skin. "You've imagined my butt?"

"I sure have. Umm, sorry, it's kinda chilly in here. Lemme warm things up." Lucas turned on a rotating heater in the corner, and in a matter of minutes the small room grew toasty.

"Sorry to keep things so cold," Lucas said, sitting astride Brice's thighs before anointing his hands with the rub. "We were so poor growing up that Daddy and Mommy were always running around behind me, turning off lights and turning down the heat. Uncle Phil has been so good to me, letting me stay here free, that I hate to run up his heating bill."

"I was raised the same," Brice sighed as Lucas's fingers began to do their work, kneading Brice's shoulders and neck only briefly before focusing on his lower back. "'Never waste anything' was pretty much my family's motto. Hell, the whole town's. My parents grew up in the Great Depression, so—uuuuhhhh! Wonderful. Where'd you learn to do all that?"

"I used to be on the baseball team back in high school. Had an older cousin, Rex, who was studying sports medicine at WVU. He sorta interned with us some, taught me some things. Wish he'd taught me more. He was pretty hot. Died driving drunk the second year I was in prison. Damn fool. I still miss him. Anyway, I learned some stuff from him, and the rest I just fake."

The distinctive scent of Bengay filled the room, reminding Brice of Phys Ed classes of long ago. Lucas dug his thumbs into Brice's sacroiliac joint.

"There's the little fucker. Swollen."

"UH!"

Lucas paused. "Am I hurting you?"

"It hurts good. Keep it up. Uhh! Man, if I had the money...and I sure as shit don't any more...I'd send you to massage school."

"Sounds good. Though I'd rather...."

"Rather what? Oh, Lucas, that feels wonderful. Thank you. You'd...ummmmm... rather what?"

"Well, I was always into biology. I was always good at it. I had dreams, stupid dreams."

"Dreams of what?"

Lucas was silent for a long time, working the enflamed joint.

"Lucas?"

"I wanted to be a forest ranger. Or a wildlife biologist. Maybe work at a state park or forest like Kumbrabow or a wilderness area like Dolly Sods. Instead, I ended up a professional cocksucker and penitentiary butt-bitch."

"Well, those are skills I admire and hope to enjoy real soon. But you ought to consider going back to school, maybe WVU, and getting a degree."

"Uncle Phil says the same thing. He's even offered to pay. Who knows? Right now, I just...I just need more time to.... It's hard for me to be around strangers. Real hard. I know I can't stay here in this valley forever, but part of me sure would like to."

"Yeah. Right now I'm feeling the same. I'm just glad I have you to hole up with. With luck, we can both figure out what to do with our futures. At this point, I don't have the slightest idea."

"Me, I think you should get cracking and write a new album. How could the music not be pouring out of you with a new muse as sexy as me?"

"True. Let's see. I could write a song called 'Bearded Beauty and the Bare-Assed Beast.' How's that sound?"

Lucas ran his palms gently over Brice's bared buttocks. "Like a big hit." He probed the bunched mounds of muscle. "Man, you're really tight down here. Can you relax more? You seem super tensed up."

Brice closed his eyes and took a few deep breaths. "I'm trying. It's hard."

"Sooo tense. Rex used to talk about how folks can carry their anxiety and sadness around in their bodies. I used to think that was bullshit, but after a few weeks in prison, it really made sense. I walked around waiting for those guys to jump me again, and my shoulders and neck used to hurt so bad at night it was hard to sleep."

"It makes sense to me too." Brice took another long breath and slumped deeper into the sheets. "I think I've been carrying tension around since.... I think I've been armored all my life. Or at least since I realized I wanted men, and I figured out what that could mean if anyone found out. In my hometown. In college. In Nashville. It's like I'm always tensed up for a fight. Poised to take on attackers at any moment. You know?"

"Shit, *yes*, I know."

"It's the reason I started lifting weights in college. And took some Phys Ed classes in self-defense and boxing. And why I carry a hunting knife underneath my truck seat. It's like a siege mentality I can't turn off."

"I can relate. What's been thrown at you since last fall has made it even worse, no doubt." Lucas's strong thumbs moved in slow, probing circles over Brice's buttocks. Despite his throbbing back, Brice's cock began to stiffen beneath him.

"It sure has. I've—oh, man, keep that up, please! I've been even more on my guard since the minute I heard that interview with Zac got published. It's been one shithead after another coming at me. One blow after another. Who knows what direction the next attack will come from? Who knows what I'll lose next? Damn. I've been drinking too much for months, taking pain pills...."

"Getting drunk, shoving pore lil' ex-cons around. You're a brute, Brice Brown." Lucas returned his strong hands' attentions to Brice's lower back. "A big savage mess. A burly, furry-assed brute." Lucas took a deep breath. He bent down and kissed Brice on his right shoulder blade. "I'm so glad you found me, furry-assed brute."

"I'm so glad *you* found *me*. I am a brute. Yes, indeed. A mad hillbilly of the first order. Yet God has still seen fit to send me a hot little redneck angel."

"Redneck angel. I like that. Don't it piss you off how folks use the word 'redneck' as an insult? Or 'hillbilly?' I'm kinda fond of both those words."

"I feel the same. Though I guess those are terms that we can apply to ourselves but outsiders damn well better not."

"Exactly, yep. 'Redneck angel.' How about that for a song title?" Lucas gave Brice's ass-cheeks gentle slaps and then slipped off the bed. "Sorry. My hands are tired. It's nearly midnight. Ready for some sleep?"

"Yeah. My back feels so much better. Thank you. Will you do me two more favors tonight?"

"Sure. What are they?"

Brice pushed himself up and over onto his side, trying to veil his erection by bending his leg. "Will you help me up here in a minute? I need to piss pretty bad."

"After a couple Yuenglings, I'll bet you do. Let me wash this stuff off my hands first. What's the second favor?"

"I'm naked now. Would you get naked too? It's not like I'm going to cruelly ravish you in this broke-back state I'm in, right?"

Lucas gazed down at Brice, mouth askew with amusement. "I ain't too sure about that. Looks like your Big Johnson there is raring to go. But I guess I'll take my chances." Casually, he slipped his black briefs off. "Be right back."

Half-hard cock swaying, Lucas strode toward the bathroom. Brice watched him go, staring at the boy's superlative ass, two tight winter-pale mounds covered with the faintest dusting of chestnut hair.

CHAPTER FORTY

BRICE WOKE IN THE MIDDLE OF THE NIGHT, bladder full yet again. Lucas was lying behind him, his warm frame pressed against Brice, his left arm flung over Brice's shoulder. Brice extricated himself with difficulty, trying not to wake the boy. He trudged his way to the toilet, moving carefully, afraid the wrong move might throw his back out again. When he clambered back into bed, Lucas whispered, "Hey. How you feeling? You all right?"

"Yeah. Pretty creaky and stiff and sore, but holding up. Thanks to the hot tub and the Bengay and your miraculous hands."

Brice slipped an arm around Lucas. Lucas rested his head on Brice's shoulder and began fooling with the fur on Brice's plump belly. Wind mourned around the eaves.

"Brice?"

"Yep?"

"I been thinking. Well, wondering. When I'm ready…when I'm ready for more…ready to do all those things you're wanting us to do together…."

"When you're ready for us to become lovers, not just bedmates?"

"Yeah. Well, what…whadda you…whadda you like? Whadda you have in mind? In terms of messing around. Fucking around."

Brice smiled into the darkness. "Oh. Oh, so much."

"Like?"

"Well, first of all, it won't be 'messing around' or 'fucking around.' It'll be much more. It'll be, well, making love to you."

"Making love?" Lucas's voice was tight. He sounded almost fearful. "D-do you…? Are you saying…?"

Brice took his hand and kissed it. "I'm not gonna toss the L word around just yet, since we only met—what? A few weeks ago? I am saying that I've come to care about you a lot. I'm not out on that limb all alone, am I? Don't you feel…? You did say earlier this evening that…."

"Yeah, you heard me right. I care a lot about you too. After the shitty history I've had with men, it's kinda amazing to be able to say that."

"Me too. Timing is everything, I think. We've met one another at the right times in our lives. I've had loads of passion and caring inside of me, but I've never really let it out before, but now I am. Because you're so damn beautiful, and because I feel a kinship with you—kind of a kinship of suffering, I guess—and because you bring out this fierce protective instinct in me, and because I feel safe with you. And pretty soon, I'm hoping, you're gonna feel just as safe with me. Why are you asking me this tonight? Wanting to talk about us getting sexual together?"

"I don't know. I…. Okay, that's a lie. I know why. Bigger men have intimidated me all my life, at the same time that I've wanted a lot of 'em. Bigger men hurt me in prison." Lucas squeezed Brice's thick biceps. "You're nearly twice my size, Brice buddy. I'm a little scared of you, to be honest. I know I'm strong, but you're way stronger. You could do anything you wanted to with me. But tonight…."

Brice laughed. "I'm broken down and harmless, huh? I have half a mind to show you how wrong you might be, but the joke would definitely be on me if my back went out again."

"Don't risk it, horndog. So will you tell me? How you'd…?"

"How I'd make love to you? Yes. I'd be glad to. But I'll get hard in the telling, so beware."

"I s'pect I will too. Worse things have happened. Go on."

"You bet. So." Brice kissed Lucas's cheek. "Here we go. Ready?"

"Yep."

"First of all, I'd kiss you. Long and deep. May I do that now?"

"Yep," Lucas whispered, wrapping an arm around Brice's neck and nuzzling his face. The two men embraced. They spent long, sweet minutes sharing kiss after kiss.

Brice pulled away. "Yeah. Like that."

"Then?"

"Then I'd lie on top of you and move my mouth down to your nipples. I love your nipples. Tiny little pink points just aching to be licked and lapped and sucked. Would you like that? Are your nips sensitive like mine?"

"Yeah, they are. I play with 'em when I jack off. But another man's never done that. Other than a couple truckers who wanted to suck me off, about all the guys I've been with have just fucked my face or my ass. Just used me as a tight hole."

"Even Eric?"

"Yeah. He'd hold me after he butt-fucked me, but, naw, he never fooled with my tits."

"So no man has really, truly made love to you? That's incredible."

"Not really. It's not like there's a lot of opportunities to meet other gay guys in Randolph County, West Virginia. I didn't really admit to myself that I wanted men till I was seventeen."

"Having a gay uncle didn't help?"

"Not a lot. Mommy 'disapproved of his lifestyle,' as she put it, and he lived way up in DC, so I never saw him all that much. Plus he was kinda flamboyant, and that put me off. I mean, like most country boys around here, I was raised to be real manly, y'know? If you're not masculine, you get a lotta shit. So a sissy kinda gay guy, I didn't know how to handle that, and I sure didn't relate to it. Took me a while to figure out that you could be gay and manly too."

"I get you. It took me years to realize all that too. So what happened when you were seventeen?"

"I got to working in Walmart. Before you know it, I had a crazy crush on a married man, a manager there. Big, brawny, bearded guy a lot like you. About your age too. Chris Gilbert. Man, he was fine, though he hardly knew I existed. Then I started whoring, and then there I was in prison."

"And you've been with no one since you got out?"

Lucas snorted. "Hell, no. Not a one."

"Not even some of those WVU guys? Some of 'em spent time here last summer, right? That Travis Ferrell kid is pretty cute."

"'Kid' is the operative word there. Travis is sweet, but he's a kid. I'm attracted to men. So go on. You'd treat my tits just right, and then?"

"Then…I'd hold your arms above your head and get my face in those fuzzy armpits of yours, lick and snuffle around, get my beard all rich with the smell of you."

"You like the way I smell?"

Brice chuckled. "You bet I do. Especially after lifting weights. Screw cologne or deodorant. I like your natural musk. Just a whiff of it starts to get me hard."

"Damn. Okay. Then?"

"Then I'd spend more time on your nips. I'd bury my face in that chest hair of yours, that little cinnamon-brown meadow you got there, and then I'd lick all those sexy tattoos, and then…. Well, I'd suck your cock. For a long, long time. I'd tug on your balls and get the taste of your pre-come all over my tongue."

"Sounding *sweet*. Then?"

"Then I'd…. This is driving me crazy, Lucas. My dick's about to explode."

"Mine too. Hold off. Keep going."

"Then I'd push my cock into your mouth and hold you down and make you suck me till I was almost there. Then we'd take a break and I'd hold you and kiss you again, work your tits till they were getting a little sore. Then I'd get you on your belly and spread your butt-cheeks, and I'd—"

"Screw me?"

"No. Not yet. I'd eat your ass. I'd bury my face between those beautiful butt-cheeks of yours and lick your hole."

Lucas sighed. He pressed his hard cock against Brice's thigh. "Oh, man. No one's ever done that."

"It'll make you open up. Make you want me inside you. I'd eat your pretty ass for a long, long, long time, till you were begging me to—"

"Fuck me. Yeah?"

"Yeah. Lucas, I'm really hurting here. Major blue balls. Do you mind if I…?"

"Jack off? Naw. Not yet. So then?"

Brice groaned, with great effort keeping his hand from straying down to his dick. "So then I'd fuck you. Real slow and with lots of lube, so you won't hurt. On your belly. On your side. On your hands and knees. On your back, so I can look down into your eyes. I'd tug your nipples and work your cock, and—"

"Oh, damn," Lucas groaned. "Okay. That's enough."

Lucas gave Brice a quick peck on the cheek, then rolled away from him. The sudden gap created between their bodies made Brice flinch, as if a half-healed flesh wound had reopened.

"Did I say or do something wrong?" Brice asked.

"No. No."

"Does any of that…?" Brice cleared his throat. *Damn, this is hard. I'm hard. But I knew what I was getting into. There are more important things here than shooting my spunk.* "What I just said. Does any of that appeal to you?"

"All of it. *All* of it," Lucas muttered low. "I know you're hurting. I'm hurting too, man. I'm starved. I'm starved for a man to…. I'm starved for you to…. Real soon, maybe. Please be patient. I think we're almost there. Please?"

"You got it," Brice rasped, his throat dry. He gave his maddened cock a quick stroke, gazing over at the dark silhouette of Lucas beneath the blanket.

"Brice?"

"Yeah?"

"Are you always Top?"

"Yeah, pretty much."

"Have you ever bottomed?"

"I got screwed pretty regular in college. Fraternity brother, Gerry, I had a big crush on. I didn't like it. He always went too damn fast. Hurt like hell. I used to bite down on the pillow to keep from crying. I was kinda crazy about him, though, so I took it just to keep him around, to keep the sex going between us."

"Would you bottom for me?"

"What? You wanna top me?"

"Maybe. We're just exploring future options here, right?"

"Right." Brice hesitated. "Hmmm. It's been nearly twenty years since I got fucked. Plus, from what I've seen, your cock is pretty big. But…."

Brice laughed quietly. "Hell, why not? Yeah, Lucas. Sure, I'd bottom for you. I'll do anything that pleases you. When you're ready to start something, ready to go further, I promise I'll be ready too. Ready for anything you want."

"Yeah?"

"Yeah. Anything, anytime."

"Okay." Lucas took a long breath. "Good night."

"Good night."

Heart and groin throbbing, Brice positioned himself onto his side, pulled one of the pillows from beneath his head, positioned it against his chest, and wrapped his arms around it. He gazed at Lucas, gazed at a shaft of moonlight, then closed his eyes. Sleep, he knew, would take its own sweet time returning.

BRICE WOKE TO FIND LUCAS'S WARM and naked weight on top of him. The room was very dark, the moonlight gone. Lucas's stiff cock pressed against Brice's belly. Lucas's mouth pressed against Brice's lips.

"Just lie there, okay?" Lucas whispered. "Let me do everything." The boy's tongue brushed against Brice's own. "I don't want you to hurt your back."

Brice nodded, heart thrilling and cock hardening. "Whatever you want," he murmured against Lucas's moist-mouthed attentions.

Lucas cupped Brice's right pec and tugged on his nipple. Brice groaned, arching against the boy's touch, wrapping his arms around him. "Yeah. That's great."

Lucas gripped Brice's wrists and pushed them down to the older man's sides. He took Brice's right nipple into his mouth and sucked hard, a sensation so firm and sudden it was nearly painful. He shifted to the left nipple and sucked even harder. Brice moaned, bucking his hips, already trembling with long-delayed delight. Lucas rubbed his thick erection against Brice's own. Brice wrapped a leg around Lucas's waist and urged him closer, trapping both cocks between them. Breathing hard, they ground against one another. Soon, both men were thrusting steadily, grunting with rising rapture.

"Oh, *damn*. I'm *already* getting close," Lucas whimpered.

"Yeah. Me too. Ohhh, man," Brice panted, biting Lucas's shoulder and humping the boy's lean loins faster.

"Oh! Oh, yeah!" Lucas jerked and gasped, shooting his come over Brice's belly hair. Seconds later, Brice finished too, with a shout and a shudder, his semen spouting over Lucas's thigh.

Lucas slumped on top of Brice, releasing his wrists. Brice wrapped his arms around the boy. The two slipped into a smiling, post-orgasmic drowse. Their first lovemaking had lasted a little over a minute.

After a sleepy interval, Lucas roused. "That didn't take long," he said, stroking Brice's chest hair, gently pinching a nipple.

"No, it didn't. I guess we were both pretty pent up. That was just wonderful. I'm surprised that you.... I mean, man, I'm grateful! But the way you've been talking, I figured it'd be weeks, maybe months before we...."

"Me too." Lucas kissed Brice on the chin. "I honestly figured that I wouldn't be ready to get sexy with you for a while yet, but then tonight, I had a dream. A real intense dream. It woke me up."

"Yeah? What'd you dream?"

Lucas rested his head against Brice's chest. "I dreamed about Eric. He was naked, and I was too. He was lying on the floor of that penitentiary bathroom in a puddle of blood, his throat slit open and a knife in his chest, just like the night he died. He was staring up at me…those big blue eyes.… Then he gripped the shiv in his chest and pulled it out, and his chest broke open, and blood started welling out. It was like a little fountain, then it looked like flower petals arching up."

"Damn. That sounds horrible."

"It was horrible. But it was beautiful too, in a weird way. When I bent down to help him, Eric gripped my hand and pulled me closer, and he smiled and kissed me on the forehead, and he dipped his fingers in that brimming blood and he smeared it across my bare chest, and it burnt like fire."

Lucas cupped Brice's limp cock in his hand. "I woke up with a jolt, shaking like a leaf, and I remembered that night two years ago, the look in Eric's eyes as he died, and then I watched you sleep, and I looked at those huge shoulders of yours, and your handsome face and your bushy beard, and I remembered all the ways you said you wanted to make love to me, and I got hard thinking about all that and started jacking myself, and then I started to think of all the ways I want to make love to you, and then I said to myself, 'Fuck, fool, time's awastin'. Seize the day! You want this big, hot man, and he wants you. It's a fucking miracle, and how often do those come along? Hell, we could die tomorrow. What are you waitin' for? For you to heal up?'"

Lucas gave Brice's cock a soft squeeze. "I may never heal up, but that's no reason to postpone the future. I ain't ready for butt-fucking yet, but I'm guess I'm ready for more than I thought I was. Big surprise, huh?"

"Big surprise, indeed. I'm awful glad you feel that way," Brice murmured, running his fingers over Lucas's muscled back.

"Me too. I'm only now getting to the point where I even know what I'm feeling."

"Sure you're not gonna have second thoughts tomorrow?"

"I'm sure. I'm real sure. I know what I want now. I want more with you. More of you." Lucas paused to wipe Brice's semen off his own thigh. He licked it slowly, luxuriously off his hand.

"Ummm. Yum. One taste, and I think I'm already addicted to this stuff." When he kissed Brice again, Brice could taste his own salty juice on the boy's softly probing tongue.

"Addicted? I hope so."

"Yep. I think I might have to milk you regular-like."

"I think you might, 'cause I intend to stick around. After tonight, no way you're getting rid of me." Brice chuckled, rolling them over and pulling Lucas into his big arms.

"You better stick around," Lucas said, taking Brice's hand. "I've waited too long for a night like this."

"Me too. And now it's here. Unbelievable."

"Unbelievable. Truer words were never spoken. More to come. More to come," Lucas whispered, voice already hoarsening with sleep.

"I sure hope so," Brice said, kissing the boy's back and caressing his whiskered cheek. *Hope? Yep. At last. We've both been starved. Now, looks like God's decided it's time we were fed.*

CHAPTER FORTY-ONE

Brice opened his eyes to first light and the greatest happiness he'd ever known. Lucas lay sleeping only a few inches away, on his back, his left forearm sprawled above his head. Brice ever so gently pulled the blankets down to Lucas's waist and gazed on the boy's bare chest, scarred ribs, and belly. He lifted the blankets far enough to see his limp cock, reddish-brown pubic hair, and fur-coated thighs. He studied Lucas's sleeping face: the close-cut chestnut beard, the blunt nose, the long eyelashes, the thick eyebrows, the full lips, the black hoops in his ears.

Brice pulled the blankets up over Lucas's torso, lay back, and closed his eyes. *Thank You,* he prayed. *Whoever You are. Whoever made me. You made this universe…the Great Bear and the crescent moon, the spruce forests and the sunsets, the bluebells and the rivers and the scarlet amaryllis…You made this handsome kid lying here beside me…his sweet face, his muscled body, the feelings that flood me every time I look at him. It's like I was dead but now I've been born again. Thank You! All praise to Your Name! All the pain I've been through, it's been well worth it, 'cause it brought me here, to this hillside, to this bed, to this sweet, wounded, beautiful boy. He looks like a scruffy lil' angel sleeping. He….*

Brice rose. Back aching, he slipped out of bed, moving stiffly to the desk. There he found what he was looking for: a legal pad and a pen. The melody he'd composed in the newly created "Lucas Tuning" came to him, and now words came too. He began to jot down a flood of lyrics.

Half an hour later, Brice tore the sheet off the notepad and read through the messy scrawl he'd made, stanzas already pocked with cross-outs and scribbled revisions.

First time I've ever written an honest song, he thought, *complete with the correct pronoun.*

He carefully folded the paper. Locating his jeans, which Lucas had draped over the back of an armchair, he slipped the lyrics into a pocket before clambering back into bed.

CHAPTER FORTY-TWO

"Hey, handsome," Brice muttered, rubbing his eyes. Lucas was snuggling against him from behind, the boy's hand ranging lazily through Brice's belly hair.

"Morning." Lucas rubbed his whiskers along the back of Brice's neck. "How'd you sleep?"

"Great. You?"

"Great. I had a big ole man to keep me warm all night. You put off a lotta heat. Think I'm gonna nickname you 'Furry Furnace' from now on."

Brice rolled over and took Lucas in his arms. "Sounds like another song title. Speaking of which, I wrote a song about you this morning."

Lucas grinned. "This morning? Really?"

"Yep. I woke up at dawn and watched you sleep, and then I got to thinking about how sweet last night was."

"You're telling me." Lucas nibbled Brice's chin. "Too short, though. Next time, let's make it last longer."

"So you still don't have second thoughts? There's gonna be a next time?"

"Damn straight there will be. As a certain Nashville cohort of yours would sing, 'I like it, I love it, I want some more of it.'"

"That's mighty fine to hear." Brice fingered Lucas's right nipple. "Next time, I'm gonna be wanting to play with these tasty little things. Long as that's all right with you."

"After last night, I'm pretty sure I'm ready for that. So you gonna sing me that song?"

"Give me a few days to polish it. Then maybe I'll play it for you." Bending, Brice kissed the patch of rust-colored hair between Lucas's well-shaped pecs. "But only if you let me spend a couple of hours making love to that beautiful chest of yours. Those nipples.... Man, I—"

A hard pounding on the door downstairs interrupted Brice.

"What the shit?" Lucas bounded out of bed and peered out the window.

"Cain't see who it is. Better not be more reporters." Lucas threw open a drawer and jerked out an over-sized pair of black gym trunks.

"If it is, I'll—" Brice sat up, only to gasp at the sharp pain in his back.

Lucas frowned. "You take it easy. I'll handle this," he said, tugging on the shorts. "Tell you what. There's the phone. There's the number for the police on that notepad there. If it's more of those assholes, you can sic the cops on 'em. Okay?"

"Okay." Brice, wincing, managed to balance on the edge of the bed. "So much for me being your great protector, huh?"

Lucas cupped Brice's chin in his hand, tilted his head up, and kissed him on the mouth. "We're in this together, buddy. Sometimes you protect me. Sometimes I protect you. Deal?"

"Deal," Brice sighed, trying to smile despite the discomfort. "But Lucas, don't—"

"I know what you're gonna say. I ain't getting in any scrape with anybody, I promise. I *really* have a reason to stay outta prison now."

With that, Lucas pulled on a ball cap and stomped downstairs. Brice moved gingerly along the edge of the bed till the phone was within reach. When he heard the sharp sounds of Lucas shouting and cussing, he punched in the number. When a woman answered, he cleared his throat and began.

"Yeah, this is Brice Brown up at Philip Roger's place, up Brantley Valley. I'm calling for his nephew, Lucas Bryan. We need a favor. Chief Willey told us to call if...."

"It was that same *Star* reporter," Lucas said, peeling off his gym shorts. "That West guy, the fucker." Brice watched as Lucas pulled on another maddeningly skimpy pair of briefs.

"Him again? I figured Amie's gunfire would have sent him away for good."

"I wish it had." Lucas fetched a pair of jeans from the closet. "This one's stubborn. He got a few more photos before all my threats about calling the cops drove him off."

"Good. The police said they'd be here in half a hour."

"I'll call 'em here in a minute and tell 'em the shithead left." Lucas tugged on the pants, then, sitting on the desk chair, pulled on socks and then a pair of lace-up work boots. "After that, I have a few chores to do."

"What? Where are you going?"

"I'm driving up to Buckhannon to Lowe's. I'm gonna install a goddamn gate today, and I'm gonna set some electric fence. And get some 'Trespassers Will Be Prosecuted' signs. I'm sick of this shit. You came here for some peace and quiet, and peace and quiet's what you're gonna get."

"You want me to—"

"Naw. I think you should take more of those pills and stay in bed."

"Do you know what kind of helpless old man that would make feel like? At least let me come along. Are you gonna install all that yourself? In this shape, I ain't gonna be much help."

"Grace is handy that way. So's my buddy Ray, the guy you met at the restaurant in Helvetia. He's unemployed right now. I'll give him a call, promise him a little money. You sure you don't wanna stay in bed?"

Brice shook his head. Stiffly, he rose. "Nope. Let me take a few pills and get dressed, and we can head out. I'll treat us to breakfast in Buckhannon."

FEELING SUPERANNUATED AND WORTHLESS, BRICE spent the overcast afternoon in an overcast mood, sitting on the tailgate of Lucas's truck, sipping coffee from a travel mug, while Lucas, Ray, and Grace installed first the gate and then the electric fence.

At day's end, after Ray's departure, Grace invited Brice and Lucas down to dinner in the big Victorian she and Amie shared. The two couples spent a quiet evening drinking red wine, telling coming-out stories, and enjoying Amie's fried chicken, gravy, mashed potatoes, green beans, fresh yeast rolls, and homemade Boston cream pie. The men said good night early, since Lucas was visibly exhausted and Brice's back was acting up again. Back at Phagg Heights, they went straight to bed and cuddled close all night.

The next day was blessedly uneventful. That morning, Lucas drove Brice down country back roads to the county seat of Elkins. There, they picked up more pain pills and a heating pad at the pharmacy, opened a bank account in which to deposit the latest residuals from Brice's ex-label, and made an appointment with a chiropractor. They shared a fancy lunch in Graceland, the vast nineteenth-century mansion converted into an elegant inn and restaurant that overlooked the town. That afternoon, back at Phagg Heights, while Brice napped atop the heating pad in the great room, Lucas roasted a chicken with oatmeal stuffing and made a big salad with blue cheese dressing. After some Scotch by the fire, they retired early yet again, medication and alcohol having made Brice drowsy. They watched CMT videos in bed till Brice drifted off to sleep in Lucas's arms.

The next morning, Lucas was in the midst of grating Cheddar for a cheese-and-mushroom omelet and Brice was frying bacon, sipping coffee, and feeling very content with the easy togetherness he and Lucas had come to share when the phone rang.

"Couldn't be anyone but Uncle Phil, Grace, Amie, or Mommy," Lucas said. "No one else has the new number."

He picked up the phone. "Hello. Yep. What?"

Lucas listened. Lucas frowned. Lucas rolled his eyes. Lucas groaned. Lucas chuckled.

"Yeah, sure. Bring it on up. We can all enjoy it together. Hell, I'll even do a dramatic reading. Yep, okay. Bye."

"What the hell?" Brice said, anxious again.

Lucas hung up the phone, his mouth twisted into a sardonic grin. "That was Amie. Latest issue of the *Star* is out."

"And?"

"And now…it looks like you gotta share your celebrity status with me."

"Oh, no. You mean…?"

"Yep. Front cover. Scandalous headlines. Lots of photos. The two of us together. A shot of me in nothing but gym shorts screaming at the guy." Lucas shook his head. "It's kinda funny, really."

"It isn't funny! Now folks are gonna be hounding you too."

Lucas shrugged. "They're already hounding me, in case you hadn't noticed."

"Yes, they are, and it's because you were kind enough to protect me."

"Well, Brice, buddy, you're gonna have to get used to that. Like I said the other day, we're in this together. We'll protect one another. So, Amie's coming up with the magazine. She's gonna stay for breakfast. Would you get some biscuits out of the freezer, wrap 'em in foil, and stick 'em in the toaster oven?"

CHAPTER FORTY-THREE

Outside, snow flurries speckled the dead grass of the lawn. Inside, the three friends sat by the fire, drinking coffee on the couch and poring over the cover of the *Star*.

As Lucas had warned, the issue sported provocative headlines: "ANOTHER BRICE BROWN GAY LOVE NEST EXPOSED!" and "COUNTRY STAR SHACKING UP WITH TRUCK-STOP HUSTLER!" Two large color photos featuring the two men filled in most of the cover. In one, Brice was gesticulating on the porch of the lodge, his lips set in a snarl, with Lucas by his side, looking equally furious. In another, Lucas stood on the doorstep of his cabin, wearing nothing but gym shorts and ball cap, mouth open in mid-shout, one fist clenched in the air. In the bottom right-hand corner, a tiny close-up of Amie accompanied a question set in smaller type: "MYSTERIOUS BEAUTY! MÉNAGE À TROIS?"

Brice sighed, kneading his scalp. "Amie, I'm so sorry you've been dragged into this."

Amie's smile was broad and bright. "Actually, I'm enjoying the fifteen minutes of fame and the intoxicating perfume of notoriety. Grace is already calling me 'Mysterious Beauty.' I'm surprised they haven't dug up my burlesque past."

"Oh, hell. What if they do?" Brice slumped back into the couch.

"It won't matter. Most people around here already know about it. They figured out years ago that Grace and I are together, and that hasn't made much of a difference. Other than a couple of preachers trying to get their parishioners to boycott our business—and that failed miserably because we're the only restaurant around here—locals have been pretty friendly. It's not as if their opinions matter all that much to me anyway. Wasn't it Oscar Wilde who said something like, 'The only thing worse than being talked about is not being talked about?'"

"Yeah, I don't much care what folks think either," Lucas said, handing Brice the magazine before rising to put another log on the fire. "I figure every person in this county knows about me being a cocksucking hustler and ex-con. A few folks I've run across have been nasty about it, but lots more have acted afraid of me, which is actually kinda cool, since they leave me alone and stay the hell outta my way. Fuck 'em. I care what Mommy thinks about me, but she wrote me off years ago as a hell-bound sinner." Lucas crossed his arms and hung his head, looking grim. "Nothing I can do about that. I ain't gonna change, and she ain't gonna change her mind. Maybe when she hears about this article and finds out that Brice and I are together—"

"We're together?" Brice interrupted, smiling.

"Yeah, we're together. Didn't you read those headlines? They may be printed on the cover of a scandal sheet, but they're dead on anyway." Lucas looked at Amie. "He can be mighty dense sometimes."

"So you two *are* a couple? This is glorious news," Amie enthused. "You're adorable together. Your uncle will be pleased, Lucas. He's been hoping you'll find someone to take care of you."

"Yeah, I figure Uncle Phil will be happy. He likes you real well, Brice. But Mommy.... I kinda doubt it."

"I'm sure part of her wants you to be happy," Amie said. "If only she weren't poisoned by that swinish pastor of hers and his hateful dogma. Reverend Davis, that corpulent poltroon. In my dreams, I sometimes have the pleasure of shooting him through the head."

"You know him?" Brice asked.

"Oh, yes. He was one of the preachers who unsuccessfully encouraged the members of his church to boycott our store. So, Lucas, how about that dramatic reading you promised me?"

Lucas chuckled. "Sure y'all don't want a shot of Bailey's in your coffee first? This might be pretty rough."

"No need for liquor," Brice said, handing Lucas the periodical. "Who cares what those jackals have said about us? We know the truth. Go ahead, Lucas. Read it."

"Okay. Here we go." Lucas sank into the armchair and flipped to the relevant pages. "The official title of this piece of no-doubt priceless prose is 'THE COUNTRY SINGER AND THE HILLBILLY HUSTLER,' written by none other than that Robert West guy. The one you drove away with your pistol, thank you very much." Lucas flashed Amie a brief smile before continuing.

"'**Where's Brice?!** Folks have been asking: Whatever happened to country-music star and infamous homosexual Brice Brown? Now we know! He's been caught cavorting with a young hillbilly hustler in the remote mountains of West Virginia!'

"'**BIG GAY SCANDAL!** Last November, as the astute reader will recall, Nashville guitarist Zac Lanier came forward with a shocking story: he and Brice Brown had conducted a clandestine homosexual affair while Lanier was still a member of Brown's band and Brown was still married to beautiful socialite Shelly Brown. Soon after this shocking and unsavory revelation....'"

Lucas broke off long enough to interject, "Unsavory? I think you're pretty savory myself. Anyway, '...Brown fled Nashville in disgrace and hid out for weeks in his hometown of Hinton, West Virginia. There, the *Star* caught up with him, discovering that he had apparently seduced a married man, Wayne Meador, a hot-tempered construction worker who physically attacked our reporters. Hinton locals told the *Star* that Brown and Meador were most probably high-school sweethearts rekindling their affair.'

Lucas paused to give Brice an inquiring glance. "Who's this, huh? I remember reading that article last December. He was a real good-looking guy, from what I could tell from the photos. I've been meaning to ask you about him."

Brice rested his elbow on his knee and his forehead in his hand. "Wayne's an old friend from my high school days. I've always been a little in love with him."

"I've got competition?" Lucas's tone was joshing, but Brice thought he could detect barely veiled concern.

"Glad to see you're jealous. No, no competition. He's straight, and he's married. He lives in North Carolina. He was in Hinton for the holidays and came down to my house to offer his support. When that damn article was published, I told him to keep his distance, and he has."

"Okay, sorry. I ain't got any right to be possessive."

"I think it's cute that you're possessive, actually. Go on."

"Okay. **Lost and Found!** In late January of this year, Brown left Hinton for parts unknown. *Star* reporters based in Nashville have since discovered that his recording contract has been canceled, his agent has dropped him, his lovely and long-suffering wife is divorcing him, and he's had to sell most of his properties. Many have speculated that Brown left the country rather than face further shame. But a few days ago, thanks to an anonymous tip, this reporter found him hiding out high in the wilds of Randolph County, West Virginia, in remote, forested Brantley Valley, not far from the tiny town of Pickens! He's apparently found erogenous escape from his troubles in the arms of a much younger man, an ex-con with a trashy, sleazy past!'"

"Trashy and sleazy? Oh, great." Lucas chuckled. "Here we go. The truck-stop whore achieves fame at last. 'THE SODOMITE STAR, THE HOMO HUSTLER, AND THE GUN-TOTING VIXEN! Yes, as if we need any further proof that Brown's perverse erotic appetites are insatiable, only weeks after his cozy time snowed in with Wayne Meador, the *Star* has discovered the shameless sodomite singer, age forty, shacking up with Lucas Bryan, age twenty-seven, a boy young enough to be his son and a homosexual hustler at that!'"

Lucas paused. "Huh! Young enough to be your son? Even I know that math is off. Anyway, 'The *Star* caught the two cohabiting in a large compound of log cabins—the former Lost Creek Guest House, now owned by a wealthy lawyer, Philip Rogers, and managed by his nephew, the aforesaid Bryan. When this reporter expressed his interest in interviewing Brice Brown so as to give the disgraced singer a chance to tell his side of the story, Lucas Bryan initially lied, claiming that Brown was not in residence. Later, Brown revealed himself, fell into a profane rage, and threatened this reporter with physical violence. Soon thereafter, a glamorous femme fatale in their company drew a pistol from her purse and fired, driving off this beleaguered representative of the *Star*! Was this bewitching madwoman merely a friend, or do Brown's sexual proclivities lean toward the infamous ménage à trois?!'"

"Lovely. Said femme enjoyed the target practice immensely," Amie interjected. "If only circumstances had allowed her to be more *fatale.*"

"You're telling me! Okay, here's the rest of that section. 'A few days later, this reporter returned to the compound, determined to give his readers a more in-depth glimpse of Brown's indecent adventures, only to be met at the door by Brown's nearly naked lover. Who knows what bed of pederastic passion the well-muscled Bryan had tumbled from? The irate young man drove off the *Star's* representative with many a vulgar and graphic threat.'"

Lucas scratched his chin. "Well, that's true. I told him I wanted to take a maul to his balls, grind the tiny lil' thangs up in a blender, and feed the grainy paste to the hawgs.'"

"Well done," said Amie. "I've always admired the deftness of your profanity."

Brice laughed. "He got another detail right: well-muscled. The headline ought to read 'Torso of the Year.' Now everyone can see what a fine body you have. With that hot pic of you on the cover, horny gay guys are going to be pouring into Brantley Valley, wanting a piece of you."

Lucas raised an eyebrow. "I think I'm pretty much taken at this point. Their coming a'courtin' would be a waste of everybody's time." He gave Brice a warm glance before resuming.

"So here's the last segment of it. 'THE COUNTRY HAS-BEEN AND THE JUICY JAILBIRD! TRUE LOVE AT LAST? Since these frightening incidents, researchers at the *Star* have confirmed several disturbing facts: Lucas Bryan began frequenting West Virginia truck stops and offering oral sex in exchange for money as early as age seventeen. Having stabbed a trucker he was attempting to rob, he was sent to prison at age twenty on charges of prostitution and malicious assault. Sources inside the penitentiary indicate that Bryan, thanks to his youth, handsome features, and athletic form, was quite the popular item among his fellow inmates there. Bryan was released on parole in May of 1997. Now, apparently, his boyish charms and seedy sexual talents have won the heart and groin of washed-up country singer Brice Brown. The *Star* wishes them the best in their high hillbilly homo hideaway! Hopefully, at some point in the near future, Brown will give the *Star* the interview we've all been waiting for and share with our readers all the salacious and unseemly details of their forbidden romance!'"

Lucas laughed low in his throat. Rising, he tossed the periodical on the coffee table. "Lord, lord. So this is what fame feels like."

Brice groaned. "Oh, Lucas. Oh, Amie. It's all my fault. Christ. I should never have come here."

"Bullshit," Lucas said. "Mizz Amie, do you agree?"

"I do. Bullshite indeed, Mr. Brice. It's been a pleasure getting to know you, a man I've admired for many years, and I do believe I've never, ever seen Lucas here any happier. Besides, I've always dreamed of being an infamous, gun-toting madwoman, à la *Thelma and Louise."*

"See? You belong here, big Daddy." Lucas offered Brice a hand and pulled him to his feet. "Okay, it's time for that ménage every *Star* reader is wondering about. Except, instead of sharing our bodies, I think we'll opt for a big breakfast instead."

Brice squeezed Lucas's hand and kissed him on his bearded cheek. "That's one thing you two fine cooks have reminded me of: good food's a helluva consolation in times of trouble."

"One of my many mottos," Amie said, finishing her cup of coffee. "Since Lucas got back to Brantley Valley, he's become a fabulous chef."

"I've had good teachers: you and Uncle Phil and Doris Ann. Let's head down to the kitchen now. I'm famished. We're gonna have biscuits, bacon, and a nice cheese-and-mushroom omelet. Plus I got a few store-bought tomatoes we can slice. They're half-decent for February. Nothing better'n tomato and mayonnaise on top of a hot biscuit."

"So you had fun hiking today?" Lucas said. He propped a hand against the wall of his cabin's narrow shower stall while Brice scrubbed his muscular back with a loofah.

"I sure did," Brice said, patting one of Lucas's buttocks. "Helped me forget all that *Star* shit. The landscape was nearly as magnificent as this one here I'm feeling on."

"Sweet talk'll get you everywhere. Yeah, this is an awful pretty part of West Virginia. That view today from Dolly Sods, the snow lingering in between the rocks, the way the wind shapes the spruce into green flags...."

"Yep. And all that space in Canaan Valley. The wetlands, the view from Bald Knob. I needed the exercise, after the great meals you've been feeding me."

"We'll get back to lifting together once your back has gotten better. You were walking pretty well today. Want another back rub before bed?"

"I'd love that," Brice said. "So tell me the truth. You really aren't upset about that *Star* article?"

"Naw. I've sorta had to make my peace with being a notorious homo whore and convict. Most folks in this state, except for the real religious types...well, okay, there are lot of real religious types, but...most mountain people are into 'Live and let live' and 'Don't mess with me and I won't mess with you.' So I don't think that article is gonna make much difference in terms of day-to-day living around here. Plus, shit, I'm proud to be named as a country star's boyfriend! Coolest thing that's ever happened to me."

"Boyfriends. Amazing. I guess I've never had a boyfriend. Not really. Zac was the closest I've ever gotten."

Lucas turned around and wrapped his arms around Brice's waist. "Yeah, Eric has been it for me. Boyfriends. Lovers. That's what the tabloids say. And since every scandal-rag reader now thinks we're lovers, I guess we should act like lovers, huh?" Lucas nuzzled Brice's mouth.

"Really? You mean it?"

"Sure do."

"Then I think you're absolutely right." Brice nuzzled back, squeezing Lucas's wet ass-cheeks. Both of them grew hard, kissing and embracing.

"I've been wanting to get you naked all day," Lucas murmured, kneading Brice's beefy pecs. "It's like I been fighting back this…hankering for you, this crazy need for you…for weeks, and now all of a sudden, it's all broke free, and I…." He dropped a hand to Brice's prick and gripped it. "God, Brice, I want…."

"What? What, boy? What do you want?" Brice groaned against Lucas's lips as Lucas commenced a tight cock-stroking. "Tell me what you want. Whatever it is, it's yours. Just do it."

"First, I wanna feast on those big tits of yours." Lucas shoved Brice forcibly back against the wall. Bending, he began licking and sucking Brice's nipples while continuing to fist Brice's dick.

Brice nodded, cupping the back of Lucas's head and riding his hand. "That's great. Yep. Oh, yeah. Rougher. Yep! Make 'em a little sore. Yep!"

Lucas alternated between the two fur-swathed nipples, sucking harder and harder, nibbling the arousal-stiff nubs till Brice was whimpering with rapture. Just when Brice thought he was about to shoot into Lucas's grip, the boy released Brice's cock and dropped to his knees. He gazed up at Brice, face wet and blue-gray eyes urgent. The shower's warm water sluiced over his shoulders and down his gym-sculpted chest.

"Now I wanna suck you off. Okay?" Lucas whispered, running his bearded chin over the tip of Brice's cock. Taking Brice's balls in his hand, he gave them a gentle tug. "Okay, Daddy? I need that big thang down my throat real bad."

"Hell, yes. I've been wanting my dick in your mouth since the first moment I saw you."

"And I been wanting to kiss you and suck you and get screwed by you from the very same moment, you standing there in that library by that glowing crystal like some kinda burly, bearded god."

Grinning up at the larger man, Lucas flicked his tongue over the tip-slit in Brice's dick. He took the glans in his mouth and sucked softly. Brice gripped Lucas's head and slumped back against the shower wall, trembling.

"My God. My God, you're good," Brice gasped as Lucas sucked harder, tightening the delicious pressure around Brice's cockhead and sliding his lips up and down the shaft. "Oh, Jesus. W-well worth the wait. That's w-wonderful. That's...."

Lucas kneaded Brice's balls and sucked tighter and faster. Grunting, Brice thrust into Lucas's mouth. When Brice's thighs began to tense with imminent climax, Lucas stopped.

"This time it's gonna last," Lucas muttered, getting to his feet. For long, moist moments, the two men kissed passionately, jacking each other's cocks, grinding their loins together. Then Lucas dropped to his knees and again took Brice into his mouth.

After several more alternations between fucking Lucas's face and deep-kissing the eager boy, Brice had had enough. "God, Lucas, please. Please," he groaned against Lucas's probing tongue. "I can't take it anymore. I'm hurting bad. Please let me come!"

Lucas snickered. He bit Brice's chin. "Was that 'Please' I heard?"

"Yes!" Brice panted. "Please!"

"You got it." Lucas knelt yet again, lapping Brice's shaft, taking the big man's balls into his mouth and sucking them firmly, then returning his oral attentions to Brice's aching cock. He paused long enough to look up at Brice and mutter, "My turn to say 'Please.' I need you to come in my mouth. Please? I need your juice on my tongue and down my throat."

"Oh, yeah. Uh huh. Uh huh!" Brice nodded, teeth gritted. He gazed down at the beautiful youth, even more beautiful in such a state of need and submission, and then closed his eyes, bent his knees, gripped Lucas's head between his hands, and commenced a frantic thrusting.

CHAPTER FORTY-FOUR

BRICE STOOD BY THE FRONT WINDOW OF THE great room, watching late afternoon snow falling over Brantley Valley, still amazed at the ease with which Lucas had trounced him four times in a row at the pool table. He was considerably more amazed remembering the bodily pleasures he'd shared with Lucas the night before and yet again that morning.

"Planting time will be here before you know it," Lucas said. Having just returned from a grocery run, he sprawled on the couch, flipping through a seed catalog. "I grew a nice big garden last year for me and Uncle Phil, and I want to do the same this time around. What you like in terms of fresh vegetables?"

"I'll eat anything you grow. God never invented a vegetable I don't like." Turning, Brice regarded the ruddy-bearded boy. *These quiet winter days spent with Lucas, lounging around in nothing but sweats, stoking up the fire, reading, working up new tunes on the piano, cooking together…or hiking in the leafless woods, far from the surly world and, at night, making love, holding one another close…. These are the best days of my life.*

"Seed catalog, huh?" Brice settled down onto the couch beside Lucas. "I figure you got your fill of seed last night, not to mention this morning."

"Vulgar! That's what Mommy would say." Lucas tossed the catalog on the coffee table before stretching luxuriously. "Yeah, I got my fill. For now. But that's the thing about appetite, right? You can sate it as often as you want, but it still keeps comin' back."

"True enough. A fact I'm wildly thankful for, now that I have a glory like you to share my bed. Before that, desire was just an agony and a curse, a monkey on my back."

"God, ain't that the truth?" Lucas rearranged himself, stretching out on the couch, resting his head in Brice's lap, and pulling an afghan over himself. "Damn, this is all so cozy and perfect," he said, looking up at Brice with a happy smile, then gazing over the great room with its hues of stone, wood, and leather. "The snow, the fire, your big, butch body. It's the man-on-man hideaway I've waited for my whole life."

"Me too," Brice said. "Honestly, I'd given up all hope that such a thing could happen, that I could find a place like this, and, more importantly, meet a guy like you."

Lucas nodded, tugging the blanket up to his chin. "I used to be so horny, so miserable. The one good thing about prison was that, as bad as he could treat me, Eric made me feel desired, and he always made sure we both came. Then I was here alone, celibate and jacking off every damn night. Actually, I hope it doesn't creep you out to hear this, but—"

"I doubt anything you could ever say would creep me out," Brice said, running a hand over Lucas's brow, then plucking softly at his bearded chin.

"I hope not. So, I have all your CDs, you know, and I went to a bunch of your concerts, and I used to buy country music magazines with articles about you and pictures of you, and I used to watch your music videos...and, well, I used to jack off thinking about you. I mean, not just you, there were other Nashville stars I fantasized about, but you were sure prominent in the pantheon, so to speak. That one shirtless pic of you at your Daytona condo, the one that *Country Weekly* published—it was just before I went to prison—wow, I just about came in my shorts over that one."

"Really? That doesn't creep me out. I think that's hot. I'm flattered."

"Well...good. Who the hell would ever have thought that we'd end up here? Together? With me gulping down your come like some kinda sweet syrup? I think this is definitely the time to use my Mommy's favorite phrase, 'Praise the Lord!'"

"You're right about that. Praise the Lord indeed. Talk about God working in mysterious ways. Who else got you all het up?"

"Ah, before prison, it was Travis Tritt and Brooks and Dunn...and you. After I got out, it was Toby Keith and Tim McGraw, plus Ty Herndon and Billy Ray Cyrus if they were looking especially scruffy...and you."

"So have you always been attracted to older guys? It doesn't bother you that I'm thirteen years older?"

"Bother me?" Lucas snorted. "Why would it bother me? Thirteen years ain't all that much older. Plus the age difference turns me on."

"Well, I guess some folks would say that it would be more appropriate if—"

"Appropriate? Appropriate to who? People can't tell people how to feel. None of us can choose what turns us on. I like big, chunky, older guys with beards. Hell, if the Greeks could do it, why can't we?"

"Greeks?"

"Yep. Athenians and Spartans and all those guys. When I got out of prison, I was one big fucking mess, as you might imagine, after all the shit that went down in there, so when I moved in here with Uncle Phil, he got on this quest to make me feel better about who I was. God knows it's hard growing up in West Virginia once you figure out you're gay—you get all torn up with self-doubt and guilt and other negative shit—so one of the things Phil did was buy me a buncha books about homosexuality. They're all in the library here. I've read every one."

"Yeah? I've never read much about the topic. I don't know why. I guess I.... Up until a few years ago, I guess I was trying to convince myself I wasn't really gay, since I knew somewhere deep inside that if I decided I was, I'd have to do something about it, and then I might lose everything if the news got out, and...that's exactly what happened."

Brice bent to kiss Lucas on the brow. "Except, after I lost everything, I found something better. So those books helped you, huh?"

"They did help. I especially liked the books about the Greeks. Stuff about myths and heroes who loved one another, a battalion of ferocious soldier-lovers called the Sacred Band. A couple cool novels about Alexander the Great and his honeys. Imagine that! Alexander-the-fucking-Great, one of the greatest military leaders in history, and he loved other men! After being told all my life that homos were big sissies and sick sinners, it was pretty cool to read about butt-kicking warriors, about the *erastes*—that's the older man—who teaches his younger lover—his *eromenos*—how to hunt and fight and make love. Hell, even Zeus, the king of the gods, took himself a young guy as his cupbearer boy-toy. Ganymede."

"So you're my hillbilly Ganymede, huh?"

"Yep," Lucas said. "Except you got it even better than Zeus, 'cause not only do I mix you drinks but I cook for you too. Speaking of which, I should start those stuffed peppers. Wanna help?"

"Sure. You said you're making macaroni and cheese too, right?"

"I am. Or I will. But only if you promise me two favors first."

Brice rubbed his belly. "As you no doubt suspect, for homemade mac and cheese, I'll do just about anything."

"Ravenous, ain't you? Okay, I really need to get back to studying for the GED, 'cause the test is coming up in a couple of months. So let's lay off the booze before dinner—or, okay, limit ourselves to one drink apiece—and this evening I'll stay down here in the lodge and study, if you wanna get in bed and read or watch TV."

"Your bed, you mean?"

"Yes, my bed, Mr. Brown. Now that I've spent several nights all snuggled up to you, it's become a habit I don't intend to break."

"Great. How about you give me one of those Alexander novels you mentioned? Guess it's time I read up on gay lit some, now that I've taken the beautiful Ganymede into my bed."

Lucas tossed off the afghan and sat up. "Good idea. I got loads of good books waiting for you. We'll make a well-educated *erastes* out of you yet."

"What's the second favor?"

"I wanna hear that song you wrote for me."

Brice blushed. "I don't know how ready it is."

"Ah, c'mon! Please? I'm dying to hear it. I just confessed that I used to fantasize about you and jack off. Least you could do is give your number one fan another private concert."

"All right." Brice coughed. "I just hope you like it. I haven't written anything new in a long time, so I'm kinda rusty."

Brice fetched his guitar from its case in the corner, then sat on the footstool by the armchair. He fiddled with the tuning pegs till the instrument sounded right.

"It's in a weird little tuning I made up. Most folks play guitars in standard tuning, but I figured there was nothing standard about our relationship, so I wanted to try something new. So I call this 'the Lucas tuning,' and the song's called 'Redneck Angel.' Remember when you said it'd make a good song title?"

"I do. Cool." Lucas leaned back into the soft couch and folded his hands behind his head. "Let's hear it, country star."

"Okay." Brice cleared his throat and began fingerpicking the initial chord. He gazed into the fire, suddenly unable to meet Lucas's eyes. "Here we go."

> *You made it all, Lord, mountain sunsets and winter rain,*
> *the thick spruce forests and the crescent moon,*
> *April's breezy bluebells by the river's green rushing,*
> *walnut boughs, and fireflies starring in dusky June.*
>
> *You shaped this lump of stone, this buried bulb*
> *afraid to wake, coward sleeping long inside my chest.*
> *You broke down my lies, you cast me out, you made me*
> *envy the many men a more common love had blessed.*
>
> *Thorny troubles led me here, a high wooded hill,*
> *to count my loads of losses, to shroud myself in pain.*
> *A coffin of stone and silence was my only future,*
> *a lonely bed, a tale of defeat, dark-tarred shame.*
>
> *Then, like a savior's suffering*
> *thorn-bound heart, the dead*
> *earth split, the amaryllis opened,*
> *a spout of scarlet light.*
> *You sent me a miracle*
> *of mercy and of might.*
> *You sent me a wounded stranger,*
> *a beautiful, bearded boy,*
> *   a redneck angel.*
>
> *He's a wonder of pale muscle and cinnamon fur,*
> *brave arms scrawled with ink, strong with sinew.*
> *His warm aroma's forest-dark and musky-rich.*
> *He holds me hard, helps my brokenness continue.*
>
> *Let me kiss his furry breast and feel his fragile heart*

pulse beneath such dense muscle, such soft skin.
Let me hold him in my arms, give his manhood shelter,
live for his long-lashed, gray-blue wink, his ornery grin.

You made it all, Lord, the golden pollen and the orchard bloom,
the redbud's pink flush, cornfields hot with August heat.
You made me too, and the beauty I'm given grace to love
in this warm bed. His nakedness is Your greatest gift, honey-sweet.

Like a savior's suffering
thorn-bound heart, the dead
earth split, the amaryllis opens,
spouting scarlet light.
You sent me a miracle
of mercy and of might.
You sent me a wounded stranger,
a beautiful, bearded boy,
>   *a redneck angel.*
He's my beautiful, bearded boy,
>   *my redneck angel,*
my tattooed and fuzzy savior,
my sweet and strong and scruffy
country boy,
>   *my redneck angel.*

Brice slowly strummed the last chord and stopped. "Wh-what do you think?" With difficulty, he met Lucas's gaze.

Lucas was staring at Brice, his cheeks wet with tears. "Oh. Oh. I...."

He wiped his face with the back of his hand and stood. "It's so beautiful. It was like a prayer. Thank you. I can't believe you wrote that for me. That's...that's the best thing anyone's ever done for me. Thank you."

Smiling with relief, Brice returned the guitar to its case, then took Lucas into his arms. "I'm the one who should be thanking you. You're the best thing that's ever happened to me. And that fact deserved a song. My guess is that this is just the first piece of music you'll inspire. Being with you, it's opened up some kind of deep well inside me. You're my new muse, Lucas. I've already told you that."

Lucas, on tiptoe, kissed Brice on the lips. "You know what, I'll get back to studying for the GED tomorrow morning, good and early. Tonight, I wanna split a bottle of champagne. I think we got a lot to celebrate."

"That's for damn sure," Brice whispered, nuzzling Lucas's cheek. "In the space of a few wintry weeks, I've gone from being a pathetic pariah to feeling like the luckiest guy in the world."

"Funny how that works, huh? All the days you wake up and it's the same-old, same-old, week after week, month after month, year after year, and then one day—no way in hell of knowing when—you wake up and think, 'Oh, shit, more of the same,' but that day you're wrong. That day, either...."

Brice nodded. "That day, everything changes. Everything's transformed. Everything goes straight to holy hell, to total ruin. Or suddenly everything gleams like gold."

"Yep," Lucas whispered. "A golden gift. Something priceless you gotta hold onto as hard as you can."

"As long as you can," murmured Brice, pulling Lucas closer.

For a few moments, the two men embraced without words, each listening to the other's breath as the light of a snowy dusk dwindled around them. Then Lucas kissed Brice firmly on the lips, led him to the bar, flipped on a lamp, opened the little fridge, and began uncorking a bottle of champagne.

CHAPTER FORTY-FIVE

As planned, Lucas rose at dawn the next morning to study, leaving Brice to sleep late. When Brice arose, the cabin's bedroom was bright with sunlight, and chickadees were quarreling noisily outside the window. Brice climbed into camo pants, boots, and hooded sweatshirt and made his way down the hill toward the lodge. About him, snow melted, plopping down from the branches of the trees.

Brice found Lucas in the library, papers and booklets spread out before him, a mug of coffee at his elbow.

"Morning, Schnoozy. How's your back?"

"About back to normal. I think I could try some lifting today. Maybe fewer sets and lighter weights to start with, and definitely with a lifting belt. Can you join me?"

"Yeah, eventually. Mid-afternoon, maybe. I've already got a lot done. Want some coffee? There's a pot of that fancy steel-cut oatmeal Uncle Phil favors on the stove. He's due home in mid-April, by the way. Just got an e-mail from him. He always gets back to see the spring wildflowers. Speaking of spring, check that out."

Lucas swiveled the desk chair and pointed out the library window. In a bed just below the glistening quartz point, tiny white flowers were sprouting from the black mountain earth.

"Snowdrops. They look like lil' bells made of ivory. So pretty. First thing to come up. Not even March yet, but there they are, shouldering up despite the cold. They look delicate as glass, but, hell, ain't that strength? Ain't that—"

The phone rang at Lucas's elbow. After so many quiet days together, the sound made both men jump.

Lucas scowled. "Now what?" He plucked the receiver up.

"Yep? Hey. Hey, Mommy. Good to hear from you. How you—? Okay. Sure. Yeah, I'll be here. That time's fine. Yeah. Yeah, he will too. We have a new gate, so I'll have to come down to the road and let you in. Okay, bye."

Lucas hung up the phone and gazed up at Brice, a blank look in his eyes. "That was my mother. She'll be here in about two hours. She wants to talk to me. And she asked if you were here."

"Uh oh. The *Star* article?"

"Yep. No fucking question about it. I was afraid of this."

Lucas bit his lip, staring out over the pool deck and its scattered patches of snow. "Okay, let's grab some oatmeal. Actually, screw the oatmeal. Let's have some country ham, eggs, red-eye gravy, and biscuits. I think we're gonna need our strength."

LUCAS ENTERED THE LODGE, LOOKING sour and already annoyed. The woman he ushered in was so plain that Brice's first thought was, *Huh. So Lucas's father must have been a looker of the first order.*

Kim Bryan was a short, square woman in her fifties with a stern face, big glasses, a high forehead, and long straight brown hair that hung to her waist. Beneath a bulky winter coat, she was dressed in black slacks and a baggy beige V-neck sweater. A purple pillbox hat perched atop her head, and she carried an enormous bespangled purse.

"Good morning, Mrs. Bryan," Brice said. Mustering a smile, he stepped forward and offered his hand.

Lucas's mother glared at Brice. "I didn't come here to make nice. I came here to say my piece and then leave."

Well, shit, thought Brice, taking a step back, as if he'd just caught himself from treading on a baby copperhead. *This is, I'm guessing, one of those oncoming disasters you can't avoid. You just have to steel yourself and shoulder through.*

"Mommy, please don't be rude to Brice. Let me make you a cup of coffee. Would you like a piece of Miss Amie's cranberry bread? It's got orange and nuts in it, just the way you like it."

"I don't want your hospitality, Lucas, or that woman's cooking. I've been talking to my pastor—"

"Oh, shit," Lucas groaned.

"Don't curse in front of me. Yes, my pastor, Reverend Davis. He—and my prayer group—suggested that I meet with you just long enough to make my position clear about…all this."

She looked around the room with an expression of repugnance, as if she were seeing not a cozy country lodge but a steaming heap of fresh dog dung or an oozing venereal sore. Then she looked Brice up and down. For a split-second, she appeared so revolted that Brice was afraid she was going to retch onto the carpet at his feet, but instead she put her hands on her hips and said, "You corrupter. You're disgusting."

Brice's mouth dropped open. "I beg your pardon?"

"Mommy, don't." Lucas crossed his arms and glared. "Just don't."

Mrs. Bryan turned to her son. "You're disgusting too. Breaking all of God's rules, pleasuring those trashy men with your trashy mouth. Doing God knows what in prison. Probably more of the same sodomitic filth. How many criminals did you take to your bed? It's a wonder you can still walk straight."

"Really? You wanna get nasty and talk that way? Okay, you got it. You asked for it."

Lucas gritted his teeth, and his face hardened. "You're right, Mommy. It *is* a wonder. My boyfriend Eric used to pound my tight little ass till I was sobbing with rapture, with heavenly bliss—kinda like what fills you up in church, when you're moaning and rocking back and forth and shouting the Lord's name. Eric was so fucking good. Every night, he had me on my back, legs in the air, him grunting like a bear and me howling like a whore in heat."

Mrs. Bryan's face flushed red, and she clutched her chest. "Abomination! Foul-mouthed *abomination*. How did the sweet child I bore become such a horror?"

"In the fullness of time, to use one of your expressions. And now big ole Brice here pleasures me just the same. Damn, Mommy, ain't you *happy* for me? I finally have a man—and a famous one, at that—to hold me and love me and screw me raw."

"Vulgar! Despicable! How can you speak to me that way? As if you weren't already debased enough, after those years you worked the truck stops."

"Yeah, I worked the truck stops. Do you know why? Do you know why? For you!"

"Don't you dare say that. Don't you dare say it!"

"For you! 'Cause Daddy was dead. And I was working my ass off at Walmart and you were doing rich ladies' hair and it still wasn't enough to pay the mortgage and keep the power from getting shut off. So, yes, I was a lot lizard. A sleeper leaper. And that money I made selling blow jobs, that money paid for your fucking house. And now you come here, all high and mighty, all fucking sanctimonious and incensed, 'cause that senile ole shit, Reverend Davis—"

"Hateful! You know how much I admire that man. He's the soul of compassion. He's taught me so much."

"Well, he sure as *shit* ain't taught you compassion. I was in prison for six years, Mommy. Six years! How many times did you visit me? Four times! Plus once in the hospital, 'cause you thought I was gonna die and you wanted to get me right with Jesus before I did."

Lucas clenched his fists as if tempted to strike her. Instead, he turned away, staring out the window over the snowy valley. "And then I get out, and I'm broken. Fucking *broken*. And what do you do? You tell me I'm a sinner, and you say you can't stand the sight of me and you're ashamed of me, and you tell me to stay away. If it weren't for Uncle Phil and this place, I woulda been out on the street. I would have fucking killed myself."

Briskly, Lucas rubbed at his forehead, as if he were trying to erase a stain there. "Do you have any idea how many times I got close to blowing my brains out? Do you? After the way you turned your back on me? My own mother?"

Mrs. Bryan's first response to this confession—that her only child had contemplated self-destruction—was simply to look smug. Then, voice stern, she replied.

"Suicide? That would have been another grave sin on your account book. As it is, if you continue in this way—with this evil man, this infamous man, this immoral, whoring homosexual—there's no way you'll make it to heaven. I'll have to sit by the side of Jesus and look down upon you, upon your fiery torments, as demons tear you limb from limb for all eternity."

Lucas snorted with contempt. "As if a God who was wise and great and powerful enough to make these beautiful mountains, to make this beautiful man...." Lucas nodded in Brice's direction. "As if such an amazing, all-knowing deity would send folks to such a horrible hell. Where's the compassion in that? Torturing folks just 'cause they love? So your God's a divine terrorist? A holy sadist reveling in our sufferings? Does Reverend Davis tell you that?"

"He does. And so does the Bible."

Lucas shook his head. "I can't fucking believe you. You're crazy. Your religion is *crazy*. You can tell your reverend he can kiss my Rebel ass. My Rebel *homo* ass. And you know what?"

Lucas brushed his hands together dismissively and looked her in the eye. "You can too, Mommy. You can too. I'm done with you."

"No, child. That's why I came here. To tell you that *I'm* done with *you*." Mrs. Bryan stepped forward and spat in her son's face.

Lucas flinched. Brice gasped with disbelief.

"You miserable old...." Lucas whispered, wiping his face with the back of his hand.

Brice stepped forward and seized Mrs. Bryan by the arm. "Ma'am, it's time you left. If you don't get your precious piety out that door now, you're gonna regret it."

"Don't touch me!" The woman kicked Brice in the shins. "I'm not finished with my son!"

Brice's response was to growl deep in his throat, dig his fingers into her arm until she winced, and drag her toward the door.

"Don't, Brice." Lucas's voice was dead calm. "Let her finish what she wants to say. Please. And then she'll never darken this door again. Will you, Mommy?"

"No. No, I won't. I can promise you that. I'll never enter this habitation of perverts and sinners ever again."

As soon as Brice dropped the woman's arm, she reached up and slapped him across the face. "Don't you ever dare touch me again."

Brice grinned at her. "Ma'am, I should warn you that men like me are raised with very specific instructions in regards to dealing with vicious women like yourself. A Southern gentleman isn't allowed to strike a lady...unless she's struck him three times already. So you have one more free go at me. If you choose to indulge yourself in a third time, all bets are off."

Mrs. Bryan wrinkled her nose. "You wouldn't dare."

"Try it." Brice's grin widened. "You see, I love your son."

Brice paused, surprised by his own words. He glanced over at Lucas, who blinked very wide eyes at him.

Brice nodded. Feeling suddenly strong with certainty, he turned his attention back to the belligerent little woman.

"I love him. I've been alone all my life. I tried to live a lie for decades, but I'm done with that, come hell or high water. So now I'm learning to tell the truth. I love your son, and I'd do anything for him. He's wonderful. He's smart and tough and kind. You should be proud of him. Instead, you revile him. I'm afraid your faith has made you stupid. Vastly stupid. Stupid as a frigging stump. Brainless as a goddamn fishing worm. You, as we say back home, ain't got the good sense God gave a goose. *Look* at him. He's magnificent. You should thank your God that you have him in your life, that you were the instrument that brought such a splendid, sweet young man into this world. You should—"

"Shut up, Mr. Brown. You're raving. I birthed a monster. How could I have known, holding that precious baby in my arms, that he'd...."

Mrs. Bryan teared up. She clasped her purse to her breast, pulled a violet handkerchief from it, and dabbed at her eyes. For a split-second, Brice felt sorry for her, before the desire to break her neck achieved ascendance again.

"Love him? Homosexuals can't love. It's all just lust, unnatural lust, when it comes to your kind. Reverend Davis has made that so, so clear to me. First Satan steered my brother into depraved wickedness, and now Satan's taken my son. Lucas, you don't know how I suffer. Thinking about the evils you've sunk yourself in, like a pig in—"

"Shit." Lucas snickered, moving over to stand beside Brice. "Ain't that the *vulgar* expression you're reaching for?"

"Yes. A pig in shit." Mrs. Bryan's face contorted with repulsion. "And as if it wasn't bad enough—you going to prison, everybody in the county knowing what kind of sick criminal you'd become—all that shame wasn't enough for you, was it? As if my heart weren't already broken by the *ignominy* of it all. Now there's that wretched magazine everywhere, telling its hideous truths! Sold in the 7-Eleven, in the grocery store checkout line, lying around the beauty shop. The pictures of the two of you together. A photo of my son looking like a shirtless poor-white-trash gigolo! If you saw the look in the eyes of my fellow churchgoers on Sundays, you'd weep tears of blood! Everyone I know knows that you two are shacking up here! Copulating like animals!"

Mrs. Bryan pointed a finger at the two men. Her voice rose to a screech. "Dissipation and scandal! Offensive and degrading sin! God will punish you! He will rain down torments upon you!"

Lucas took Brice's hand and squeezed it. "Mommy, I *believe* you. I'm in torment right now. Shit, you're hurting my ears. Are you done now? Are you done?"

"Almost." Mrs. Bryan paused to catch her breath. "I don't know how I could have ever loved you, Lucas. Reverend Davis tells me that this sin has been inside you all along, like a venomous snake waiting for the right circumstances to squirm awake. He says that I should feel nothing for you now—now that you've made me a laughingstock, now that you've brought down such public shame upon my head. He says I should feel nothing for you but pity and contempt. Sadly, I've come to understand that he's right."

Lucas's grip tightened on Brice's hand. "So that's all you feel for me, huh?"

"Yes." She adjusted her hat on her head. "And the reverend says I should cut you out of my life like a dangerous tumor. I'm afraid I agree. I never want to see you again."

Lucas's grip grew tighter, and then it went limp.

"You're serious?"

"Yes."

Lucas took a long breath and cleared his throat. "Well, him and you and me agree on something then. I think that'd be best. Is that it?"

"Yes. I'm finished."

"Good. How about you show yourself out? I'll lock the gate up later."

"Certainly." Mrs. Bryan shot Brice a viperous look, then pulled a scarf from her coat pocket and wrapped it around her neck. For a brief instant, Brice felt the urge to step forward, seize the ends of the scarf, and throttle her till her face turned purple and her dying body ceased its convulsions. Instead, he wrapped an arm around Lucas and watched her open the door, step onto the porch, and slam the door behind her.

"Oh, buddy," Brice said, wrapping an arm around the younger man. Lucas stiffened, and then he slumped against Brice.

"Oh, God, I'm so angry," Lucas groaned. "I'm so *angry*. How could she…? So vicious, so…."

Lucas stiffened again, pushing Brice away. "Look, I gotta take a drive, okay?"

Brice wrinkled his brow. "Do you think that's a good idea? As worked up as you are? I don't want you to—"

"Don't worry." Lucas patted Brice's arm. "I ain't gonna drive into a tree or over a mountain. I'm done with those thoughts, I swear. I just need some time alone. Get it?"

"Yeah, I guess so." Brice wanted to take Lucas in his arms and comfort him, but the boy's body language—his averted glance, and the way he stood, as if he were poised to lunge into a long-distance race—made Brice think better of it. "Just please be careful. I'm gonna be real worried about you till you get back. You know that, right?"

"Yeah, I do." Lucas pulled his ball cap and jacket off the hall tree. "I'll be back by dinnertime, I promise."

Brice nodded, trying to smile, trying to push back a sudden gnawing panic. "Okay, I'll hold you to that. Watch the roads. They might still be icy. I'll have something ready for us to eat when you get back."

"Okay. Great." Lucas pulled on his coat and hat. "Later."

With that, he was out the door. Brice collapsed on the couch, his hands shaking. He stared at a patch of sunlight stretching across the hearthstone and listened as Lucas's truck rumbled to life outside. In another minute, the boy had torn out of the parking lot. Soon Brice could hear nothing but snowmelt dripping off the eaves and his own frightened heart throbbing in his ears.

CHAPTER FORTY-SIX

IN THE LODGE LIBRARY, BRICE LOCATED THE section of books about Greece and settled into an armchair, trying to focus on the first novel about Alexander the Great, *Fire from Heaven*. As good as the book was, it was impossible to concentrate longer than the length of a couple of paragraphs. He was listening unconsciously, intensely, for the sound of Lucas's return. Tiny noises distracted him: a crow cawing, the wind soughing around the corners of the lodge, the hum of the heating system, the ticking of the grandfather clock in the great room. He stood, walked to the window, and watched patches of snow dwindling. He watched the sun fade and clouds thicken. He watched vultures in the distance ride the air.

Omens? Omens of disaster? Omens of death and loss? Is Lucas all right? Will he come back? Jesus, that was terrible. What heartlessness and evil. What will happen to us? And I said I love him! I do love him. I do. Incredible. But now that I've said it, how will that affect him? Will it change what's between us? Will it make him afraid? Will it drive a wedge between us? Oh, God, please, no. I've waited so long to feel this way. Please help us. Please let us be together, no matter what the odds. Please, Lord, please.

After Brice pushed through the first chapter of the book, he tried to take a nap on the couch. He failed. Sleep's comfort remained elusive. Grumbling, he rose. Grumbling, he checked e-mail.

Shelly announced that their divorce was final. She'd read the *Star* article, she said, and though she felt humiliated now that everyone on earth knew that she'd been "duped into marrying a homosexual," she hoped Brice could find some kind of happiness with his "new squeeze." She'd sold the Franklin house for a fine profit, and she was dating a wealthy Atlanta banker and being invited to "all the right parties."

His sister Leigh wished him well too, admitting that his nephew Carden, in the aftermath of the *Star* article, had gotten into another big fight with his father and several brawls at school over the subject of Brice's sexual orientation. A local man, she said, had been caught painting the word FAGGOT on Brice's porch. Officer Bailey had summarily arrested the vandal and thrown him into jail, and Leigh was encouraging the county prosecutor to throw the book at him. Other than that, she was glad to report, Brice's house had been left alone. She hoped that the *Star*, "despite its sensationalism," was right in claiming that Brice had found a love interest at last, and she hoped that Brice could come home soon.

Phil's note was written in all caps, causing Brice to chuckle despite his profound state of anxiety. "I SAW THE *STAR*! YOU MONSTER! YOU PREDATOR! SEDUCING MY NEPHEW? HOW COULD I HAVE TRUSTED YOU??!!! JUST TEASING, HA, HA! CONGRATULATIONS ON BEDDING THAT WILD BOY! I'M DRINKING A PIÑA COLADA IN YOUR HONOR! SPEAKING OF WHICH, DO I GET TO BE LUCAS'S MATRON OF HONOR? I HAVE JUST THE PEARLS FOR THE OCCASION. SEE YOU IN APRIL!"

Brice took a walk around the compound, taking deep breaths of cold mountain air, trying to calm himself, trying not to imagine or expect the worst. In Lucas's cabin, he gathered up their dirty clothes, grinning at the sight of Lucas's skimpy underwear mingling in the hamper with his own much larger boxer briefs, and did some laundry on the lower level of the lodge. He contemplated lifting weights, but, without Lucas to spot him, and fearing for his back, he took a lengthy dip in the hot tub instead.

As twilight fell, Brice's worry increased. Cooking, he decided, might prove to be a decent distraction. He tuned the kitchen radio to a country-music station, reminiscing regretfully about his Nashville years and the fellow musicians with whom he'd socialized, most of them still successful presences on the airwaves, not one of whom had shown him any support during his downfall. After rooting around for provisions in the cupboard and finding a copy of *The Joy of Cooking* on a shelf, he put together a passable chowder with some canned clams. Letting it simmer, he found the ingredients for mulled wine and warmed that up as well.

He was sipping on a mug of the wine and sitting in a rocking chair in a corner of the kitchen when he heard the very welcome sound of a vehicle crunching into the gravel drive before the lodge. He stood, wanting to look busy rather than paralyzed with concern, and was dumping a can of kale into a pot when footsteps clumped down the stairs and Lucas entered the kitchen, an open bottle in his hand.

"Hey. Smells good. Whatcha cooking?"

Heavy with relief, Brice ached to embrace him, but, imagining the deep state of Lucas's emotional turmoil, didn't know what kind of response he'd get. Instead, he lifted a ladle.

"New England clam chowder. Canned clams, bacon, cream, potatoes, carrots. How's that sound? With oyster crackers? And kale? And a salad?"

"Shit. Sure. I'm starved." Lucas tipped up the bottle and took a long drag. "Thanks for making dinner."

"You may be starved, but you ain't thirsty, are you? You haven't been drinking and driving all day, have you?"

Lucas groaned. "Don't go getting all parental on me. I've had enough of that today. No, I haven't been drinking and driving. Well, I have, but just from Radclyffe's Roost up to here."

"Where'd you go?"

"I drove up to the top of Spruce Knob. Five thousand feet up gives you a little perspective. Had lunch at a little place near Seneca Rocks. I took a long walk in the state forest. Stopped by to see Grace and Amie. I bought this bottle at their place and opened it on the way up the valley. Grace recommended it. Try it. It's good."

He handed the bottle to Brice. Brice took a bubbly swig before handing it back. "It's tasty. What is it?"

"It's another Prosecco, a lot like that one we had on Valentine's Day. I figured, since we celebrated last night, we could celebrate again this evening."

"You feel like celebrating?"

Lucas took another long swig and smiled. "*Shit*, yes, I sure do. It's the party season around here. Grace reminded me that tomorrow's Fasnacht in Helvetia. Wanna go with them? The Hutte's got a holiday buffet I'm dying to sample."

"Sure, kid. What's Fasnacht?"

"Ah, it's a Swiss thang. Kinda like Mardi Gras. There's a parade—they call it the Lampion parade, since it's done with lamps and candles—and a masked ball, and at midnight they burn an effigy of Old Man Winter to celebrate the coming spring."

"Sounds fun. I'm up for it if you are."

"I sure am. We could do with some fun, huh? What's that there?"

"Mulled wine. *Glühwein,* the Germans call it. It's got a bunch of spices in it. Shelly used to serve it at our Christmas parties down in Franklin."

"Great! More to drink. Good." Lucas took another long gulp from the bottle and handed it to Brice. "You finish this. I'm gonna get into that wine. Smells great."

Worried by Lucas's show of cheeriness, Brice sipped the Prosecco, watching Lucas as he poured out a mug of *Glühwein.* "You ready to eat?"

Lucas sat with a sharp exhalation of breath in the rocking chair. He slurped the wine and smacked his lips. "Naw. I wanna drink first. In fact, I might get a big ole buzz on tonight. You mind?"

Chuckling, Brice shook his head. "Nope. After what happened this morning, I figure you deserve a good drunk."

"Ain't that the fucking truth?" Lucas propped a booted foot on one knee. "You gonna join me?"

Brice shook his head. "Huh uh. I need to keep my wits about me. The rest of this and a mug of that wine are all I need. Someone needs to stay sober tonight."

Lucas leaned back into the chair and rocked. "And why is that?"

"So someone can take care of you. That job falls to me. And it'll fall to me as long as you want it to."

Lucas stared at Brice. He chewed his lower lip. "Yeah?"

"Yeah." Brice tipped the Prosecco bottle up and drained it.

"Promise?"

Brice nodded. He put the bottle on the counter and crossed his arms. "Promise."

Lucas nodded. He took another slurp of wine and dropped his gaze to the floor.

"So what we celebrating?" Brice said, taking up the ladle and stirring the chowder.

"What you think we're celebrating? I'm done with that harpy."

"Looks like it." Brice kept his voice noncommittal, waiting to see where Lucas's mood was tending.

"I'm shitting you." Lucas's voice dropped lower. "That's not why we're celebrating."

"Oh?" Brice opened a cabinet and pulled out a bag of oyster crackers.

"Did you mean it?"

Brice took the salad spinner from another cabinet, put it on the counter, and turned to Lucas. The boy was slumped in the chair, head on his chest.

"Did I mean what?"

Lucas looked up, still rocking. His eyes bored into Brice. "You know. What you said this morning."

Brice leaned back against the edge of the counter, pushed his hands into his pants pockets, and bowed his head. "I know it's hard to believe. It's hard for me to believe. I know I've only known you for a short time. Maybe I'm deluding myself. Maybe my desire and my need are hoodwinking me. Maybe what I feel is just a passing infatuation. But I don't think so. I think I've met you at just the right point in my life, and I think you and I could have something deep and lasting. If you're interested."

Lucas said nothing. His chair rocking ceased.

Chest tight, Brice refreshed his mug of mulled wine. He stared into the cloud of steam that rose from his cup. "Am I in this alone?"

"Brice," Lucas muttered. "Oh, Brice."

Brice put his cup down and cleared his throat. "I know you've been through a lot. I know that intimacy, physical intimacy, is a difficult thing for you. I'll understand if you're not ready for more. I'll understand, and I'll be all right. But, honestly—I guess I just realized this too—if you don't think you'll ever want more, if you don't think you'll ever be able to love me back, I don't think I can stay here and just be buddies. I don't think...."

Lucas rose from the chair. He held out his mug. "Can I have some more?"

"Sure." Brice took the cup and filled it.

"Spring's coming," Lucas said. "It's just around the corner."

"Yes."

Lucas lifted his mug. "So here's a toast to spring."

Brice lifted his mug. They clinked.

Lucas reached over, resting a hand on Brice's shoulder. "I'm too tore up now to...."

"Yes. I know. I'm sorry. This is the worst possible timing, to say what I did on a day when...."

"Yep, I guess I'm officially an orphan." Lucas shook his head. "Amazing. She's just amazing. But here's another toast, okay?"

"Yeah?"

"To...to you staying here with me. To me getting better. Stronger. 'Cause, Brice?

You ain't in this alone. You ain't. Far from it. I don't know what I'd do if you…."

Lucas coughed. He knocked back the wine and gulped till it was gone. He poured himself another mug. His hand shook and he put the steaming mug down. He slumped back against the counter and looked up at Brice. His eyes, rimmed with tears, spilled over.

"Lucas. Buddy." Brice put his mug down and gripped the boy's arm.

"Oh, hell." Lucas wiped his eyes. Then he threw his arms around Brice, pressed his face against the bigger man's chest, and began to sob.

CHAPTER FORTY-SEVEN

BRICE GUIDED LUCAS UP TO THE GREAT ROOM. They sat together on the couch in the dark before the flameless hearth, and Brice held Lucas, and Lucas trembled in his arms and wept, his sides shaking, till Brice's shirt was moist with the boy's tears. He cried as if he never had before, as if it were a novel release and a passionate luxury he'd never allowed himself: wracked coughing, choking, shaking, cursing, punching the couch pillows, blowing his nose, hacking up phlegm, and hugging Brice so hard the older man had to suck in air to catch his breath.

After a quarter of an hour, Lucas subsided. Without words, Brice directed him downstairs. They made a brief meal of chowder, crackers, salad, and kale. Lucas, wet-cheeked, red-eyed, and stony-faced, insisted on cleaning up. Then he took Brice's hand and led him out the door and up the hill.

In Lucas's cabin, they stripped and climbed into bed. As soon as Brice pulled Lucas to him, the naked boy began shaking and sobbing once more. Brice held him and rubbed his back and stroked his face till Lucas's grief-stricken sobs tapered off and he fell asleep. Heart hurting, Brice spooned him from behind, knowing what every lover comes to know: no matter how strong or smart you are, there is no foolproof way to shield your beloved from sorrow.

BRICE WOKE TO DAYLIGHT AND the sound of water. He rolled over to find Lucas gone. For a split-second, he panicked. Then he realized that the rushing sound was the shower. He made a pile of pillows, folded his arms behind his head, and waited for Lucas to emerge.

In a few minutes, the boy did so. He stood naked by the bed, drying his wet head and beard. "Hey," he said hoarsely, smiling down at Brice.

"Hey," Brice said, studying him. Lucas's eyes were still red, and there were faint bags beneath them. "How you feeling?"

"Headache, congestion. As much from the crying as from the wine. Sorry I made such a fuss last night."

Brice shrugged. "No need to apologize. If my mother had ever treated me the way yours did—"

"Like a dog?"

"Yes. Like a dog. If she had, I would have had the same reaction you did. Get back in here, okay?"

Lucas hung the towel on the back of the bathroom door and climbed into bed with Brice. He sighed, leaning his head against Brice's shoulder, and pulled the blankets up over them.

"I would be so fucked, so fucked, so fucked if you weren't here," Lucas said.

Brice took his hand. "Maybe. But if I'd never come here, that article in the *Star* would never have been published, and your mother would never have shown up to… say the things she did."

"That show-down has been on the agenda for years, Brice. It was gonna happen sooner or later. I'm glad it's over. Wait'll I tell Uncle Phil. He'll snatch her bald-headed if she ever crosses his path again."

"That's a process I'd like to see," Brice said, sniggering. "That snatching bald-headed. But it'd take a while. She's got lots of hair."

"True." Lucas nuzzled his chin against Brice's right pec. "Man, she made me feel like the lowliest turd. I know she's full of shit—her whole version of religion is full of shit—but still…when your own mother…. I mean, I already have problems feeling worthless. I sure didn't need all that."

"No, you didn't. Honestly, I wanted to knock her teeth out."

"I love that protective streak in you, though I guess punching a woman, no matter how mean, wouldn't have been the right move. Do you know what I mean, though? About feeling worthless? I felt so goddamn no-account last night, I coulda died. Thank God you were here to hold on me. Who knows what kinda crazy shit I might have done without you around?"

"Feeling worthless? Hell, yes, I know what you mean. My father was, well, demanding. And it was all about him, you know? Which meant I spent my whole life trying to impress him, to get his attention and make him proud of me, but he was too self-absorbed to even notice. Nothing I did was ever good enough. That's why I got into music, I guess: to get noticed. That's why being a big star in Nashville meant so much to me, and why it was so awful to lose my audience. It made me feel like such a big fucking failure. I'm sorry. I'm going on about myself when I should be focusing on you."

"No, go on. Sounds like more stuff we got in common. Besides, I don't wanna talk about Mommy no more. Do you miss Nashville bad?"

"No. Not Nashville exactly." Brice rubbed his eyes and sighed. "Not the city of Nashville, but…the idea of Nashville—living there, being in the music business, making all that money, getting all that publicity. Nashville meant success. You know? The success I'd ached for. The big dream come true."

"Yeah, makes sense. I mean, hell, you were on the Grand Ole Opry. You were giving concerts all over the nation, right?"

"Yep. Australia and Europe too. Like I already told you, the Country Music Museum even had a little exhibit about me. That meant the world to me. It meant that all my struggles had paid off. It meant that I was finally part of that long, glorious tradition."

Brice tugged at the whiskers on Lucas's chin and slumped back into the pillows. "Then they took the exhibit down, due to 'revelations about my sexuality,' I think that's how they phrased it. Just like the bridge was renamed. God, what an insult."

"Bridge? What bridge?"

"I guess I didn't tell you. Once I got famous, the bridge across the New River in my hometown was named after me. Once the big news got out that I was a fag, the shitheads renamed the bridge after a local girl who's working in D.C. politics now. The Brice Brown Bridge is now the Suzanne Matthews Bridge."

"You've got to be kidding."

"Nope. It's like I've been deleted. Like everything I've ever achieved has been erased. You call yourself a mess? Me, I…I'm sick. My ego's sick. Fuck."

"What? What do you mean? Go on, buddy. Go on. Please."

Brice nodded. "Yeah, okay. I hate to admit this, 'cause it sounds neurotic as hell, kinda pathetic, really, but it's like I'm some big fucking narcissist who can only feel good about himself when folks are making a big fuss about how great he is. *Man*, I miss the attention. The concert crowds, the awards, the adulation.... It was like a drug. And withdrawal has been hell. I was so depressed around Christmas that I thought about killing myself."

"I know those feelings, and don't you fucking dare. Am I not audience enough?" Lucas gently bit Brice's shoulder.

"You're a sharp-toothed lil' wildcat, ain't you? Well, as much as I wish that were enough...."

"Yeah, I get it. There's love." Lucas took the fur-coated flesh of Brice's pec in his palm and squeezed it. "And there's work. That's what Freud says."

"Freud?"

"Yep. I had a lot of time to read in prison. Freud says you need both love and work to be happy. As much as I'd like to stay in this valley with you, snuggling till kingdom come, at some point we're both gonna have to figure out what to do with our lives. Me, who knows? You—your work, your career is music. No way around it."

"I think you're right...but you're using the L word now too?" Brice tweaked Lucas's nose. "Be careful. Don't get my hopes up."

"Yeah, I am using that word. And we'll have a big conversation about all that, soon as I recover some from that verbal beating Mommy gave me yesterday. Anyway, back to career. A guy's gotta have a career. And a man as talented as you should have loads of fans. Millions of fans. As much as you've accomplished, you have every right to expect that. Every artist wants his work to be noticed and admired and respected. Man, it irks my ass that the world's so full of pious, mealy-mouthed homo-haters that so many fans have abandoned you."

"That's the way of the world right now, Lucas. I gotta cope with this fragile, hungry, malformed, big baby of an ego of mine and grow up and adjust my expectations and stop wishing I could be back where I was. All that before—my whole Nashville career—was based on lies anyway, me posing as straight. I don't intend to lie any more, so it's very likely—if not downright certain—that I'm never gonna have a big mainstream audience again."

"Maybe not. But you are gonna keep writing new stuff, right?"

Brice fondled Lucas's limp dick. He bent Lucas's arm back and took a long whiff of the boy's armpit. "As long as we share a bed, you're damn right I'm gonna keep writing. Beauty and desire are always grist for the poetic mill."

"Well, then, who knows? Get together a new album of material, and maybe....

A collection of gay country-music songs? It'd be a first! You could have a whole new audience. I've already told you how much music like that would mean to queer folks, especially folks like us who don't run to the cities, who are ornery enough to stay out in the boonies or in small towns and take the risk of being ourselves."

"Anything's possible, I guess. But Nashville—"

"Fuck Nashville. That's not the only way to go. There's gotta be some other way to get your music out there to folks who'd appreciate it."

Lucas tugged at the coarse hair around Brice's navel and slid out of bed. "So, how's about we have some of that oatmeal I whipped up yesterday, and then we go looking for some seeds and onion sets and sprouts and such at Lowe's? It's nearly March, and I wanna grow me up some baby broccoli and cabbage in the greenhouse, so they'll be a decent size when planting time comes around."

"Greenhouse? There's a greenhouse here?"

"You ain't seen it? Uncle Phil set it up just for me, since he knows we come from a long line of gardeners. Lord, every spring Mommy used to...."

Lucas's face clouded over. "To hell with her. Anyway, late afternoon, we can head down to Helvetia with Amie and Grace and see some of the Fasnacht festivities and have dinner. Maybe hang around and watch Old Man Winter go up in flames. Planting time's a'comin'. You gonna help me in the garden this spring?"

"Depends. If it's warm, will you work bare-chested?"

"Hell, sure."

"Then you got it."

"Great." Lucas winked, flexing his triceps. "Okay, lemme trim my beard up for tonight. You wanna take a shower?"

"Yeah, once you're done. I think I'll trim my beard too, come to think of it. No reason the ladies should have to be seen in public with a couple of wild barbarians."

"True," said Lucas. "We can keep the wild to ourselves. And I'm thinking, you stick with me, there's gonna be a lotta wild, a lotta glorious wild, to come."

"I'm counting on that." Brice settled back onto the pillows and smiled, watching Lucas stride bare-assed into the bathroom. He was already imagining Lucas working in the garden, wearing nothing but muddy boots and jeans, his pale shoulders growing pink under the spring sun, his nipples hard under the tongue of some lucky breeze, getting sweaty and working up an appetite for first a big country meal and then a long night of love.

My hunky, shirtless farmboy. Yep, thought Brice, *that's a sweet image, and this is gonna be a sweet spring. We're gonna rise outta the cold together, Lucas and me. I'll bet there's gonna be another song or three in that.*

"SO YOU TWO REALIZE," BRICE warned, "now that our shocking sodomitic affair has been exposed by the *Star*, if you're seen with us, you'll be tarred with the same brush. Maybe we shouldn't go to Helvetia together. If there are reporters there, things might get ugly."

Brice sat with Amie, Grace, and Lucas at a table in the dining area of Radclyffe's Roost. The four friends were finishing off a pot of Amie's ginger tea before attending the Fasnacht celebrations. Brice, Lucas, and Grace were dressed in simple jeans and earth-tone sweaters, but Amie, ever the fashion plate, was wearing a string of pearls and a long crimson dress with high-heeled black boots. Beyond the big window, a light snow was falling.

"Do we look like we're worried?" Grace said. "'Mysterious Beauty' here is waiting for her next appearance in mass media."

"True! And the next excuse to pull her pistol." Amie pursed her red lips and struck a second's seductive pose before waving off Brice's concern. "I've already told you: locals know that Grace and I are a couple. We've had very little trouble."

Grace chuckled. "That's because everyone in the county is afraid you'll refuse to serve them your sterling cuisine if they piss you off."

"Also true." Amie poured the last of the tea into Lucas's empty cup. "Lucas, I'm so sorry your mother chose to be such a raving termagant."

"If you mean 'bitch,' yeah, me too." Lucas swigged down the tea and drummed his fingers on the tabletop. "I was always closer to Daddy, but Mommy and I used to get along pretty well...till she found out I was gay. Of course, that lil' secret was revealed in the worse way possible. Hustling was the stupidest goddamn thing I ever did. Gotta admit I liked the attention even more'n the money, but, man...."

"I felt the same as a burlesque dancer, honey." Amie patted the back of Lucas's hand. "Admiration can be as intoxicating as cash. Don't blame yourself. We know you did all that to help your mother keep her house."

"Yep. And now she never wants to see me again. Mean as she's gotten, I guess that's fine with me." Lucas rose. "Okay, folks. My stomach's growling, and that buffet's a'waitin.' Let's head on out."

"I'll drive. Our car has more room," Grace said.

"Let me just get my purse," Amie said, smiling wickedly. "In case we encounter more vile reporters."

"Honey, you can't just wave a pistol at folks in the middle of downtown Helvetia," Grace said.

"Isn't that a pity? Law and order can be such a pesky obstacle. Why, given the opportunity, I could teach all sorts of folks better manners."

Grinning, Lucas pulled on his black denim jacket. "That's something I'd sure like to see."

"Come on, Annie Oakley," Grace said. "Let's get our coats. I'm hungry too."

As soon as the women left the room, Lucas pulled a flask from his jacket's inner pocket, opened it, and took a long drink.

Brice raised his eyebrows. "Starting early, aren't you?"

Lucas shrugged. "It's almost five. Want some?" He offered Brice the flask.

"Sure. What is it?"

"That Scotch you like. They don't serve booze at the Hutte, so I figured this'd keep us warm during the parade later. It's pretty damned cold out."

"Thanks." Brice took a long sip and handed the flask back. "You ready to be seen in public now that everyone knows we're—"

"Lovers? Hell, yes, I'm ready. Everybody's gonna look at us and think, 'What's a guy so talented doing with holler trash like that?'"

Brice snorted. "No, everybody's gonna be thinking, 'What's that old has-been doing with a guy so staggeringly hot?'"

Lucas laughed. "Flattery, huh?" He took another big drink, then sealed the flask, slipped it back into his jacket, and wrapped an arm around Brice's waist. "You don't need to sweet-talk me, big man. Tonight, when we get home, I'm gonna get you nekkid and deep-throat your dick. Then I'm thinking it's high time that you—"

Lucas's erotic murmurings were cut short by Grace and Amie's entrance. "Ready?" Grace asked, jingling her car keys.

"Ohhhh, yeah," Lucas said, patting Brice's ass. "I am ready indeed."

CHAPTER FORTY-EIGHT

WHEN THE FOUR ENTERED THE PACKED DINING room of the Hutte, everyone in the place stopped talking and stared, just as Brice had feared.

"Oh, hell, here we go," Brice muttered beneath his breath, bracing himself for lobbed insults and the hostilities bound to escalate after that. For a second, he caught himself hoping that Amie had indeed brought her gun.

The tension was almost immediately broken by Eleanor, the owner, who rushed over to seat them. "Welcome, y'all. So glad you could join us for Fasnacht!" she shouted, giving each of them big hugs one after another. She turned then, giving the rest of the room a stern glance. Cowed, the other patrons dropped their eyes to their plates and continued eating.

"Like oil on troubled waters," Lucas said. "Thanks, Miss Eleanor. You seen any reporters roundabouts?"

"Hard to tell, honey. Lots of out-of-towners make it to Helvetia for Fasnacht. I'll let you know if I notice anyone suspicious. And let me know if anyone in here gives you any trouble about that trashy *Star* article. If they do, I'll toss their butts out into the snow. I won't abide meanness in this place."

"That'd be much appreciated," Brice said as Eleanor showed them to a table in the back. His hands, he realized, were shaking slightly as he scanned the room, tensed for trouble. *Full-blown siege mentality I got going here*, he thought. *Think I need me another swig of Lucas's flask.* "Lucas tells me you have a special holiday buffet tonight. What's on it?"

"Oh, we have quite the tasty array. Sausage,

chicken, bratwurst, parsley potatoes, sauerkraut, green beans, homemade cheese, homemade bread, plus peach cobbler for dessert. We also have some local beer. Does that appeal?"

"Hell, yes. I mean, 'Yes, ma'am,'" Lucas enthused, rubbing his hands together. "That's well worth the risk of running into more scandal-rag guys. Y'all want to start with some beers?"

"Absolutely," said Grace, pulling a chair out for Amie.

To Brice's relief, the meal passed without incident, other than the occasional curious or judgmental sideways looks from other restaurant patrons and a full-on glare from an emaciated old man near the door, a disgusted expression that Lucas returned in kind. Lucas's buddy Ray made it a point to come over and be friendly, as did a pretty blonde girl that Lucas had grown up near, and Eleanor stopped by their table often to make sure that they were enjoying themselves. The only thing that concerned Brice was Lucas's steady drinking. By the time they'd emptied their plates, the boy had put down four beers and was looking flush-faced.

"I'm payin' for this," Lucas insisted, snatching up the check and slapping down several big bills. "We all know I'm a big ole mess, but you three have really saved my life lately. Now let's check out that parade."

"THIS IS GREAT," BRICE WHISPERED. "Really magical. I'm so glad we came."

The two men stood on the side of the road in the dark and the softly falling snow, watching the procession of people pass. Many of the participants were costumed, several wearing huge, grotesque masks, and all carried candles or lanterns. A few feet away, Grace and Amie stood together, Amie pointing out especially interesting costumes and Grace taking photographs of them. Across the road, locals gathered around a bonfire, laughing and chatting. Inside the nearby Community Hall, the sounds of banjo, fiddle, and guitar signaled that the square dance had just begun. Both Brice and Lucas had pulled the hoods of their sweatshirts up over their ball caps to keep the snow out of their collars, and that concealment, plus the celebrants' own party-mood enthusiasm and the winter dimness, seemed to shelter them from being recognized or receiving any negative attentions.

Lucas leaned into Brice and took a quick sip from his flask. "Glad you like it," he mumbled. "That food sure was delicious."

"It was. I'd never had Swiss food before you brought me here. Don't you love being from West Virginia?" Brice looked up into the winter sky, opened his mouth, and caught a few flakes on his tongue. "Beautiful landscapes—rivers and hills—and, on top of that, events like this. Amazing cultural variety. Folks preserving their heritage. The music, the food, the costumes. Sometimes I miss Nashville, and I sure miss the money and the fans, but this…. Man, it's good to be back in the mountains. Sweet little small towns like this…."

"Holy fucking shit," Lucas blurted, stiffening against Brice.

"What is it?"

"There. That big bald guy in the blue peacoat. There across the road."

"Yeah, I see him. Who is it?"

Lucas lifted the flask to his mouth and noisily slurped it. "It's Reverend Davis. My mother's minister. The son of a bitch who convinced her I was a hell-bound sinner she should cut out of her life. I wanna go over there and kick his ass."

"Lucas, don't," Brice said, laying a hand on the shorter man's shoulder. "You've had too much to drink. You're on parole, remember? Don't do something we'll both regret. I don't want to lose you to the legal system, okay?"

Lucas stuffed the flask inside his jacket. His left hand cupped his right fist. Then he released a long breath and unclenched his hand. "Shit, you're right. Fuck him. He ain't worth getting worked up over. Let's head on into the Community Hall and listen to some music."

"That'd be best," Brice said. Clasping Lucas by the arm, he led him over to Grace and Amie. "Hey, ladies," he said. "Want to head inside? Looks like the parade's about over, and my toes are getting numb."

"Surely," Amie said, brushing snow from her stylish felt hat. "Let's see some of the dancing and the masked ball. Do you want to stay till the effigy of Old Man Winter is burnt? That won't happen till midnight."

"Lucas, what do you think? Maybe we—"

Brice was cut short by the sound of someone shouting Lucas's name. "Lucas! Lucas Bryan!"

"Son of a fucking whore," Lucas growled. "Here he comes. Charging like a goddamn bull."

"Who the hell?" Grace said. "Is that—?"

"Mommy's minister," Lucas said, fists clenching up again.

"Reverend Davis," Amie said. "The bloated toad."

By the time the portly man had lumbered across the road, the four friends had formed a tight defensive line. Amie, Brice noticed, was unzipping her clutch purse. *Amie said that she had dreams about shooting him through the head. Oh, hell, I hope we don't all end up in jail,* Brice thought, fixing the minister with a glare.

"Lucas Bryan! How dare you show your face in public?" the pastor wheezed.

"Fuck off, Reverend," Lucas said, his voice low and stony. "This is a free country. We got as much a right to celebrate here as anyone."

"Your kind have far more freedoms than you should. You should be put in camps, in my opinion."

"Camps?" Brice blurted. "What kind of crazy Nazi asshole are you?"

Davis ignored him. "Lucas, you're a criminal and a whore. You're a chancre on this county."

"You'd better shut the fuck up and move on down the road, Reverend," Brice growled, squaring his shoulders and stepping in front of Lucas. "That'd be the wise thing to do."

The minister looked Brice up and down, his mouth twisting. "You. The pervert singer. Sharing a bed with this misguided child, encouraging him in his corruption. Is it true? Are you two engaging together in carnal knowledge?"

"You're damn right we are," Lucas said, moving around Brice to stand beside him. "And I thank God for that."

"Don't even mention the name of God. The name of the Lord on those lips? Those lips you've used for abominable pleasures? You're a pestilence. A horrible punishment will be dealt you, I have no doubt."

"Punishment?" Brice cracked his knuckles. "You're the one's gonna see some punishment, unless you get out of my face."

The reverend folded his arms atop his belly and smirked. "You wouldn't dare touch me here. Attacking a man of God? In public?"

"I wouldn't risk it if I were you," Brice snarled. Inside his chest, a fury was building, one fueled by all the abuse and injustices of the last three months. Part of him ached to thrash the abusive pastor till he bled. Another part struggled to resist that impulse, knowing the legal consequences if Lucas were to become embroiled in a brawl.

"Brice is right," Lucas said, moving closer to Brice. "Stuff it up your ass. Leave us the fuck alone, or you'll regret it."

"You're threatening me too? Exactly what I'd expect from a ex-con like you." The minister shook his head and scowled. "You're a ruffian and a delinquent. How your mother has suffered since the enormity of your sinful prostitution was revealed. And now you're infamous. Everyone in the nation knows of your rampant immorality. Your mother is such a good, fine, upstanding woman, but you seem to have devoted your life to breaking her heart with your disgusting blasphemies."

"Maybe her heart needed broken," Amie said, shifting her purse from her right hand to her left. "Considering that it's become a vessel you've filled with poison."

"You two as well?" Davis sneered at Amie and Grace. "Sapphists and sodomites. It makes sense that you four would band together, drawn together by perversion and evil. For too long, your sinister lesbianism has—"

"Watch out how you speak to ladies, you damn fool," Brice interjected, nostrils flaring. "We've had enough of your nastiness. If you don't leave us the hell alone, I'm going to break that fat face of yours."

"No need, Brice," Amie said. "I've been wanting to have a little chat with Reverend Davis for a long time, and tonight I'm going to have it."

"Uh, oh," Grace said, smiling faintly.

Amie left Grace's side to position herself between the minister and her friends. "I believe you have it wrong, Reverend. We're drawn together by faith and hope and love. Faith in our camaraderie, hope for a better future, and love for one another."

"Here she goes," Grace said, giving Brice a wink. "Better stand back."

Amie gave Grace a fond glance before regarding the minister with a cold glare. "Despite the many pressures and adversities we've faced, Grace and I have been together for nearly twenty years. And now these two men, thanks to some kind fate, have found one another and have decided to share their lives together. This is a reason for celebration, but you're too stupid to realize that."

Davis put his hands on his hips. "Stupid? No, I'm simply saying what Christ—"

Amie cut him off, her voice steely and composed. "I believe that any Biblical scholar can point out to you an important fact. It's knowledge that might ameliorate your state of vast ignorance, knowledge that any people with a modicum of sense already possess. That fact is this: in the Bible, Jesus never once speaks against homosexuality. He speaks of forgiveness and love, but perhaps you've forgotten that, stewing as you are in your own toxic virulence."

"Madam, how dare you—"

Amie cut him off again, her voice rising. "Yes, virulence. Perhaps a man of your embarrassing limitations isn't familiar with the word. Let me speak more simply, since you appear to be a simple man…simple in so many ways. You're poisonous, Reverend Davis, and that poison infects the people around you. You're poisonous the way a scorpion is, or a wolf spider, or a Gila monster, or a diamondback rattler. Except that Nature has armed those creatures with poison in order that they might protect themselves, in order that they might feed, while you—"

"You're comparing me to those nasty—"

"Be quiet, Reverend. I'm not done. You are indeed like them in your toxicity, but, unlike their venom, yours has no natural purpose. Your poison, your hatred, are unnatural. They are a sign of disease, like a burgeoning tumor."

"Unnatural? You four are the unnatural—"

"Be silent, I told you! This is not your time to give a sermon, it's mine. Your hatred is that of a little man with a little soul. I would reach for a vulgar analogy here and impugn the size of your manhood as well, but I suspect that your genitals have long ago atrophied, dwindling past the reach of metaphor."

Davis gasped. Lucas sniggered. Brice guffawed.

"Holy as you supposedly are, what need would you have of genitals anyway? Your flesh-hating faith has turned you against the teeming beauties and blessings of this sensual world. You speak of Lucas's blasphemous behavior? There is nothing blasphemous about this boy. Be sure of it. There's nothing blasphemous about the bodily pleasures these two men might take together. No, what's unmitigated blasphemy is your attitude toward this universe of wonders that God has made. *That's* blasphemy."

Amie raised a black-gloved hand and pointed it at the minister, as if aiming her gun at the space between his eyes. She took a step forward, and immediately Davis took a step back, as if they were rehearsing a dance move together.

"Even more blasphemous is that you, like so many conservative Christians, have taken a religion of compassion and perverted it. You have twisted it into a weapon of viciousness, persecution, and exclusion. You've used it to try to close our store and turn the county against us. Now you're using it to try to make this sweet-souled young man suffer. I assure you, he has suffered enough. Christ didn't torment the suffering,

Reverend. He consoled them. How could you have forgotten that? You are the pervert, Reverend Davis, not we."

Davis gulped in deep breaths, his face red and his eyes bulging. "You-you're a foul slut. You have a history of harlotry. Why should I—"

"You're devoted to those Old Testament slurs, aren't you?" Amie sighed, fluttering her gloved fingers in his face. "I'm neither slut nor harlot. I'm a woman who celebrates her appetites and her body. I'm a woman who cherishes the world because of all it gives us to love. There is so much to love, Reverend Davis. A man of your profession should be sharply aware of that. The cosmos is full of gifts both spiritual and corporeal. These men together have found a profound gift. Grace and I together have found a profound gift. Yet you would seek to hound and harass us. Just as your kind have hounded and harassed gays and lesbians for centuries. You spread the spores of misery like some stubborn fungus. You seek to make outcasts out of anyone who doesn't subscribe to your vicious faith."

"Vicious? You madwoman! You heretical—"

"Silence, reverend! I have only one thing left to say." Amie lifted off her hat and shook out her long black hair. Her voice rose yet again. "Perhaps God is as hateful as you think. Perhaps He is! And if He is, if He is as dedicated to punishment and reprisal as you believe, then you have a terrible day of doom coming. I can foresee it, yes."

Amie stepped closer to Davis. To Brice's relief, she tucked her purse into her coat pocket before gesticulating dramatically against the falling snow.

"Yes! I predict your end! Ignominious, and excruciating, and soon. Soon! Your selfishness, egotism and cruelty will be crushed. God will hold you like a loathsome spider above the pit of His wrath."

"No! You're insane!" Davis's red face paled. "I'm God's servant!"

"No! You're His foe! You have intimidated and threatened and connived. You have turned fathers against daughters and mothers against sons. You have fomented wrath rather than love."

Amie stepped forward, stabbing him in the chest with her right forefinger. "He will exact an agonizing chastisement! Before Him, all those you have tormented will speak against you. See their faces! So many. So many. All those you have wronged! A long, long line of sad shades and spectral outcasts."

"I've wronged no one! I speak for the Lord."

"You speak lies! The Lord says you lie! On the Day of Judgment, angels will separate the chaff from the wheat and the goats from the sheep and the cruel from the kind! And you, you—"

"No. Shut up!" Davis moaned. Big as he was, he visibly quailed in the face of this small woman's stentorian wrath. About them, four of the last parade participants had gathered, mouths agape.

"You shall be cast into the Lake of Fire. Serpents will feast on your fatty flesh. Gouts of flame will incinerate your bones!"

"Shut up!" Davis howled, taking another step back. He ran a hand over his bald pate as if he were sweating despite the wintry night.

"You *must* hear the truth! You *need* to hear it! You *know* what I say is true! What woes you have caused! Innumerable woes! Confess it!"

"No. No!"

"Yes! You think you can dissemble before God, who knows and sees all? And now you must pay the price! Soon your intestines will be gnawed by ravenous lizards. Soon vipers will intertwine about your spine. Soon vultures and kites, the rapacious birds of the air, will feast on your eyeballs, snapping them between the sharp edges of their beaks as if they were tender grapes."

"No. What outrageous falsehoods. Stop it! No!"

"Yes. Yes! I see it so clearly! And then, most horribly, behold! The Beast of Revelation, that slouching horror, with its many heads and its many horns, will rise from the churning deep to take its turn, to sate its hideous hunger. Feel it now! Feel its clammy limbs embrace you. Feel its teeth devouring the throbbing mass of—"

"Shut up!" Davis screamed, his eyes wide with panic. "No! I won't listen to this. I refuse to listen to this. Too horrible! No!"

"Horrible, yes! Feel the beast's fangs sink deep into the rotten tissue of your heart, black and dripping gobbets that it will—"

Amie's next delicious detail was drowned out by Davis's scream. Clasping his hands over his ears, he turned tail and bolted away. Seconds later, he'd disappeared into the dark.

For a long moment, there was stunned, snow-stippled silence. Then a bug-eyed bystander muttered, "Damn, lady. I guess you told him."

Amie chuckled. "Why, thank you. I do believe I did."

"Holy shit," Lucas gasped. Pulling his flask from his jacket, he drained it.

"Damnation," Brice rasped. "You told me once that you had dreams about shooting him through the head, and now I believe you have."

"In a manner of speaking." Smiling, Amie replaced her hat on her head. "That'll teach him to cross us. It's always fun to use their language against them."

"That, gentlemen, is what several seasons of *Designing Women* can teach you," Grace said, taking Amie by the arm. "Come on, Julia Sugarbaker. Let's get out of here before that shattered bastard limps back here with the law and accuses you of assault and battery."

CHAPTER FORTY-NINE

"I'LL DRIVE," BRICE SAID, BRUSHING SNOW OFF HIS shoulders. Having said their goodnights to Grace and Amie, the two men stood by Lucas's truck in the parking lot of Radcliffe's Roost. Across the road, Lost Creek burbled noisily. Otherwise, the winter night was utterly silent.

Lucas shrugged his shoulders. "Whatever." He dropped the keys into Brice's outstretched hand.

Neither spoke on the drive up Brantley Valley. Lucas slumped back into the corner of the truck cab, eyes closed. When they reached the compound, he clambered unsteadily from the truck.

"Whoa. I'm pretty shit-faced," he said, swaying.

"So I see. You gonna be sick?"

"Naw. Not that shit-faced. Give me a hand?"

"Sure. I got you." Brice took his arm and helped him up the few steps to the porch. Once inside, Lucas staggered over to the couch and collapsed onto it.

"Guess I've had enough, huh?" Lucas asked.

"Yep. Some water'll help fend off a hangover." Brice fetched Perrier from the bar fridge.

"Thanks." Lucas guzzled the mineral water. "You gonna tell me to stop drinking so much?"

"Naw. You're an adult, and I'm not your father. Mind if I cuddle with you? It's chilly in here."

"Cuddle away." Lucas gave Brice a lopsided grin. "Too late to make a fire. We'll head up to my cabin once I'm done with this."

Brice plopped down beside Lucas, wrapped an arm around him, and arranged an afghan over their laps and legs. "This all right?"

"Hell, yes," Lucas said, slurring his 's.' "I still can't believe how Miss Amie told that frigging preacher off."

"Me neither. She was magnificent."

"Uncle Phil can be the same way. Folks like that, you never wanna piss off…unless you like getting publicly humiliated. I'm glad she went off on him. The crap he was saying got under my skin."

"It shouldn't. It was all pure bullshit."

"I guess." Lucas gulped Perrier. "It was still hard to hear."

"Yeah, I know. A preacher in my hometown…we got into a pretty loud altercation a few months back. I sort of lost it."

Lucas didn't respond. He simply nodded, staring at the cold hearth.

"Lucas, you wanna talk?"

"Sure," Lucas said. "What about?"

"Why you're drinking so much. Same reason as yesterday, that's my guess."

"Mommy? Yep. Guess so." Lucas took another gulp of Perrier and looked Brice in the eye. "Goddamn, you're handsome. Do you know how goddamn handsome you are?"

"That's just the booze talking." Brice rubbed his knuckles over Lucas's scalp. "No wonder. You've been swilling steadily since about 4:30. It's nearly ten now."

Lucas shrugged. "Feels good to get so soused every now and then. I get tired of…."

"Of what?" Brice pulled him closer.

Lucas turned his head and pressed his brow against Brice's shoulder. "Of feeling. I feel too much. That's always been my problem. A tragic flaw, like in those Greek plays I read in prison. I just…."

"Go on." Brice squeezed him gently. "This is another thing we have in common, I think."

"Yeah. Probably." Lucas nodded, leaned back, and took another drink. "Ever since I was a kid, knee-high to a grasshopper, I've just…felt too much. I'm too damn sensitive. I try to be tough, to be a grown-up, to be a man, but…everything gets to me, y'know? I'm so easy to hurt, so thin-skinned. It wears me out. It wears everybody out."

"It doesn't wear me out," Brice said.

"Hell, you've only been here for a few weeks. Watch out. Pretty soon, I'll wear you out too."

"You're not gonna wear me out, Lucas. Just the opposite. You've…how do I say this? You've reinvigorated my life. You've brought me back from the dead."

Lucas laughed. "You're a crazy man. You're gonna get tired of me any day now and head on out of here. I'm a loser. I broke my Mommy's heart, that minister said, and he's right."

"He's wrong. I think she broke *your* heart, and that's because she's too judgmental to love you for who you are."

"Maybe. I don't know." Lucas shook his head. "If you don't get out of here, who knows? I'm liable to break your heart too."

"You may do that," Brice said, taking Lucas's hand. "That's entirely within the realm of possibility. Every time a man lets himself love someone, that someone has the power to break his heart. But I don't think in this case that's gonna happen."

"No?"

"No."

"So you ain't going anywhere?"

"No, I'm not. I've already told you that. I'm only leaving if you want me to."

Lucas drained the Perrier bottle, swayed forward, put it with exaggerated care onto the coffee table, and stared at the carpet. "I don't want you to leave. I don't want you to leave. Please don't leave me."

"Lucas, listen to me." Brice lifted Lucas's hand to his lips and kissed it. "I ain't going *anywhere*. I swear. You hear me? I love you. I love you for who you are. I'm staying here with you."

Brice cleared his throat, feeling tears trying to gather but fighting them back. "I love you. You're my life now. What kind of man decides to leave his life unless he has no choice but to do so?"

"You're my life too." Lucas choked up a sob. He pressed his face into his cupped hands for a long moment before turning his wet gray-blue gaze back to Brice. "I want you to stay. Stay, okay? Please stay. Stay and take care of me. I need you to take care of me. I need you to take care of me."

Brice stroked the boy's furry cheek. "You got it."

"You swear?"

"I swear." Leaning forward, Brice kissed Lucas on the brow.

"Good. Will you help me now?"

"Sure. Do what?"

"Help me stand up and get up the hill to my cabin and up to our bed. 'Sall right?"

"All right. I'm gonna get more water and some aspirins in you before bed. Okay? To ward off a hangover."

Lucas nodded slowly. "Good idea. Good idea. Maybe a nice quick hot shower too. Thank you, man. Thank you."

"Sure." Brice stood. With difficulty, he pulled Lucas to his feet. "For what?"

"For being so good t'me," Lucas groaned. "So good t'me. My hero. Write me another song? Promise?"

Brice wrapped an arm around Lucas's waist. "Yes, buddy. I'll write you another song. I promise. Here now. Let's get you buttoned up. It's still snowing out."

"How you feeling?" Brice asked, as he toweled Lucas off.

"Better. Lot better. The shower helped."

"Come on then." Brice took Lucas by the hand, helped him into bed, and switched off the lamp. Lucas snuggled back against Brice, Brice kissed Lucas on the shoulder blade, and both men were asleep within minutes.

In the middle of the night, a bad dream broke apart Brice's sleep. Muttering peevishly, he rose, his bladder full, and hit the bathroom. Returning to bed, he wrapped an arm around Lucas, nestled close, and did his best to forget the details of the dream. He was beginning to drift off again when Lucas's soft voice roused him. "Brice? You awake?"

"Yeah. Had a stupid nightmare."

"What about?"

"It was real subtle. I was performing in the Ryman to a house of completely empty seats." Brice chuckled. "What do you think that could mean?"

Lucas chuckled too. "You're right. Mighty subtle. Mighty mysterious. Too complex for me to interpret."

Brice ran a palm over Lucas's buzz cut. "How you feeling after all that booze?"

Lucas rolled over onto his back. "I'm fine. No headache or nothing. I woke up a little while ago and started thinking."

"Yeah?" Brice yawned. "What about?"

"Guess." Lucas reached over, took Brice's hand, and pressed his erect cock into his palm.

"Aha," Brice said, smiling into the dark. He gripped Lucas's prick and stroked it slowly. "After all that's happened in the last two days, I was wondering when you might—"

"Get back in the mood after the family trauma and drama?"

"Yeah. Well put." Brice tightened his thumb and forefinger around Lucas's cock-shaft, just below the head, and stroked more firmly. "I love the way your dick feels. Big as mine. But thicker, I think. Makes a glorious handful."

Lucas groaned and thrust into Brice's grip. "Uhhhh. You sure know how to handle it. Mmm, yeah. So, Brice?"

"Yeah?"

"A couple of times now, you've said you love me. Right?"

"Right. Absolutely. Do you believe me?"

"Yes."

"Does that bother you? That I love you? Do you want me to love you?"

"Bother me? I'm fucking ecstatic. Of course I want you to love me."

"You do?" Brice flicked the tip of his forefinger over Lucas's come-slit, found moisture there, and began to rub the tiny opening.

"Ummmmm. Yes. I believe you...you love me...because...you listen to me, you care how I feel, you make me feel...wanted...mmmmm...you protect me, you stand up...for me.... I can't express how...uhh...how much all that means to me. So now...."

"Now?"

"Now I'm ready for you to show me...how you care about me...in ways that you've been waiting for." Lucas arched his back and thrust steadily into Brice's hand. "You've been so patient, Brice. I appreciate that so damn much. I still ain't quite ready for butt-sex, but just about everything else...uhhhhh uuuuunnn...yes."

"So you're saying...other than ass-play, you're giving me permission to love you in the ways I've mentioned before?"

"Yeah. Mmm! Oh, yeah. You up for that tonight?"

Brice heaved a long sigh, a sound welling with pleasure and relief, full of the knowledge that long-awaited raptures were imminent. "You bet," he said, jacking Lucas's cock. "One warning, though."

"Yeah?"

"I tend to get a little rough when I'm really into a guy, and I don't think I've ever been into anyone as much as I'm into you. So just tell me if...."

"I'll tell you if you're getting too rough. Go slow, okay? Make it last. I don't wanna shoot too soon."

"It's a deal. You're not still drunk, though? I ain't gonna make love to you while you're drunk and then have you wake up sober, regretting all we did."

"I'm sober. I promise. Make love to me, Brice. Please. I want it bad."

Brice heaved another deep sigh. "All right, Lucas. Here we go. You ready?"

"I am ready indeed. Go for it."

Still gripping Lucas's dick, Brice climbed on top of him. "Oh, God, you're such a gift," he groaned, nuzzling Lucas's face.

"Same to you, big guy." Lucas nibbled Brice's lips. "I love the way your big beard feels against my face." He wrapped his arms around Brice's broad back, kissed him, and pulled him closer, all the while riding Brice's fist.

Brice luxuriated in Lucas's kisses for a long time, till both men's whiskers were wet with spit. Brice released Lucas's prick and pulled away, only to slide down Lucas's body till his head was level with his lover's torso.

"Ummm, your sweet, sweet tits," Brice said, kissing Lucas's right pec. "You mind if we turn on the bedside light? I really want to see you."

"And I wanna see you," Lucas said. "Gotta feast all five senses, right?"

Lucas flipped on the lamp. The two men grinned happily at one another. Then Brice lowered his gaze to Lucas's bare chest.

"Oh, God, you're so built. You're so beautiful."

Entranced, Brice ran a reverent hand over Lucas's torso. His pecs were low mounds of muscle, hills forest-fuzzy with a sparse coating of reddish brown hair. The nipples were tiny and erect. Brice squeezed the right pec gently in his palm, reveling in the dense strength embodied there, and then bent to the nipple and lapped it.

Lucas tensed up, gripped Brice's shoulders, and whimpered. "Oh, man."

"You like that?" Brice gave the little nub another lick before looking up at Lucas.

Lucas nodded, gray-blue eyes very wide. "Hell, yes. The sensation goes straight to my cock. Keep it up, man. Please."

Brice licked the nipple again and again. He took it into his mouth and sucked gently. Then he moved to Lucas's left pec, kneading its hard flesh and treating the left nipple to the same eager adorations.

Lucas ran his hands through Brice's short, receding hair. "You can do that harder, man. I ain't gonna break."

"Be glad to," Brice muttered, sucking more intensely. "Just let me know if I get too rough." He trapped Lucas's hard-on between his own chest and Lucas's belly before reaching up to pinch and tug Lucas's right nipple.

"Oh, yeah. Work 'em both. Oh, yeah," Lucas groaned, gripping Brice's head. "That's…. Do it even harder, okay? Yeah. Yeah. Yeah, that…almost hurts…but it…feels so damn good."

"I've been wanting to suck your tits for weeks," Brice muttered, taking Lucas's left nipple between his teeth and biting down gently.

"Yeah. Oh! Yeah!" Lucas gasped. Reaching down, he seized his own prick and began stroking it.

"Not too rough?"

"N-naw. N-naw. Just right. Just…right."

Brice took his time, shifting from firmness to gentleness and back again, reveling in Lucas's blissful moans and euphoric squirming. Brice lapped, sucked, nibbled, bit, chewed and tugged Lucas's tiny nipples, moving from one to the other like a honeybee between two especially succulent pink roses.

Lucas fisted his cock faster and faster. "Oh, man, I'm already close."

"Let me help with that," Brice said. He slid further down Lucas's body, kissing his scars, licking the line of cinnamon hair descending from his navel to his pubes. Squeezing the boy's nipples between his thumbs and forefingers, he nuzzled his cock, lapped its sticky head, and then took the thick column into his mouth.

Brice sucked steadily, loving the smell and taste of Lucas's crotch-musk, laving the head and shaft with his tongue. "Oh, yeah!" Lucas groaned. He ran his fingers over Brice's dick-tautened lips and saliva-moist beard, then gripped Brice's head and fucked his face with quick, shallow thrusts. Deep in his throat, Brice laughed a low laugh of consummation and triumph—as well as he could with his mouth crammed happily full of his lover's dick. Squeezing Lucas's tits, he bobbed faster and faster, deep-throating Lucas's cock as drool spilled from the corners of his mouth and strung off his chin.

"I'm…ohhh…getting real, real close," Lucas gasped, bucking against Brice's face.

"Do it," Brice mumbled around the hard flesh in his mouth, his nose buried in the boy's sweaty pubic hair. "Gimme a big load."

"Huuuuhhhh. Okay. Huhhhhhh!"

Lucas pumped faster. Brice sucked harder. Lucas tensed, his fingers digging into Brice's scalp.

"Here we go," Lucas panted, his thighs trembling. "Here we go."

Brice released Lucas's nipples and cupped Lucas's buttocks in his hands, pulling the boy closer, taking Lucas into him even more deeply. In another moment, Lucas stiffened, jerked, released a great shout, and climaxed, his come coursing over Brice's tongue.

Bittersweet, Brice thought, savoring the taste, rolling it around in his mouth as another spasm of semen hit the back of his throat. *Finally, the come of a man I love on my tongue. My lover's virile come. Like liquor his body's distilled, ale his manhood's brewed. Love's come. Bittersweet. Thank You, thank You, You who created this cosmos and permitted me to come into being and walk the path that brought me to this beautiful man and take his flesh and his sap inside me. Thank You.*

Lucas lay limp beneath Brice, his eyes closed, his chest heaving. Brice let Lucas's cock slip from his mouth. He leaned his head against Lucas's furry thigh and watched his penis slowly soften. When, every now and then, drops of fluid beaded like tiny opals on his prick tip, Brice took his time licking them away. The creamy droplets reminded him of his childhood in Summers County, back when he'd helped his grandfather collect sap to make maple syrup; mornings, he'd watch sugar water dripping from the elderberry spiles of tapped maple trees, the droplets glinting in slants of late winter sun, so pure and sweet when caught on the tongue.

Lucas sighed. "That was wonderful. I knew you'd be an amazing lover. Why the hell did I wait so long? Get up here and kiss me."

Brice obliged. The two men lay on their sides beneath the blanket, fondling and kissing. "You need to come now," Lucas said, taking Brice's half-hard penis in his hand.

"Naw." Brice nibbled Lucas's plump lower lip. "Tonight's all about you."

"Sure?"

Brice nodded, brushing his beard against Lucas's own.

Lucas snuggled his head into the space between Brice's neck and shoulder and threw an arm over Brice's chest. Brice fondled Lucas's ear, tugging gently at his metal hoop.

"I'm not gonna drink so much any more," Lucas said. "I don't need it with you around."

"Good. I won't either. I always do stupid shit when I get drunk."

Lucas kissed Brice's collarbone and fell silent. Soon his breathing deepened. Just when Brice thought Lucas had fallen asleep, just when Brice was about to roll him onto his side and spoon him, Lucas murmured his name.

"Hmm?"

"You make me real, real happy. Happier'n I thought I ever could be. Good night."

Love welled up in Brice, constricting his throat and tightening his chest, making it difficult to speak. By the time he was ready to reply, Lucas had begun a gentle snoring. Brice kissed the boy on the temple, sent up another prayer of thankfulness, and closed his eyes.

CHAPTER FIFTY

THE NEXT MORNING, BRICE CAME TO consciousness in a particularly heaven-sent manner: he woke to find his young lover sucking his cock while late February sunlight poured over the boy's freckled shoulders and shapely ass-cheeks. Brice fucked Lucas's face for a long time, then pulled him up into his burly arms for some tit-tweaking and good-morning kisses. Caressing led to wrestling and laughter, which led to more kissing and then a rhythmic sixty-nining, which led to grunts of ecstasy as the two men filled each other's mouths with welcome loads of come.

For a few minutes, they panted drowsily, sunk in post-orgasmic contentment, Brice fondling Lucas's balls and Lucas stroking Brice's hairy ass. "Lie on top of me for a little while," Lucas murmured, after they'd caught their breaths. "I love to feel you on top of me."

Brice rose on one elbow. "Just tell me when I start crushing you. I'm a pretty big boy."

"That's one of the things I like about you," Lucas said, running his fingers through the fur on Brice's ample belly.

Reversing his position, Brice straddled Lucas's thighs and slowly lowered himself on top of the boy. He slipped his left arm under Lucas's head and stroked Lucas's tattoo sleeve with his right hand.

"Like they say in the movies, where you been all my life?" Lucas said, nipping Brice's ear.

"Married to a woman. Living a lie. You?"

"Eating prison food and getting beat up regular."

"Seems like things have improved a good bit then." Brice gnawed Lucas's ginger-bearded chin.

Lucas sighed. "Thank God."

"Thank God indeed," Brice rasped. They fell silent, gazing into each other's eyes.

"I love all this hair on your chest. And how big and chunky your pecs are," Lucas said, tugging at the fur around Brice's right nipple.

"They're as much fat as muscle, I fear."

"That's fine with me. I love the way you fill out a shirt."

"I love the way you fill out a pair of jeans. Or those skimpy black Speedos I bought you. And I love your tattoos." Brice ran a finger down Lucas's left arm. "When did you get them?"

"Once I got out of prison. I couldn't afford 'em, but Uncle Phil said I could have anything I wanted for my welcome-home gift, so I said a bunch of tattoos. He about fainted at first. Told me he thought I'd grown up but he guessed he was wrong. But then he changed his mind. I think he gets a kick out of my rebellious side. My 'Fuck You' stance, as he calls it."

"That tends to be a healthy attitude in a world that's always trying to control who we are and what we do. When's your birthday?"

"April twenty-fourth. Yours is August eighth, right? You're a Leo. That figures. Charismatic. Talented. Ambitious. Loves attention. Loves an audience."

"Sounds about right. And you?"

"Taurus. Stubborn. Loyal. Earthy. Loves stability and comfort. Cherishes the good life. Tasty food, cozy spaces." Lucas squeezed Brice's biceps. "Skillful lovers."

"Skillful? Well, you inspire me, both in and out of the sack. So your birthday is coming up in just a couple of month. Got any plans?"

"Not yet. How about we take a hike at Blackwater Falls State Park? It's about two hours from here. Super pretty."

"It is. Some frat brothers and I went there one fall when I was back in college and rented out a cabin to party for the weekend. I'd love to go back. How about we rent a cabin too? My treat."

"That'd be great. It'd be a perfect setting for you to give me the birthday present I want the most."

"I'd be glad to, if I knew what that present was."

"You'll find out," Lucas said, patting Brice's butt.

"I'll give you anything you want. As long as I can afford it. My finances ain't what they used to be."

"This won't cost much, I promise."

"Then you got it." Brice kissed Lucas's cheek.

"Great. I'll be counting the days." Lucas patted Brice's butt again. "Guess we better get up. Lots to do. Get on off me, cowboy."

Brice rolled off Lucas and slid off the side of the bed. He stretched out his back for a brief moment before offering Lucas a hand and hauling him from the tangle of post-sex sheets.

Brice squeezed Lucas's inked left shoulder. "You've never told me about your tattoos. What they mean to you."

"You wanna know?"

"I do."

"Okay. Then I got to get to studying and woodcutting and some planting in the greenhouse. Wanna help with that? Last night, we missed it, thanks to that jowly motherfucker, Reverend Davis, but the Helvetia folks burnt the effigy of Old Man Winter. Spring's acomin' and I got a big man to feed," Lucas said, running his palm over Brice's belly swell. "So I gotta get a big garden in."

"I'd be glad to help. Been many a year since I had my hands in the dirt. So, the tattoos?"

"Okay. Well. This up here on my shoulder, see these flames? Can you make out letters in 'em?"

Brice finger-traced the inked swirls. "CSA?"

"Yep. Like I said before—I guess it was the first day we met—like you, I had an ancestor in the Confederate army. He was a cavalry guy. Got wounded bad at Brandy Station and sat out the rest of the war. It pisses the ever-loving hell outta me when people talk shit about the Rebel flag."

"Oh, I know. Folks see the battle flag on my ball cap and assume all kinds of nastiness. It really irks my ass."

"Well, fuck 'em. It's a free country. We can honor our ancestors if we want to."

Lucas gave a sharp salute before continuing his explanations. "Okay, so here on my biceps, that's the male symbol, the Mars symbol."

"With a big ole arrow." Brice gave Lucas's crotch a quick grope. "Not unlike yours."

"Behave now, Daddy. So this is a shamrock," Lucas said, pointing to his left forearm. "With Celtic knots, see? 'Cause I got Irish blood. And this is the sign for Taurus, here with the horns. Since I got some Scots blood too, this is a Scottish shield with crossed spears, and this is a Scottish thistle, and this back here, this flaming sword's a Scottish claymore. Weapons, 'cause the world's hostile and you gotta defend what's yours and fight for what you believe in."

"Appropriate," Brice said, fondling Lucas's muscular arm. "Prickly thistles, swords, and shields. You're an ornery little warrior."

"So're you. Otherwise neither of us would have survived this long. This back here on my triceps is a Norse rune, Tyr, that actually means 'warrior.' So, over here on the right arm...."

Lucas flexed, giving Brice a brief but appetizing muscle show. "This biceps band is barbed wire, and this wristband's thorns. They're both about how strength can come from suffering. This here on my forearm is a Thor's hammer. I spent a lot of time in the library when I was in prison, and Eric—his family was originally from Denmark—he got me into Norse mythology. I thought Thor was super-cool 'cause he protected the people he cared about and 'cause he was...well, I imagined him as a big, sexy man, the kind of protector I needed. Guess I found him, huh? First in Eric, and now in you."

Lucas stood on tiptoe and kissed Brice firmly on the mouth. "Okay, stud, ink tour's over. Gimme a few hours of alone time. I'm planning on taking the GED in May, so I gotta study. How about we meet in the great room about two? I'll fix us a couple sandwiches and then we can get to that planting. Tonight, I'm gonna make us spaghetti and meatballs."

"One of my favorites."

"I know. I read about your favorite foods in *Country Weekly* a good while back. And then the hot tub?"

"Sounds great. Let me grab a quick shower, and I'll get out of your hair...such as it is."

Brice tousled Lucas's buzz cut and headed to the bathroom, his brain swimming with swords and shamrocks, dripping maple sap and spurting semen, and the pale, hard muscles of his lover's naked youth. Already, he could sense, fragments of a fresh lyric were piecing themselves together inside his newly awakened heart.

CHAPTER FIFTY-ONE

Two drizzle-chilly days passed quietly and without interruption, free of phone calls, visitors, traumatizing e-mail messages, or trespassing reporters. Brice relaxed, read, played his guitar, drove to Elkins for his chiropractic appointment, and, after browsing cookbooks, made a loaf of French bread and an old-fashioned buttermilk pie. Lucas chopped wood, drove to Buckhannon for groceries, and steadily worked through more GED preparatory material. Together, they lifted weights, soaked in the hot tub, watched television, hiked around the February-gray compound, and played games of pool.

Now, as night came on, they sprawled on the couch, enjoying glasses of red wine and big bowls of French onion soup. Firelight illuminated the great room, as did a few candles set on the coffee table and the mantelpiece. Outside, a cold rain poured down.

"This soup's delicious," Brice said. "I love these quiet evenings with you."

"We are sorta acting like an old settled-in, long-married couple, but you don't hear me complaining, do you? I got enough excitement in prison, believe me. It was always so noisy, and I was almost never alone, so quiet and solitude with you are mighty welcome. So, Ole Brokeback, you ain't told me yet. How'd your visit to the chiropractor go today?" Grinning mischievously, Lucas gave Brice a gentle poke in the ribs. "Was he hot? Did his hands feel good on you?"

"Jealous, huh? He wasn't hot—far from it— but he helped a lot. He showed me some exercises and he moved me around some. I'm feeling a lot less stiff. Like some stress had been building and building and he released it."

"Good. I need you limber for all that wrestling and spit-swapping I got in mind. Man, listen to that rain against the windows. Not for nothing they say that this area has the highest precipitation in the state. Good for the gardens, though. We're gonna have a helluva harvest this year, I hope," Lucas said, nibbling melted Swiss cheese off his spoon. "Those greenhouse seedlings are looking good."

"I've been in the city and the suburbs too long. It's been decades since I did any serious gardening. What all are you planning to raise, other than those broccoli and cabbage sprouts?"

"Lots. Asparagus and rhubarb will come up first. Then we'll get some leaf lettuce and peas and new potatoes. Strawberries after that. Later, it'll be beets, squash, and okra. Eggplants, if I can keep the fucking potato beetles off 'em. Melons: cantaloupe and watermelon and honeydew. Sweet peppers and hot peppers. Half-runners, Blue Lakes. Then tomatoes and corn and more potatoes. You stick around here, and you'll eat well."

"I have no doubt of that. I'm eating well now, thanks to you." Brice chewed a beef-broth-sodden crouton. "So you'll pass the GED in May. What then? Good a cook as you are, you ought to attend chef school."

"*If* I pass the GED, I'm thinking about taking the ACT and applying to college. Uncle Phil insists I go, and he insists he'll pay. I don't wanna be any more of a parasite than I already am—he's given me a free place to live since I got outta prison—but honestly there ain't no other way I could afford to go back to school."

"College where?"

"WVU. Forestry or biology. I've already asked 'em to send me information about those programs."

"So you'd move to Morgantown?"

"Yep. That general area. Uncle Phil owns a lil' family vacation home on Cheat Lake I could stay in. The thought scares me to death. I know I gotta get on with my life, figure out some way to make a living, but leaving Brantley Valley...."

"So what happens to us?"

Lucas took a long sip of wine, leaned his head back into a pillow, and stared at shadows that firelight cast against the raftered ceiling. "I don't know. Guess we need some more time to see...."

Brice nodded. "How serious this is? Whether it's something to arrange a life around?"

Brice moved closer, resting a hand on Lucas's thigh. "It feels pretty damn serious to me, but I guess we're both inexperienced when it comes to love and romance, so, yeah, we should be cautious still."

"Cautious, yeah. Part of me is so happy, and part of me is so afraid. Part of me is terrified you'll bolt." Lucas covered Brice's hand with his.

"And leave what I've found here with you? No way. Every now and then I'm afraid *you'll* bolt. I'm afraid you'll put up that prickly distance again."

"My insecurities have made me do some pretty dumb shit, that's for sure."

"Well, I have a couple of surprises that should ease that insecurity." Brice pulled a small gift-wrapped box from his pocket. "After my appointment, I found a little something for you in Elkins." He placed the box in Lucas's lap. "Open it."

"Wow. Okay." Lucas tore off the wrapping and opened the box. Inside was a smaller box of rusty velvet. He opened that and stared. "Oh. Oh, wow."

"Don't get scared. It's just a ring. A thumb ring. Nothing all that serious. Nothing all that expensive. I figured the silver would look good with those necklaces you wear, and the knotwork reminds me of the Celtic knots in your shamrock tattoo."

Lucas, with an expression of wonder, lifted the ring from its box. "How...how'd you know what size—"

"I emailed your uncle. We guessed at the size."

"No one's ever bought me a ring before."

"Consider it an early birthday present. And it goes with another gift."

"Another gift?"

"The ring was bought. The best gifts are made." Brice rose to fetch his guitar from its hard-shell case in the corner. He sat by Lucas, propped the instrument on his knee, and fine-tuned it.

"The other morning," Brice explained, "I got to thinking about your tattoos. This is called 'Country Boy.' Here we go. I hope you like it."

Wake me, boy, with your hot hunger,
And then I'll love your mouth with mine,
caress thorny ink, your ginger beard,
taste maple sap, your virile wine,

your country muscles, hill-bred and fine,
torso forests, scents of mountain pine.

You're the storm and you're the thunder,
the shamrock and the thistle too,
my naked warrior, my Rebel rain,
furry devotions strong and true.

You're country muscle, hill-bred and fine.
Mountain boy, your love's my shrine.

Shields and spears, your flaming sword,
Barbed-wire biceps, thorn-bound wrist:
I taste tattoos beneath my tongue,
grip your blade inside my fist,
      burning, burning inside my fist.

Your salvation's worth any risk.
Country boy inside the mist,
      Inside the swirling highland mist,
Come give this country boy a kiss.

Musky boy, you're starry sweat-shine,
Mountain boy, make your body mine,
Your love's my salvation, my body's bliss.
Country boy, make our love a shrine.
Country boy, make our love a shrine.

Lucas swallowed hard. Eyes averted, he slipped the ring on his thumb and turned it around and around.

"It fits just right. 'Make our love a shrine.' That's wonderful, man," he said in a voice so low that Brice struggled to hear him. "You buy me a ring and you write me songs.... After all the shit I've survived...all this is like a godsent dream."

"I'm glad you like the song." Smiling, Brice returned the instrument to its case. "For a while there, I thought I'd never write a decent tune again, but meeting you, holding you…music and lyrics are bubbling up in me now."

"Wonderful music. We need to get it out there somehow. You sure that Nashville—"

Brice shook his head. "No way. Believe me. I know how that world works. Openly gay lyrics? There's just no way."

"Some other way then." Lucas held his hand up so that firelight could glint off the ring. "This means so much to me. I wanna head up to the cabin and get naked and hold on you and listen to the rain on the roof. Maybe get frisky and give you a little reward."

"Yes to all of that," said Brice with a wide smile. "You want some of that buttermilk pie first?"

"I do. But before that, I guess I got a big question."

"Shoot."

"Would you…? Now, I ain't asking you to, I'm just asking if you'd be willing to…. What are your plans? I mean, for the future?"

"I told you I'd stay here with you. I'm gonna stay here as long as you want me to."

"But if I leave to go to school? What'll you do then?"

"I don't know. I can't take advantage of your uncle's hospitality forever. I still have a good bit in the bank, thanks to my investments and everything I sold a month or so back, but that won't last, since no new money's coming in. Like you, I need to figure out how to make a living. As much as I'd like to stay here and make love to you and make music about you and take hikes and cook big meals and spend cuddly fireside evenings with you…."

Lucas cleared his throat, bowed his head, and fiddled with his new ring. "So, if I moved to that Cheat Lake house? If I asked you to, would you be willing to, to move there with me? Not that I'm asking yet. But would you be willing?"

Brice chuckled. "What do you think? There's nothing for me in Nashville, and there's no reason to move back to Hinton until all the *Star*-brewed 'homosexual scandal' dies down. I don't know what I'd do in Morgantown, but I'd figure something out."

"You could give guitar lessons. Or, better, you could be my houseboy. Or housedaddy." Lucas leaned into Brice, grinning. "When I get home after class, you can meet me at the door wearing nothing but work boots and a jock strap and a dog collar. How's that sound?"

Brice guffawed. "Whatever appeals to you. Yes, I'd move there with you. The two of us parting is definitely not in my plans. What's that line in the Bible? 'Whither thou goest, I will too?'"

"Something like that. It was two ladies, not two guys, but yeah."

Lucas patted Brice's thigh and rose. "Something to think about, the big scary future. Might be easier to face with this magic ring. Now how about that pie? With a big ole hairy man like you to love on, I gotta keep up my strength."

PART
FOUR

CHAPTER FIFTY-TWO

"Yooooooooo hoooo!"

Brice jumped at the shrill sound, then laughed out loud. "Down here! In the kitchen!" he shouted, putting down the paring knife.

With a heavy clumping, feet descended the stairs. The door between dining room and kitchen flew open, and Mr. Philip burst into the room. He was dressed in a cabbie cap, pale blue slacks, and a black shirt adored with pink flamingos, and he carried two big shopping bags.

"Darling! Did I miss the wedding?" he said, dropping the bags before giving Brice a bear hug.

"You did not," Brice said. "That event has yet to be scheduled."

"The bride's deflowering then?"

"Ummm. Uh. Yes and no. Our, uh, intimacy is…coming along but still incomplete."

"I retract that last query as unseemly." Phil stepped back and poked Brice's belly. "I see that you haven't starved. Looks like there's more of you to love."

Brice blushed. "Yeah. Lucas has been feeding me mighty well."

"I'll bet." Phil leered, deepening Brice's blush. "Feeding you his sweet favors. Is he still thin as a rail?"

"No. He's actually put on weight too. His hips are as lean as ever, but there's the cutest little fuzzy bit of plump just below his navel I can't help but dote on."

"About time he filled out." Phil began pulling packages from the shopping bags. "Have you written a song about that yet?"

"What?"

"Lucas tells me via e-mail that you've been writing up a storm this past month."

"I have, thanks to him. He really gets the creative juices going."

"Indeed." Phil winked. "I know they're two weeks late, but I have some belated April Fool's Day gifts for y'all. Where is the prodigal son?"

"He's down at Radclyffe's Roost, but he should be home for dinner. He's been helping Grace around the property and working behind the counter some. So have I, actually, just to make a little money. Other than a gaggle of prissy ladies who come in after church for Sunday brunch and give us both raised noses and cold shoulders, customers have been pretty nice to us. We've had to tell a few reporters to fuck off, but media interest in us has died down, so incidents of journalistic harassment have tapered off, thank God."

"Thank God indeed. Though I was able to parlay my intimate knowledge of your outrageous affair into invitations to some of the best gay parties in Fort Lauderdale. Those queens were all hysterical with envy over the fact that I knew a famous gay star. Did y'all get the citrus yet?"

"No. You sent citrus?"

"I did. Grapefruits and navel oranges. Fresh juice for celebratory mimosas!"

"What you celebrating?"

"Why, you two, of course. Courting in this romantic woodland getaway all to yourselves! It's like a fairy tale…in a manner of speaking. Did the erotic enchantment of the Homo Hideaway work its magic or what?"

"It did," Brice said. "It sure did. I'm head over heels. That boy's the best thing that's ever happened to me."

"You do look like you're in love. Is he?"

Brice sighed and shrugged. "I don't know. He hasn't said." Moving back to the counter, he recommenced chopping stalks of rhubarb. "He sure acts like it, though."

"When it comes to love, actions really do speak louder than words. And speaking of loving actions, I brought y'all loads and loads of condoms and packets of lube to contribute to your orgiastic shenanigans. They pass 'em all out for free at the gay bars in Fort Lauderdale. Plus, there's some cute shirts for y'all, and some alligator boxer briefs, and a plush alligator to guard your bed, and all sorts of other things charmingly Floridian. Oh, and a shark's tooth cock ring."

Brice winced. "Ouch! Really?"

"You butch boys can be so gullible. It's actually a shark's tooth necklace. Lucas can wear it when you two play Fay Wray and King Kong during your next fantasy fest. I can just see him beating your gorilla chest with his tiny starlet fists." Phil pulled a bottle of white wine from the fridge. "Shall we share a welcome-home drink and some welcome-home gossip?"

"We can indeed. Dinner won't be for another couple of hours. I have a pork shoulder in the oven with some dry rub on it, and some barbecue sauce simmering. We're gonna have pulled pork sandwiches and cole slaw, since Lucas says you and I share an unnatural passion for barbecue. Plus this here's a strawberry/rhubarb pie I'm making."

"Sounds fabulous." Phil poured them out glasses of wine, then sat on a counter stool and opened boxes. "I bought the stuffed alligator from the hottest young store clerk with an Australian accent and shoulders about a league wide. Miss Emily—that's my bridge partner—she said, 'Why, Philip, why are you ogling that young man? He looks dumb as a box of rocks. Bless his heart, he looks like he couldn't pour water out of a boot if the instructions were on the heel.' And do you know what I said?"

Brice took a sip of wine before pulling a lump of plastic-wrapped piecrust dough from the fridge. "Oh, Lord, I'd forgotten what priceless stories you tell. What did you say?"

"I said, 'Honey, I don't want to suck his *brains!*'"

Brice guffawed. "Great!"

"Yes! And another time Miss Emily and I were driving past this gated community, and I said, 'In there live the Cresswells and the Burgoines and the Bermans and the Silversteins and the Brights. And that fit and charming bachelor, Kip Young. His cock's too big.' And Miss Emily said, 'Why, Philip dear, mercy me! How do you know his cock's too big?'"

Brice began rolling out the dough. "I *know* this'll be good. So what did you say then?"

"I slapped her on her bony knee—she has stockings in every shade of purple—and I said, "Honey, I done SAT on it!"

"Oh, fuck. Did you really?"

"Say it or sit on it?"

"Both, I guess?"

"Both! Poor thing, Miss Emily's been so traumatized lately. Back in March, she suffered a spiritual shock of the first order. You say, 'Do tell' now."

Brice sprinkled the dough with flour. "Do tell."

"I'm glad you asked. Well, she's a devout Methodist, and sometimes she drags me to her church. The hats she wears! Egregious! At any rate, a scandal nigh about tore that congregation apart. Why, I was there when it happened. The minister, who's a distinguished, silver-headed man about my age—his wife, I'm sad to say, looks like a two-bit whore half the time, with feathers and furbelows to beat the band—why, Minister Bush was in the midst of the most moving sermon about the seven deadly sins—just holding forth, just holding forth!—when who should sashay down the aisle but this plump young girl of Cuban hue—about twenty, I'd say—wearing, of all things, black stiletto heels and a baggy orange something that I could swear was a housedress, and she had a teensy-tiny ruby tiara in her hair—Can you imagine? A tiara!—and clutched to her voluptuous bosom was a cinnamon-colored child half-wrapped in a scarlet blanket."

"And then?"

"Minister Bush, he turned pale as toilet tissue and his eyes bugged out, and he started stammering, but he kept on as best he could as she commenced on down the aisle, and then she came to a dead halt right in front of the pulpit and she raised the baby on high like an offering, and the baby started to howl like a little banshee, and just about the time the minister got to the text about 'the works of the flesh,' she said, 'Donald, why you not return my calls? Your son, your *hijo*, little Luís, he needs you!'"

"Holy fuck. Really?" Shaking his head, Brice lifted the dough on the rolling pin and slid it into the pie plate. "What happened then?"

"The place exploded into pandemonium! The pastor began shouting denials and denunciations, and the two-bit whore of a wife flew at the little Cuban girl with her red fingernails bared like some kind of fearsome bird of prey, and the little girl threw her hands up in the air, and that baby sailed across the room, and a parishioner just barely caught it, and then the unwed mother took the wife by the bottle-blonde hair and the two started jerking one another all over that room. It was a frenzy! So I saw only one way to calm the waters. God showed me the way!"

"And how was that?" Mouth twisted with amusement, Brice crimped crust.

"Why, I picked up a hymnal, and I started singing 'What Child Is This?' at the top of my lungs, and pretty soon everyone in that church had joined me. I've never heard such a rousing rendition! We were all filled by the Holy Spirit!"

Brice's sides shook. "You are shitting me. You have got to be shitting me."

"Not at all. It's the God's honest truth. All kinds of wonders and marvels manifest in Florida. Well, 'enough about me. What about you? What do *you* think of me?' as the Divine Miss M put it in *Beaches*. What have y'all been up to? I hate technology, so I rarely turn my computer on. If you've sent me any e-mail lately, I might not have read it. Last I heard, soon after my wicked sister had showed y'all her ass in the worst way, y'all had made a frightful scene in the snowy Fasnacht streets of Helvetia."

"Right. Amie tore that bastard a new one. Well, after that unpleasantness…you remember I asked you about Lucas's ring size? I gave Lucas a ring."

"Really? Is the engagement official?"

"Naw, not yet, but I'm keeping my fingers crossed. So then, after the weather warmed up last month, Lucas took me on a bunch of day trips. Spruce Knob, Seneca Rocks, Smoke Hole Caverns. We've hiked in the state forest a good bit. Let's see, what else? We had Grace and Amie up for St. Patrick's Day. Lucas made corned beef and cabbage, and I made cornbread. The four of us went to the Pickens Maple Syrup Festival and about ate ourselves to death. Lucas and I put in the garden. Yesterday, we planted corn. Lucas said it was time to do that since the dogwood's blooming. He's still studying for his GED, and I'm still writing songs. We're both wondering what's next for us."

"He's still planning to apply to WVU, I hope?"

"I think so. Me, I need…I need to get a real job and stop mooching off you, for one thing. Or at least pay rent."

"Mooching?" Phil raised his eyebrows and sipped his wine. "Rent? You owe me nothing. You've been helping keep this place up in my absence, and you've made my nephew happy. He's no longer the sulking, brooding, heart-maimed little introvert he was when I left, is he?"

"Well, no."

"Then you've given me a gift worth a king's ransom. After all those years in prison… the scars…I thought the poor boy would never…."

Phil slipped off the stool, stepped over to the fridge, and pulled out some cheeses. "Brie and cheddar. Very nice. Let's let these warm up a bit for cocktail hour. After today's flight delays and the long drive I've endured, I could do with a daiquiri or three. When is Lucas due home?"

Brice looked at the wall clock. "Not sure. Pretty soon."

"Then you and I have time to discuss something. I have a proposition for you."

Brice began hulling strawberries. "Okay. What's that?"

"I'm thinking about retiring to Florida permanently. The warm weather is a balm for my aging joints, and I love my condo down there, and the friends I've made. There are lots of retired gay men in Fort Lauderdale. Here, I feel fairly isolated. I have only Lucas, Grace, and Amie…and the occasional game of bridge with some local ladies. And I must admit all those years of living in DC have made me want more of a social life than I could ever find here."

"Well, we'd sure miss you, but moving down there for good makes sense, I guess. But what's the proposition?"

"The proposition is that you stay here and make this place a real retreat for queer youth. I've had several kids come and go over the last year, but I haven't put much effort into getting the word out, other than through my contacts with the WVU gay and lesbian student group. You could make Phagg Heights serve many more people than it has."

"Well, wow. I don't know." Brice wiped his hands on a dish towel, leaned back against the sink, and folded his arms. "I've got to admit I have no idea what I'm going to do in the future, since my time on the big stage is definitely done with. Lucas asked me if I'd be willing to move to Morgantown with him if he enters WVU, and I told him I would."

"Morgantown is only a two-hour drive from here. If he goes to school up there, you could visit one another on weekends. Just think about it. I haven't mentioned any of this to him yet, but—"

Phil paused to cup his ear. "Listen there. On the stairs. I do believe the little brute has arrived."

In another few seconds, Lucas strode into the room, carrying a toolbox and wearing an oil-stained gray T-shirt, a ball cap, work boots, and dirty jeans with holes in the knees. "Hey, Uncle Phil! You're home! We missed you."

"I gather that y'all managed to entertain one another without me," Phil said, giving his nephew a hug. "The Dionysian revels of the young. Mercy, you're a muddy mess. And you smell like rotting leaves."

"Sorry," Lucas said, stepping back and scratching his ribs. "I been working down at Grace and Amie's. Cleaning their gutters and patching a hole in the roof. They said to say Hi."

"Well, go shower up, odoriferous!" Phil waved Lucas away. "It's approaching cocktail time. And I have tales to tell."

"You always do," Lucas said, slipping off his cap and rubbing his scalp. "I'll meet y'all in the great room, okay?" With that, he sauntered back the way he'd come.

"My God. The change in him," Phil said. "He's completely different. Almost lighthearted. You've worked a miracle."

"He's the one who's worked a miracle. Before I came here, God, was I grim. Nothing to look forward to. But now...."

"A mutual miracle, then. A reciprocal redemption. Well, finish cobbling together that pie and let's head upstairs. I'm standing in profound need of a frozen cocktail. Complete with tiny umbrella."

PHIL WAITED TILL EVERYONE HAD drinks in hand and little plates heaped with smoked oysters, cheese, and crackers before he began.

"First of all, boy, let me see that ring."

Lucas grinned proudly and held out his hand. "Check it out. Handsome, ain't it? Kinda studly."

"What? No diamond? Is the famous Brice Brown a cheapskate?"

Brice bit his lip. "I thought a diamond might be a little over the top at this stage in the relationship."

"I don't want no fucking prissy diamond. I love this. The design matches my tattoos, see?"

"I do see. With that buzz cut and all those trashy tattoos and bulging muscles and ratty clothes, you look like more of a baby Hell's Angel than ever...rather than the refined Southern gentleman I dreamed you'd become. Oh, I had such high hopes that you'd grow up to be an elegant invert like me."

"Fat chance. Don't you know I'm bad to the bone?" Smirking, Lucas propped a sock-covered foot on the coffee table and slurped his beer. "Give it a rest, Uncle Phil. The tougher I look, the less likely local assholes will bother me."

"True. The threat of local assholery is a real one, especially now that you're both Notorious Homosexuals and Figures of Public Scandal. Beware! A convocation of the Randolph County devout might head up here yet to tar and feather the both of you."

"Oh, shit. Don't even say that. We've had enough crap driving off reporters."

"I'm teasing you, boy. I'm proud of you. I'm proud of the man you've become. You seem so much better adjusted than you were before. No thanks to your gorgon of a mother. I gave Sister a little visit on the drive back from the airport."

Lucas sat up straight. "What? You did?"

"I did indeed. The sad sow was deep into a passionate assignation with Cheez Whiz when I stopped by. Lord, the fuss she made, detailing her many sufferings and humiliations. The way she talked, you two were both avatars of Beelzebub. What weeping and wailing and gnashing of teeth! The tears, the wringing of hands, the tearing of hair! I let Sister have her little say before I lit into her." Phil took a sip of his daiquiri and smiled with satisfaction.

"Holy shit, Uncle Phil. What'd you say?"

"Several ferocious things. I fear that my normal mannerly composure slipped a wee bit."

"Did you snatch her bald-headed? I told Brice that you'd snatch her bald-headed once you heard how she treated me."

"He did," Brice said, in between bites of Brie. "I've been trying to imagine her bald ever since."

"Well, as a matter of fact, I did give that rat's nest of hers a good tug before I left. I also hit that portrait of her imaginary friend—that black velvet Jesus she so cherishes—upside the head with that vile vat of Cheez Whiz. I told Sister that she was a savage ogress and a rampant hag. I told her that her piety was pustular in the extreme, and that only someone afflicted with a serious case of cretinism would allow a tuskéd warthog like Reverend Davis to turn her against her own child, especially a boy as sterling as you."

"Damn, Uncle Phil. Really?"

"'Damn' is right. That must have been hard for you."

"Hard? It wasn't hard. That heifer gave me grief all through my adolescence for being 'a sinner and a sissy,' as she put it. The only reason she's had anything decent to say to me over the last three decades is because she's always trying to cadge money. It was one thing for her to be hateful to me, but once she pretty much disowned Lucas when he got out of prison—a time in his life when he desperately needed support, as would any of us in such a position—I saw then what an ungenerous, mean-spirited heart she has. If there weren't Christians like Doris Ann or that sweet Eleanor woman down in Helvetia, I'd write the whole religion off entirely. No wonder I'm an atheist. And for her to come up here and say what she said to Lucas, and spit in his face? Oh, no. Oh, no."

Phil tapped the rainbow-colored umbrella in his lime-green drink. "So I told her if she ever came up here to Rump-Ranger Ranch again—I called it that just to see the look of puritanical horror on her face—I'd loose the dogs on her. I described in some detail how they'd disembowel her before I chucked that Cheez Whiz at Our Lord, gave her hair a yank, and made a glorious exit to the sound of her outraged blubbering."

"Dogs? We ain't got dogs."

"Well, we can buy some. Some horrendous hell-hounds with gruesome fangs, perhaps. For your birthday? It's coming up next week."

"No, thanks. I could do with a new pair of cowboy boots. That's about it."

"Then you shall have them. They'll contribute to your ribald redneck glory. Would you like me to bake your favorite coconut cake?"

"That'd be great, though I think Brice 'n me're going up to Blackwater Falls and rent a cabin for the night, maybe hit Helvetia's Ramp Supper the day after. You still up for that, Brice?"

"Absolutely. But you said you wanted a special gift from me. Your birthday's next Friday, and you still haven't told me what you want."

Lucas gave Brice a wink and took a chug of beer. "We'll get to that. Don't worry. According to Ole Granddaddy there," he said, indicating the tall clock against the wall, "it's getting on time for dinner, but before we chow down.... Uncle Phil, I think we should celebrate you cussing Mommy out in a special way."

"How's that, boy?"

"Well, you've told Brice some of your best stories, but not the one about...." Lucas held up his hand, curled his index finger and middle finger into fangs and stabbed at the air. "Big Creek?"

"Oh, Lord, yes! How appropriate." Phil forked up a smoked oyster, popped it into his mouth, and gave it a vigorous chewing. "Well! Here we go. As Sophia on *The Golden Girls* would put it, 'Picture it. Big Creek Holler, by the Gauley River, 1968.' Dear Sister Kim is visiting her Bible camp friend, Opal Meadows, down in Fayette County. It's a hot and humid summer morning, and they're making their way down the riverbank, swatting at the beastly swarms of bitey gnats with goldenrod stalks. And Sister says, 'Now, Opal, there better not be no damn snakes at this church, you know I'm scared to death of those things.' And Opal says, 'Kimmy, I've told you a dozen times there ain't gonna be no snakes! Now quit your worryin'!'"

"Uh oh," said Brice.

"Exactly," said Lucas.

"So there are quite a few cars parked along the road and even more folks are coming on foot by the time the two get to the Holiness church. Sister and Miss Opal head on in and take a seat. The place is about as plain as can be, with worn pine floors, a couple windows, a raised stage and podium, and a couple lights hanging from the ceiling."

"Too plain for Mommy. She likes her stained glass, don't she?"

"True. She's always had a vulgar taste for gaud. So the service gets under way and the preacher man starts off as soft as can be but pretty soon he's getting het up and hyperventilating and tossing in 'Haahh!' at the end of phrases to emphasize things. About fifteen minutes into the service, he shifts into real high gear and the congregation does too, with lots of hand-waving and stomping and shouts of praise. Sister, who's a Southern Baptist, is thinking maybe this is all too wild for her and maybe she's stumbled into some kind of backwoods bedlam."

"Sounds like some holler churches we have down in Summers County," Brice said.

"Yes, they're thick as fleas in this state. So, the church is shaking with the word of the Lord and overcome parishioners are taking to the aisles, dancing and gibbering about in pure holy bliss. And then...."

"And then?" Lucas drained his beer, propped his elbows on his knees, and gave Brice a Cheshire-cat grin.

"And then the preacher reaches down behind the podium and comes back up with two huge timber rattlers."

"Holy shit," breathed Brice.

"Holy shit, indeed. And the deacons grab rattlers of their own and start a'mingling with the crowd."

"And what does Mommy do then, Uncle Phil?"

"Sister Kim bolts right up and lets loose a scream that can shatter glass and wake the dead up on the hill! No one thinks anything much of it—they think she's just as seized up by the Lord as they are—until she stands up on the pew screaming like a banshee with urine running down both legs!"

"Oh, my God! Really? She pissed herself?"

"Yes! Yes!" Phil slapped his knee with a howl. "Quick as a streak she's walking on the back of the pews, screaming bloody murder, falling down, flailing about, clambering for the center aisle. Half-leaping, half-falling, she makes it, and the people are cheering her on, assuming that the Holy Ghost has grabbed ahold of Sister's soul real good. With even more hooting and hollering from the congregation, she stands up, white skirt piss-stained with more a'coming, and lights out for the door like she's on fire."

"My face and sides are aching," Brice gasped. "Stop!"

"I'm about done. So Opal catches up with Sister in the tiny parking lot and grabs her by the arm and says, 'Kimmy, for God's sake, what the hell is wrong with you? You embarrassed me in there!' and Sister goes from blind terror to blind rage in a split second. The Spirit really does grab her this time, but it isn't the Holy Ghost, it's the spirit of pure Irish rage, and she starts beating the living shit out of Opal, and Opal runs for the road with Sister in hot pursuit, throwing rocks and snatching handfuls of hair from the back of Opal's head all the way back to Brownsville. I don't think they ever spoke again. As for that snake-handling preacher, he tempted Fate one too many times and one day went off to have lunch with Jesus, if you get my drift. Sister, bless her heart, never set foot in a Holiness church again."

Brice's violent laughter graded into a coughing fit. He collapsed back against the couch. "My God. My God. I may have to lie down for a while."

"You do that, honey. Meanwhile, just like Mrs. Venable in Tennessee's *Suddenly, Last Summer*, I'm having another daiquiri—frozen! Let's not rush the evening. After dinner, I do intend to go to bed early. It's been a long day of travel, plus I figure I should leave you two to snake handling of a safer sort."

CHAPTER FIFTY-THREE

BRICE SAT BACK AND WIPED HIS MOUTH. "BEST barbecued ribs I've had in a long time. Great view too," he said, looking out over the forested gorge of Blackwater Canyon. "The only view I know that's any finer is you buck naked."

"Hush." Lucas gazed worriedly around the dining room of the lodge. "Enough folks are staring as it is. This celebrity status thang can be a pain in the ass." Frowning, he popped the last bite of lasagna into his mouth.

"I'm fine with it, as long as they don't refuse to serve us. You want dessert?"

"I do want dessert. In a manner of speaking. But not here. I'm tired of being looked at like a circus freak. You ready to go back to the cabin?"

"Yep. We can split that bottle of champagne I brought."

The two men rose. They passed their waiter—a handsome, clean-shaven blond kid—as they moved toward the exit. "Thanks, Mr. Brown," the boy said, smiling shyly. "I love your music. It was real cool to see y'all here. I hope you two have a wonderful evening."

"Thanks. It was a great meal," Brice said. "Tip's on the table."

The boy nodded and hurried off. "Family, I think," Brice said to Lucas. "A member of the fraternity. Funny how much a little friendliness can mean when you're feeling like a pariah."

They drove through the April dark, Lucas leaning against Brice in silence. Back at their cabin, they stood on the porch for a long moment, taking in the forested stillness and breathing in the cool highland air. Then Brice took Lucas's hand and led him inside.

"You ready for some of that champagne now?" Brice asked, after locking the door behind them. "It should be cold enough to—"

"Not yet, big guy," Lucas said, shoving Brice back against the wall. "I've been aching for dessert all damn day, and I got several courses in mind. Here's the first."

Lucas pressed his lips to Brice's and began kissing him hungrily, all the while unbuttoning the front of Brice's plaid flannel shirt and slipping it off him. Soon the two men's tongues were tussling, and Lucas was pinching Brice's nipples and rubbing his erection against Brice's own.

"Here's dessert course number two," Lucas muttered, unzipping Brice's jeans and hauling his hard-on out. "Follow me."

Using Brice's prick as a handle, he led the big man over to the couch before pushing him down onto it. Lucas dropped to his knees, wrapped his arms around Brice's waist, and took his cock into his mouth.

"Ohhhh, yeah," Brice breathed. He gripped Lucas by the shoulders and thrust into the tight wetness of Lucas's skillful mouth. Lucas gazed up at Brice with happy submission, sucking and nibbling and licking his dick with spit-moist abandon.

"I love looking down into those pretty eyes of yours while you're sucking my cock," Brice groaned. "Nothing better."

"You like my Truck-Stop Special, huh?" Lucas mumbled around Brice's dick-head.

"Hell, yes, I do. You keep that up too much longer and I'm gonna shoot."

Lucas pulled off. "As much as I'd like a big mouthful of your load, I got other things in mind. I got this evening all planned. Why don't you fetch that champagne now? But leave your dick out, okay?"

"Sure. It's your birthday." Brice clambered to his feet, cock jutting from his trouser's zippered gap. "I'll do whatever you want."

"You bet you will." Lucas snickered, giving Brice's butt a slap.

"Vicious!" Brice gasped with mock shock. Erection at full mast, he shuffled to the kitchen. He returned carrying two tumblers of golden champagne, with a couple of boxes wedged under his arms.

"No champagne glasses, but these'll do." He dropped the boxes on one end of the couch, then sat beside Lucas. "Here's to age twenty-eight. May the year to come be full of wonderful surprises."

"Here, here. I'm pretty sure it will be."

Brice and Lucas tapped glasses, sipped, kissed, sipped, kissed, and sipped.

"These boots are pretty sharp, huh?" Lucas said, pulling off his new footwear. "Justin's. Uncle Phil has great taste."

"He does. So you never did tell me about that special gift you wanted," Brice said, putting the boxes on Lucas's lap. "I got you these little things instead. Sorry I didn't wrap them. My attempts at gift-wrapping always look like the Frankenstein monster did it."

"Cool. Okay, let's see what we have here." Lucas opened the top box. "Oh, yeah, nice! I needed a new belt. Brown suede. Pretty needlework. And a CS belt buckle. Confederate States. Great! And what's this? A black jockstrap? Hah!"

"That gift's more for me than you, got to admit. There's a couple things in this other box. Well, two things and a future jaunt."

"Hmmm. Okay," Lucas murmured, opening the second box. "Oh, so cool! A book about Norse myths."

"Yep. I didn't see that one on your shelves."

"Naw, I don't have this one. And *Forest Trees of West Virginia*. Great!"

Nodding, Brice gulped champagne. "I thought that'd be helpful when you go to WVU. Look inside it. There's something else."

Lucas flipped through the little book, pulled out an envelope, and opened it. "'All-expense paid weekend in Rehoboth Beach.' Where's that?"

"It's a beach in Delaware where all the DC and Baltimore queers go, your uncle tells me. We can go this summer, if you'd like. Or off-season in October, when it's less crowded. It was Phil's idea. He told me that you've never seen the ocean."

"I haven't. A beach trip'd be wonderful. Let's go this summer. I hate crowds, but if I'm gonna see the ocean, I'll wanna get in it. Thank you!"

Lucas wrapped an arm around Brice and kissed him. Then he took Brice's dwindled dick in his hand and squeezed it. Bending, he nuzzled Brice's bare chest. "So you said you're gonna do everything I ask, huh, Daddy?"

"Yep. It's your birthday. Everything's possible."

"Good to hear." Lucas nibbled a nipple, then sat back, took a drink, and folded his arms behind his head. "Why don't you strip? Down to your boxer briefs."

"Whatever you want." Smiling, Brice drained his glass. He pulled off his lumberjack boots and his socks. Standing, he shucked off his jeans.

"*Real* nice. Leave your dick out now." Lucas poured them both more champagne before moving over to the boom box he'd brought and flipping it on. Soft music filled the room.

Brice smiled. "'Where or When.' That was my mother's favorite song."

Lucas offered Brice his hand. "May I have this dance?"

"I don't dance. Uh, not real well."

"I'll show you. I feel like leading tonight."

Lucas took Brice by the hand and encircled his waist. Brice shuffled backwards, feeling clumsy and overweight, but in a few minutes, with Lucas's bearded cheek pressed to his, Lucas's lips grazing his, he forgot his discomfort and simply basked in his lover's closeness.

"Ain't you gonna get naked?" Brice whispered, nipping the smaller man's earlobe.

"Naw. Not for a while. Not till it's time to sample my birthday cake."

"Cake? I'm afraid I didn't bring any cake."

"Oh, you brought cake." Lucas squeezed Brice's right butt-cheek. "You got my birthday cake right here."

Brice halted. "Huh? You mean…?"

"I mean…I've been thinking about the ways we've been together. We've shared ourselves, our bodies, in all the ways you said you wanted. All the ways but one."

"Yeah," Brice sighed. "I've tried not to push. I figured when you were ready for that, you'd tell me."

"And I will. It's just…'cause of all that happened…in prison…those guys…Eric…." Lucas rested his forehead against Brice's shoulder and took a long breath.

"I know, Lucas, buddy. I understand. I do."

"I know you do." Lucas nudged Brice back into the dance. "It's sort of the ultimate… giving, y'know? The ultimate trust."

"I guess so. And it makes sense that you'd still have some trust issues after…."

"Yeah. But I'm almost ready. I've been fantasizing about you screwing me."

Brice grinned. "Yeah?" He patted Lucas's trouser-covered butt. "Yeah?"

"Oh, yeah. Thing is, I've been fantasizing about something else too. I was thinking… it'd make it easier for me to trust you in that way if…if you…."

Lucas slipped a hand down the back of Brice's briefs. "If you went first. Y'know?"

"Aha." Brice paused in the dance for a moment before moving with Lucas again. "I get it. My butt is your 'birthday cake,' huh? Is *this* the special gift you were talking about?"

Lucas looked up at Brice and gave him an impish smile. "Yep. It is indeed. I been planning to cruelly ravish you for weeks and weeks now." Lucas's finger slipped between Brice's furry rump-cheeks. "What d'you say?"

"Uhhh. Well. Like I told you before, it's been a while. I never enjoyed it before. And you're mighty big. But…."

Lucas lifted his hand, slipped his finger into his mouth, moistened it, and then returned it to Brice's butt-crack. He probed gently. "Go on."

Brice pressed his hard-on against Lucas's hip. "I guess being with you…. I feel so much for you that…."

Lucas's wet finger found Brice's hole and stroked it. "Yeah? Go on."

"Uhhhmm," Brice sighed, pulling Lucas closer. "Yes, Lucas. Yes, you can fuck me. I told you I'd give you anything you wanted. I meant it. I trust you to treat me right. If anyone can teach me how to enjoy getting plowed, you can."

"Fantastic." Lucas kissed Brice on the chin and pushed his fingertip against Brice's hole, inserting the slightest millimeter. Brice jolted and released a guttural groan.

"I'll going to make you feel real fine, big Daddy, I promise. We'll take our sweet time. Does that feel good now?"

Brice closed his eyes, leaned against Lucas, and wrapped his arms around the boy's back. "I-I…. Yes. Yes. Yes, it does."

Lucas wetted his finger once more before delving into Brice a little farther. "You want me to keep going?"

Brice nodded. The feeling of being entered, albeit only by Lucas's finger so far, was far more pleasurable than he'd imagined. The enjoyment was intensified considerably when Lucas took Brice's cock in hand.

The two men circled to the music, Brice slowly humping Lucas's hand and Lucas gently finger-fucking Brice's butt. "Where or When" came to an end, and then "Not A Day Goes By," and then "Time After Time," and still they circled, both of them breathing heavily. Brice squirmed against Lucas's hand, trembling as the boy dug deeper, finding and probing his prostate.

"Oh, God, Lucas," Brice moaned, his groin grinding against Lucas's loins. "That f-feels super. No one's ever touched that…spot inside me before. It's like…a cross between a throb, an itch, and pure ecstasy. You're driving me fucking crazy. I feel like I could come any minute. My balls are aching."

"Ummm." Lucas shifted the angle of his arm and burrowed a millimeter deeper, evoking another gasp from Brice. "Ummm, your hole is so sweet. Soooo sweet. You're getting kinda open now. I think it's time you said, 'I'm ready to get fucked, boy. Take me into the bedroom and fuck my ass, boy.'"

Brice trembled against Lucas and pushed his butt back against his hand. "Ohh. I, uh...."

"Say it," Lucas huskily ordered.

"I, uh, I'm ready to get fucked, boy. Take me into the bedroom, boy, and fuck my ass, boy."

"That's right," Lucas said, slipping his finger from Brice's ass only to lead him by his erect cock across the room and into the bedroom.

"Get those briefs off. Now get on the bed. On your back. Lean back on those pillows. Good. That's right. Good."

Once Brice had positioned himself, Lucas leaned over and kissed him on his moist brow. "You enjoying this? You want some more?"

Brice lay back, looked up at Lucas, and fisted his cock. "God, yes. I sure do. You have me so turned on."

"Good." Lucas took his duffel bag off the dresser before pulling an armchair to the foot of the bed. He pulled out a tube of lube and lobbed it over to Brice before settling into the chair.

"Okay, finger your butt, big man. Get it good and open for me, okay? And look me in the eyes while you do it. Look down here between those furry legs of yours and give me a show."

"Y-yeah. Okay. Okay."

Lucas pulled off his shirt and sat back, grinning. Brice worked the first two knuckles of his right forefinger up his ass while jacking himself with his left hand.

"Beautiful. How's that feel?"

"Ummm. Pretty good." Brice eased his finger in and out. "It felt better when you were doing it."

"I'm just trying to get you all relaxed down there so it won't hurt when I fuck you. Check this out. Uncle Phil fetched me this from Florida." Lucas pulled a dildo from his duffel bag and tossed it onto the bed. "For just this purpose. It should help break you in."

"You want me to...?"

Lucas's lascivious grin broadened. He unzipped his pants and pulled out his hard cock. "Ohhhh, yes, I do. And I want to watch. I want to watch until you think you're ready for the real thing. And when you're ready, Brice my man, I'm going to give it to you so slow and so sweet you'll think we just entered Eden together."

BRICE SWAYED ON HIS ELBOWS and knees, the dildo buried in his ass and his rump up in the air, just as Lucas had ordered. A trickle of sweat ran down his temple. He squeezed his cock and bowed his head.

The mattress sagged as Lucas climbed onto the bed behind Brice. The boy's thighs nudged Brice's further apart. The boy's hand pushed at Brice's lower back, angling him a little lower.

"You ready for this?" Lucas murmured, running a hand over Brice's back, brushing his lips over Brice's right buttock.

"Yeah, I think so."

"And you want it? For real? Not just as a way to get up my ass eventually?"

Brice looked back, taking in the sight of the lean youth kneeling behind him: his red-brown beard, warm gray-blue eyes, muscular torso, and large, hard cock. "Yeah, I want it. Give it to me, Lucas. Teach me how to love it. Teach me how to love you inside me."

"You got it, Brice buddy." Lucas took the base of the dildo and fucked Brice with it for a good minute before pulling it out and positioning his own condomed cockhead against Brice's hole. "Okay. Here we go."

Lucas pushed against Brice's well-lubed entrance. Brice winced as the boy's cockhead slipped inside him. Hands gripping the sheet, he gave a hoarse groan.

"Hurt?"

"A little. Uh. Not bad. The finger-fucking and the dildo really made a difference, I think. Gimme a minute." Brice took his own cock in hand and stroked it.

"Okay. I think I can take a little more. Gimme a little more."

Lucas slid his cock another inch up inside Brice. Five minutes later—five minutes of Brice wincing, Lucas easing a little farther in, Brice flinching, Brice nodding and sighing and encouraging Lucas to continue, Lucas kissing Brice's shoulders and soothing him, Brice reaching back to spread his butt-cheeks, Lucas encouraging Brice to relax, Brice stroking himself, and Lucas thrusting ever so slowly, ever so softly—the entirety of

Lucas's cock was buried inside Brice.

Lucas bent over, resting his torso on Brice's back. Slipping his arms around Brice, he worked his nipples and kissed his shoulder blades as he thrust slowly in and out.

"Feel good? I'm all the way in."

"Yeah, I can tell. I'm full up with you. Uhhh! I'm full up with you, man. To the brim. Wow. Amazing. It hurt some there at first, but now it's feeling fantastic." Brice clenched his ass-ring around Lucas's cock and bucked back against him.

"Umm, that's great," Lucas sighed. "Keep that up. So you're into this, huh?"

"I sure as hell am," Brice said, jacking himself. "Work my nips a little harder."

"You got it." The two men rocked together for a long time, groaning and grunting with happy heat.

"New position now. On your side," Lucas ordered, giving Brice's butt-cheeks a slap before abruptly pulling out. Brice complied, rolling over and cocking his butt. Lucas pressed against Brice's back and entered him again.

"Ummm, yeah," Brice grunted as Lucas's cock slid home.

"Ohhh, Daddy, my dick feels so good up your hole," Lucas sighed, kneading Brice's right pec.

"And my hole's so happy stuffed fulla your dick," Brice moaned, resting his right thigh upon Lucas's bent leg. Lucas cupped Brice's bushy-whiskered cheek and Brice turned his head. They kissed, long and deep, as Lucas thrust in and out, pinching Brice's nipple as Brice worked his own cock. Soon Brice was rapidly jacking himself, and Lucas was pounding Brice hard and fast.

"Oh, fuck," Brice grunted. "Oh, fuck! Your cock's hitting.... Oh! My God, I've never felt.... Oh, fuck!"

"Your sweet spot? Good. Hand that hot prick here. I'll finish that thang off for you," Lucas said, nudging Brice's hand aside. Lucas fisted Brice's cock and hammered his ass even harder.

"Yeah. Christ, fuck me, man! Christ. Fuck me, Lucas! Oh, yeah. Ohhhh, yeah. Ohhh."

"Close?"

"Uh huh. Uh huh!"

"Me too. Me fucking too. You're so tight and hot and.... Oh, damn, here...we...go."

Brice roared and spasmed, spouting come into Lucas's grip. Lucas tensed up, heaved a raspy shout, and finished as well, cock still firmly buried up Brice's butt.

The two men slumped together. After a while, Brice rose, first to piss, then to moisten a washcloth and clean them both up, then to toss the lube-smeared rag in the sink.

When Brice climbed back into bed, Lucas took the bigger man into his arms. "Thank you," he said, kissing Brice tenderly on the lips.

"Thank you. That was more wonderful than I ever would have imagined. Happy birthday."

"It was a perfect birthday. The best I've ever had, without a doubt. Can I be big spoon tonight?"

"Sure you can." Brice rolled over and snuggled back against Lucas. Lucas threw an arm over Brice, and Brice took his hand.

Lucas cuddled closer. "That was just fantastic. Will you…will you let me top you again one of these days?"

Brice chuckled. "I sure will. In fact, fine as that felt, I'm thinking you need to screw me again in the morning."

CHAPTER FIFTY-FOUR

"No place to park," Lucas said, frowning as he drove through the car-lined roads of Helvetia. About them, the forested hills rose steeply, casting midafternoon shadow. Beside the road, the trout stream burbled busily by, freed from winter's shackling ice. "It's really busy this year. I'm gonna turn around at the Hutte. We'll park back up on the Pickens Road."

"So Phil isn't meeting us here?" Brice asked, studying the clusters of people. Some stood on lawns, some sat on porches, some congregated about parked pickup trucks, but most strolled down the road toward the Community Hall, where the Ramp Supper was being served.

"Naw. He's back at Sodomy Central baking me that cake. He hates ramps. Eating them reminds him of being poor when he was a kid, before his daddy started to do legal work for the coal companies and made a shitload of money."

"Coal does run this state. I'm damned glad my home county doesn't have much of the stuff."

"Daddy died in a mine." Lucas pulled into the Hutte parking lot. "Buncha sonofabitchs tearing up the land. I'd castrate 'em if I could. I wish one of the legendary monsters around here would take a personal interest and go after 'em. The Snarly Yow, maybe, or the Braxton County monster, or that vampire they say's lurking around German Valley."

"Sounds like a gratifying novel or horror movie," Brice said. "I love that righteous-warrior side of you."

"I love that in you too," Lucas said, turning the truck around. "The way you cussed that journalist out when he called me a truck-stop whore? Classic."

"Yeah, kicking his teeth in would have felt mighty good." Brice puffed out his chest and flexed a thick arm. "Nobody messes with my lil' sweetmeat and gets away with it."

"Sweetmeat, huh? You're the one with the sweet meat, Daddy." Lucas pulled out of the parking lot and headed back the way they'd come. Along the Pickens Road, long lines of cars and trucks were parked on the berms, so Lucas kept driving up the forest-lined slope, looking for a spot.

"Shit, it's really crowded. I hope they don't run out of ramps by the time we get there," he groused. "That big pancake-and-bacon breakfast at the Blackwater lodge was delicious, but I'm already hungry again."

"You worked up a big appetite last night, screwing me cross-eyed," Brice said, rubbing Lucas's knee. "And then again this morning."

Lucas grinned over at Brice. "You ain't complaining, are you?"

"Complaining? I asked you to give it to me again, didn't I? Though I gotta admit I'm a little sore after all that pounding. You're a young man of impressive, uh, genital vigor."

"Sore, huh? Good. Something to remember me by. Ain't it hot, to think that what we do together is what guys have been doing since before the days of Alexander the Great? That's pretty cool, ain't it?"

"It is. A long and lascivious legacy of succulent and salacious sodomy, your uncle would probably put it." Brice chuckled. "After finding out how great it felt, you plowing me, I gotta admit I've been missing something all these years of being on top."

"I'm real, real glad you enjoyed it. I was sorta worried, since I…I'd never done that before."

"What? Really?"

"Yep, really. With the truckers, I sucked cock. In prison, it was me getting my rump rammed, willingly or not. So you were my first."

"I-I'm honored. Truly." Brice reached over to caress the soft fur on Lucas's forearm. "You were such an amazing Top that it's hard to believe you've never screwed a man before."

"Well, I remembered the way Eric.… He was real rough with me sometimes, beating me up and all, but when he fucked me, man, he really did it right. So I just recalled all the ways he used to…make me relax and make me feel good. Poor Eric. The people you care about, they really are kinda with you always, huh? In one way or another."

"I guess so," Brice said. "You talking about Eric makes me think of Zac. It's been a good while since I've even thought of him, all wrapped up in you the way I've been. I wonder how he's doing, health-wise. I guess I forgive him. It's a lot easier to forgive someone when you've found happiness."

Lucas flashed Brice a tender sideways glance. "So you're happy, huh?"

"I am. I sure am. You make me so happy, Lucas."

"Here's a place at last," Lucas said, pulling the truck over onto the gravel berm, beneath a green overhang of hemlock. "Well, if you think you're happy now, big guy, you're gonna be even happier tonight. I think it's finally time for you to claim that prize you been waiting for so patiently."

"Really?" Brice's face lit up. "You mean…?"

"You get to pluck my lil' rosebud, yeah. What I gave you this morning, you get to give me tonight."

"Hot damn. Yeah? Oh, man. Ohhhh, man."

Lucas laughed. "You're looking pretty eager, Mr. Brown. I'm pretty eager too, actually. More eager'n I'd ever thought I'd be, considering my checkered past."

Lucas turned off the engine and set the parking brake, and the two climbed out. "Got a little bit of a walk," Lucas said, pulling on his black denim jacket. "It must be a quarter mile back to town."

"No problem," Brice said, adjusting his baseball cap. "It's a little chilly, but it's a beautiful day. Look at those flowers up the slope."

"Dog's-tooth violet and wild geranium," Lucas said. "And look at the new leaves on the buckeyes and the tulip poplars. Daddy taught me all the trees and wildflowers."

Brice looked both ways before lifting Lucas's hand to his mouth and kissing it. "You're my wildflower."

"And you're full of it," Lucas said, pulling his hand away at the sound of a car approaching around the bed. "You just can't wait to see me with my legs in the air."

"Painfully true. God knows I've waited long enough."

"Yes, you have. The soul of patience. Well, I'm finally over my hang-ups, and your patience is gonna be rewarded real soon. But first, let's get down the hill to those ramps. I'm gonna be majorly irked if they've run out."

"Brice Brown!" said the burly man in denim overalls who took their money at the door. "You come outta seclusion to eat our legendary ramson, huh?"

"Uh, yeah," Brice said, steeling himself for hostility. Instead the big guy smiled.

"You've been through the wringer, I know. People can be shits. Some Christians, they act like they've never read any of those red-letter words Jesus spoke. Screw 'em, I say. You just keep on keepin' on with little Lucas here." The man pounded Lucas on the shoulder. "He's a good kid, a smart kid. And enjoy the food, okay?"

"You bet," Brice said, shaking the man's proffered hand. "I really appreciate the friendliness."

The man shrugged. "Friendly's easier than being mean. We're all God's children, right?"

"Who was that?" Brice asked Lucas as they moved into line to be served.

"Mr. Honaker. He was my biology teacher and the assistant coach at my high school. He was always mighty nice to me." Lucas tipped the brim of his cap down. "Glad he still is. Every time I see someone I used to know, I wonder if they're gonna be decent or downright nasty."

As smiling women poured them sweet iced tea and heaped up their plates with fried ramps, brown beans, ham, fried potatoes, cornbread, and applesauce, Brice surveyed the room.

"No rabid reporters or fundamentalist assassin squads that I can see," Brice said as they headed, plates full, toward the long lines of communal tables.

"Good. How you've stood being the center of hostile attention for months, I can't imagine." Lucas shook his head. "Every time we leave the compound, I tense up with screaming paranoia. There's some spots over in that corner, away from people. Let's head over there and snarf up this chow. I'm ravenous."

The two men took a seat at the far end of a long table and dug in. Every now and then, Brice looked up to scan the noisy room for hateful glares. He found a few, but fortunately, most people, including those seated closest to them, were too busy devouring their meals and interacting with family and friends to notice that a notorious homosexual singer and his young lover were feasting with them.

"As usual, it looks like we're the only queers in the entire room. I'd hoped that Grace and Amie might show up," Brice said, forking up potatoes. "I'd call them if there were any cell phone service around here."

"They said they might drive down if business was slow at the store, but if they didn't show up by three-thirty, they weren't coming. If we miss 'em, they'll be up later to have coconut cake with us and Phil. Hey, Brice?"

"Umm, yep?" Brice mumbled around a piece of cornbread he'd topped with applesauce.

Lucas lowered his voice. "You get tired of being the only queers in the room? I mean, if we're gonna stay in the country, that's gonna be pretty much the way it'll be all the time."

Brice shrugged. "Sure, I get tired of it sometimes. I sure felt isolated growing up in Hinton knowing I liked guys, though it was easier in college. The gay bars in Morgantown were mighty fun. When I was in Nashville, though, I was too closeted to take advantage of any gay life there. Now, well, I don't think I want to live in a city again. It'll be hard to stay here, yeah, and isolated some, but as long as I'm with you, and I have a few cool friends like Grace and Amie, I'll be fine."

"Yeah. Having someone makes a big difference." Lucas's eyes met Brice's own. "I really want to hold your hand right now, but I can't, 'cause I'm afraid."

"You insisted that I hold your hand at the Hutte on Valentine's Day. You practically dared me. What's changed?"

Lucas looked around the crowded room and scowled. "I don't know. With the *Star* publicity and reporters hounding us and all that shit, I just feel.... I don't know. Exposed? Outnumbered?"

"Yeah." Brice took a deep breath. "And I'm sorry about that."

"Stop apologizing." Lucas chewed on a morsel of ham. "I ain't got no regrets. I just get tired of being on my guard. I was on my guard all the time before, but now...."

"It's even worse."

"Yeah." Lucas scooped up a spoonful of brown beans. "Sometimes I wish I could live in a city, where folks might be more accepting, but I know I can't. The few times I've left the country—some family trips when I was a kid, a couple school field trips.... Ugh. I hated it. Damn crowds and noise and traffic, red lights and delays, prissy people with fancy clothes looking down on me, making fun of the way I talk. Those big-city gay boys can have their discos and glamorous ghettos and expensive lifestyle. Besides, how would a penniless redneck like me even afford to live in those places? It's small-town West Virginia for me, no doubt about it."

"Whither thou goest...as I've said before." Brice checked his wristwatch. "It's three fifteen. I don't think Grace and Amie are coming. How about we get them some plates to go and drop by Radclyffe's Roost on the way home?"

"Good idea. Grace does love her some ramps. Lemme just gobble up the rest of this ham and finish this tea."

BRICE AND LUCAS, CARRYING PAPER plates covered in plastic wrap, trudged up the Pickens Road, enjoying the leafy shade, the soft breezes, and the purling of the brook in the gully below. They'd nearly reached Lucas's vehicle when a much larger truck, bright red with a double cab, came around the turn in the road uphill. It drove slowly past them. Two men sat in the front seat and two men sat in the back. All of them were staring.

Brice's stomach constricted. He looked up and down the road. Wooded hillsides and lines of empty cars. No one else was around. Instead of continuing down the slope toward Helvetia, the big vehicle pulled into a turn-around, reversed direction, and crawled past them again. It slid off the road and crunched into gravel only a few yards uphill, right behind Lucas's truck.

"Lucas, we might want to move a little faster. I think—"

The driver of the red truck, a big man with glossy black hair and a thick goatee, leaned out his open window. "Hey! Don't I know you?" In a less remote, less potentially perilous context, Brice would have found him handsome.

"Oh, hell," Lucas muttered. "Great. Just fucking great."

Fight or flight. This is how it feels, Brice thought. *There are four of them to two of us. I can't yet tell how big they are.*

"Know me? No, I don't think so," Brice said loudly. Though his voice was steady, both his feet and his heart picked up their pace.

"Yeah, I recognize you! Aren't you Brice Brown? The queer singer?"

"Here we go," Brice muttered. "Lucas, get out of here, okay? Get in the truck fast, or run back toward town. With your parole—"

"Fuck my parole." Lucas gritted his teeth. "Leave you? Are you crazy?"

All four men clambered out, with wide grins on their faces. The dark-haired driver sneered. "Oh, yeah! It *is* you. The famous Brice Brown! We've read lots of shit about you. Hell, I used to hear you on the radio when I drove to work."

In a split-second, Brice had assessed them, studying their physiques, their faces, and their postures. *That's malice in their eyes, no question. In their thirties, I'd say, all of them. Those two—the driver and that other guy—are as big as I am, though the bald one's more fat than muscle. Those two, the blond and the redhead, are smaller than me, but they look scrappy, hard, and lean. They're all four bigger than Lucas. Goddamn it. Where's Amie and her deadly purse when we need her?*

Brice gave Lucas a glance full of warning and stepped in front of him. For the thousandth time in his life, he was torn between two wildly disparate impulses: should he prepare for a brawl or drag Lucas into the truck and urge him to drive off as fast as he could?

I won't be a coward. Not in the eyes of the man I love. Fuck that. Brice placed the wrapped plate of food in the open truck bed and crossed his arms, regarding the quartet of strangers.

"Yeah, I'm Brice Brown. So?"

The four men exchanged grins and glances. "So we're big fans of yours, man," said the driver. "You and that little sweetie there. Word is he's real talented in some departments."

Brice curled his lip. "Why don't y'all get on down the road, boys? Before you miss the ramps. I think they're almost out."

"Ain't you gonna give us your autograph first?" said the little blond guy, stepping closer. "It's kinda hard to believe a thing like you exists. A faggot country singer. Will wonders never cease?"

Lucas placed his plate of food on the hood of the truck, then moved over to stand beside Brice. "What'd you call him?"

"A faggot," replied the blond guy. "And you're that little cocksucker who's been selling hummers all up and down the interstate, aren't you? I got some money in my pocket. Five dollars? Will that do you? You in the mood? You want to suck my cock, little man?"

Brice's curled lip quivered. "I'll give you an autograph, you frog-faced sonofabitch, right across that nasty mouth of yours, if you don't get the hell out of here and take your brain-dead buddies with you."

"You're pretty ferocious for a fag," the goateed driver said. "Big too. Too bad for y'all we outnumber you." The four men moved closer, the two smaller ones fanning out to flank Brice and Lucas.

"Of course you outnumber us," Brice said, putting up his fists. "Your kind are like jackals. You always work in packs. Fucking cowards. None of you would dare take me on alone. I'd wipe up the fucking road with any one of you."

"No need to take you on alone," the big bald man growled. "We're buds, right, guys? One for all and all for one."

"Right," said the redhead, pulling a knife from his jacket and unsheathing it.

"Fuck off now. Fuck off," Lucas snarled, lowering himself into fighting stance. Pulling his car keys from his pocket, he grasped them in his right fist, fanning them out threateningly between his fingers. "We don't want no trouble, boys, but we'll deal it out if we need to. I learned some pretty vicious things in prison. You mess with us, and I might just have to show y'all some. Gouge out some eyes, flatten some balls, break some windpipes."

"I doubt that," the driver said. "Fetch that bat from the back, Ed."

"Well, fuck," Lucas muttered as the blond man threw open the truck door and pulled out a baseball bat. "Really?"

This is what I've been dreading ever since I realized I wanted men. This here, right now. This is the nightmare I always feared would come. Brice did his best to choke back the sick terror filling him. *Lord, don't let it all end like us. Give us the strength to fight. Nothing to do now but fight.*

"Back to back, Lucas," Brice muttered. "Now."

"You got it."

The two larger men lunged forward simultaneously, the goateed driver swinging at Brice, the bald guy going for Lucas. Brice blocked his opponent's blow with his forearm and then punched him smack dab in the belly, knocking him backward. Lucas dodged his foe's blow, then swung his fist of clasped keys high, catching the bald man in the face. When he fell back howling, scrabbling at his bleeding cheek, Lucas kneed him in the crotch.

"Shit!" the blond guy said, brandishing the bat. "Watch out, Fred. The little one's mean as a snake."

Brice and Lucas regrouped, pressed back to back again.

"Don't pay to fight fair in circumstances like this," Lucas said. "Tear 'em up any way you can. Rip off their balls, if need be. Rip out their throats."

"Right. I love you."

"I love you too. Watch out!"

The blond leaped forward and swung at Brice with the bat. Before he could dodge it, the hard wood glanced off Brice's shoulder. "Fuck!" Brice yelled, staggering back against the truck.

"Motherfucker!" Lucas swung at the blond, stabbing him in the neck with his sharp handful of keys. The man screamed, dropped the bat, and fell onto his knees, clutching his bloody wound. Snarling, Lucas kicked him twice in the ribs.

The driver, on his feet again, charged forward, slamming into Lucas and knocking him backward. Gasping, Lucas dug his keyed fist into the man's side. Cussing and grappling savagely, the two staggered around the hood of the truck, over the berm, and into the shallow ditch beside the road.

Gripping his wounded shoulder, Brice pushed up off Lucas's vehicle. The bald man was nearly on his feet. Brice brought his elbow down on the back of the man's head, and the guy collapsed. As Brice turned, the redhead stepped forward and stabbed at Brice's chest with his knife. Brice parried the blow with his left forearm, roaring as the steel slashed into him. Gritting his teeth, he drove his right fist into the man's nose, knocking him flat.

Brice turned toward the ditch. The big driver held Lucas several inches off the ground. The man had Lucas's right arm twisted behind him and his own arm wrapped around Lucas's throat. Lucas scrabbled at the man, gasping and kicking wildly.

"Drop him, you bastard!" Brice shouted.

Before he could charge forward, a great blow caught Brice on the left hip. He staggered sideways in agony, hit the hood of Lucas's truck, and dropped to his knees. He had just enough time to turn, to see the big bald guy holding the baseball bat, before the man swung the bat, agony exploded inside Brice's skull, his face slammed into gravel, and all his senses snuffed out.

CHAPTER FIFTY-FIVE

EYES CLOSED, BRICE BEGAN TO HUM ALONG.

I know that song. Love it. Used to play it.

Fare thee well, my own true love,
Fare thee well for a while.
I'm goin' back where I came from
But I'll come back again
Even if I go ten thousand mile.

Brice licked his lips. "Whoa. Cotton mouth. My head hurts. How much'd we drink last night, Lucas?"

Smiling, he opened his eyes. His smile faded as bits of memory returned.

Brice sat bolt upright and took in his surroundings at a glance. Lime-green room. Medical machines. Tubes in his arms. Bandage on his left forearm. A man he'd never seen before was sitting in a chair by his bed.

"Hey! You're awake," the stranger blurted. He was a short, stocky guy in his early thirties, with thick brown hair to his shoulders, hazel eyes, dense eyebrows meeting over the bridge of his nose, hillbilly-length sideburns, and a bushy biker goatee grading into several days' worth of stubble.

"Who're you? Where's Lucas? Where am I? Where's Lucas?"

The man stood and took Brice by the hand. "Hey, relax. Lucas is just downstairs in the cafeteria. I offered to sit with you while he got something to eat."

A wave of weakness washed over Brice. He rubbed his aching head, only to find his scalp shaven clean. "He's all right? He's all right?"

"Well, his face was mighty bruised up, and his

shoulder was dislocated, but otherwise—"

"Dislocated? How? I—"

"You don't remember what happened?"

Brice rubbed his jaw. His beard was shaggier than ever.

"I, uh. I, uh. Yeah, some. I remember some. Those bastards. Those motherfucking—"

The man released his hand. "I should probably fetch a nurse. We been waiting for two weeks for you to wake up."

"Wake up? Two weeks?"

"Yeah. You been in a coma that long. You took a helluva blow to the—"

"Where's Lucas? So he's all right? Find me Lucas. Will you find me Lucas? I need—"

"Hey, man, relax. He should be back real soon, but, sure, I'll—"

At that moment, the door to the room opened. To Brice's vast relief, Lucas stepped into the room. He was wearing a black T-shirt and black jeans, and his arm was in a sling. He stared at Brice, open-mouthed.

"Oh, my God. Oh, thank God. Oh, thank God. You're awake. You came back!" Lucas was beside Brice in an instant, kissing his face all over.

The stranger stood back and laughed. "Glad I was here for the reunion. I was just setting by the bed singing an old song I play on my guitar sometimes, and then who should start humming along but my favorite country-music star, Brice Brown."

"Oh, man, I'm so, so glad you're awake! How do you feel?" Lucas asked.

"Kinda shitty. My head hurts. I feel feeble. My arm throbs."

"Yeah. You got a big scar under that bandage. That prick with the knife cut you bad."

"But you're all right?" Brice said, caressing Lucas's cheek and kissing his hand.

"Good enough. My shoulder's still sorta tore-up, but otherwise I'm in good shape, considering what happened. God knows it coulda been worse. If Matt here hadn't come along, we'd both be dead."

"Matt?"

The stranger raised his hand. "That's me. Matt Taylor."

"So what happened? I only remember bits and pieces."

"I'll tell you here directly. Matt, would you go fetch a nurse? They'll want to know Brice is conscious, and I'm sure they'll want to check him out. They been poking and prodding him for half a month."

"Be glad to fetch 'em. Mr. Brown, I'm damned glad you're finally conscious. You scared the shit out of all of us." With that, Matt shambled out of the room.

Lucas pulled the chair closer to the bed, sat in it, and took Brice's hand.

"Maybe you should just rest now. We can talk later."

"Naw. Naw. I need to know what happened. Why can't I remember?"

"'Cause you got cracked in the head, man."

"Cracked in…? Lucas, tell me. Please. Tell me!"

"Okay, okay. Don't get all riled up. Here we go. Matt's a state park employee who lives here in Charleston."

"Charleston? We're in Charleston?"

"Yeah. They brought us both here after the attack. So Matt's driving up from Charleston to get him some of that ramp supper, and he rounds the corner just about the time that bald bastard clobbers you with that fucking baseball bat. Do you remember that?"

Brice lay back. "I do, just barely. Like it was a bad dream. Could I have some water? My mouth's parched."

"Ah. Sure." Hurriedly, Lucas poured a plastic cup full from a pitcher nearby.

Brice took the cup with shaking hands and gulped the water down. "Ah. Ah. Better. Okay, go on."

"So the bald bastard hits you upside the head with that bat and down you go. I'm thinking you're dead, and I'm thinking I'm next, 'cause that big goateed guy has wrenched my right arm so hard he's dislocated my shoulder, and he has his arm around my neck and is doing his level best to choke the life out of me. But then I make a fist with my left hand, and I bring it up and swing it back, and I catch him right in the balls, and he yowls like a cougar and drops me fast."

"Holy hell. Thank God you got away."

"Thank God indeed. Right about then—speaking of divine intervention and heaven-sent timing—that's when Matt drives up, and he takes it all in real fast, and he pulls a crowbar outta his truck, and in a flash he's on top of the bald bastard, who's fixing to bash your skull open, and Matt brings that crowbar down on the guy's arm, and the fat turd drops the bat, and then Matt clocks him in the jaw with the crowbar, and the fat turd goes down, and then Matt, he leaps—Man, you shoulda seen it! It was like some kinda slow-motion Olympic event!—he leaps over the bald bastard's body and starts swinging the crowbar at the goateed guy. Well, Matt catches him hard in the chest, and the guy flies through the air and hits the hillside, and then Matt's helping me up, and the goateed sonofabitch scrambles up and hops into his truck, and he's outta there like a bat outta hell, leaving his bloodied buddies behind."

"Damn. I guess we owe this Matt guy our lives."

"We do indeed." Lucas bent to kiss the knuckles of Brice's hand. "He's real cool. He's come by a lot to keep me company while I've hung out here by your bed."

"So then what?"

"So then, well, Matt hands me his crowbar, and the baseball bat for good measure, and he spins off in his truck to fetch help, and I guard the three pricks—the redhead you put out, the blond I stabbed in the neck, and the bald guy that Matt knocked the shit out of—and I watch the blood pour outta your arm and ooze outta your nose, and I check your pulse and pray you ain't gonna die. Pretty soon, Matt's back with folks, and then the emergency people show up, and the cops, and we're both on our way here."

"So why was I out for so long?"

"That bald pig gave your skull a hairline fracture and bruised your brain. The doctors considered operating but decided against it, said you'd likely come to on your own, once the swelling went down. They did have to stitch up your arm. That knife wound was real deep. But why should I tell you all this when you can read about it? We're in the news again."

Grim-faced, Lucas tapped a magazine lying on the bedside table. "*Country Weekly* did a whole cover story on it. It was written by that Johnson guy, the one who came to Phagg Heights, the one you sorta liked? It was real sympathetic, focusing on the gay-bashing aspect and pointing out how dangerous homophobia can be. The *Star* did a story too, of course, and the *Charleston Gazette*, and all sorts of other newspapers. A few journalist types, including Mr. Johnson, have been lurking around, waiting for you to wake up."

"So your parole? You didn't have to…?"

"Go back to prison and resume my career as a butt-bitch for a series of big bruisers? Naw. Only guy whose butt-bitch I'm ever gonna be is Brice Brown's. There was a parole hearing, but your sister Leigh came up to help with all that, since she's a lawyer, and Matt testified that the bastards had attacked us. Plus my dislocated arm and bruised-up face, your injuries, and the fact that all kinds of homophobic bullshit had been published about us, all that convinced the judge that it was a clear case of gay-bashing and self-defense."

"And the guys who did it?"

"Well, the three of 'em we took out all ended up in the Elkins hospital. The guy I key-stabbed is still there. The cops tracked down the one who got away. They're all facing big charges and are liable to get prison time. We'll have to testify, of course."

Brice set his lips. "Be glad to. The fuckers. They could have killed us."

"They'll get theirs, your sister says. Especially with Matt's testimony. The priceless thing is that Matt's gay too."

"Really?"

"Oh, yeah. And a part-time musician. He's crazy about your music. When he figured out whose asses he'd saved, he about pissed himself with pride and joy. So those guys all got their butts kicked by a trio of ferocious faggots. Hah! That'll teach 'em to mess with country queers. Hey, look here."

Lucas handed Brice a paper. Brice squinted at it.

"Vision's a little off. What is it?"

"Good news. While I was waiting here for you to wake up—Grace and Amie and Uncle Phil and your sister have all been by to give me breaks—I finished studying and I took the GED. I passed! With really high scores. Now I gotta get ready for the ACT. After that, I'm gonna apply to the forestry program at WVU like I planned."

"That's wonderful, Lucas. I knew you'd—"

A short, stocky white woman entered the room, followed by a tall black woman with high cheekbones. "Mr. Brown, you're up. Welcome back to the world," said the black woman.

"This is Dr. Boone," Lucas said, indicating the taller woman. "That there's Nurse Bugg. They've been real, real nice to me."

"And Mr. Bryan here has been equally pleasant," said the doctor. "If you'll leave us for a bit, Mr. Bryan, we need to do some tests on Mr. Brown here."

"I figured." Lucas lifted Brice's hand and kissed it. "I'm gonna go call your sister and Uncle Phil and let 'em know you're outta that coma. Be right back."

Dr. Boone looked after him fondly. "He's been here every day, Mr. Brown. That boy's the soul of devotion. So let's see how you're shaping up. With any luck, we can send you home soon."

CHAPTER FIFTY-SIX

"BRICE IS REAL TIRED, AND HIS HEAD HURTS, SO let's keep this short, okay?"

"Whatever you say, Mr. Bryan. I know you've both been through a lot. I'm just grateful that you've agreed to speak to me. *Country Weekly* readers really want to know your side of the story."

Larry Johnson settled into the chair by Brice's hospital bed, then pulled out a notebook and a tiny tape recorder he clicked on. "So how shall we begin?"

Brice took a sip of orange juice. "How about this? I'm gay. I denied it for years, denied it to the world and denied it to myself. No more lies. I'm gay."

"And why did you deny it?"

Brice rolled his eyes. "Why do you think? So I could keep making music, keep making a living at making music. So I wouldn't lose my career."

"Or his life," Lucas added. "As you know, we both nearly died a few weeks back. Brice came to only five days ago."

"Yes. So Zac Lanier was telling the truth? About your affair?"

"For the most part. I hurt him, and I'm sorry about that. I was too much of a coward then, an emotional coward, to let myself care for him the way he needed to be cared for."

"And now you two, you and Mr. Bryan, are indeed a couple?"

"Yes." Brice took Lucas's small hand. "We are indeed. I never really let myself love before. Never had the guts. I was afraid of the consequences. But then I met Lucas, and I guess he gave me the courage to be true to myself at last."

"And you two plan to share a future together?"

"Yep." Lucas nodded. "We're not sure what's next, but we'll do it together. Brice is getting outta here tomorrow, and we're heading back up to Randolph County. Some friends got a welcome-home party planned."

"Brice, you wanted to keep this brief, so we will. I have just one more question. What would you like to say to your fans, to the country music community?"

"I'd like...I'd like to say...." Brice took a deep breath. "I never chose to be who I am. Who does? I didn't choose to be gay. I didn't choose to love men. I didn't choose to be a country boy, a Southerner, or a mountain man either. 'Southern by the grace of God,' y'know? Some would say God made me all those things. Some would say that my upbringing, and my genes, I guess, gave me those identities. Who knows? I just know that I didn't choose any of 'em, but I've finally learned to accept 'em, the complex, the... contradictory passel of selves I am, and to be truthful about that. So now, other folks— Nashville, country-music fans, whoever—are just gonna have to learn to take me as I am."

Brice paused to sip his juice. "I also want to say to the country-music world... please stop hating gay folks, and please stop using your religion as a free pass to being nasty. If you saw me a few days ago—sprawled out here in a coma—you would have seen the consequences of hating. Lucas and I both could've died that day. Those guys didn't even know us, but they hated us so much they did their damned best to kill us."

Brice closed his eyes and settled back against the pillows. "So I say, folks, if you don't like who I am, just leave me alone and fuck off. Leave me be. If you've got love in your heart for anyone, then be happy that Lucas and I have found love too, that some men can find love with men and some women can find love with women. I don't know what the future holds, but I do know this: I'm gonna love Lucas and I'm gonna be honest, and I'm gonna keep making honest music, authentic music, no matter what."

"That's long enough," Lucas said.

Larry flipped off the recorder. "Great. Thank you. I'll send the transcript along for you and your lawyer to vet."

He rose and shook first Brice's hand, then Lucas's. "My photographer is a little late, but she should be here any minute. You don't mind a few photos? I think it would do Nashville good to see the two of you together."

"I think you're right. We'll hold hands. That'll certainly give 'em something to talk about," Lucas said, brushing his palm over Brice's shaven scalp. "Just give big Brice here a few minutes to straighten up that mussy, fly-away hair of his."

"Cut it out." Brice swatted wearily at Lucas's hand.

"I'm just messing with you, Daddy. He looks pretty tough and manly all bald, don't he, Mr. Johnson? The perfect studly image for the cover of *Country Weekly*."

"You're back! You look wonderful!" Amie enthused, throwing her arms around Brice. Next in the hugging line was Grace, then Philip, then Doris Ann, then Eleanor from the Hutte Restaurant, and finally Matt Taylor, who'd reserved a room at Helvetia's Beekeeper Inn and driven up from Charleston to attend the celebratory event.

The dining area of Radclyffe's Roost sported "Welcome Home" banners, vases of flowers, piles of cards from well-wishers, and platters of finger food Amie had prepared. In the background, Brice's CDs played softly on the stereo. Brice, feeling detached, dizzy and weak, sat back in a cushioned armchair, listened to the happy chatter, and savored the refreshments Lucas brought him: cups of Amie's rum punch, as well as plates crowded with sausage balls, steamed shrimp, cheese straws, and ham biscuits.

Within an hour, Brice nudged Lucas's knee. "I'm sorry," he muttered, "but I'm dead tired. Can we head home? I just wanna lie down and close my eyes. I still can't see well, and I'm wobbly as hell."

Lucas nodded. The two said their goodbyes and received another round of hugs before Lucas bagged up the as-yet-unread letters and cards, helped Brice out to the pickup, and drove them up the hill to Phagg Heights.

In the cabin bedroom, Lucas undressed them both, led shaky-kneed Brice into the shower, and bathed him. After drying them off and doling out Brice's pain medications, Lucas helped him into bed. There, he stroked Brice's scalp and massaged his face.

"Thanks, man. That helps the headache," Brice sighed. "But my vision's still blurred, and my hands keep trembling."

"The doctors said there'd be lingering symptoms, buddy."

"What if they're permanent? What if I can't play guitar? What if—"

"Stop it with the what-ifs. I'll take care of you, no matter what. You're gonna be fine, that's what Dr. Boone predicted. It's just gonna take some time."

"Yeah. Sorry. Patience has never been my strong suit."

"You've sure been patient with me. Time for me to return the favor. How about tomorrow I make us some mimosas, scrambled eggs, and sausage? We can have breakfast out on the porch with Uncle Phil, and I can read you some of those cards you got. You got so many."

"That'd be nice," Brice whispered. "God, I feel so washed-out, so weak. All my life I've tried so hard to be strong, but now...."

"Brice, honey...."

"I couldn't protect you from them." Brice shifted over onto his belly, buried his face in a pillow, and started to shake. "I wasn't strong enough or fast enough. I—" His voice broke.

"Brice, stop it. No one's a superman. That's in the comics and movies, big guy. This is real life, whether we like it or not." Lucas wrapped an arm around him. "Roll over here. Kiss me, okay? Just kiss me, okay?"

"Okay."

The two men shared a series of gentle kisses. With his thumb, Lucas wiped the tears from Brice's cheeks.

"Hey, your sister wants us to come down to Hinton and visit once you're feeling better," Lucas said, resting his cheek against Brice's furry pec. "You can show me where you grew up."

"That'd be good. I want you to meet my nephew. I'm so glad to be here, Lucas. I'm so glad to be home. I'm so glad...." Brice murmured, his speech trailing off into deep sleep.

"WAKE UP, BIG BALD BEAR."

Brice opened his eyes to find Lucas sitting naked on the bed and holding two mugs. Behind Lucas, gauzy curtains wafted in the May morning wind.

"I got fancy. I used Uncle Phil's recipe for café au lait."

"Thanks." Sitting up with difficulty, Brice took the cup. The tremors in his hands were less noticeable this morning, though the pain in his head lingered still.

"How you feeling?" Lucas stood, resting a hand on Brice's shoulder.

"A little better. Nightmares, though."

"Yeah, I heard 'em. I've had some of those too. PTSD. Bound to happen. You hungry? Up for that porch breakfast with Uncle Phil?"

Brice looked up at Lucas and nodded. The boy's sweet face and beautiful body made him want to break down and sob. Instead, he muttered, "Yeah. Yeah, I am. God, I'm so grateful you're all right."

"Darling! I love what you've done with your hair," Phil said, joining them on the porch.

"You had to say it, didn't you?" Lucas screwed up his mouth.

"It's the baseball bat special," Brice said, handing Phil a mimosa. "It costs quite a bit. Thank God for health insurance."

"I think it's real sexy, now that the big bruise is gone." Lucas doled them out plates from a tray. "Y'ought to keep shaving your head for a while to see if you like it. Dig in, guys, before it gets cold."

The three ate happily and heartily. A soft rainstorm drifted over the valley and dripped from the leaves. Phil went off to his office to pay bills, leaving Brice and Lucas to themselves. Lucas prepared another round of mimosas and began the process of sorting through the cards Brice had received at the Charleston hospital. Brice rocked in the rocking chair, fingering the red scar on his forearm, and looked out over the countryside, feeling profoundly thankful that he was still around to see the mountains gleaming with rain and spring's gold-green.

"Here's one from Tim McGraw and Faith Hill. Wow. And one from Mary Chapin Carpenter."

"Liberals. Makes sense." Brice dug a thumb against his temple, trying to drive off the dull hurt there. "The conservatives, they probably wish I'd died."

"Here's one from McGavock Confederate Cemetery. Where's that?"

"That's where my Rebel ancestor's buried, down in Franklin, Tennessee. I send 'em donations every now and then."

"Here's one from your nephew. Another from that Travis kid up at WVU. And one from your ex-wife."

"I guess she can afford to be forgiving." Brice sipped his mimosa and watched a breeze shake raindrops from black locust blossoms. "Is there one from Lorrie Kershaw? She's Shelly's cousin. She was real sweet to me, even after the big scandal last fall."

"Yes. She sent one. This one's from Steve Morgan. He was your manager?"

"Yep. Who else?"

"An official-looking one from Molasses Mount Records. They the label who dumped you?"

"Yep. Anything from the Country Music Museum? The Country Music Association? CMT?"

Lucas scowled. "Nope. Not a damn thing."

"That figures. Anyone else familiar?"

"Let's see. Wayne Meador. Your high-school crush?"

"Yeah. Cool. You've got to meet him one of these days. Anyone else we know?"

"Ummmmm. Yeah." Lucas's brow bunched up.

"Who?"

"Zac. Zac Lanier."

Brice stopped rocking. "Hand that here." He opened it, peered at it, rubbed his eyes, cussed under his breath, and handed it back. "Read it to me, would you?"

"You sure?" Lucas raised an eyebrow. "It might be private."

"I'm sure. Go on."

"Okay. It's real short. It says, 'Brice, I'm so sorry. Sorry for everything. I hope you're recovering. I hope you're happy. Z.' That's it."

"Ghosts, ghosts. We all got ghosts." Brice stood up and drained his mimosa. "I'm gonna take a nap on the couch in the great room. Wake me in a couple of hours, okay? If the rain's stopped, let's drive out to the state forest and take a walk. I'm still feeling weak, but exercise might help. Maybe you can teach me a few more wildflowers."

CHAPTER FIFTY-SEVEN

"THAT WAS GREAT COCONUT CAKE," BRICE SAID, pulling his T-shirt over his head and shucking off his camo shorts.

Lucas flipped on the bedside lamp and opened the window to the breeze and the shush of night rain. "Well, Uncle Phil figured, since we missed my birthday cake before...."

"Right. Cake redux. Plus filet mignon, baked potato, and broccoli with hollandaise sauce? He went all out. I'm liking this 'welcome-home' diet, though I may have to buy larger pants. My belly's getting prodigious."

"Bullshit. You lost weight during those weeks in the hospital, and you know it. You may have to press that furball belly up against me here in a minute." Lucas sat on the edge of the bed and pulled off his hiking boots. "So, would you do me a coupla favors?"

"Sure. Name 'em."

"Tomorrow, would you give me some guitar lessons? I used to pluck on Daddy's banjo when I was a kid, and I wasn't too bad. I think I'd like to learn to play guitar so you and I could play together."

Brice peeled off his underwear and climbed into bed. "That would be fun. If my damn hands behave."

"They're better, aren't they?"

"Some. So's my head, though my vision isn't back to normal. But I'm feeling a lot better all over now that I'm back home. That little hike in the woods today was a good idea. Now that the weather's nice, let's get outside more."

"We will." Lucas stood to peel off his black T-shirt and climb out of his ratty black jeans. "I'm gonna spend time in the garden tomorrow, and you can help me if you want. But speaking of getting out, that's my second favor. How about we drive up to Morgantown in the next week or so and check the place out? If I go to school up there, I'd like to know my way around. You can show me the places where you used to live and hang out, and we can stay at Uncle Phil's place on Cheat Lake. I e-mailed Travis, and he said he'd love to have us over for dinner. He has an apartment in some woodsy neighborhood called South Park."

"Lucky kid." Brice stretched out, folded his arms behind his head, and closed his eyes. "When I was a student, I always wanted to live there. Sure, Lucas. We'll do that."

"Good. So how tired are you?"

"Ah, not terribly tired." Brice shrugged. "The nap today helped. My head hurts hardly at all."

"Good. Keep your eyes closed, okay?"

Brice smiled. "Okay. What you up to?"

"A little surprise. Be right back."

Brice listened to the sound of Lucas descending the stairs. Brice listened to the rain outside, pattering down among the forest trees. Brice listened to his own breath—a few breaths among the finite number allotted him—and sent up yet another prayer, full of a survivor's thankfulness.

A loud pop resounded downstairs. In another minute, Lucas' feet ascended the steps. "Don't look yet," he said.

The sound of water in the bathroom commenced and continued for a few minutes. The toilet flushed. Footsteps crossed the room, and a finger traced the upper edge of Brice's beard.

"Okay," Lucas said. "Open your eyes."

Brice did so. He grinned with concupiscent delight. "Ohhhh, man."

Lucas was standing by the bed wearing nothing but his black ball cap, silver neck chains, knotwork thumb ring, and the black jockstrap Brice had given him for his birthday. He held a tray upon which sat an opened bottle of champagne, two glasses, and a tiny box.

"Yet more champagne?" said Brice, looking not at the bottle but at Lucas's well-packed jock.

"You bet." Lucas sat the tray on the bedside table, poured out champagne, and handed Brice a flute. "I thought it was high time you and I had a welcome-home celebration of our very own."

"You're absolutely right."

Lucas sat beside Brice on the edge of the bed. They clinked drinks and sipped.

"I have something for you," Lucas said, picking up the tiny box.

"Another welcome-home gift?"

"More than that. Open it."

"Okay. Hmm? Well, I'll be…." He plucked the gift out. It was a chunky ring, with a silver setting resembling palm fronds that framed a big oval of polished hematite.

"Some folks might say our rings should match, but I saw this in a Charleston jewelry store and thought you'd like it. Hematite's supposed to be healing and grounding, and it's good for relationships. At least that's what the Internet says. Folks used to believe that it grew where warriors' blood was spilled. Since you're my warrior," Lucas added, patting Brice's scarred forearm, "I figured it'd be appropriate."

"And since I got my blood spilled a few weeks back? I love it." Brice slipped it on his right forefinger. "Butch. Substantial."

"Like you. It means…. It's a commitment ring, Brice. You don't remember what I told you in the middle of that brawl, do you?"

"I…I remember them surrounding us. I remember I punched some of them. I remember being angry and terrified all at once. What happened after I got hit in the head, I only know about 'cause you've told me."

"Okay, let me refresh your memory. The fight started when the two big ones attacked us. You punched the driver, and I cut the bald guy with my keys. You remember that?"

"Maybe. Sort of. The memory's fractured. It's just a bunch of scattered sensations."

"Then you and I stood back to back, ready for the next onslaught, and you said to me, 'I love you.' Do you remember what I said then?"

Brice sat up. "I…I don't. I…. No, wait. Oh, my God. I do. I do. You said…."

Lucas nodded. "I said 'I love you too.'"

"How could I have forgotten that?" Brice rubbed his forehead. "My God."

"How? A blow to the head with a baseball bat? I think that's a pretty good excuse. I didn't just say it in the heat of the moment, Brice. I been wanting to say it for weeks. I think I knew I loved you when you played me that song, 'Redneck Angel.' And then I almost lost you. I sat by your bedside, regretting I hadn't told you before, regretting how I'd let my hang-ups get between us. I'd study your handsome, sleeping face and hold your hand and pray you'd wake. My big ole sleeping beauty…."

Brice chuckled. "Beauty? More like a sleeping beast. Or bear."

"A beautiful snoozing bear, yeah," Lucas said, caressing the fur around Brice's navel. "Anyway, I promised myself that as soon as we had some time alone, I was gonna tell you how I feel. So here we are. I love you, Brice. I'm sorry I waited so goddamn long to say it. I've only known you for a few months, but you were dead-on when you said we met at the right time in our lives. I want a future with you."

"Really? You're serious? You're sure?"

"Hell, yes, I'm sure. I've never been so sure of anything in my life."

"Lucas, lover, you got it!" Smiling happily, Brice shifted around to sit beside Lucas. He hugged him hard, kissed him, and lifted his glass in a toast.

"When it's right, it's right. Here's to us. Two brawling, ornery country boys who waded through a lot of crap to find one another."

"Well said." Lucas gulped from his glass. "So drink up, 'cause you have one more surprise. You remember what I promised before we got to the Ramp Supper at Helvetia? A certain long-awaited prize?"

"That I do remember. Oh, yes. Your rosebud, I think you put it." Brice reached over and stroked the base of Lucas's spine.

"Exactly. Well, if you're feeling up to it, tonight's the night." Lucas bent forward and brushed Brice's bearded mouth with his own. "I'm so ready and so randy. It's been so long since we made love. Nearly a month, with you in the hospital. I been wanting you so bad. Thinking about you on top of me. Inside me. I've even…."

Lucas ran his fingers over Brice's chest and squeezed his pecs. "While you were in the coma, I used to go back to my motel room near the hospital—Uncle Phil paid for it; I'd stay there when visiting hours were over—and I'd lie in bed and alternate between crying, scared shitless that you'd never wake up, and jacking off, thinking about sucking your cock and taking your dick up my butt. I even, uh, broke myself in again with that dildo I brought to Blackwater Falls."

"Really? God, that's hot." Brice gulped his glass empty. Reaching over, he took Lucas's right nipple between his fingers and tugged.

"Umm, yeah. My nips need some rough use. So you're up for it?" Lucas slipped his hand between Brice's legs and grasped the tumescence there. "Feels like you are. Up. Very up."

"God, yes. My hands may still shake and my scar may still throb, but my dick seems to be working fine."

"I think you're right. Let's conduct a lil' test."

Lucas dropped to his knees. Grasping Brice's balls in one hand, he took Brice's cock into his mouth. "Mmmm, yaahh," he mumbled in audible relief. "Mmmmmm, yaaaahhh."

Grunting, Brice gripped Lucas's head with both hands. Gently, Lucas gnawed the cockhead, then began a soft sucking.

"Ohh-h-h-h, yes," Brice sighed. "I've missed how that feels."

Lucas bobbed tighter, harder, and faster. When Brice's thighs began to tense, he pulled off, grinning. "I've missed how that tastes. Good to know you're ready to go, since I just spent time in the bathroom cleaning myself out and lubing myself up."

Brice's eyes gleamed. "Ohhhh, sweet. Really? You're already lubed?"

"Check for yourself," Lucas said, getting to his feet. He straddled Brice's lap, facing him.

Again they kissed, Lucas pinching Brice's nipples as Brice cupped Lucas's buttocks and slipped a finger between them. Sighing, he fondled the fuzzy crevice and found the lubed-up hole.

"Go on," Lucas whispered, biting Brice's lower lip. "Get inside me."

"God, you're hot. God, you turn me on. God, I love you," Brice said, pushing his finger up Lucas's hole and moving it and out. Lucas nodded, stiffened, and groaned.

"Feel good?" Brice muttered against Lucas's cheek.

"Jesus, yes." Lucas leaned against Brice. "Deeper. Hit my...yeah, there. There. Uhhhhh."

Brice took Lucas's hard-on in his free hand and stroked it. Lucas wrapped his arms around Brice's neck and pressed his lips against Brice's bald head. Riding Brice's finger, Lucas gasped, bucked, and writhed.

"Yeah, deeper. Two fingers now, okay? Put 'em in me. Hell, yes, Daddy, finger my hole. Get in there deep. Get me good and open for you. Get me ready to get plowed. I want you to pound me into tomorrow."

"I love your sexy talk," Brice said. He finger-fucked and jacked Lucas till the bearded boy was sweating and trembling.

"God, I need your dick. Oh, man, I need your dick," Lucas moaned, nuzzling Brice's cheek. "Are you ready to put your dick in me?"

Brice chuckled, working in a third finger. "You know the answer to that. I've been ready to fuck you since the day we met. Feels like you're ready too."

"Oh, yeah. Oh, yeah. I'm soooo ready," Lucas muttered, his ass-ring pulsing about Brice's bunched fingers. "How you wanna fuck me, Daddy?"

"Sweetest question I've ever heard." Brice rubbed preseminal juice over the head of Lucas's prick. "We'll start with…you on your knees. We'll finish with you on your back. I wanna see your face when you come."

"And I wanna see *your* face when *you* come. Okay, let's do this."

Lucas slipped off Brice's fingers and scrambled off the big man's lap. He positioned himself on the edge of the bed, his elbows on the mattress and his pale butt in the air.

"Put it in me. Put it in me, man," Lucas begged, gazing back at Brice. "I need it bad. So damn bad. Put it in me and screw me stupid."

Brice stood by the bed on wobbly legs. He looked down over the naked and kneeling youth, full of wonder, gratitude, and awe. *I could have died. But I survived. And now I'm being given this most splendid of gifts.* With shaking hands, he caressed Lucas's buttocks. He bent and kissed them. He ran his bearded chin over the fuzzy crevice between them. He reached between Lucas's thighs and tugged on his erection.

"What you wanting for?" Lucas moaned. "Put it in me, man."

"Just taking the moment in. Where's the condoms?"

"Forget the condoms. We're both clean."

"No condom? You sure?"

"I'm sure." Lucas nodded, brow pressed against the bed. "Do it! Don't make me beg."

"Why not?" Brice said, working lube-slick fingers inside Lucas again.

"Brice!"

"You're begging now?" Brice pushed in and out.

"I'm begging!" Lucas looked back at Brice again, face flushed. "Fuck me!"

Brice slid his fingers out. He positioned his cockhead against Lucas's little hole, took a deep breath, and pushed. There were only a few seconds of resistance before Lucas's tightness opened and took him in.

Lucas whimpered and shook. He pushed back onto Brice till the bigger man's cock was completely inside him.

"Ohhhhh, yes," Brice gasped.

"Mmmmmmm, yeah," Lucas grunted, rocking back and forth. "Give it to me."

Brice began a slow thrusting. Lucas bucked back against him, jacking himself and panting.

"Harder, man. Rougher. Faster. I can take it. Plow me. Fuck me hard."

Brice obliged, slamming into the boy and pounding his ass. Weak his big body still might have been, but within minutes he was tensing with imminent climax.

"Damn, you're so sweet. So hot. So tight. I'm almost there."

"Me too," Lucas gasped, fisting his dick. "After all these weeks wanting you, wanting this, I'm about to shoot."

"Not yet." Pulling out, Brice wiped sweat from the furry cleft between his pecs. "On your back, boy," he ordered. "Legs in the air."

Lucas flipped over. He grinned up at Brice, raised his legs, and grabbed his ankles. He rolled back, exposing his taint. "Finally got me where you want me, huh?"

"You're damn right." Brice knelt before Lucas, pressed his shoulders against the boy's legs, and worked his cock back inside. He pushed forward, bending his lover double, until Lucas's knees were level with his ears. Kissing deeply, the two men rocked together, Brice thrusting wildly in and out, Lucas jacking himself just as wildly. Their eyes locked. Both grinned in rapture and in triumph.

"We...did...it. We're here," Brice gasped.

"We sure are," Lucas said, crossing his ankles behind Brice's neck.

"I'm gonna...."

"Me too!"

With ecstatic shouts, both men came, Lucas only a few seconds before Brice.

Brice slumped atop his lover, panting. He heaved a hoarse laugh. Lucas laughed too, squeezing Brice's butt. Brice rolled off him, wiping sweat from Lucas's temple, and gathered the boy into his arms.

"That was everything I'd hoped for," Brice said quietly. "Everything I've been waiting for."

"Me too," Lucas sighed. "Everything."

They lay there together for a long time, stroking one another's bare chests, playing with one another's limp dicks, and listening to the rain.

Lucas ran a finger over the sealed wound marring Brice's forearm.

"Guess we're both scarred now, huh?"

Brice touched Lucas's ribs. "That seems right. But now all the scars are worth it."

Lucas flipped off the light, rolled onto his side, laid his head on Brice's shoulder, and plucked at the hair between his pecs. "I love the sound of the rain. Good for the garden. Tomorrow, I'm gonna put in squash and melons. Wanna help?"

"Sure," Brice said. "We'll plant and harvest together."

PART
FIVE

"I DON'T KNOW IF COUNTRY WEEKLY WILL EVEN run this," Larry Johnson said, in between sips of cappuccino. "You used to be a big story, especially right after the gay-bashing, but now...."

"2004 has more interesting tales to tell, huh? No more cover stories for me?"

"I suspect part of you is relieved."

The two men sat in a shadowy corner of The Black Bear, a coffee shop in Morgantown, West Virginia. Around them, university students hunched over small tables, tapping on laptops or listening to their headphones.

"Part of me's glad to be out of the spotlight. It almost killed me."

Brice poked his scone with his fork. He looked out the big plate glass window into the April afternoon. City traffic crawled up Spruce Street. In the distance, the hills were green.

"Another part of me—that neurotic brat of a starved ego I carry inside—will miss the attention, the affirmation, the fame. I got an early taste of all that just down the block, at the Last Resort, a coffeehouse where I used to play in college. Guess I got addicted. The sound of applause is a hard thing to give up."

"Well, I'll nudge the magazine to carry the story. It might help you raise money for your retreat."

"Please do. We need it bad. Our budget's shoestring."

"I'll do my best." Larry pulled out his small recorder. "So tell me about all that's happened since we last talked, since you came out of that coma."

Brice took a big bite of scone and chewed, his

mind ranging back over the preceding six years.

"Well, so…it took me a good long while to get over that attack. My head hurt and my hands shook and my vision was screwed up for nine months. Lucas and I both still have nightmares, to be honest. We're cautious to the point of paranoia every time we leave the house. I don't think that's likely to change. Don't put this in the story, but…I've been on and off antidepressants ever since."

Larry nodded. "I can understand that. Your assailants are still in prison?"

"Yes. All four of them. Ironically, in the same penitentiary where Lucas spent time. We're damn lucky we had the sympathetic judges and juries that we did. Justice for once."

"Moving on to more positive topics, there have been lots of good things going on with you too, right? I've heard a few tidbits through the grapevine."

"You mean the occasional sidebar in the *Star*? Yeah, lots of good things. Lucas started the Forest Management program here at WVU in the fall of 1999. It's going to take him longer than four years, 'cause he's working a full-time job in a local greenhouse to earn his living expenses, but his uncle's paying his tuition, thank God. He should graduate in a couple of years."

"So you two have been living apart since 1999?"

"Yeah. We've adjusted. We're both good at being alone, and the time apart makes our time together even more precious. We take turns on the weekends: he drives down to Randolph County, or I drive up here. He's been staying at a little place his uncle owns on Cheat Lake."

"The *Star* had a big, oh-so-shocking article about your commitment ceremony. Tell me about that."

Brice grinned. "Oh-so-shocking, yes. We had the ceremony last summer by the sea at Rehoboth Beach. Super informal: we were dressed in swim trunks, tank tops, and ball caps. A crowd of gays and lesbians we hardly knew stood around and cheered us. We held the reception in a gay bar, with cases of champagne and a whole bunch of fancy hors d'oeuvres our friend Amie made."

"So what happens when Lucas graduates?"

Brice took a sip of coffee and smiled. "Then he moves back to Randolph County to live with me and hopefully work at the state forest nearby. He jokes a lot about moving from felony to forestry."

"Tell me about the retreat."

"Lucas's Uncle Phil owns it. He retired to Florida a few years back, but he asked me to run it and expand it."

"How's it funded?"

"We've gotten some grants and a bunch of folks have donated, though most of the funding is Phil's. Off the record, Larry, I'm not exactly well-off. My investments haven't been all that successful, though I'm still getting residual checks." Brice chewed his lip and looked down into his empty cup. "I teach guitar to WVU students when I'm up here on the weekends. Luckily, a lot of them think it's cool to have a former celebrity as an instructor. Plus I work part-time at a store called Radclyffe's Roost, down the hill from the Randolph County retreat. I could certainly do with some of that Nashville dough I used to make, but at least now I'm living an honest life."

"Honesty has its price, I know. So who stays at your retreat?"

"Now that queer newspapers have publicized us, we've had gay and lesbian kids from all over the nation. Just about all of them have been turned out by their families. Right now, we have three boys—one from Missouri, one from Wayne County, one from Florida—and three girls—one from Cincinnati, one from Fayette County, and one from Pennsylvania."

"On to your music. You have a concert tonight at the Mountainlair, WVU's student union, the first concert you've given since 1997. I'm looking forward to it. I really appreciate the invitation to attend. Tell me about your new songs. What inspired them?"

Brice rubbed his hands and sat back. "Before I was outed by that interview Zac Lanier gave, I hadn't written a song in around a year. I didn't feel free to write about the truth, and so I'd just stopped writing at all. But as soon as Lucas and I started to get close, new tunes started pouring out of me. I have a whole bunch of 'em now. I guess they're kind of revolutionary: country songs with openly gay lyrics. And thanks to iTunes, online music, and my webpage, I have a new generation of fans. I'm pretty sure I'll never get to release a hard-copy CD again, at least not one supported by a big Nashville label, but who knows? This iPod thing looks like it's up and coming."

"So who are your new fans?"

"I get a pretty regular series of supportive notes from 'em, both hard-copy and e-mail, so from what I can tell, they're liberal folks into country music. Or they're gays and lesbians, many of 'em who live in small towns, in Appalachia, in the South, or they're city queers who grew up in the country."

Brice took another sip of coffee and gazed at a patch of sunlight on the floor. "Those letters, those fans, mean the world to me. They mean, I guess, that what talent I have hasn't gone to waste. It's wonderful to have an audience again. It may be a small one, but it's sure appreciative and enthusiastic."

"Good to hear. Anything else you'd like to add?"

"Naw. Just give your readers—if you can get the piece published—the address where they can send donations to the retreat. Some of those scrawny little queer kids have ferocious appetites."

BRICE STOOD IN THE BACK of the Mountainlair's Gluck Theater, greeting folks as they entered. Most were strangers, except for Grace, Amie, Doris Ann, and Philip—who gave him their customary hugs—plus journalist Larry Johnson and Travis Ferrell, the kid whose advice had proven to be such a life-transforming boon. Matt Taylor and his brooding, black-bearded new boyfriend, Derek, also attended, having driven up from Charleston for the concert. Many audience members, Brice surmised, were members of the sponsoring organization, WVU's LGBT student group. They all sat near the front, around an animated Travis.

"Brice!"

Brice turned to see Jason Mullins, the organizer of the event, hurrying over to him, face furrowed with concern.

"Brice, did you get my messages?"

"No, sorry. Lucas and I gobbled some burritos at Wings Olé and took a long hike up at Cooper's Rock, so I haven't been on the computer, and I've had my phone turned off. We just got back to town. What's up?"

Jason wrung his hands. "You're not going to believe this, but about two hours ago I got hate mail about this event. A death threat, actually."

Brice grimaced. "You've got to be fucking kidding me."

"I wish I were." Jason pulled a paper from his back pocket. "Someone stuck this note under my office door, right across the hall."

Brice unfolded it and read it out loud. "'Brice Brown is the Beast. I will execute the Beast and throw him into the Lake of Fire.' Ohhhh, hell."

"Anonymous, of course. I called the campus cops, and they said they'd get back to me, but they haven't. They haven't sent an officer over either."

Brice scanned the room. "No one looks suspicious, but who knows? Shooters don't come with convenient labels on their foreheads, right?"

"So what should we do? Are you still going to go on? We're due to start in ten minutes."

Brice pondered. *All these folks have been kind enough to come tonight to hear my music. They might be in danger, and they don't even know it. If I'm up on the stage, I'm a sitting duck. If there's a shooter here, I'm likely to take a bullet in the head or the chest. Up there, I sure as hell won't be in any position to protect anyone. Shit. But if I cancel, I'm a coward. I will have been silenced again. Another queer will have turned tail and run off. Screw that. What's the likelihood of anything happening, really?*

"Yes, I'm going on," Brice said. "You bet your ass I am."

Turning, he headed down the aisle toward Lucas, who was chatting happily with Amie in the second row. "Hey, honey," Brice asked, "can I talk to you?"

"Sure, buddy," Lucas said, face gleaming. "Your big night, huh?"

"Yeah. Come on over here. Now listen—"

"Brice Brown!"

Brice looked up the aisle and caught his breath. Wayne Meador and a good-looking redhead, both nattily dressed, were striding down the aisle toward them.

"I guess you showed all the assholes, didn't you?" Wayne said, seizing Brice in a big hug. "I knew you'd have a career again."

"My God. You came? All the way from North Carolina?"

"Ah, we broke it up with a visit with Roy in Hinton. The ole bastard's hanging on. Too mean to die, I figure. Brice, this here's Gail, my wife."

Brice took her hand. "Nice to meet you. I gather that you finally tamed this ole dog."

Gail looked amused. "Tamed? Not sure about that. Who wants a tame man anyway?"

"True enough." Brice rubbed his whiskered jaw. "I couldn't agree more. Gimme a man with a little warrior, a little wild in him, right? Speaking of which, this is my partner, Lucas Bryan."

Lucas shook their hands. "It's great that you could come. Brice has talked about y'all a lot."

"Let me introduce you two to my Randolph County friends," Brice said, leading them down the aisle. "After that, Gail, if you'll give us a minute, I need to chair an important little guy-chat before this concert begins."

"So HERE YOU GO, FOLKS," said Jason Mullins. "The revolutionary, one-of-a-kind Brice

Brown!"

Carrying his old Yamaha, Brice strode onto the stage to the achingly welcome sound of applause. The huge room was hardly packed. Indeed, it was only about a fifth full. Lucas, Wayne, and Matt Taylor had arranged themselves throughout the room, all three scanning the space for trouble and ready to act if necessary.

I've got me some pretty fierce protectors out there, Brice thought, waving and grinning at the audience as he made his way into the center of a soft spotlight. He gave Jason a hug before the anxious-looking organizer loped off the stage.

When the applause tapered off, Brice yelled, "Hey, folks, thanks so much for coming out to see me on this fair April evening!"

He settled onto the stool, adjusted the microphone, and took a long look at the room, the rows of faces both familiar and strange, fans who cared for him to one degree or another, fans who were waiting for him to share his music. He smiled out at them, remembering the many venues in which he'd performed: the coffeehouses and bars, the state fairs, the slew of Nashville honky-tonks, the Ryman and Opryland, London and Melbourne, and that last concert, in Daytona Beach right before he was outed.

And now here, my alma mater. I might maybe die tonight, he thought, strumming the guitar, tuning a flat string. *And I sure hope I don't, 'cause there's so much to live for. But if I do, I'll go out doing what I love. Plus I'm pretty confident that Lucas, Matt, and Wayne will tear anyone dangerous or hostile into little bitty pieces.*

"I'm so glad to be here. It's been a long road back to the stage," Brice said, leaning into the mike. "I really wanna thank y'all for inviting me. Especially Jason Mullins and the LGBT student group. So, let me start with the first really honest song I've ever written. It's called 'Redneck Angel,' and it's dedicated to my honey, a lil' West Virginia country sexpot named Lucas Bryan."

In the back of the room, Lucas raised his hand in salute. Then Brice began to sing.

CHAPTER FIFTY-NINE

A NEW MOON HUNG OVER CHEAT LAKE, ITS midnight light interrupted by the occasional passing cloud. Weary after the long evening, Brice and Lucas sat bare-chested and barefoot in deck chairs, gazing out over the waters, sharing a glass of single-malt Scotch and enjoying the unseasonably warm breeze.

"No blood and violence, just happy people and great music," Lucas said, his fingers loosely intertwined with Brice's. "First anticlimax I've ever appreciated."

"Me too," Brice agreed. "For the first minute, I was stiff-backed and braced to take a bullet, but then I just forgot about it and sang."

"I can't believe campus security didn't send any cops over. Assholes. We had your back, though. That boyfriend of Matt's had an eye out too. We would've been on top of a shooter in a heartbeat."

"I know. I just wish we didn't have to live this way. Always on the lookout for trouble."

"Checking the perimeter. Protecting your people. It's the warrior's way, Brice. It's what men do. We got broad shoulders. We can handle it."

"I know we can. I just get tired sometimes. But, man, in the midst of the anxiety tonight, I thought about how much I've been given to love. I'm so lucky…to have you, to be in a position to help those Phagg Heights kids, to be composing again. The friends we have…few but so, so cool. Just a few years ago, I had no hope, and I was thinking about suicide. Now, wow. I love our life."

"Me too." Lucas squeezed Brice's hand. "The music tonight was wonderful. You're in top form. With these new iTune outlets, I think you should seriously think about putting together an album we could sell online."

"I'm planning on doing that." Brice stood and moved to the railing, looking up to the high steeps of Chestnut Ridge, and then out over the lake, and then up to the spring sky. "You see those clouds drifting over the moon? They remind me of the sea foam I used to see on the beach, when I had that condo at Daytona and used to walk at night and feel lonely and horny and listen to the surf. The foam'd gleam in the moonlight like bubbly strands of silver, and it'd make little boats, little pirate ships that'd drift down the sands at the mercy of the winds."

Brice turned, leaned back against the railing, and smiled at his lover. "I guess we're like that, huh? At the mercy of fate. Except this time, fate turned kind and led me to you. Who knows how long it'll last, but...."

Lucas rose. He strode over to Brice, passed him the glass of Scotch, and took his hand.

"Who knows how long anything'll last?" Lucas said, standing on tiptoe to kiss Brice on the cheek. "Don't mortality make what sweetness we find even more intense? And, man, are you sweet. I ain't going anywhere. Count on what we found, Brice. Count on what we got."

"I will." Brice drained the glass. "It's late. I'm tired. I want to get naked and climb into bed with you and cuddle and listen to the lapping of the lake and the wind in the trees."

Lucas wrapped an arm around Brice's waist and nibbled his bare shoulder. "Sounds sweet. Tomorrow morning, I'm thinking you should plow me raw. After that, I'll make us a big breakfast, maybe some fancy omelets. Before you have to head back to Phagg Heights, we can play a few country tunes together on our guitars."

"Country tunes. Yep. You're my country, Lucas." Brice ran his hand over his partner's naked torso. "You're the landscape I cherish the most, the hills and forests and valleys I want to travel through, the homeland in which I plan to abide."

"Kinda poetic. Sounds like you got a new song coming on. Come on now, Daddy," Lucas said, giving Brice's butt a gentle pat, "and take your mountain muse to bed."

MORE TITLES BY JEFF MANN
FROM LETHE PRESS & BEAR BONES BOOKS

Non-Fiction

Edge: Travels of an Appalachian Leather Bear

Binding the God: Ursine Essays from the Mountain South

Fiction

A History of Barbed Wire

Fog: A Novel of Desire and Reprisal

Desire & Devour: Stories of Blood and Sweat

Purgatory: A Novel of the Civil War

Salvation: A Novel of the Civil War

Cub

Insatiable (forthcoming)

Consent (forthcoming)

Poetry

Rebels

A Romantic Mann

CPSIA information can be obtained
at www.ICGtesting.com
Printed in the USA
LVOW08s0018200317
527767LV00001B/89/P